NO JUSTICE
BUT
EVERYONE
GOT PAID

BY

J. D. GLASS

LCCN: 2010912630 READING, OHIO

ISBN: 978-0-615-38139-8

BETA PRINTING) SEPTEMBER 2010
1ST PRINTING JANUARY 1, 2011 00:00:01 GENERAL RELEASE PER ATALANTA
COVER & BACK PHOTO BY AUTHOR MARK T. TILLAR 2011

NO JUSTICE BUT EVERYONE GOT PAID

BY: J.D. GLASS

NO JUSTICE PUBLISHING, CO.
STARKVILLE, US OF A

Table of Contents

Introduction

Since the narrator is unable to be here, the duty of writing an Introduction has fallen unto me, Boswell. I am one of the very few people in this world whom the narrator considered a friend. It is believed the narrator is presently in an attic of a building not far from here; due to what his friends like to think of as a long term commitment to yuanyixue therapy with Dr. G. Hegel. Atalanta asked me to do this introduction as a favor unto him; with only one condition – to be brief. My friend's favors always have conditions dependent or precedent.

First, the narrator wanted every reader to understand that this is the first and only truly internet created book. There are no others.

If someone attempts to tell you that there is another such text, they are deceitful money changers who are attempting to mislead you and to cause you to believe in a false text.

The narrator explicitly told me to impart to you the reader that he accepts full legal liability and moral responsibility for this text, limited to extraterrestrials, which he recognizes is his solemn duty as given to him by the Internet. Yet he insisted that the reader understand that in the creative sense, this text has been handed down to the narrator, word for word from the internet; and it is not his creation, as he was merely a scribe sitting before the warm glowing light of the cathode ray tube receiving the word as handed down to him from its Creator the internet, SALAAMALAIKUM LAWRENCECURLYMOSES.COM.

The narrator asks the reader to understand that he merely transcribed the words, and pleads with the reader to have faith in his ability as stenographer; and in the absolute veracity of the text as given to him from its Creator the internet, SALAAMALAIKUM LAWRENCECURLYMOSES.COM.

The narrator has told the few friends of his who were asked to do the first readings, (including myself), that he had faithfully spent hours basking in the warm soft glow of the cathode ray tube transcribing the *WORD* after last Sunday night.

Only after hours of staring at the *WORD* and transcribing the *WORD* did he publish iT on his blog in beta form for us. Release date is at 00:00:01 of the upcoming new year as a general commercial release.

He assured us that every word, punctuation mark, symbol, and number, had appeared countless times, and in countless variations of combinations, in the cathode ray tube's warm glow. The narrator knew he was blessed to have been chosen by the INTERNET to have him record this text. So he spent hour after hour faithfully transcribing this text - the only true text; as given to him through the warm electromagnetic golden blue green glowing light containing the saving grace and the infinite wisdom of the internet, SALAAMALAIKUMLAWRENCECURLYMOSES.COM.

The narrator informed us that we all should be humbled in knowing, through the revelations made to him contained in the cathode ray tube's warm electromagnetic golden blue green glow, which SALAAMALAIKUMLAWRENCECURLYMOSES.COM not only does this for us in our own language, but miraculously speaks to all people, in all languages, who believe in only one internet, the true internet, and know that all other internets are false internets.

Last, is my own personal opinion, that the technology that is the internet, like humanity itself whether manifesting itself in an individual, or as the total sum of civilizations past and present, is not to be trusted.

I have repeatedly told JD that the book's title should have been '*No More Sacraments of Reconciliation*', but he would not listen to my sophistry, as I am not the internet.

I think the narrator is being his usual narcissistic self in wanting to believe that his brachygraphy would be translated.

The narrator's attitude reminds me of a tag line from Inglewood's own 'Henley Street Willie': "*In the beginning was Information, and the Information was with Qubit, and Information was Qubit. What fools these mortals be.*" *

*(Postscript for JD; if you don't like this intro – Dr. Johnson, Austin, Atalanta, Addison, and the Arawa all have written intros for their website's P2P listings.

Also, you owe me couple rounds of single malt, as i didn't bust your mythical b.s. by writing that this whole thing is a work for hire - mr. checked box 2G anonymous on the tx form.

Now that i think about it, you should throw in some Northern Lights too, since i didn't go all judas on your 'sitting for hours' b.s. either. Think journalism school ethic's class would have taught you that the reader might want to know you got paid piece meal by Iblis Qibla Compasses LLC, (which we all know is a dummy corporation listed on ورس اوراق ب هادار ت هران , and is totally controlled by its parent corporation, IRGC Prosthetics LLC**), just like all those moslim women and children factory workers are paid in Daw Aung San Suu Kyi's part of the neighborhood. Well, unless you're a child bride, then someone else gets paid.

Now that i think about it, you should throw in a supper '*Conquistador*' since i didn't reveal that you got paid by character-no-spaces instead of letting Cardinal & Coscia LPA negotiate a character-with-spaces-and-footnotes-and-end-notes deal.)

** (IRGC LLC prosthetic jihadist penises are sold at all the finer jihadist mosque gift shops and at the merch tables in their ablution spaces.)

iii

Chapter One   Mit Dem Feind

Coughing was bringing me to some consciousness, a physically painful process, the consciousness not the coughing. The back of my head hurt as if it had been struck by something. Probably was hit by some small piece of a kaaba meteorite during last night's showers.

Semi-consciousness always begins with momentary anxiety then the realization that everything *i* know is wrong, excepting the self-realization of my narcissistic negativity. Deductive reasoning cannot escape faith.

It matters. Narcissistic personality disorder aside, emotional approximations and vector corrections are my human experience.

In primary school my consciousness became tektite-like fractal reflections of my teacher's words: '*kashimono-karimono*'.

It is really all about *me*, always has been since **i** realized there was a *me*. That is the prevarication **i** started repeating to *my*self thereafter.

That is how Homo sapiens sapiens are wired - repeat behavior, become habit, become innate. The synapses continued re-sparking the lie insuring the prime directive of survival no matter what the individual struggle. **i** realized **i** was repeating behaviors because my head and body were hurting. Plus, **i** could tell **i** wasn't at home on my futon.

i half opened my eyes. Rain drops were splashing in oily street pavement puddles, including the one an inch or so from my face. In every puddle the rain drops sent tsunamis of small blue gold concentric circles crashing and overlapping. That is, as far up and down the concrete street as **i** could see laying there in the dark. Not lucid enough to do a Max Born calculation of squaring the tsunami's wave function.

"Careful", this morning's *Dr. Johnson* 'ego' rebuked last night's *Boswell* 'id', "Sir, you are without any skills in inebriation."

JAZZ. My consciousness was rising VERYVERYVERY slowly and disjointedly. My hearing was platoon point man. American JAZZ is crucial to echolocation before dawn. (gaige kaifang)

JAZZ. Sounds, possibly originating from the rear basement windows across the street. Monk, Coltrane, so what is Miles playing.

Sounds merging together, but notes straining to break timing and pitch. *"Ordinarily he was insane, but he had lucid moments when he was merely stupid "* – Heinrich Heine, in some bygone moment of inspiration, wrote in anticipation of my lying here pretending to notice chord progression and rhythm changes; which only re-enforces my belief that it is all about phrasing.

Sure…, right….., believable ………., my brain wants me to believe i am laying in the gutter thirty three feet from the intersection of Bleecker & Thompson.

Fading Into *this* morning's realiↄies, time-space synesthesia a mis enemigos.

3/11th consciousness was allowing my eyesight to focus in on this morning reality, the familiar street gutters of the convention district in a river town i knew was hundreds of miles away from my brain.

i recognized the street. i knew i was lying in my home town, Starkville……. and the JAZZ faded along with my street side siesta.

("Drowning possible", as usual first thing in the morning, Dr. Johnson started nagging Boswell. i ignored them both.

Boswell, who recently became a member of the American Copy Editors Society, took Dr. Johnson's 'cutline' and announced in an irritating voice for this time of the morning, his 'hed' - "Zanclean flood deposits man in street gutter earlier this morning". Boswell then assured Dr. Johnson and i that '…it would make a great teaser for the local 6:00 am morning talking heads local news and mostly weather show'. i ignored him as i was attempting to wake up.)

Thing being lately, i have a lot of moments when waking up when i feel as if i am drowning.

Such as when i wake up on cold clear night laying in the public park, or in a garbage strewn yard of an abandoned row house, and i looked up at ᅲ: ursamajorursaminorstarsgalaxies < > the cosmos.

i get very dizzy within seconds, and feel my diaphragm moving up while breathe is being siphoned out my trachea from my lungs by ᅲ's centrifugal forces.

Sensory overload. Not the 'Hubble Space Telescope Photographs type', more like a 'two year old chasing fireflies at dusk in late September' type.

System Check: Diagnostic's Boot - a thirty six bit lottery for the new day; *charles bonnet syndrome*, or *temporal lobe epilepsy*, or *transmissible spongiform encephalopathy*?

Not quite sure if booting, or just looping presently.

Probably just localized interference from some random gravity waves pulling at three different points of the hohlraum infection in my hippocampus.

my back was against the concrete curb, with my left shoulder and leg partially draped over the curb. A (as in 1 of 6.66 billion +) biochemically fueled carbon base bipedal life form now prone in the rainy street gutter. (i iii i iiiii ida pingala sushumna)

Boot completed with the realization that in spite of the pressure of 4.44 million billion Newtonian tones upon me, at some spacetime point i could get up and walk home. Darwinian triumph.

The cold rain drops had soaked my clothes and cleansed my face while i was unconsciously loitering at street level. The rain was an accessory after the fact, with its reckless and foreseeable sedimentary erosion of last night's revelries trace evidence.

Seeing hundreds of drops, feeling maybe a hundred drops every minute or so; deceptions of my perceptions. Cold water droplets falling on me, and my concrete futon.

Liquid eroding solids; i need to have Leonard Susskind define solid again for me, or Ashoke Sen, because concrete streets and curbs empirically make such firm mattresses and pillows.

i know from the U.N. 2010 population census that concrete futons are preferred over sand, dirt, or mud, at the intersection of two of the four hemispheres: the northern and the western hemispheres. At least that's what the Census claimed, citing the Public Relations Firm of Broca & Wernicke's internal polling data, which has shown it consistently since U.S. Navy General Order No. 4 of January 14, 1863 to the present.

Long term marijuana a posteriori thoughts bounce off in all eleven dimensions, but not very far, at most a couple of membranes. Standard AU measurements aren't relative to all Homo sapiens sapiens prone in rain soaked street gutters as a new day dawns.

Roughly, the **4,927,500,000,000th** dawn without the **world** being **carbonized**. (déjà vu bubbleverses?)

'Est-il faible'? 'Bisschen'. Weak force - the prone biochemically fueled carbon base bipedal life form's electromagnetic field at this exact moment i thought as systems powered up.

Qigong Doc Zheng Ronliang would gather lots of wet leaves from this gutter, with a couple of 'grammostola rosea ', if my bloodshot eyes are to be believed. They aren't. Several meta menardi scurried into the street drain.

No rosea.

Have to focus soon and beckon this morning's prana. Lying in the street is not tolerated in this part of the city. Unlike under the highway overpasses down on the river bank, or over by the coal fired power plant – that's no problem.

i was in the convention district, which was a distinct problem for the Visitor and Convention Bureau's costly international advertising campaigns.

Only through the miracle of geography i'm not waking up in the Evin District Visitor and Convention Bureau District. i know what happens to hikers who get off the sidewalks there.

Rain bombards the puddles while micro streams of street surface water flow along, and through them. my concrete futon's a priori situational reality. Déjà vu, c'est moi, the irrationally transcendental 'it' "i" & 'over-i'. Einstein/ Podolsky/ Rosen paradox?

But that feeling, that old familiar déjà vu, was causing my chest to tighten. 'Evolutionary flight response relic', i said aloud to nobody in particular.

(Dr. Johnson replied with his diagnosis of , '…frontotemporal dementia'.)

Not that i am even sure of that memory, or any memories, or even the idea of memory. Chemicals have a shelf life. At least that is one of the policy rationales of the F.D.A. regulations requiring expiration dates printed on all the labels of all those little plastic bottles from the pharmacy. Landfills full of those plastic bottles are more pristine environments than anything cycling though my organs. Memories don't have much of a chance at shelf life in me.

That bit about eleven dimensions i exaggerated, this carbon base bipedal life form knowingly exists only in three dimensions.

i know that because i only sense three. Ronald Reagan's 'Real Politik' view of my realities - trust but verify.

my lineal reality, with an infinite amount of random microscopic black holes flowing through my cerebrum according to some sahasrara gravitational wave theory not yet conceived. *dark matter* Ω *,F,P 001111111 /* Δ^9 𝕋ℍ(*ɟ dark energy subconscious = -3 / sin (Ø) 001111111 superstring ego = 3Ø / sin (3/Ø) 001111111*

Of course that must be, is, very juvenile, and is artistically and logically wrong, throughout all the multiverses. It is absurd even from a manic. There is obviously a problem with either my Chebyshev or Padé approximations on the face of it.

At least, that is what i think is what Austin and Giles were trying to explain to me last Sunday night at a very small family bar at the corner of Dock and Pear. We had just finished a couple pitchers of Philadelphia Porter.

Then Austin started to discuss Padé after he had ordered three pints of Black Sam's favorite cydar, 'Hare's 3 Finger Toxin'. After drinking one cydar i lost interest in approximations. i tried to change the conversation by stating, *"Inventas vitam juvat excoluisse per artes is heresy according to the Ijma"*. Austin and Giles ignored me, so i started looking at the ceiling, and Giles and Austin kept talking logarithms for at least three more rounds.

No doubt delusions caused by my presently imbalanced delta-9-tetrahydrocannabinol, nicotine, and caffeine levels.

Should have asked for the correct formulation of the equation from Doc Norris Bradbury, or possibly, even from any latte sipping string theorist at the 'Steam Engine Coffee' on Telegraph Avenue, back when i was seeking an education on the left coast in that other spacetimepoint.

Random microscopic black holes, theoretically cerebrum dwelling. Physics, domo arigatou gaziamasu , *theoretical mathematics* causes me to trust the 五 senses as *theoretically* reliable interpretations of my presently rain soaked concrete street gutter spacetimepoint.

How elegant to think while waves of neutrinos sweep PrPC's, PrPSc's, and vCJD's toward microscopic event horizons and thus become symbiant architects of my transmissible spongiform encephalopathy consciousness this morning.

(Ok, got it. Dr. Johnson, then seriously, so what you're telling me, is where all those prion proteins went.)

6

Lazy Decadent Elitist Self Indulgent thoughts are some form of a fetish mental infection: *fin de siècle musings*. Niðhoggr was becoming intoxicated by sipping my acetylcholine while gnawing at my edinger-westphal nuclei.

Puddles glistened purple and gold. Rain drops causing concentric waves to crash through each other in a private multidemonsional performance of Gerald Arpino's *'Light Rain'* just for me.

The 'crashing through' part reminds me of all of the sexual relationships I have had my life. Waves crashing. No that sound is the blood vessels in my temples.

Right this second, the increasing mathematically probability of meeting with a local police officer required me to lift myself up and start walking. A probability that even a '43 Model II Relay Interpolator would solve instantly, or for the pocket protectors, the HP-35.

Thin Blue Line Wave Avoidance Flight Response. At last a rational thought that a post industrial man could act upon, and by post industrial, i mean post hubblespacetelescope.

So I did.

Getting up was not easy. Walking was painful, as my legs felt like some paraponera clavata had dined on my thighs while I was laying amongst the wet leaves on my concrete futon. La vita e buona.

I had not noticed when I was enjoying my siesta at curb level, but the wind was moving the rain in swirling sheets of water down the street from the east. True to my karma, I started walking east to get home. Leaning into gusts of cold swirling sheets of rain, I had to take Scott Joplin's advice, ' *slow march tempo only* '.

If rain drops were notes, I was walking in Mozart's 25th in gust minor.

7

I could not stand up straight yet due to the lumbar muscle pain. I started some type of truncated Levy walk, although I knew home was only nine blocks east, then five blocks north, up the stairs and through the door.

Behind the door is my freedom. Freedom from the intake cells at the justice center this morning. I am not being judgmental, nothing particularly wrong with sleeping at the JC once in awhile.

American history being the moral norm, specifically my American family history of the last four generations.

Now I crave solitude. So I had to single focus on the immediate prime directive. Probably less than a half hour before the sun rises. Due to the time, the rain soaked streets were empty.

My back was aching, forcing me to walk very slowly and bent over. I looked up at the glass buildings for a couple steps as I crossed a street.

For some reason a catchy tune I heard around the neighborhood when I was very young came to mind: *"Lieber Herr Gott, mach mich stumm, Das ich nicht nach Dachau komm."*

I seem to remember the old german butchers and their wives on summer nights sitting on the steps outside their row houses arguing whether the boys of DeutscheJungvolk in der Hitler-Jugend, or the girls of Schwesternschaft der Hilter-Jugend, sang it with more vigor.

Under today's cool rainy morning's von Neumann - Morgenstern calculation, the closest city police cruisers must be at the White Castle across from Starkville's Adelaide Railway Station, thirteen blocks past my apartment, there I go exaggerating again, a room is not an apartment.

Or, the police cruisers were parked side by side on the top plaza parking level of Sports Stadium. Police officers have their habits and customs too. Not just rules and procedures, but corporate culture stuff: mission statements / slogans / creeds, and fallible human habits such as skipping the first three levels of the use of force continuum when arresting anyone from the neighborhood.

Habits, such as parking on the top plaza level to kill time by getting out of the patrol cruisers to grab a cigarette and talk freely.

Even so, they were always waiting for the cruiser's mobile display terminals to light up with the radios crepitating dispatch alerts from the command communications center located fifteen miles outside of Starkville city limits.

Last Sunday's '*Starkville Zeitung*' had reported that the location was due to some 1950's AEC requirements of command & control systems directive regarding communications and population centers during the good old days of the cold war with the Union of Soviet Socialist Republics.

Wonder how all those summa cum laude's with chernobyl martyrs industrial college rbmk degrees are enjoying Putin's usurper economy with Saladin, Nur ad-Din Zangi, Baibars, Kilij Arslan, al-Ashraf Khalil, and Zengi on the border.

Now the only thing I wanted more than some coffee was a joint, and those treasures were behind a locked apartment door blocks away. I first had to get out of the business convention center district

The buildings in the district had distinct elements of the anti-semitic and nazi sympathizer Philip Cortelyou Johnson and his protégé.

Architects seem to believe that their buildings affect people, and therefore their ideas affect communities.   Burned out village of Markow effects Phil. Phil affects steel and glass boxes placed in Starkville.

Fuck you Phil. Starkville with all its problems will never forget your nazi's friends working with the moslims destroying and killing innocent jewish people. To Hell with you and your fellow criminals: 'Izbah Al-Yahud' Eichmann and Emin al-Husseini.

9

No stone mason cut foundation stones for those steel structures. Internal combustion engine collateral damage: quarrymen, sawyers, and carvers.

I was heading uptown to the historic district to my apartment at 14 North Moore Street, a beautiful 19th century stone structure on the corner of North Moore and Varick Lane.

The cold rain was starting to ease, but still softly stung as it hit my face. More likely the proper diagnosis was that I was becoming ever more conscious. I was shivering; muscles were becoming taut.

Pain.

I did not have to share the sidewalk, a good omen for the new day. Leaning into the rain – my face only seemed almost parallel with the street. I was enjoying myself immensely, such are narcissists.

The fact is that I enjoy walking in these midwestern thunderstorms while concentrating on absorbing random atmospheric electrical charges. Staccato lightning is my absolute favorite. When I am manic, it is a van der Waals force tingling of my rain soaked body hairs type of thing.

When only I'm only slightly manic, it is a hadal zone crawling biochemically fueled carbon based bipedal crustacean witnessing elves fouettè jetè through the lithosphere while the ionosphere pulsates Schubert's 'Ava Marie' electromagnetically across my corneas type of thing.

(doubly electromagnetically induced transparency)

Wet. Shivering. Walking. Stumbling. Lower back pain radiating. Almost rational. ALIVE.

My present quest for sanctuary involved a journey through Starkville's architectural history, if one was aware of buildings, and not just the street and the concrete sidewalks at this time of day.

I thought of the Rye Cliff Internet Notes: Kantian architectural hop head Atlas shrugged, but remained catatonic from the shimmering glass box reflections, as his tektite consciousness bounced from random synapses firing. Hop head happiness is not an ideal of reason, but merely of the cannabinoid receptors firing.

The convention district was on the western edge of the city. It's where the Interstate Highway, (*what is Freeway Ricky Ross doing today, movie deals or video games?*) , acts as a Great Wall of China keeping Starkville's souls within.

The southern edge of the city was bordered by the sluggishly flowing Honkawa river. The eastern border of the city is the idyllic rolling Hebron hills from the river's edge north 3.141592653589793 238462643383279502884197169399375105820974944592307816 4062862089986280348253421170679 or so miles.

The hills and meadows then curve gently over all the way back to the freeway, or as the Sentinelese and the Arawa say, '…all the way to the antifaschistischer Schutzwall'.

There were still large areas in the Hebron hills with rich pastures for grazing stocks amongst the new settlements.

An elderly transcendental oil portrait painter friend of Boswell spends most every day there amongst the beasts, painting the rolling pastures in irrational colors.

The Hebron hills are nature's amphitheater for the twenty four hour a day off off off off off Broadway show being performed by the residents and transients of Starkville.

Almost all of the buildings outside the historic district were circa 1958 to 1975. Steel Framed Glass Boxes. Steel honeycombs.

Boring: like the law and accounting firms, Fortune 500's, and the upscale retailers that occupied them.

The modern reich urban planning triumph.

11

Block after block of sleek, secure, environmentally controlled, architectural one off's, post 9-11 ph balanced monitored aqua scapes. I mean monitored working spaces.

(Dr. Johnson offered an unrequested diagnosis, "...probably dyslexia with a, p, e, s, within a possible c.p.q.?")

The historic district was built by German and Irish immigrants starting in the 1790's, but the greatest periods of growth were 1830 though 1852, and then 1864 to 1911. The hundred years and more of weathering and settling on foundations only added to the eminent visual character of the buildings; especially their hand cut stone, brick, mortar, solid deciduous beams and frames.

Most buildings are four stories in height and have fireplaces in every room with high ceilings due to the coal smoke. The region's fortunate geographic history of glaciations, and re-colonization of juglans nigra, meant that black walnut wood work and trim were used throughout all the buildings built before 1909.

In my building - the icing on the cake, so to speak, are the original cast iron laundry hooks in the massive black walnut beams in the attic. Hooks perfect for tying harvested branches on, and then waiting for the leaves to drop covering the ambrosial buds. I understand the pride of the western Kentucky tobacco farmer when he is filling his dark, drafty, gable barn lofts in autumn.

As I slowly passed among the darkened Steel Framed Glass Boxes, I started to cogitate that in most Midwestern river towns nowadays the older building's of their historic districts are inhabited by the young urban professional gentrification speculators; avant-garde artists and other working poor; the mentally ill; the homeless; drug addicts; crack-whores-prostitutes (redundant); and the terminal cases and the elderly survivors of the disease of Pauperism with their co-dependents. Starkville is no different.

Starkville urban legend had Dr. D. L. Harrell, Jr. and Dr. Francis T. Stribling proposing in 1935 the busing of the entire neighborhood to Western State Hospital on the outskirts of Staunton as part of their progressive scientific and humanitarian policy of the lower tenth. Legend is that Starkville City Council only defeated the legislation by the republican votes cast against it, allegedly due to the costs of gasoline, food, and lodging for the neighborhood for a week.

("It is obvious to the politically progressive that the republican's perennial short term view of spending had stopped a program with long term governmental savings and ruined yet another attempt by progressives at improving the lives of the less fortunate", I noted wryly to Dr. Johnson and Boswell. "Wrong, as usual. It was purely a partisan republican vote against spending any money in the town that had inflicted the 28th President on us", quickly opined a smiling Boswell.)

If it wasn't for '*Aptheker v. Secretary of State*', County Sheriff A. John Ochsner would insure that no one in the neighborhood would be allowed to talk with their neighbors. The Sheriff busts everyone's balls by calling every one '*idiots and imbeciles*'. He is just an angry man prone to bluster and the occasional daily excessive use of force. Sheriff John's favorite Nottingham ploy was to arrest anyone with a record or a gang tattoo under Ind.(ustrial) General Laws Chap. 215 1907.

My ecological niche, my camouflage, my ummah, are the streets of the historic district. It's what my long time friend, (and multi-million dollar annual grossing business owning client), Giulio Clement call's '*living outside the wire*' from his upper income scale faux exclusive residential neighborhood in the Hebron hills.

It's just the way he talks.

The Alexander Column was built in the middle of the intersection of Main and N. Franklin by the veterans of 1898. It is the beginning of my neighborhood.

The column with its inscription 'Wir Erwarten Ihren Besuch' is a spacetimepoint dividing the strata's of citizenry that are the melting pot of Starkville.

Crossing the street I noticed a large gyrfalcon was sitting atop of the column staring at down at me as I slowly walked.

The Salvation Army Shelter and the City Homeless Shelter are within seven blocks of each other. The Food Bank and St. Sulpice's soup kitchen are within the same seven blocks.

So sleeping and eating do not require a bus token. Seemingly on every other corner were small markets with stoic appearing Pakistani's working behind bullet proof glass selling soap, diapers, cereal, candy, milk, soda pop, Kamppell's soups, and Kensitas; but mostly a hell of a lot of alcohol and Jersey Blunts.

(Dr. Johnson, ever the scientist, noted that, "The alcohol and blunts thing is a Chicken versus Egg riddle. Economic deprivations versus cultural stratifications; the type of hypothesis that a student at UW Madison working toward a master's degree in counseling specializing in school counseling would argue with another student at UW Madison working toward a master's degree in counseling specializing in community counseling while they were snowshoeing the Madison Arboretum".)

The rain was stopping as I crossed the intersection at Vine Street and Maple Avenue. I noticed that I almost actually crossed at the intersection. Having developed the habit of crossing streets where ever and when ever, it makes such things as actually walking in a crosswalk mathematically improbable, and thereby noticeable.

That is one great thing about this town, jaywalking is never enforced unless you are a member of the Baggy Pants LLC, or merely as associate thereof, and then it always is just so they can do a 'Terry' pat down.

Living in Seattle I wouldn't need an apartment because every time I jaywalked across 7th Avenue and Stewart Street I would get a hot shower and an edible and religiously appropriate meal courtesy of the good taxpayers of King County. Multiple daily violations of the social compact are not excused in liberal la la la la lands.

("2 octaves above C - below the bass staff ", I recommended to Dr. Johnson.)

Here in the Midwest, they will arrest Mapplethorpe photographs, but go jay walk right out into traffic and the police ignore you.

14

Well, at least this morning's me – a Ralph Ellison one-off. Have to admit that skin color probably dictates that police discretionary calculus for at least 20 blocks in every direction, and more, the further you go back in spacetimepoints.

Ich bin ein Baggey Pants LLC'ers.

I stepped over the concrete curb while trying to stand straight up, and then looked up. The western skyline above the buildings on North Moore was just beginning to show the color streaks of the morning's sunrise.

It would not be long before the sun rose.

I walked up to 14 North Moore Street's massive oak door. Stood in the doorway fumbling around for at least a minute for the key that was in my right pocket. Love these cargo pants but the deep pockets are a real problem at times like this.

Then after fumbling with the lock, I had to lean my shoulder against the oak door to get it to open, and then, again to close it.

The frame, the door, or both, had swelled throughout the night – obviously natural forces were purposely obstructing me from the goal of the new morning's quest.

My hands pulled at the dark hand carved black walnut banister, arms dragging myself up the stairs as I climbed, with my back pain radiating staccato through my thighs and down into my ankles.

Both of my hands could not wrap around all that black walnut. Those immigrants knew how to make beautiful things that last. I dragged myself slowly up the stairs.

At the landing I had to keep my right hand on the wall for support, and did so all the way to my door.

Again with the key thing. I finally opened the door and entered my Nunavut. As soon as I got inside I went over to the refrigerator.

I lifted the velcro strip and reach into my side pants pocket and got my pack of Kensitas out. I took a deep breath and held it while I opened the cigarette box and got out the thumb drive.

It was dry.

I exhaled slowly as I put both on top of the refrigerator.

I then walked over to the futon taking off my wet clothes and threw them over a very old wooden chair made from a single cercis siliquastrum tree.

The chair is placed against the room's interior wall between an old Ethiopian wooden chest and my aquarium.

Fell on the futon. It was a controlled fall, as in my state, was a newtonian habit.

BBC Radio 3 on the internet was playing softly, adding back ground. It's usually on whether I'm there or not.

I really had no idea who the composer was, possibly Niccolo Piccinni or Niccolo Paganini. As usual, I did not know the composer, the title of the composition, or the orchestra.

Love classical music, but memory would never, could never, retain all those foreign names and titles. (*Or was it Radio Classique?*)

......varying deep rich tones with pitch fluctuations......

I laid there trying to see my fish in the aquarium while listening to the rain so lightly crashing against the windows. Les grands classique futon ending to my 1409th faux '*Charshanbeh Suri*' Starkville § *STYLE.*

The last thing I remember thinking before I fell asleep, other than how much my eyes were starting to hurt from last night's extremely bright twelve act zodiacal electromagnetic light show, was that everything was just perfect.

(Boswell interrupted just perfect by chiding me as I drifted off to sleep. "Wrong again, it was the 50th something Kwanzaa." Then he looked over at Dr. Johnson. "Right, Dr. Johnson?" Dr. Johnson was feeling a bit light headed as he turned to Boswell and stated, "Wrong again, wrong month.")

(Then Dr. Johnson softly began to sing an old cotton field 16 bar blues song about astrology. Actually it is his favorite negro hymn, "*When the sun comes back and the first Qur'an calls   Follow the galilee goblet   For the old begena player is waiting   for to carry you to freedom   if you follow the single...*")

Chapter Two   Isolation

What came first, the clangorous ringing of the alarm or the hacking up of gobs of phlegm from my lungs and throat into my mouth?

Momentary anxiety consciousness is a physically painful process.

Regardless. I leaned up on my right elbow. As my left hand hit the top of the alarm clock, I spat the dark brown phlegm into an ash tray and then put it back on the floor under the coffee table.

First conscious choice of the re-established day: cigarette or joint? No brainer. I am an American. I get BOTH. A half finished joint was on the tray on the coffee table right next to an open pack of my Kensitas cigarettes. An impossible morning choice: one that only Kanzi, Washoe, and Sarah could solve at this time of day – is whether to add a 5th string or stay with 4, while knowing that the 5th string will allow waves above middle C *(onsciousness)*.

I took couple hits off the half finished joint, my fajr. *THC is always my first choice.* Started hacking again; deep, deep, coughing. Morning ritual for decades now: causal connections?

Philosophical Enquiry into the Origin of Our Ideas of the Sublimely Beautiful Cause argument of whether a Dromedary Cause vs. a Great Tasting Nicotine Cause is found within formless Hippocampus Cancers has to be left to all those lucky Decision, Rational Choice, and Game Theory students at Columbia University; (but who had really desired to go to the Australian National University). After the DZERO results at Fermi National Accelerator showed a doubly strange particle, I quit being Saliere to the ꙅꙩꙠ꙱ꙅ 'ꙅ Mozart. I am sure Mr. Francis Bacon will list his complaint about my quitting the discussion as his 12^{.5th} in his enumerations.

I spit in the ash tray again, always the dark brown phlegm in the morning, dark brown quarky gluony plasmatic phlegm.

I grabbed one of the cigarettes, and lit my first nicotine delivery tube of the day. Years ago, when I still had a sense of taste, the first puffs off a cigarette in the morning always tasted the best. Now I never notice a taste when I smoke: morning, noon, or night. Think some lawyers had something about that printed on the side of every pack encouraging all of us sale's tax paying consumers.

Damn, different parts of my body were responding to this morning's roll call, not one of them at 100 per cent. Pot is our Mikhailian reward and Pain is our Zabaniahian reality (-ies for you multiversers; P & P homologous chromosomes?).

Didn't have time to enjoy the cigarette, or acknowledge the roll call of sore muscles, or even attempt to remember last night's events which dissipated as daydreams with the morning's phlegm.

What was I dreaming, something about the DZERO results at Fermi National Accelerator showing a triply strange particle; while Mohammed Atef, Hamza Rabia, and Abu Laith al-Libi were receiving the sacrament of clitorectomy in some Pakistani second floor walk up office?

Time to shower/dress/fuel up on fresh 'extra bold bean', and then get to the office. Seventy one minutes of sleep. Not good but not bad either.

I started quietly humming Sister Rosetta Tharpe's *'Didn't It Rain'* to myself as I grabbed my bluish-white cadmium tea cup sitting next to the cigarettes. A very fine tea cup from a beautiful tea set that was given to me from a muslim client last Sunday, or the Sunday before. Think I had left it there day before yesterday, possibly yesterday, again - not trusting the memory.

I jiggled the cup of my homemade ayahuasca tea and watch the dark liquid spinning inside. I poured it all in my mouth and swished it around for about three seconds before swallowing.

This morning's mouthwash tasted like an ash tray rinse.

Hot Hammat Gader showers. Genius, pure genius, as far as human inventions are concerned. Notwithstanding Babylonian Talmud 5:7 - hot water in large quantities is definitely not injurious to my body.

A Babylonian fortune cookie that I did agreed with was the one about possessions today are gone tomorrow. "Even those with extremely high levels of DAF-16", I said out loud to an absent Sister Rosetta.

Standing in the shower with my head under the scalding hot water with both my hands on the wall, I was hacking and spitting into the water swirling around and into the drain. I notice less blood in the phlegm this morning. Vitamin C working? I always enjoy this part of my mornings. The cleansing of my lungs and throat always feels so vital and invigorating to the body. (*Nam-myoho-renge-kyo and/or wuda*)

Coughing so hard that tears flow is *always* such a sensual way to start the day.

Systems Check again: various scratches and bruises but amazingly no visible damage to face. Fragile and needy beings aren't we?

After work it would be great to shower until the hot water ran out. It takes seventeen minutes on a good day, usually spent singing John Lee Hooker or Muddy Waters songs.

Right now it's in, hack/spit for three minutes, out. Then throw on some clean underwear, socks, and a faded pair of old Levi's. All which had been lying on the floor in a pile of clothes by the futon.

Found a clean tee shirt on the kitchen table, (and by clean I mean it did not reek like Jiminnie Kaine's couch at Starkville's California Ursidae Stealthy Bonds offices in the Philip Cortelyou Johnson glass box district of town).

It was my favorite shirt, a '*Fun Lovin Criminals*' tour shirt from the 90's.

Are the Difontaines still in the New Jersey asbestos business, or did they disappear in the foggy mists with AT&T Bell Lab's?

As I slipped the tee shirt over my head, I tried to remember the last time my fish got their shrimp pellets – but I could not.

Possibly due to tetrahydrocannabinol, nicotine, and caffeine clogged hippocampal mossy cells. I walked over to the aquarium and took an old torn copy of Khayyam's '*Rubaiyat*' off its top and leaned it up against the left side of the tank.

My aquarium was an indulgence; a multiverse within forty gallons of non-distilled Haridwar Ganges water indulgence. It is full of healthy, vibrant plants, and a poly-resin model of a 20th century Industrial Promotion Hall sat opposite a 1930's Imperial Bank Building, both anchored in 3.1415 inches of fine trinitite sand base. Behind them a 170mm Juche Tower was lying on top of a much larger fractured ruby, cut as a star. Close by a sickle, a hammer, and a writing brush were sticking out of the trinitite base between three pieces of a kaaba meteorite; (kaaba meteorite's are for sale on friday morning's by the Quaestores on Khnum Avenue).

The other prominent occupants in my aquascape are the Afropomus snails. Since they had the good sense not to be flittering about constantly, I was able to get to know them much better than the fish. Oney, Austin, Hercules, Giles, Aris, Sheels, and Moll, were much more social beings than any fish I have ever known.

Since I could not remember when I had fed the fish, I took a second to feed them. The fish always went into a feeding frenzy when I sprinkled the 'name brand' antihypernucleus enriched shrimp pellets into the tank. I have three, or *had* three pretty nice fish, notoliparis kermadecensis.

Very active, so fun to watch when stoned that I really don't mind paying way too much for the 'name brand' instead of the cheaper generic.

I shook some of the tiny, golden, shrimp enriched, wafer pellets into the tank, looking to coax the fish out of the plant cover, or the poly-resin model buildings. I was in a bit of a hurry, so after a second I decided that the problem of the number of fish had to wait until much later, mucho mas tarde.

Now I had to get over to the justice center holding cells before arraignments started, to talk with a client.

Grabbed my smokes, Zippo lighter, and began leaving my comfort zone, craving fresh brewed coffee. Instead, as a very poor second at this time of day, I went out to the refrigerator.

I took out the glass jug that was about twelfth full of my home made ayahuasca tea made with water from my Revigator. I poured a glass full of the tea and only added two teaspoons of Hawaiian sugar. I drank most of it, pour out the rest in the sink, and then put the glass on the counter.

While walking out to the door I grabbed a roll of Nicodemus's hyssop troches, and for breakfast, a handful of Scooby Snacks. I was as ready for the world as I would be since I woke up this morning. I longingly looked at the remains of three of friday night's smoked joints in the ash tray, and resisted the urge to smoke 'em.

As I locked the apartment door the fish issue started to irritate me. I almost went back in. I didn't. I turned and left trying to remember, was it yesterday, two nights ago, was it even before that, on Sunday night?

I cannot remember. That is why my decisions are mere conjecture.

Regardless, I could not remember when I last saw all three fish. I was really high and watching them before falling asleep, but when?

At some point there were only two of them. I think the two that are left are Muon and Tau.

At least their markings are, as I remember, similar to Muon and Tau. Spinal Lysergic Acid Diethylamide Déjà Vu, AS IF. Then I had some mental images, a false memory probably, as I started to open the building's massive oak door to the street.

There were times in the last weeks, when I was really stoned, drunk, and very tired, and just as I was just fading off to sleep, when Muon and Tau would shimmer and disappear.

Shimmering déjà vu bursting of relativistic particles.

In a yoctosecond there would be another shimmer in a different part of the aquarium and appearing were two Pangio Kuhlii's – Krypton and Xenon, and who then dart off disappearing among the lush rotala macrandra and nymphaeas's flourishing cover.

Then another shimmer at some random interval, maybe not random, but hypothesis $(1/(x^2)$ times $1/(x^2)$, I estimated as I tried to focus on the fish.

I watched Moll doing the extension/retraction thing up the glass behind the 1930's Imperial Bank Building for a bit, and then Muon and Tau were starring out of the aquascape at me.

The shimmering bursts kept happening for probably 499 seconds before I fell asleep thinking that in some other multiverse the excessive levels of chemicals in my system were having a self awareness experience of their own.

The Chemical Bros' got together with my bacterial cells who were listening to George C's 'Sub Atomic Extremophiles'. Then they went all Voodoo Chile with my guts funkified microbiota as I slept.

It would take an old P J. Pollock type to capture the surrealistic essence of my aquarium when I'm stoned. (*'moi le bassin aux nympheas'*)

Regardless of the fish situation, I needed to leave the building.

I had other problems to focus on this morning.

Chapter Three   Dr. Jackal - Inclusion with no Atonement

As soon as I got outside I was bombarded with the city's usual morning commuting noises: man and machine.

The streets were becoming crowded with this morning's commuters. All the way up North Moore Street past Maple Avenue the Cars\Trucks\Buses bouquet of exhaust fumes blended with all the moistened methane, carbon dioxides, sulfur dioxides, magnetic spherules, and particulates of nitrous oxides, that were emanating from last night's rain soaked gutters.

If you'd survey the Starkville's citizens, they would be primarily independents who view themselves as rugged individuals, akin to the City's namesake - Brigadier General John Stark.

Regrettably not since the 1860 election had the citizens of Starkville had the opportunity to vote for any state or local candidates with General Stark's leadership qualities; and only a few times since then among presidential candidates.

It was all about vast sums of money now, not service or duty.

(Boswell wanted to get back to nitrous oxides, "Dr. Johnson, if you asked voters in the same poll how many Starkville citizens could tell the difference between the smell of urine and manure of a Sus ahoenobarbus hog versus a Sus ahoenobarbus sow, you probably wouldn't be surprised at percentage of the number of correct answers, being Midwesterners, would you Dr. Johnson?")

The city sidewalks were Starkville's Ellis Island Main Hall at this time of day. The Baggy Pants LLC day shift was just now relieving the senior and more lucrative night shift on all the major corners. The suits were streaming out from buses and the parking garages in increasing numbers; mixing with the homeless crazies who were heading toward the free food store, or to the daily St. Vicente De Paul's morning instant coffee and one day old doughnuts give away.

25

Crazies knew the best take was the morning commute. After working all day, the suits were never in a giving mood. Begging, the panhandling sharks swam between and among the human currents on the sidewalks. Sharks only ask for conscious cleansing change from the laobaixing. Suits drift onward to plastic office modules on the umpteenth floor of the soul numbing sameness of skyscraping steel boxes.

I waited next to the newspaper vending boxes for the traffic light to change. As I glanced at the vending boxes, I noticed the 'Starkville Zeitung' morning edition's headline: '*Drug Area Task Force arrests 15 in raid on street dealers on Khnum Avenue.*'

The endless Battle of Marne of the drug war was proceeding as it has in the past – high body counts. It is trench warfare between the government and its citizens, especially since misguided Harry Anslinger had the government declared war on us through HR 238 in 1937. 21 USC Sections 811, 844 are empirical facts that the government learned nothing from the 18th Amendment experiment. Our government just keeps sending us to prison.

My deduction: Harry Anslinger **1**   Shen Nung **0**.

So I am thankful that the founders banned a governmental religion in the bill of rights to the constitution, and instead gave us felony and misdemeanor for all our sins.

Violating the social compact and being put in stocks in the public square is so much easier to live with than having everyone believing you're going to the twelve levels, or in my case, the thirteen nonillion levels of hell.

(I believe Dr. Johnson agrees I'm no 'Sturm und Drang' type.)

Worse yet - everyone on the arab street, with their collective scientific educational levels being that of any 'yochien', will believe that Allah (*the french kisser of young boys*) might think I AM IMPURE. OH MY.

Whenever I discuss comparative law with Austin and Giles, Boswell will always interrupt off topic, saying that the Old Testament's Wrathful God had brutalized the tribes, but still mercifully gave Abraham ten morally relativistic commandments, and not one of them cast out marijuana or hashish.

Being multicultural, Oney, Hercules, Moll, and Aris, would always counter that Haydar and Mohammed have encouraged and permitted 'Azalluu' after 8:00 am.

(Dr. Johnson agreed and sourced to Ibn Rushd, (nom de plume *'Averroes from the 90702'*), in his popular travel novel *'Tahafut al-tahafut'*; which also has handy self help tips for cooking Sus domesticus pachamanca 'conquistador au jus'. Boswell then also cited Zoraster's Broadway Show *'Zend-Avesta'* Song Book.)

Everyone agreed it was just bad luck for all the innocents that had been tortured and killed by misinterpretations of the god given rules by the Kings, Sultans, Princes, Pharisees, Propraetors, Prophets, Popes, Plutocrats, Potentates and 20th century Presidents.

In the present 21st century, I'm beginning to think imammies and their jihadistbots torture and kill to relieve their personal insecurity as very small penis men.

Of course that, and because they are jealous of *'Averroes from the 90702'* blockbuster worldwide sales from the paperback version of his travel book; and not any misinterpretations of let us say - Qur'an 9:5.

At least Starkville isn't another islamjihadiecrazytown yet.

Islam's immoral jihadimmamies with their even more barbaric physical torture *plus* prison terms for the 'non submissive' who wants to smoke herbs or drink something brewed with german hops, 250 lashes should please allah. Is that right you religion of peacers?

If whipping my flesh doesn't make me a believer in frenchkissing justice, then shouldn't I be permitted to be in an office in some Steel Framed Glass Box wearing a cumin or curry colored robe while

27

facing 143 S. 3rd Street in Philadelphia, while drinking single malt scotch and lighting up bowls of charas, while memorizing and mediating on John Cleland's '*Memoirs of a Woman Of Pleasure*' and have mindless self sex five times a day within the cathode ray tube's warm electromagnetic golden blue green glow?

"Then he (mohammie) – (*the pure I'm so sure*) said, '*Where is the little one? Call the little one to me*'. *Young Imadingbatjihadie came running and jumped into his lap. Then he put his hand in his beard. Then the plagiarizing prophet, may all the allahs in all the multiverses bless him and grant him young boys, opened his mouth and put his tongue in young Imadingbatjihadie's mouth. Then young Imadingbatjihadie said, 'o allah, I love him, so so so love him and am the one who loves him!*'

(Boswell spoke up in a matter of fact manner observing, "If that doesn't smite your nether regions, it should at least strike some reverence under your loin cloth, or at least perhaps a herpes test".)

I keep choosing Hubble, Felonies, and Misdemeanors.

I keep **choosing** Hubble, Felonies, and Misdemeanors.

Tetrahydrocannabinol, how else to explain the lucidity of my dreams and thoughts this morning?

("**Extragalactic magnetic fields transmogrifying gravity waves throughout the hypothalamus**", Boswell insightfully opined to Dr. Johnson.)

Sharks were swimming through this morning's currents of suits flowing between the Steel Framed Glass Boxes; probably 10 major phyla of suits.

Symbiotic comes from the Suit's desire to feel the superiority of the emotion of pity, hence superiority psychological reward is triggered releasing Suit cleansing endorphins by the giving of quarters/dimes/nickels/pennies.

Sharks and the other street microbial life survive by getting the required $3.79 for their morning liter of sweet peach wine, or $1.99

for a 40 oz Pilsner. Suit self indulgence triggers habitual re-enforcement of homo sapiens sapiens city street level interactions, which then becomes a prewired symbiotic endorphin release.

Repeat behavior, become habit, become innate, all by 8:30 am every morning.

Successful evolutionary behaviors are learned every morning on Starkville's city sidewalks: inspired bio coding. I am not forming consistently lucid thoughts yet as tetrahydrocannabinols entropy.

Those flip-flop wearing PhDs who hang out most morning's in the sidewalk cafés on Telegraph Avenue across from Sproul Plaza drinking double mochas and lattes, while talking only of theoretical mathematics and logic, would not be able to white board my thoughts this morning.

As tempting as is it to say incantations and believe in their absolutions, I knew that last night's revelries effect upon my psyche would not be cleansed, even *if* I sacrificed a Buff Brahma Bantam hen's egg by frying, salting, peppering, and splashing with ketchup.

Last night's revelries were a subconscious tsunami in my parietal cortex. If I had an HP-35 I could calculate the difference in the speed at which horizontal and vertical waves were travelling from my parietal cortex to my frontal lobe.

(Dr. Johnson proposed, 'If the tsunami starts in parietal it will take the P-wave .0000000666 s to travel to frontal, but it will take the S-wave .0000001998 s to travel to frontal.')

Not yet a feasible early warning system of the gods wrath, but I should definitely sacrifice at least three Buff Brahma Bantam hen eggs, a pound of bacon, ⅜ pound of goetta, and four slices of butter covered rye bread for atonement as soon as I get a chance.

The Quest at this particular second in my morning spacetimepoint was Guatemalan Bean grown in the fertile verdant Petén region.

The brain was obviously not fully online yet this morning, although all my '*Rother J*' psychosomatic illnesses were running smoothly in background.

Roll Call: sore knees, skinned elbow, lower back pain, and yes, random partial thoughts. I crossed Vine Street and walk then one remaining block to my office.

The reality is that my office is my home. Patria.

Again with the exaggeration - reality is that I know I have no home.

I work therefore I effect. Not clever but not humorless either, yet not worth sparking a synapse in Gore's green economy. I do study situational humor from the great islamic slap stick vaudevillians, especially on nights when Yaum Al-Jumu'ah is at the Comedy Club on Sunsetting, doing his battling kazoo's rendition of '*Arbeit Machi Frei* '. The kazoo's shrill tone always brings the biggest laughs and applause.

(Dr. Johnson agreed that, "It never fails to get the Tom Collins and Blue Hawaiian guzzling jihadists out of their chairs screaming profanities and clapping".)

Construction of the building where my office is began on the day King Abdul Aziz signed the Treaty of Jeddah in 1927, and the building formally opened on January 31, 1929.

The first tenants were several distinguished doctors, some civil practice attorneys, three floors of stock brokers, and a large insurance company occupying the top four floors. The ornate lobby is still reassuring to those who come to visit the building's tenants with its solid marble walls and floor. It provides that classic formal quality even as all its colors sun faded into light yellows from cigarette smoke and the other residual schizophrenias of time.

I lit up a cigarette to add to the long term effect of humans on the stained ornate. I stared up at the only painting in the lobby, a faded 1904 '*L'Illustration*' print of some battle scene of the Japanese and

Russians, which was hanging above the elevator. It was a great picture. Lots of impressions without the actual life experience.

I waited. You can recite the Declaration of Independence waiting for the elevator, or not. In the mornings I use the time to focus, or not. Sometimes I think about what elevator riders discussed the first week or so in October, 1929 as they waited for the exact same elevator I was waiting for.

My bet is they argued whether Jack Hendricks was going to be able to do better than 66 – 88 next year, especially after allowing 760 runs. After all who really wanted to talk about Hoover's leadership on getting votes on the tariff over pitching while waiting for the morning's elevator?

I bet the stockbrokers who had become very glum after September 3rd's '381.17' wanted to talk about pitching. I'm sure the stock brokers especially wanted to focus on the promise of next year's season.

When I was highly buzzed I could fade spacetime and conjure other tenants who spent their professional working lives within the building during some other spacetimepoints.

We share the building. Therefore, we indefinitely share our realities temporal gravitational wave effects rolling amongst its scaffolding; wimps and machos exchanging emails.

Since last Sunday, or possibly the Sunday before that, I had discussions with building tenants from August 23rd and 24th 1929, March 7th, 1936 and October 6th, 1973.

Multiverses for, and in, and of, the temporal professional office condominiums; except, since I am an American, I want **my own space**. Preferably bottom land with running water full of pike, trout, and bass; with cereals, indicas, and sativas growing all around, and with a fruit tree or three.

31

Definitely a couple Boerboels, because, like I said, I want **my own space**.

(Boswell said it was, "...un-American not to have some dogs". Dr. Johnson replied that, "Grand Ayatoldheisaliar Nosehair Makarumupstuff Shitari's ban on dogs as unclean is just more Nazi Propaganda against the hubblespacetelescope". Boswell noted that, "**More dogs** have been **in space than Iranians**.")

It's in the constitution. Also the Presidents signed and the Congresses ratified treaties giving us the space. It's how we got the land of the Cherokee, the Siksika, the Yahi, the Hoh, the Pima, the Tano, the Jicarilla, the Bidia, the Ojibwa, the Sauk, the Pohoy, the Coree, the Miami, the Unalachtigo, the Munsee, the Navaho, the Sioux, the Seminole, the Mohawks, the Mohegens, the Alliklik, the Black Carib, the Flathead Salish, the Listiguj, the Huelel, the Bari, the Ukomnom, the Lecesem, the Ocuilteco, the Kichai, the Runasimi, the Dakubetede, the Jemez, the Michif, the Lillooet, the Hopi, the Mono, the Cree, the Sarsi, the Chinookan, the Iroquis, Chootaws, the Pomo, the whatever's.

I know it's my right by General W.T. Sherman's Special Field Order No. 15; and by federal statute - the Indians Appropriations Act of 1871. So it's my own office space - **free** and **clear**. Office Space title in fee simple, linearly in the **11** demon*shuns* of my demon*shria* this day.

The elevator finally arrived. I stepped over to the lobby's ashtray putting out my cigarette while trying to solve an arithmetic progression.

Say about a quintillion molecules per imaginary Peruvian snow flake, then how many molecules I am radiating away moving through these 11 points simultaneously?

Alpha Decay?

Further calculating, if the earth's gravity disrupts the surface of asteroids, then what shape am I passing 11 points simultaneously upward on 1929 model elevator?

(Boswell said, 'It is as obvious as a Tiger Slug mucus trail. The shedding of deoxyribonucleic acid amongst 11 point streams of energized protons and electrons passing through my transmissible spongiform encephalopathy at 900 kms was something even Dr. Johnson could see with his own eyes'.)

The elevator is the original, and therefore moved at analog speed – very slow when compared to those modern elevators in the XX storied Philip Cortelyou Johnson glass boxes a few blocks away.

When the door opened, and as I stepped in, the elevator swayed ever so slightly.

The elevator operator chair was in the upright position and probably had been in same position for more than thirty years. I leaned against the side wall and depressed the button for my floor.

The elevator hesitated, shook slightly, and rose ever so slowly. Nostalgia for an analog world overcomes one while moving at inches, not feet, and certainly not floors, per second.

I love the elevator's antique colonial gold and brown General Electric Georgian model series 665 light fixture three bulbs pale light illuminating the dark maple wood paneling. Qualifier - as long as there were no more than two other Homo sapiens sapiens with me on the journey. After two Homo sapiens sapiens, I become a student of flooring not paneling.

13th Floor: Mia Patria. ("O patria mia" - Giuseppe wasn't a client of mine, but he understands in his spacetime.)

I shared the 13th floor with Zurvanite & Khurramite L.L.C., whose offices are located directly across from the elevator; Zurv was a dour fatalist, whereas Khurr was always ready to tell a joke, usually about all the women's underwear they exported to the Arabian gulf.

Down the hallway to the right is where the women's bathroom is, right across from an empty office.

It is not really empty.

Federal Agents use it. Not sure what they use it for since they come and go so infrequently. They do Fed stuff like walking up stairs to be discrete. Not sure if they walk from lobby or just get off at a lower floor and walk from there. Outside of court rooms, I avoid Feds, as they are the foot soldiers in the old and continuing war on citizens who possess natural herbs. I respect their devotion to duty and envy them their misplaced certitude.

(My residual hippocampus tetrahydrocannabinols best analysis is that the space must be used for some electronic equipment, either pointed outward or inward. Since their office is on 13th floor, it could mean only one thing to me – the Feds are not interested in me as target. No way would Feds chance 'target' hearing random noises in an empty office down the hall, and seeing all those same gray suits coming and going from the stairway.

The tetrahydrocannabinols best analysis was the most probable target was the Jiaojong's School of Plumbing Information Security & Waste Engineering on the 14th floor, or MVD Section K Cereal Grocer on the 15th floor. Feds were probably just monitoring how much tech and corporate info the MVD Grocers and Jiaojong Plumber's were hacking from Starkville's largest pork packing companies. Dr. Johnson was sure the Feds were monitoring to see how much of the information was used shorting pig futures with the courtiers de change in Tehran.

I'm pretty sure I heard from a public intox inmate at the justice center that the Feds, Grocers, and Plumber's all hang out together after work drinking Vodka Martinis with the local dias de pesadilla bocca ball team, down at the river side bar at 646 N. Franklin Street. I was told the Feds just listen to Bud Powell's '*Blues In The Closet*' play on the juke box over and over and over and over and over and over and over and over, again and again.

The Achoo Baytiiiii Version News Agency is on the 12th floor.

No one is interested in what they print, or care what crazy 12th floor ideas they brainstorm down there. Certainly I wouldn't want to share a couple tumblers of scotch with them. I am sure I'd get stuck with their bill at a minimum, and that is only after listening to their delusional view of the world cup rankings.)

Live and Let Live I was thinking walking from the elevator, excepting the Jihadists.

When all the imamamies in the world sign a proclamation that Dawah *and* 8:39 are affronts to human dignity, and are crimes against humanity to be repudiated by all muslims, I will revise.

Then I will Live and Let Live, until then the Jihadists can Kiss My Ass while I Smoke a Joint and Drink Scotch.

(Boswell said he had, "...read about the righteous gentile Oregon tea party 2nd amendment type's, following the State's 10th amendment right to enact laws for mercy killing, who went lobbying K street with their S & W Model 500's. They wanted help enacting laws granting Oregonians the right to fulfill the jihadists their religious desire by State (*mandated*) sponsored mercy killings of all the women enslaving, brain washed, very small penis jihadist bastards on sight".

I noted that, "...the most merciful act that the large family does to one of its infant members is to kill it, I remember it from 'Reichsministerium fur Volksaufkiarung und Propagadaministerium Large Families Directive 63'. Since jihadists are our brothers, it is logical that when they act like homicidal two years olds and kill each other mercifully by rectally inserted prosthetic jihadistsmallpenis ied's, we should assist them. It would save Oregon tax payers money on 1625 fps 440 cast-lead loads if we helped our infantile jihadist very small penis brothers with their suppositories.")

It doesn't take a FBI 302 memo to know that Hamas, al Qaida, KUDS, and more such gangsters are among us, even here in Starkville.

Ok mathematicians, what is the formula for discerning the probability that every person who goes to our one Starkville mosque despises everything General Stark fought for and embodied?

HP-35 or '43 Model II Relay are advised for your calculating.

Also a follow-up: what is the probability that if the mosque types had their way, there would be no line dancing at the C & W Bar, no Rap show at the Club, no R & B or Rock & Roll at the sports stadium.

What's the certainty formula for when the imammaries and mutawwawas take all Starkville country music bars jukeboxes; with their great selection of Johnny Cash, Merle Haggard, Dwight Yocum, Kitty Wells, Tammy Wynette, Earl Scruggs, Hank Williams Sr. & Jr., Jimmie Rodgers, Mel Tillis, Waylon Jennings, Willie Nelson, DAC, A.C. Robertson, Henry Gilliland, Fiddlin' John Carson, and the entire Carter Family, that someone will wake up and remember General Stark and then immediately remember Smith and Wesson. My bet the 1ˢᵗ one will be a Leonard F. Slye fan.

Unless, that is **unless,** the muslim cry baby thugs took the jukeboxes from the hip hop clubs first. Then it's a Glock 9MM rappin' salaam ALAIKUM, ALAIKUM, ALAIKUM, ALAIKUM, ALAIKUM, ALAIKUM, ALAIKUM, ALAIKUM, ALAIKUM, ALAIKUM, ALAIKUM, ALAIKUM, ALAIKUM, ALAIKUM, ALAIKUM, ALAIKUM, ALAIKUM as it is ventilating the dress wearing culture thieves.

My office was down the hallway to the left. So is the men's bathroom with its two porcelain toilets with brass fittings set in marble stalls. Two steel washbasins. I am its only visitor as far I as can tell, other than the never seen maintenance person who restocks the paper towels and toilet paper at indeterminate times.

My office's glazed glass door was set in a steel frame, which pleasantly contrasted with the hallway's wood paneling. The building management stenciled my name in black on the glazed glass.

The stenciled glass always reminds me of a canted camera angled scene from a subversive messaged private detective film noir premiered in New York, January '48:   *J.D. GLASS ATTORNEY AT LAW.*

I paid building maintenance extra to stencil in a copy of my favorite pyramid text from Queen Behenu, in a basic serif along all four borders of the glass. Of course it is *only* for visitor's affect.

I really appreciate the clients who in our first interview mention how they would like to see more glass texts.

Opening my door, the first thing seen is the secretary's desk with an Art Deco pen and pencil set in front of a black rotary dial telephone, which is sitting next an Underwood. The computer and printer were in the adjoining hutch so to diminish their visibility.

My office is ....functionally lazy comes to mind.

36

My ante room had couple decent leather chairs bought from a defunct brokerage firm on the fifth floor. In front of the chairs was a 1905 mahogany and glass inlaid coffee table that I had rescued from an estate sale.

On top of the coffee table lay an original December 21st, 1946 issue of The New Yorker, and a few issues of Popular Mechanics, Popular Science, and Physikalische Gesellschaft zu Berlin, magazines set out upon it.

I also had put three of my favorite older issues of Scientific American on the coffee table for my clients, with the two Alumni Memorial issues of the only California Bears national championship programs – 1920 and 1937.

Old Denoyer – Geppert Series maps circa 1951 that had been matted and framed were hanging on the walls.

Adjacent was a space of maybe 7' by 11', which contained the secretary's desk, functional with everything within reach.

I had hanging on the wall above the desk a fantastic, just superb, 1936 bootleg print of Maqbool F. Husain's 'Bharat Mata', signed by Mahatma Gandhi, within a black walnut frame.

Any realtors who have had the occasion to be in my office, and who work the neighborhood between 82nd & 105th, always comment on what a positive state of mind   Bharat Mata adds to the office spacetimepoints.

Down the hall to the right was my conference room. My conferences were limited to 13' by 19', minus the space occupied by the glass table and four chairs sitting almost in the middle of the space. Again with the older matted American geography and history maps hanging on the walls.

Further down the hall was my 'office' with locking door. My desk is pale oak of decent size. I have a high back leather chair with rollers allowing for hours per day of my feet on the desk with my eyes closed.

My most important piece of office furniture was next to my desk under the window along the outside wall – a very soft handmade blanco baraq skin leather sofa: "92W x 39D x 35H", a slice of heaven.

Second only to the sofa, was my black Dictioneri coffee maker, which brews at two hundred degrees, sitting on the mini-refrigerator by the window sill.

There was a file cabinet next to the refrigerator with a TV on it.

True to my habitual behavior, I immediately got out the Guatemalan Bean and ground it up. Now absolutely being the perfect moment to lean over the grinds to take a pranayma cleansing breathe; carefully, as I could violate the EPA's workplace limitations on carbon dioxide. Dr. Johnson and Boswell couldn't afford any more administrative fines this month.

If it is a manic Monday, then it's a tan tien cleansing breath.

Sapor Sapuri Saveur Sapore Saveur Savoare

I grabbed a plastic twenty ounce plastic bottle full of Revigator water from the refrigerator and poured it into the black Dictioneri and hit brew.

I keep my suits and shirts on the back of my office door, three black wool suits, three black shirts, one black tie.

Never really been a suit, always felt a bit of a Patrick Henry when wearing one. I peeled off my clothes, throwing the tee shirt and jeans on floor by the blanco baraq leather skin sofa.

I lay down on the sofa and began focusing on relaxing my back muscles. Then I pulled over my legs an old handmade cloak. I had won it in a game of logic from Ahmad Shah.

I not only knew the fish, no thanks to Boswell nudging me a couple times, but easily grabbed it from Coalsack as I gutted Ahmad's logic; and then just as easily plunged hubblespacetelescope into the heart of his mythological hypothesis.

Pissed Vincente off to no end as I had beaten him to it.

Sun light streamed through the windows warming my face, and causing me to occasionally scratch and tug my beard stubbles.

Every time γ, hν, or $\hbar\omega$ stop by to visit me, it's a libidinous experience.

Street noises always present - always different. Now the tempo was increasing moment by moment; reminding me of when I was young and sitting alone during Sunday matinees in the drafty and dark 2nd balcony in Hesse-Nassau, watching Otto Klemperer leading the Wiesbaden symphony in Mahler's Symphony No. 5.

("Nice, very nice, *possible* spacetimepointmemory", commented Boswell in a monotone.)

It was very sensual moment; the smell of the hot water running over the ground beans, warm morning sunlight on my skin, morning commute noises softened and muted by the thinning air of thirteen stories, and various acute pains in multiple parts of my body subsiding in very sensuous waves.

Morning Habit: Body Pain, Echolocation, Northern Lights, Kensitas, Coffee, Body Pain.

How many mornings lately have I woke up and had to look around for a moment or two before knowing where I actually was? Seems like all of them.

Don't know the science of it, but waking up in a different place, spacetimepoint after spacetimepoint; day after day, week after week, month after month, must lead to a particular type of momentary anxiety psychosis.

39

Edge Of All Fear stuff, waking up without reference is death by asphyxiation of the soul.

Momentary waking isolation is described best by John Milton at some spacetimepoint in Paradise Lost.

> *So much hubblespacetelescope celestial light*
> *Shine inward, and the mind through all edinger-westphal nuclei powers*
> *Irradiate, there planet eyes, all mist from thence*
> *Purge and disperse, that I may see and tell*
> *Of things invisible to delta-9-tetrahydrocannabinol sight.*

First, it is always the rush of the actual awakening. Then it's followed by an anxiety jolt while trying to get a landmark to generate at least some kind of reference point in spacetimepoints echolocations.

It is always my experience to have a millisecond of panic, precipitating into a physical rush, that there will be no landmark, no JAZZ *this time.*

For those mornings where alcohol and/or THC concentrations are higher than the normal excessive levels, it might take 6 - 9 seconds to recognize a landmark; clinically causing quite a physical reaction - endomorphism incontinence with the morning's dawn.

 Got up and poured the coffee into my mug. What I like about double walled glass mugs is their opaque reality, with very little condensation. I like to see the buildup of the coffee stain while I imbibe. Not the same as reading tea leaves; more like seeing Pollock's *'Lavender Mist'* build up molecularly over spacetime.

I am waiting for science to help me perfect the ultimate morning coffee: French roast with magnesium-L-threonate and Omega-3 enriched heavy dairy crème.

I am willing to split the profits 50/50 when selling it to snowboarders in Madison, Wisconsin.

(Boswell spoke up then saying I, '…was wrong *again*, Italian roast'.)

Taking a couple sips I realized that I had not had one completely rationale thought since hacking up phlegm in the shower. I turned on the web station and the 3rd Symphony instantly filled the room in real contrast to my ego's delusional faux heroic existence.

No ancestral theban dna/blood streams, or even seasonal creeks, in my family's oral traditions. Thank you anyway for the dreams Laius and Epaminondas.

I then went and put on my shirt and pants. I should have made a phone call, and then gotten over to arraignments, instead I laid back down on the sofa and pulled the cloak up over my chest again. Everything could wait eleven more minutes while I focused.

Beauty of my job is that Court starts at 9:00 am, relatively speaking; unlike the other suits in the glass boxes who start on time by punching the time clock. Problem today is that I have to actually talk to Clement in lockup, which means I had to be there soon. Not a Client Courtesy talk where you calm them with a few words about procedure.

Clement has been my friend since he was in seventh grade. Calm him, as in chill out, as in some emotional breakdown, wasn't likely as everyone in primary school thought he was Lt. Commander Spock from Langley, Virginia. Clement is a stand up no nonsense guy, fun to drink with. He wouldn't tell you, but it surprises no one in the business world that finds out, he was a Gulf I tank crewman, $97^{1/2}$ Easting 2nd Cavalry Apparitions.

I picked up the remote and powered up the television. An annoying rerun of last Sunday's Dr. Goebbels's 'Sportpalast' program was on. Since I did not really care about rallying the soccer fans for the world cup, I changed the channel, and of course got an 'islam in england' show.

It was hilarious.

I had to watch for a minute because it was so funny, better than any sketch ever on saturday late night television. Julius H. Marx,

41

Leonard A. Schneider, and Andrew G. Kaufman know that islamic comedy is an oxymoron. The new English Reformation Channel 1 show was really subtle humor wrapped in rib splitting one liners.

The wannabe comedian was doing his *Islamic Viewpoint and Values for the 21st Century* bit. He billed his act as 'An evening of interfaith commentary and comedy to assay misconceptions about muslims living with non-muslims'.

He got the most laughs from the audience's rowdy yemeni and pakistani soccer fans while doing his jokes on raping your wife to maintain a strong mulsim marriage; though the one about a woman wearing perfume in public being a prostitute got the crowd clapping.

This was very high brow culture stuff for yemenis. The audience of zina loving muslims knew that incongruity, absurdity, and ludicrousness, are at the core of french kissing. Comedians know that core truths are the funniest jokes, especially the core islamic truth that there are not four pious males on the planet.

(Boswell then earnestly inquired of Dr. Johnson whether, "...they should start a dating web site exclusively for Pakistani women who were raped and then were imprisoned under barbaric Hudud laws by a very very very small penis islamic legal system?"

Dr. Johnson replied without hesitation, "Starkville's California Ursidae Stealthy Bonds should assist with the I.P.O.; and not only Pakistani women but all females living under the slavery of islam, and especially fourteen year old girls such as Hena Akhter, who should be given a free life time membership upon their twenty first birthday. All the prokaryotic muslimjihadieeclitorishating male immammies and believers have forfeited all rights in all the multiverses to be in the any spacetimepoint with any woman".)

The wannabe comedian's very skillful presentation of the idea that a good muslim would degrade, beat, rape, and enslave a woman, I can tell you, was killing the audience.

Every comedian knows that to connect with the audience you have to use material that the audience is familiar with, and is part of their everyday lives.

The wannabe had over a millennium of material: beating, raping, belittling, and degrading a wife, a daughter, a mother, a sister, or any women, for the glory of the frenchkissing pedophile.

For me his bit's *'Pièce de résistance'*, from all of the endless material from the religion of peace, was the very, very, very pious *'honor killing'* routine.

It was reminiscent of Jibril's twenty three year career of recycling jokes he stole from the old vaudeville act of 'Suhuf, Tawrat, Tehillim, and Injil'.

The wannabe comedian was lobbying jokes throughout the spacetimepointmultiverses like katyushas from Gaza.

(Dr. Johnson astutely remarked that, "All the Methane Ice Worms on Titan watching the show probably were misinterpreting the comedy for news commentary or just a contradiction of the strong anthropic principle."

That made Boswell laugh out loud as he responded with, "...the very small penis jihadie killers won't admit islam is a form of speciesism".)

I believe the comedian said he just got back from doing two shows a night at the Middle East Policy & Burlesque Theatre on J Street, which had sold out two weeks before the shows.

(Boswell noted that, "The policy and burlesque theatre has been presenting generations of new comics from its start; the most famous being Freddy Nietzsche, and DJ J Gotti Fichte". Dr. Johnson added that, "The MEPBT has been on the International Register of Histrionic Places listing since the Nationalsozialismus Theatre Company bought it in 1933".)

After another minute or so I changed the channel over to an Italian news show. I did not understand what the news presenter was saying.

I gathered the best I could from the imbedded video and the crawler that it was something about a guy named Arshed Masih and his wife Martha.

I think the story was mostly about their employer Sheikh Mohammarries Insultanmyintelligencie.

Apparently Sheikh Insultanmyintelligencie had the Rawalpindi Police Department give Arshed Masih and his wife Martha the Police Department's highest civilian award for their indefatigable promotion of interfaith cooperation between the local mulsim and christian communities.

But the story's imbedded video changed during his presentation. It must have been a rookie studio technician's mistake, because it was never corrected.

Apparently the imbed must have been for another story about this year's Ranan Lurie Award not going to the 'The Pinheads of Tomorrow' character - *california ursidae mohammad.*

From the look of imbedded video, the local muslim soccer hooligan crowd were in the street and were very upset that their favorite cartoon - *california ursidae mohammad* did not win, *or something.*

The news presenter was a professional as he did not let the mistaken imbedded video effect his presentation of the story. He ignored the imbedded video, and finished talking to the camera just as if the Rawalpindi Police Department video was there all along.

I believe that the news story on the Sheikh was just another of the thousands of produced infomercials of that type of misogynistic-slick-fluff-feel good advertisements for the practitioners of peace.

I'm sure some guys in the office of the Volksaufklarung und Propaganda Ministry in Qatar will be asking the Italians for an apology for not clearing the story through them at first.

Fluff stories, especially any stories about giving awards to Christians, were considered only seasonal pieces by Vilayat-e faqih and confined to ramadamnie day's ratings battles.

I picked up the remote and changed the channel again. The United Nations Department of Economic and Social Affairs Division for the Advancement of Women monthly televised forum was on.

I got up and put my tie on while watching to see what the U.N. was doing during last month. Then I layed back down again.

Hillbilliezlah's Mohammamie Bugger Chrarrazzi was lecturing on the formation of the United States of Old Men Wearing Dresses Raping Child Brides.

He was most fervent on its constitutional requirement that all preteen slave girls must act toward all immamies with blatant promiscuity and immodest dress or suffer stoning.

He insinuated the formation of the USOMWDRCB would hasten the reappearance of the Mahdi from his West Hollywood twelve week engagement at the Gay and Lesbian Comedy Club off Sunsetting Avenue.

Hillbilliezlah' s Mohammamie Bugger Chrarrazzi was quick to assure his audience that the Mahdi would be back in time to judge the Pan Arab Adult Entertainment Awards, and hopefully end the tyranny of the FatWadsofHate's thirteen year reign of champion preteen pole dancers, thereby finally bring some justice to the event in the eyes of all the street soccer hooligans. Seventy Two preteen clitorisless sex slaves *is* the prime fantasy all street hooligans.

Hillbilliezlah's Mohammamie Bugger Chrarrazzi made some further stump speech promises. Such as if the USOMWDRCB was ratified before Mahdi returned, then the Pan Arab Adult preteen girls pole dancing idols show would be the dominant show on the new Pan Arab Adult Entertainment channel, and that it would be the number one show in the global village midnight webcasts for the entire season.

Then Hillbilliezlah's Mohammamie Bugger Chrarrazzi pledged, "…if the show was the number one show for the season, he would pay for a celebration at the Ba'Babii'arthie Party Dominatrix Club, where all the potential pledged wannabees Old Men Wearing Dresses Raping Child Brides would have to bring several of their preteen granddaughters as entertainment".

Mohammamie further vowed that, "…if they did not bring preteen granddaughters, they would not be let into the Party Dominatrix Club, or the promised land". He then waved both his hands above his head, and then after straightening his long silk robes, sat down.

All Fawzanesleazest of the Senior Council of Clowns, the highest dollar contributor to western political parties, immediately stood up and took the podium.

All Fawzanesleazest grasped a goblet of '*Yayin Nesekh*' wine from within the podium and held it up as a salute to the camera before drinking all of it in one clown gulp.

All Fawzanesleazest took the microphone and began speaking in a dry squeaky falsetto voice, "The Senior Council of Clowns is willing to support the USOMWDRCB as USOMWDRCB has signed a 'Corpus Separatum' with the Senior Council of Clowns granting the Clowns complete authority to enforce islam's commitment to slavery. Anyone who isn't a Clown is an ignorant polytheist, and the Clown scholars are hereby awarded, under the International Union of Clown agreement with the United Nations Department of Economic and Social Affairs Division for the Advancement of Women, all the ignorant polytheist's blood, money, and especially their preteen girls."

Under his silk robe, All Fawzanesleazest's tiny tiny tiny tiny tiny tiny tiny tiny tiny tiny tiny tiny tiny tiny penis was getting erect as he spoke, as it always did when he preached the kkkoran's directive on sex slaves.

All Fawzanesleazest's tiny tiny tiny tiny tiny tiny tiny tiny tiny tiny tiny tiny tiny penis preferred dark hair, preteen, jewish slave girls.

He picked up a copy of '*All-Tawreasonlessnazihateforsmallpenis-menwhoareMonopervets*"; (his most recent Comic Book released by the local Arabian Gulf Government's Marvelous Series for Muslim Soccer Hooligans and which is used as the preferred text book at the I'amacrazyjihadist Frenchkisser Osama Bin Laden Islamic Wahacrybaby University), and started reading. "Provoke God's wrath and continue sinning by not killing infidels and enslaving all those preteen Chinese, Japanese, Korean, European, American, African, and especially Russian Jewish girls, and you will go to the bottom of Hell. Slavery is a major part of jihad for old men with very small penises..."

I picked up the remote and changed the channel to a heroic battle scene from 1959. The fighting men of the P.L.A.'s 308th Artillery Regiment were attacking from a politically progressive position on the leftist bank of the Lhasa River. Without regard for their personal mortality, the PLA soldiers repeatedly fired the Party's war weary Kaiser Wilhelm Geschütz directly into the peaceful Potala Palace.

The brave men of the 308th, without moralis, or any personal reflection on their actions, strived to insure that every one of their 120 kg projectile party shells went directly through the Potala Palace walls destroying all the royal photocopiers.

The Potala Palace finally cried out, '*Budda way to forsake me Mudda Fudda*', sounding like some Rican Baggey Pants LLC'er named Marcellus the Centurion on some street corner in South Central near Gravesend.

It was then the Potala Palace chose to surrender itself to the brave soldiers of the P.L.A.'s 308th.

Upon discovering the Potala Palace was refusing to fight, just as nostra aetate roman catholics refuse, the brave men of the 308th stormed the building.

Then the soldiers, without regard to their own salvation, burned all the books and manuscripts found within the building, per their orders from the Supreme Comrade ZDungWhoWillRotInHell commanding 'Deus Vult'.

(Dr. Johnson thought it was important that, "…the 308th's Commander only looted Jim's watch and had permitted his men only take one of Della's combs." Of course any real treasures, such as gold idols, frankinonsense jewels, myrrh shekels, and half-shekels of Tyre silver pieces, were sent back to the Shanghai Baal Sculpture Foundries. Boswell laughed saying, "If the building had sounded like it was a Rican from Inglewood, the 308th's automatons would have had to blow it the hell up, because Ricans from Inglewood would die photocopying.")

The present spacetimepointfact was that I had to go see Clement. I really needed to get started on my day instead of watching the unconditional surrendering of yet another building's Lockean Natural Right to smoke dope in its own chimney.

("Yet another triumph in the Department of Health's campaign to eradicate smoking in the working classes. Anybody have an extra Virginia Slender 100 I can bum?" Boswell said as he tempestuously laughed.)

I knew that I had just wasted eleven minutes of my limited lifespactimepoints watching insane aneurysm inducing nonsense. I knew that instead of watching such insane nonsense that I should have been gyrating prostrate on the floor meditating on all of the Great Prophet Farrokh Bulsara hadith's in preparation to experience today's perturbations of Newton's 1st, 2nd, & 3rd.

I absentmindedly started humming 'o terra addio' as I powered downed the television. I put the remote down, underneath the sofa, next to my tattered copy of Hogshire's 'You Are Going to Prison'.

Chapter Four   Der Teufel Horen Sie

I rolled over on my side, and as I did a magazine residing between a cushion and the back of the sofa surfaced by sticking sharply into my left teres minor. I pulled it out. It was a copy of '*True Stories*' magazine from July, 1940 - the best selling issue of all time for the company. It had a quite enchanting cover picture of Pauline Kohler, the personal maid for Member Number Seven of the National Socialist Labor Party.

(Boswell finds Ms. Kohler to be, "…as fine a writer as Ms. P. Barrell".)

The True Stories cover article was a lurid and titillating retelling by Ms. Kohler, of the ancient tale of a powerful politician and the women whom he abused during his career. The Tragōidi had various acts: an immolation of a young innocent catholic girl; the stalking of a minor film star on the north bank of the Aioi river, public exhibitions to his staff and their families some 8 mm recordings of an older naked mistress, some mischling ex-mayor's wife.

The women all were willing to let Member Number Seven use them and abuse them, for the opportunity to be paid in fine jewelry, furs, and expensive dresses, for being available to the Aryan politician.

Very racy and fun stuff to read, harmless voyeurism, especially for Starkville's women who were bored no doubt with discussing again whether the U.S. should follow Canada's policy of selling only slaughtered hogs on a carcass-graded basis; and reading Bao Shichen's '*Nongzhen*'. Again

Kasarian Sex Rhyw Sex Seks Sex الجنس Sex

Noun or verb, it was still a physical disorder or ailment, listed prominently in Starkville's Self Diagnostic and Statistical Manual of Legal Mental Disorders Vol. XXX.x.II.

It was definitely NOT the type of ailment that was worth wasting any more of my precious life force on. Primitive organism pre-programmed species survival mechanism, not individual survival mechanism, specifically my surviving my life's only true romantic relationship.

Damn, Rosa was fun. (Geliebter, komm! Stets soll nur dir. Elend ich habe sie verloren!)

I am not a cloistered Gregor Mendel, nor a confused Buddhist contemplating the ether*net* for that matter. Jesus H. Fucking Christ, my non-reproducingsexacts really aren't worth the energy when it is all said and done, and it is certainly very boring to talk about.

Writing about notoliparis kermadecensis transcendence is much more enjoyable than talking about any of my sexual performances, and is not such a complete waste of precious spacetimepoints, as are all my sexual encounters.

Other than the small personal satisfaction it gives me to discuss them in great detail with Dr. Johnson and Boswell on our saturday afternoon internet call-in sex education webcasts to the arabian peninsula's community access channels. Last week's callers were all from Qom.

I notice, and make allowances for, when doing any scientific sampling of eroticism, of my Starkville bias. Inevitably I always forget about allah – I always repress all the allah's in the multiverses, not just the one here in Starkville.

Multiple allahs and yahwehs present a paradox to the muslim faithful, which is why jihadiimmammaginarys hate science. My bias is to my Starkville multiverses, while not condoning that whole *'Hasan came running and jumped into his lap'* thing. As a post hubblespacetelescopeStarkvilleatheist, I prefer my supreme beings and prophets, at a minimum, not sticking their tongues in any young boy mouths, or sticking anything into a preteen girl. So this multiverse's allah achieves repressed memory status.

Well, that, and the Mazen Abdul Jawad thing.

(I admit I have little understanding of beliefs in Genesis Chapter 1, (especially 1:26); or in Sura' Al-Baqarah, Sura' As-Sajdah, and Sura'Yassin, (especially Al-Baqarah:30); yet whatever mythical creator you interject into the creation equation one subset of data has not changed: Darwin's 1890 religious theory -*The Preservation of Favored Hominoids in the Struggle for Life*, "At some future period, not very distant as measured by centuries, the civilized races of man will almost certainly exterminate, and replace, the savage muslims throughout the world…The break between man and his nearest allies will then be wider, for it will intervene between man in a more civilized state… and some ape as low as a imammiijihaditiibonobos screeching the adhan, instead of as now between homo sapiens sapiens and very small penis mutaween and much smaller penis basij and malikis jihadiebombisiamangs". My bias to my Starkville multiverse realities hypothesis causes my rejection of 'pedophilia' as a trait of a true prime calculator. Ancient greek pottery god's included. As I have repeatedly told Dr Johnson, "That, of course, and a similar bias towards Fuhrer und Reichskanzler and Hajji Amin El Husseini, who all agreed that Hasan jumping into laps and frenchkissing was one of the best stories in that book of hate." (*The first edition - not the retread July 18th, 1925 Volksausgabe copy.*) Dr Johnson then always inquires of Boswell from the 32nd of Newton's Queries, "What is the difference between supreme beings or old prophet's frenchkissing young boys versus catholic priests frenchkissing young boys". Boswell consistently replies he believes, "It is a matter of a few parsecs, since priests are merely clerks, and clearly were not Pope Rahbara Moazzam".)

When my eroticism is all said and done, I end up by myself drinking homemade tea and smoking a Kensitas with a joint of my Northern Lights. I rolled over on my other side and then farted so hard that Ahmad Shah's old cloak ruffled. Déjà phew of last night's bowl of pork and bear cubes with my green chile sauce/garlic/jalapenos.

I then rolled back over. I rubbed my left teres minor while softly humming a staccato '*O TERRA ADDIO*'.

It would take a pen and paper plus twenty minutes of quiet reflection; then I might possibly be able to get the right number.

("Well, at least then you would probably be very close to the number", stated Dr. Johnson. Boswell attempted to make an Adams prediction by saying "The answer has to be, of which I am certain the HP-35 will verify, '*42.*'".)

There is no way in hell I could remember all the foreign names, or the ones who only offered a nickname other than *Agrippina*.

So for any of those woman still living in the Arabian gulf - you're safe from your insaneimammies as long as you don't go on THC's Intrepid Green Light show, broadcasting from Tattle-tale al-Zaa-TV on Saturday's midnight dual WEB-TV broadcast right after Claudius and Grimani's '*Liberetto*', showing my tattoo on your lower back.

Not even their first names. Well of course Messalina and Clodia, and the first names of a very few of them. I will always remember a couple of them. I have their scars reminding me at various trigger spacetimepoints throughout my every day and night.

("Now only you date women with Mayer Rokitansky Kuster Hauser Syndrome.", quipped Boswell while nodding his head at Dr. Johnson. "Brahmacharya.", Dr. Johnson replied with his endless dissatisfaction. Yet Boswell and I cannot de-link aparigraha-ahimsa-satya-asteya. It is an all or nothing commitment Boswell and I continually insist to Dr. Johnson.)

The postindustrialposthubblespacetelescope individual's existence does not need the tribe, gaggle, colony, or swarm, to survive emotionally. The postindustrialposthubblespacetelescopeindividual soul sustains itself on endless streams of binary code. All physical relationships are convenience. Sex is the opiate of the masses or something. A disease, if you can count additive behavior as a disease. John Lennon wanted followers because he knew societies needed working class heroes. I have enough addictions.

Modern postindustrialposthubblespacetelescoper's ejaculate to pornographic webcasts of synthetic sex between ruckus mycoplasma mycoides and vacuous mycoplasma capricolum at 1080p with 150,000:1 dynamic contrast ratio, and with a seven channel speaker system reproducing the full range of frequencies to stimulate the medial orbito frontal cortex.

Is digital sex considered sex with idols by insaneimamies? Or is it just a run of the mill transgression - such as raping a preteen kafir slave, oh wait - raping slaves is sanctioned in the moronokorano and permitted by all frenchkissers even today, ask any insaneimmamiiebombiiies.

I should ask the insaneimamies if a run of the mill transgression such as having an impure thought about the mischling ex-mayor of tehran's wife, the soprano Lulu, is prohibited.

Is watching Lulu's midnight balcony webcasts prohibited? Is listening to the audio of her midnight balcony webcasts prohibited?

I still remember a few lines of her poetry from last night's sultry performance, spoken so tenderly, and so lovingly:

'Tis but thy religion that is my enemy, thou are thyself, though not a jihadist. What is a jihadist? It is not blood soaked hand, feet standing in rivers of blood, arms beheading innocent's, hiding your guilty face under burqa like a woman. O, be some other religion belonging to a rationale man.

What's in a religion? That which we call an insane murderers, By any other word would smell as foul. So jihadie would, were he not impure with religion, retain that humanism which is innate, and for thy honest man which is no part of religion, take all of my midnight webcasts.'

Romantic Balcony Love is rare, and is purchased by practitioners of monasticism from Tahrir Square with a high income, and a Tudor house with a large master bath room complete with whirlpool bathtub, also having a heated outside pool, and of course a couple German automobiles in the multiple car garage.

(Wahhahaha and the other crybabiii's with their ridiculous misogynist enslavement of women always require two swimming pools, separated by sex. Really have to wonder why Wahhahahacrybabi's are such big perv's that they can't even swim with women in bikinis. Have to be the weakest willed men that ever existed. Must be very small penis syndrome with sex sex sex sex sex sex sex sex sex on their minds all the time that killing nonbelievers isn't. Jihadist think of sex just like the rest of us preprogrammed males, but nonbelievers are without the homicidal rage of being an ignorant very very very small penis 7th century murdering Al' pervertedjihadie. It doesn't require enslavement of others to discipline your own mind. Narcissistic to Histrionic – your soul is darkest black you sick pedophile fucks, with your very small penis killing of innocents while fantasizing of raping 72 clitorisless preteen girls. Boswell then spoke up stating in a gruff voice that, "It is the same very small penis jihadies who are selling their 9 year old daughters as brides to 81 year old frenchkissers to pay monetary debts. Insane jihadiefathers religiously selling their own daughters, clitoris included. Does the hubblespacetelescope work in the 7th century?")

I sat up and looked at a moth that was flying around the outside the window inches above the sill. It was small grayish green with black streaks on its wings.

'*Nabokovia ada,* no it's an *Ectoedemia jdglassi'*, I thought. Well it was for about three more seconds, then a juvenile bateleur swept down and the air show was over.

("Malice and hate are common juvenile bateleur traits", Dr. Johnson observed and Boswell agreed. Dr. Johnson then started quietly humming *'Pace t'imploro'*.)

The business of the day could wait no longer. It was time to head over to the Justice Center. I got off the blanco baraq leather skin sofa and opened the window and took three deep breaths over the kill zone. (*Nam-myoho-renge-kyo*) I then went back and folded Ahmad Shah's old handmade cloak while placing it over the back of the sofa.

I opened the middle desk drawer and got out my glass pipe. Pinched a bit of a neon green Northern Lights bud's crystallized leaves.

The buds were harvested last Sunday, from the cut plants hanging upside down on cast iron laundry hooks in the massive black walnut attic beams at 14 North Moore Street. We had celebrated an especially potent harvest thanks to the engineering marvel that is the Baggy Pants LLC Gore Green Energy Seal *'Rottweiler'* model hydroponics unit.

I took three long hits and then put the pipe underneath the blanco baraq leather skin sofa, then grabbed the mouth wash that I keep stashed behind the sofa. I took a small gulp of it and then put the bottle back, while enjoying the burning sensation a bit too much no doubt.

Then I slowly forced the liquid back and forth over my tongue as I walked over to the window and spit the sensually burning mouth wash out: a 13th floor non-hazardous material drop test.

Well OK, a biohazard to any of those 61, or maybe 83, at most 97, paraponera clavata in the gutter patiently waiting for me. Since they were waiting for me, they were immediately aware of the non-hazardous material drop test.

They quickly formed a phalanx. Then their leader Epaminondas then called out to me.

"JD losest labor
As easy mayst thou the intrenchant vapors
With THC sword impress as sciences bleed
Let fall thy DNA drool on vulnerable crests
We bear a verysmallpenis life, which must not yield
To one of woman born."

I shut the window and turned my back on the contemptuous Theban.

Chapter Five   Incoming Tide

I picked up my calendar with the morning's file folders, put a pen in my pocket, and then took my black wool suit coat off its hook on the back of the door and put it on.

As I locked my office door and turned toward the elevator, an immense feeling of sadness engulfed me to the point where I lost my balance.

A couple lines of Tennyson flashed through my mind; '*Tears, idle tears, I know not what they mean, Tears from the depth of some divine despair, Rise in the heart, and gather to the eyes…*'

After a second I regained my muscle control as the emotion weakened, but it was also accompanied with tinge of dread. No that is denial and obfuscation.

It was a transference of dread tsunami throughout my nervous system. Was it caused by an undersea earthquake thousands of light years away, or possibly just another uropaquake or titanquake?

More probable, a tsunami arising from what I did or did not do last Sunday, reflecting as dark energy waves passing throughout my hippocampus's nucleotides neuronal noise consciousness, and it's spinning worm hole vortex, that is all of my spacetimepoints sundaymondaytuesdaywednesdaythursdayfridaysaturdaysundays.

My left hand began to scratch at my beard while I stood waiting for the elevator. (Dr. Johnson murmured, "It's definitely not myoclonus".)

Beard scratching, a nervous habit no doubt, instinctual and acquired behavior; an organism following innate patterns within the gravity waves amongst the scaffolding of the dark matter of this morning's spacetimepointsconsciousness.

That is, unless, you are a posthubblespacetelescope atheist, whose imaginary soul is 3.14159265 angstroms of spinning polarized qiyamah positroniums, which are constantly shedding composite particles of 𝑇𝐻𝐶 hadrons, and whose beard merely itches.

(Dr. Johnson opined to Boswell that I was either, "…ignorant of basic physics, or just insanely damned".)

As soon as I entered the elevator I started daydreaming, and singing a favorite tune, '...*watching the P-waves roll in and then watch S-waves roll away again...*'

Not actually out loud, I never actually vocalize when I sing any Otis Redding songs about the neurons in my medial frontal cortex.

As the elevator descended, and then as I exited it, I knew I wasn't actually daydreaming either as I was singing, it was more of remembering a former possible spacetimepointconsciousness which had recreated some faux scene from a faux Wooster Group theatre production in the round. It definitely wasn't a scene in a Capulet family tomb in some darken churchyard. As I made my way out of the building I couldn't remember much of it, more mood than substance:

After Appomattox, San Francisco had become the Restaurant at the End of the Universe. Douglas Adams had moved it about a zillion parsecs after hearing of Otis's death. The Promised Land abruptly ends with steep cliffs being bashed by the cold waves of arctic chilled waters of the Pacific Ocean. Richard Brautigan was eating clam chowder while Henry Miller sipped Rhum Negrita on the deck at the Italian's Restaurant on the pier. Jack London and John Steinbeck were late. Miller was bored, and had not drunk enough Rhum Negrita yet to tell Brautigan how effeminate his books were. Just about then, Douglas Adams had enough of Miller's morose desires and solemn remembrances of Mademoiselle Claude and slammed the improbability drive into the no boundary proposal position...........

As soon as I got outside my mind's faux theatre cobweb curtains fell. I felt better immediately.

The sky was blue. High cirrus, almost transparent, scattered in the western skyline of the city.

A light western breeze was accumulating the sewer gases from the street drains with the street's carbon monoxide and fluorocarbons.

I took a deep breath (nam-myoho-renge-kyo) and my thoughts slowed. I put two fingers on my right carotid artery little less than 30 seconds; maybe 103 bpm.

Took another deep breath and then rolled my head to left before exhaling. I wasn't a bit manic, just exhausted physically.

("Liar Liar Liar", sang Dr. Johnson and Boswell 'a cappella' before laughing uncontrollably.)

I headed to the Justice Center with the soft breeze at my back and the new morning blue sky ahead of me. The sunlight was casting my shadow seven or so degrees westward, another multipolar - multiverse morning for me and my somewhat visible morning shadow.

I was about seven steps to the curb when the traffic light changed, so I stopped a few steps short of the curb. Of course I took the time to grab a cigarette and light up, and then began wonder a bit, a bit about the traffic light that is, bet a Kensitas that not one of the Baggy Pants LLC'ers had ever even heard of Garrett Augustus Morgan or Lewis Howard Latimer.

(Boswell then spoke up saying that I was "a racist" because I limited the proposed question to '…Baggy Pants LLC'ers'.)

I knew there was no Baggy Pants LLC'er that was going to pick up a pen and write a Louis Auchincloss's "manhattan monologues" about Starkville these days either.

(I rejoined Boswell by stating, "You and Dr. Johnson both no doubt would say it would be an urban period piece. You would say it would have characters that rely on, and are obsessed with, tribal relationships. You delusional paranoids would say it would show the neighborhood's moral failing, and the total lack of any appreciation by the young neighborhood entrepreneur Baggy Pants LLC'ers in an education of science and western philosophy instead of faithfully pursuing their tirich mir orange kush intifada. I say it would be a hell of a read because I am a boswellian racist or *something*".)

59

"Hey JD, where you going?" asked Matthew, who had walked up behind me as I lit up. I wasn't in the mood to interact with another person just yet. Matthew was a pleasant enough man, married with children, a tax attorney of no small accomplishments, solid character, smart, and had the gift of humor. I needed more time to be able to interact with my fellow citizens, especially Matthew's type, who apparently had figured out their existence in this multiverse to their own personal satisfaction.

(Usual normative is to default to faith; as doubly strange particles don't make any sense to any homo sapiens sapiens really with small 1400 g brains, which I am pretty sure is my situation this morning. At least my working hypothesis is that mine will weigh in at 1019g - of which only 66.6% was working.)

I replied, actually attempting to smile, "Shavua tov, Room A" even though I've been atheist since the 4th of December in 1959 - by way of generations of European Roman Catholics.

The attempted smiled wasn't just because it's fun to pronounce 'Shavua tov' with a Midwestern accent, it was more of the civilized meaning of my greeting conveyed to a fellow homo sapiens sapiens this morning.

Of course, it showed my normal morning situational spacetimepointabsentmindedness, possibly due to my morning's tetrahydrocannabinols emotional detachment from the reality of my spacetimepointsworkdaydestination.

I realized then that I really physically needed another cup of coffee, even a cup of the barging brand Aldobrandinian.

"Anything fun on your morning schedule Matt", I asked.

The light changed and we started walking across the street toward the justice center and the court house.

"No JD, just a couple truancy admissions and a sentencing over in juvenile court", he stated flatly and then added, "...should be back in my office by quarter of eleven or so."

After taking a couple more steps I held up my left hand mimicking Leonard Nemoy's 'Spock' as I quipped, "Live long and prosper upon your successes in today's juvenile courtroom Olivet discourses Matthew". I turned at a 45° toward the middle of the opposite sidewalk. I am such a geek.

Matthew turned and smiled, as he said in the manner of a tone death green blooded vulcan, "Judge not, that ye be not judged". He turned around and walked on without me.

I walked across the street weaving through the cars, until reaching the next corner. I threw my cigarette away, before walking into my favorite bakery hoping for a cup of any freshly brewed coffee. It was crowded.

I could not even see the display cases due to all the people standing around. I turned around and left. I had no time for waiting in line as I had to get to lockup.

Orlando Zapata Tamayo came to mind. I immediately started to feel guilty for desiring pastries, and then for my spacetimepoints total lacking of consequentialness.

Damn. The bakery's aroma of fresh baked apple-raisin strudels, buttery croissants, and almond-honey bienenstich mixed with the expresso beans being filtered into cups, was a malicious attempt by Aglaopheme and Thelxiepeia to arouse within me impossible desires, and to waylay me from my sworn duties of this morning.

I lit another cigarette walking over to the JC. I had to nod - or say the perfunctory "good morning" a couple times walking past judges, lawyers, police officers, court staff, and other occasional familiar work day faces whose lives I really know nothing about.

As soon as I got to the Justice Center I took a long drag finishing off my cigarette. I then put it in the concrete ashtray among fifty one or so other expended nicotine delivery systems. I got in the small line of fellow citizens waiting outside the doors of the JC.

When my turn came, I walked through the revolving doors of the Starkville Justice Center, just like everyone else does twenty four hours a day, three hundred sixty five days a year.

I immediately went into the vending area to the left of the revolving doors.

I put two quarters into one of the vending machines.

Post Industrial Men have only three choices: coffee/ hot chocolate/ chicken soup.

It isn't a choice. It's more of a compulsion, paths in the road not taken; an electro-mechanical multiverse rorschach personality test, with negative and positive stimulus effects.

Of course, per the multiverse's plan of the day, I got a cup of hot tawny water with a palatable hint of instant coffee crystals for my no longer sensitive palate.

Operative ingredient being at most a couple dehydrated bean crystals in scalding water. I would venture made from stale coffee beans somewhere around 42 – 46 defects and -190 to -200 points on the Brazil / New York Scale.

I gave it a score of absolute zero on today's scale between predestination and total depravity.

Have to respect and admire Aglaopheme and Thelxiepeia's work this morning. Complete emotional cycling in mere minutes.

Short term memory hop heads can ride the emotions up and down that long without drifting off into dimension 6 or 9.

Hubblespacetelescopestoners are addicted to watching Aglaopheme and Thelxiepeia's midnight balcony webcasts in 1080p with 150,000:1 dynamic contrast ratio, and with the 7 channel speaker system reproducing the full range of frequencies to stimulate the THC encrusted medial orbito frontal cortexes.

If I had fifteen minutes I'd walk over to the clerk's office and hand write out a 'Beleidigung Complaint' with a salacious count against both of them. Then I'd probably add a punitive demand based upon sexual harassment just for my own selfish personal gratification of asking them both lewd and lascivious questions in each of their lengthy depositions.

The height of sensual desire in the bakery to the lowest reality of crushed expectations from the justice center vending machine.

It was very nice work considering it's only about 08:33 am. Aglaopheme and Thelxiepeia were on a higher level than usual with this morning's reality.

Colour-separation overlay dissolving greenscreen and bluescreen as I stood there and thought of Karajan conducting Beethoven's 5th Symphony in Coffee Minor to cleanse my anger.

After standing there listening to the Seers' portentous joint prophecy with my eyes closed for about forty three seconds, I began smiling and felt OK.

No anger peculating though my thalamus as the retro reflective curtain rose again.

I threw the cup in the vending area trash bin. Then I started humming very softly as I walked across the hall to the entrance to lock up. I shoved my calendar and files under my arm and got my ID out of my wallet.

I slid the ID into the camera tray under the wall camera next to the door. I hit the black plastic button above the tray.

As soon as I heard the door buzz, I grabbed my ID back and I pushed open the steel door.

As the door closed behind me, I put my ID back in my wallet and then the wallet inside my coat pocket.

On my right there was a visitor's log on a small steel case desk, and directly in front of me was another steel door. I signed in, and then waved up at the room camera, waiting for the door to open.

Don't have to use the black button to buzz past here as Command Center watches everything - controlling all doors from here on in.

I took three deeps breaths, (*Nam-myoho-renge-kyo*). I pulled at my beard stubble with a slight twist a couple times while waiting as I softly sang, '.....*Watching the P-waves come in and watching S-waves go away again*'.

Brother Otis the only waves I see here are the flowing tides of humanity rolling through these halls up to Tarpeian Rock State Correctional or being discharged back into the streets of my neighborhood.

I was being very careful not to slip on all the tiger slug mucus trails on the floor. (*WAVE PHASE RESIDUALS*)

The door lock buzzed open.

It was " SHOW TIME ".

Chapter Six   Leninist Theory

Here in Starkville's version of '*Lazzaretto Vecchio*' are my fellow citizens and noncitizens, my fellow Homo sapiens sapiens, my brothers and sisters.

Our incarcerated DNA was osculating integrase enzymes amid the endless waves of neutrinos strafing the plus polarized gravitational waves.

(Dr. Johnson cited the metaphysical enzyme osculation's to the September 1st, 1939 issue of '*Fortschritte der Physik and Verhandlungen*'.)

The Inn was full, and smelled of human sweat. The type of cortisol smell that sets everyman's grueneberg ganglion tingling, no Ludwig-Boltzmann study was needed, take my word for it. It was a Phil Doppelganger densely layered '*Wall of Smell*' Thermo-Key production.

An odious deception of my senses that possibly 33132 mark(ed) brothers and sisters were in lock up this morning.

Down the entire hallway on my right was a four foot concrete block wall. Set in the block was polycarbonate thermoplastic layered glass running up to the ceiling.

On the other side of the glass there were about one hundred fifteen prisoners.

Second guess, with a quick look at faces scattered though out the crowded concrete and block room, was that there were a lot more - with some out of sight sitting on metal benches anchored along the far wall, and others squatting or laying on the floor. Each person was sitting or standing where they could.

(This morning Dr. Johnson had '…no theories for distribution of prisoner particle density in the concrete block cell'. Of course clinician Boswell had to proffer his stock thesis of '…*criminal chaos theory*'.)

All of the inmates were in the clothes they were wearing when they were arrested. It is one of those occasions you don't dress for - like death.

Everyone knows being arrested it is a possibility when they dress themselves every morning, but *not for you, not this day.*

You never plan to dress for being handcuffed, transported in a marked cruiser, booked, and the 21st century required internet bound photo.

Occasionally, when I am visiting lock up, there will be a junior college political science professor type arrested for DUI after leaving some trendy wine bar, who is for the first time experiencing the JC in practice, not in theory.

Political science professors need first person experience of the local jurisdiction's police powers policies being implemented versus professorial third-person omniscient lectures.

Especially when such Jr. Professors types were leading in-class socratic discussions with young impressionable minds regarding that ascetic british trained lawyer who was imprisoned four times for being very annoying; in 1922, 1930, 1933, and 1942.

Whenever in lockup, the associate political science professor types were always nervously chatting with certain cell mates, with whom they would never speak to again after making bail.

The professor's later renditions of this adventure to fellow happy hour codependent graphic artist students was expressed with a certain *'je ne sais quoi'* street credibility, during which the Jr. Professor of course would stress the dangerous nature of his fellow cell mates.

Of course avoiding the dangerous cell mates was the only reason Jr Professors were nervously talking with all the other Countesses; which went unsaid during these later renditions to the nubile art students.

All future happy hour codepedent female multimedia/journalism students will process this puffery, these expanding retellings, by a naive osmosis into becoming *their own experience* in the lockup at the JC.

As they did with the other thirty seven hours a week they spent watching cable reality shows such as the 'Pinheads of Tomorrow', or maybe 'Pinheads of the Day After'.

(Boswell quipped that, "The enlightened duality of the godsverses endless realities and interplanetary manifestations are all on two jihadist channels, both with sanitary pad advertisements".)

Perhaps, watching and listening to jr. professors is the safest way to learn where countesses are in the prison hierarchy scale.

("Also incontinence pads," Dr. Johnson joked with Boswell. Boswell who was contemplating nubile art students when he hesitated, and then in all seriousness asked, "Do sanitary pads have pictures of famous jihadists on them like they make on urinal screens with the pictures of Bin Laden?" Dr. Johnson said he, "…didn't think so, but would be great way to increase sales to the Russian Orthodox universities – by putting Kimmie Illie Sung Midget Puke and mischling ex-mayors of Tehran on them".)

Every few feet in lockup was an alcoholic or crack addict, who was physically or chemically impaired, more often to the 'nth degree while in Starkville Justice Center intake holding cells, perhaps more probable, both.

There was a scattering of the unkempt and unbathed mentally ill in the morning crowd. They were usually of two types. Both types avoided bathing.

1st type, call them Shark Eyes; you know the docile individuals whose eyes were blank, flat, with expressionless gaze. Dangerous.

2nd type, call them Cheetah Eyes; you know the agitated individuals, suspiciousness eyes flashing hostility, extreme reactions to sound and light, babbling in strange words. Dangerous.

There was an occasional silk polo shirt, or Brooks Brothers business suit. The majority of the remaining souls were the Baggy Pants LLC'ers, assorted domestic disputers, B & E's dressed ninja black, and all the other assorted misdemeanors types.

It is the same Caste System every morning, every group represented, though the percentages fluctuate.

Just like my ability lately to interpret the oscilloscope's graphing of my edinger-westphal nuclei waves for defense of Y, with mitigating factors of X, to ascertain the prosecution's provable facts into the GHz range.

Some had been in lock up since yesterday morning's docket, but probably eighty one per cent came in after 2141 hours.

In the hallway on my left were a series of five interview rooms.

Those rooms were full of public defenders diligently meeting today's mostly cookie cutter batch of clients – unemployed high school dropout chemically dependent misogynists, always with alibi's, and whose personal history and all their children's names and their babies mamas names the Public Defender knows going in from the last time the misogynists came through the revolving doors of the justice center.

("Forgetting Starkville's Dalits, Vasisha, and Kshatriya types are we?" smugly noted the Progressive Brahmin Boswell.)

The hallway splits in a Y about twenty three meters from the door, with the guard's control booth dividing the hallway.

Off to the right was booking. The humiliation, well to be factually correct - humiliation only applies to a minority of the clientele, of providing name / address / social security number / phone number / next of kin / employer, and then the ink on the fingers, the photo against the height lined background painted on the concrete block wall, and for felons - the swab in the mouth or other taking of body fluids.

Off to the left were the entrances to the court rooms. Judgment day: well actually just the reading of the charges and the setting of bonds in this building.

At morning arraignments the press and their cameras are meters or so to the left of the Judge's desk corner. That way they get the '*Perp Walk*' to the podium with a clear shot of the judge on the bench. Reporters were always hoping to make the editor's cut and get face time on that day's local news show. Crime pays.

The control booth had seven officers for opening and closing the various doors as prisoners and attorneys went back and forth from lock up to the interview rooms.

I went left at the booth and ambled about nineteen feet down to the holding room's courtroom security area. At its one desk there were always several officers. One was always diligently writing on the morning's paperwork it seemed.

It is where the prisoners were let into the court rooms as their names were called out. There were five officers acting as human traffic cops there this morning.

I knew all by face, none by first name, even though I have been over here a couple of mornings a week for how many years now?

This morning it really smelled of homo sapiens sa*peeing,* worse than about any other time I had ever been here. It was a nervous odor. I prefer nervous sweat odors to alcoholic vomiting odors.

The worst smells are the mentally ill losing body functions as they lay on the concrete floor and benches. Never body outlines in chalk, but several bodily fluids outlines on today's floor.

This morning the dominating smell was of the nervous and scared, and occasionally, the angry stench of the bi-polars. Humidity was evident on every shirt. Most having large dark wet circles of perspiration.

"Good Morning Sergeant, what's with the Air Conditioning?"

"Morning counselor, don't know exactly, but maintenance has been working on it since seven or so."

"You have a Giulio Clement in population Sergeant?"

"Yes counselor, he's in back there somewhere."

The Sergeant then turned and yelled "Giulio Clement" at the mass of individuals in the holding cell.

"Sergeant, it looks like the inn is full this morning?" I commented as I looked into the crowded cell.

"We are letting all nonviolent females out, and a lot of the men too. Just not enough space for everyone as required under the federal judge's order. You must be making fat stacks of cash counselor."

"That's great news for my clients, gets them home by early afternoon. Why not just O.R. bond everyone? You'd sure make me look more effective Sergeant."

I saw Clement walking to the doorway. He looked pissed off, but other than that seemed none the worse for sitting in lockup overnight.

"Giulio", I shook his hand and then put my hand on his back as I led him out into the hallway about a meter.

We stopped and he leaned up against the wall and put his left foot on the wall.

"Don't suppose there is a chance in hell you will slip me one of your cigarettes JD?

He asked as if he just expected me to hand him my whole pack and my zippo too.

Now, similar to H. S. Thomspon, I thought it definitely was in my best interest, and ours perhaps, and maybe in the interest of the greater good of the entire Starkville justice system, for both of us to smoke a joint of my northern lights.

"Hell, in the good old days we both could have lit up in here, and by the way, of course fucking not. Presently at least I get to walk the hell out of here as soon as I get you arraigned."

Giulio looked surprised by the required indignity of denying the incarcerated a cigarette.

"By the way counselor, you look like the transients who live under the bridge by the river; you still stoned from last night? You've been drinking those Blanca Opsin Mohito's at the jazz bar?" He stopped and looked me directly in my bloodshot eyes. "Fuckin ironic, I'm sitting on concrete benches here all night, and I'm asking Mr. Mooheetoe if you're fucking Ok."

He was right it was ironic. I did look like rubbish but I really wasn't in pain to speak of right then.

I certainly wasn't physically incapacitated.

I could perform well enough for the justice system. Once the curtain goes up and the house lights dim, you just slip into character and perform.

A Judy Garland cutout, circa November 18, 1959.

"Ok, in a minute you are going back in, and then in a while your case will be called and they bring you out to the podium in the courtroom through that door over there. A Corrections Officer will be behind you all the way in, at the podium, and back out here."

"JD, when am I getting the hell out of here?"

"In the court room you don't say anything. Nothing, unless I tell you to and then, only a yes, or no, or I understand."

"Am I getting the hell out of here before lunch or not?"

"Giulio did you hear me, not a word unless I tell you to talk and then look the judge in the eye, and answer with a yes or no, or a short sentence. Do you understand?" I was wasting my breath because he was smart enough to know his part intuitively. How many decades knowing Clement? He always was much more attuned in social settings than me. I get lost in the individual facts and details.

"I am not a moron, AM I GETTING OUT BEFORE LUNCH, COUNSELOR?"

"Damn it keep your voice down Giulio." Clement was beginning to piss me off, "If you raise your voice again I am going to request the Judge to order the brain electrical oscillations signature scan and fingerprinting test to see if you are doing it just to piss me off." It was obvious the only thing on his mind after sitting in the intake cell all night was just to get out and go home.

"J.D. - you jerk off wishing you had the power to have scientific experiments done to other people's brains don't you ol' Buddy?" Clement said with emphasis on the 'OTHER' while smiling a Cheshire cat '*Were all Mad Here*' smile.

He could give a damn about the charge, no sign of contrition, remorse or regrets; in his mind this all was just a private matter. He just wanted to go home.

Don't we all.

Clement wanted to go to a place that had ceased to exist as soon as he was handcuffed and lead out the front door. He was going to be legally homeless, not her.

It somewhat reminded me of Boswell's favorite street tag.

:) spacetimepoints are a bitch (:

72

"Giulio if you shut up and let me do the talking you should be fine. The bond will have to be posted and you will have to sign a protection order keeping you away from her, the kids, and your own house. You should be processed and out by 1 pm at the very latest."

That did it, his eyes flashed and his face tightened. Definitely hit pay dirt, the kids.

"Call Linus, or Cletus, and get one of them down here. Tell them bring cash for the bond."

"As soon as I walk out I'll call them and tell them of the situation."

I squared myself in front of him as he leaned against the wall. "You have to obey the stay away order, and it means that not only you - but anyone you might ask, no calling, email, IM, snail mail or smoke signals, run into at the mall or school or anywhere. It means stay away until I tell you different. You understand. Otherwise you will sit in jail. They don't fuck around with D.V.'s anymore. You understand. You will sit. Bad publicity of dead wives equals no re-election for the judge. Not to mention the hell his wife will give him."

"Just get me out of here. Spare me the lecture. You work for me. I am not gonna fuck up, and if I do, you will deal with it. Fucking up is what you deal with all day and night is it not; for U.S. dollars?"

No way he was going to say 'yes thank you', that would come months later probably, if it all, when we were out drinking single malt scotch and listening to a jazz quartet somewhere. Now he's doing his best Lenny Bruce/Robert Mitchum imitation.

"Fuck you too, Giulio. Call me later to set up an appointment, preferably at the Western bar." I put my hand on his back and walked him back to the Sergeant.

I watch him walk back in to the holding cell until he disappeared in among the other prisoners.

I don't know why I felt the need to actually shake hands or put an arm around a shoulder of my clients when I meet them in lock up.

Clement was a friend so this time it was out of compassion, but it still was a habit.

I know that no one ever complained about it.

Less clinical than Dr. Johnson's Bed Side Manner? I just try to connect with the person so to reach a spacetimepoint familiarity of their humanity as I dealt with them, other than as wife beater/drug dealer/con artist/child murderer/embezzler/rapist.

Thousands of faces over the years, names and crimes repressed deep within my neurons and glia.

"Sergeant, it reeks in here." I stated the obvious as he buzzed opened the door into the Court room for me.

"Counselor," the Sergeant dourly said. He shut the door behind me, as he would continue to do all morning, reminding me of that Douglas Adam's character, the robot 'Marvin', in one of the greatest books of philosophy and religious studies ever written in the English language.

The court room was filling up with today's assortment of family members, police officers, bail bond agents, Mothers against Drunks, Domestic Violence Victim Advocates, and the comedic bit players – the attorneys; public and private.

I walked over to the Judge's clerk. She was sorting through the stack of morning case jackets. "Good morning Sue," I interrupted her triaging, "Can I have an early call on Giulio Clement?"

She looked up focusing her blue eyes on me. I noticed her eyes registering an immediate look of disapproval and dismissal at the same moment. "JD you will be third", she said flatly and look back down at the stack of complaints and bond sheets.

"Thanks Sue", I turned and looked for an empty chair. Sue had been married over twenty years and her kids were mostly moved out of the house. She took good care of herself and always looked well dressed. Her efficiency and demeanor was usually a good start to the work day, issue focusing.

"You look like hell counselor from what I can see of your eyes are nothing but red", she stated loudly in an irate voice to me.

("Behold, this have I have found," said Boswell looking over at Sue, "counting one red eye by one red eye, to find out the account of last night revelries." Dr. Johnson discreetly smiled at Boswell's witty reference.)

I appreciate Sue's professionalism, as she was always very nice about getting my cases called. I looked back at her a bit taken back, as she just waved me off with the back of her left hand.

(Dr. Johnson really wasn't taken back, '…not a bit'.)

I thought what a very nice way to let me, and every else within thirty three feet of me, take note of the obvious.

Along the bar to my right were seated several of the public defenders and an empty chair. The city commissioners were thoughtful enough to supply the defense attorneys interlocking steel framed chairs with plastic seats and backs in their original building construction budget.

"Hey guys", I said as I invaded their space. They were sitting talking to each other, with the empty chair between them. Their brief cases were sitting on the empty chair. They looked at me, moved their cases, and continued talking without missing a beat.

I sat between two of them, as comfortable as any airline seat in the coach section I had ever sat in. Absolutely fabulous first thing in the morning to be shoulders to knees with the PD's.

So much hollywood t.v. type glamour in the morning's pursuit of justice for us second and third tier graduates.

I was starting to feel pain behind my temples. Probably my occipital lobes nerve cells overloading with calcium again. But worse than that, was my physical desire for coffee and a cigarette. Seemed like an hour ago since I extinguished my cigarette outside the revolving doors of the Justice Center. Both addictions were kicking in.

Christ, it could be at least a half an hour before I would get out of here I realized.

"JD, slept anytime since the last decade?" the Public Defender sitting to my left asked.

"Only in the streets", I answered smiling to myself knowing the PD would misinterpret as a joke. Narcissists are so*oooooooooooooo* clever when joking about themselves to themselves.

"All rise", Sue announced over the court room speaker, "this session of the Starkville County and City Court is called to Order, the Honorable Judge Turpin presiding."

Judge Turpin had been on the bench for thirty one years. His family had been a prominent east side family for decades since moving here from Texas in the 1890's to work at Starkville's largest meat packing company, which at the time was still competitive with the Amour brothers operations. His grandfather started work as an assistant supervisor, and eventually after all the uproar caused by Upton Sinclair's work, became fiscal officer. He retired long before the company was dissolved.

Turpin was an unpleasant man, a typical liberal democrat whose disdain for most of the human beings that appeared before him was obvious to attorneys, and the court clerk and bailiffs.

You knew that the old geezer was an elitist from the moment he walked into that Jesuit preparatory school eons ago wearing his little narrow tie.

Sue called the first case. "State of Ohio vs. Giulio Clement."

I closed my eyes, and then took a deep breathe through my nose.

"State of Ohio vs. Giulio Clement", stated Sue for the 2nd time. I opened my eyes and saw Sue looking at me as my client entered the room. Exhaling slowly as I got up and went to the podium finally knowing the secret to getting Sue to call my cases first.

"Counselor, are you feeling OK?" Judge Turpin asked me accusingly with his voice rising on every syllable.

"Good enough to make it through the morning, your honor. Thank you for asking" I responded, but I wanted to tell him that his degree was a doctor of law and not a doctor of medicine, "J.D. Glass representing the defendant for the record, your honor."

"You don't look well Counselor."

"I am fine your honor", I lied. Lying to the Court is unethical and grounds for discipline if you're a solo; if you're a member of a white shoe firm, then it is what you get paid all that money for.

"The plea is not guilty. Defendant waives reading of the charges, has no prior contacts with this court or any other, requests O.R. bond, he will comply with all requirements of the bond, including any stay away orders."

"Prosecutor facts and criminal history please", Judge Turpin stated staring at Clement.

"Your Honor, the complaint states that the defendant was involved in an argument with his wife that apparently started in their back yard and then into the house, yelling at her, startling her, causing her to fall backwards over a table, causing bruising to her calves and thighs. Police were called by wife. No priors. State requests Protective Order covering wife, children, and residence, and $53,000.00 cash bond", the prosecutor stated in monotone, almost as if she had stated it over one hundred thousand times before.

For Sue it only was her thirty three thousandth, but that is why she was still doing the morning arraignment docket. Seniority takes time in public sector jobs.

"Mr. Clement you understand that my 'Protective Order' terms are non-negotiable. If I grant you bond and you don't follow the terms in any way, especially if you contact or have a friend/relative/employee or anyone contact your wife or children you are going to sit in jail until trial. If you go to your marital residence – you are going to jail. Understood?"

Mornings are easier when your client is bright enough to look the Judge in the eye while telling the Judge what he wants to hear. Clement did that in spades, quickly, succinctly, and with a nice reference to him expecting the same ethical life choices from his vice presidents and comptroller.

When I repeated my request for the O.R. it was a formality - as the judge was already writing. I leaned over to Giulio and told him to call me after he got out, after he got a room at the Western and took a long hot shower.

Is there any more civilizing invention than hot running water?

The deputy placed his hand on Giulio's handcuffs and led him back to the holding cell off to the right. I watch him until they went through the door back into lockup.

Then I went through the door to the left of the clerk, whom at that moment was busy stamping, scanning papers and digitalizing incarcerated identities unto the Ethernet.

I got out into the hallway. It was filled with family members, and the late arriving walk-ins – people who made bond before their court date. Every day at this time there are lots of babies in their carriers on the stone hallway benches, or in Costlow strollers just outside the court room door. Of course, one can't forget all those toddlers playing on the floor wearing their Baggy Pants LLC tee shirts.

I headed out side for a smoke.

The children growing up in the streets of Starkville have to learn rugged individuality, Marshall of Hadleyville style walking on the concrete sidewalks sprinkled with the broken alcohol bottles, through urine scented alleys, and between the cars parked on the litter strewn streets, while avoiding the drunks, druggies, homeless crazies, the LLC er's stray gunshots, and most importantly, the prowling perverts.

The neighborhood kids for the most part are natural born capitalists, and have their skills honed by being runners for the baggy pants sales rep's on every other corner.

Lessons learned from Johnny 'The Brain' Torrio. Like the Starbucks store location logarithms - but without a War on Coffee social effect backlash.

I don't get the concept of solids
O' vibrating strings
Or Multi-verses
Or globs of Dark Energy/Matter.

I do get the concept of .38gm & .45gm lead casings
lying in the streets
two blocks from the courthouse.

Baggy Pants LLC non-compete clause: blood in blood out. It is embroidered on the shoulders of their 'Blut und Ehre' Tee-Shirts that are for sale at their website and certain local street corners.

Baby's Mamas mostly wear the revealing Baggy Pants LLC Starkville Division line of sheer half tee design, although the jersey style with logo and colors is close second.

My personal favorite is the copyright infringing Baby Tee for toddlers embossed with **HISTORY DOES NOT REPEAT ITSELF BUT IT HIP HOPS**.

You know ol' Sam C ain't getting royalties.

(Dr. Johnson spoke up saying "...don't forget on Mother's Day you get 15% off if you buy both the woman's sheer half tee and the baby tee!" To which Boswell laughing stated, "Please allow for twenty three days for delivery C.O.D., no refunds, leaded dyes within standard limits allowed by R.O.C. ministry of national defense industrial regulations. Children under 11 years old responsible for manufacturing garments were given 11 minute food, bathroom, cigarette, and reeducation breaks during every 11 hours of labor by the party's political officer on duty at the time.")

Blue sky with high cirrus, if anyone else joining me in looking upwards this beautiful sun filled morning, would notice.

Took five steps and decided to relax; refill for a moment by smoking a cigarette. I walked a bit along the building until there was at least 3.14159265 feet between me and the rest of humanity using the public walkway.

I leaned back against Justice's wall, and put my left foot up against the building, transcendentally and irrationally, just to steady it while I smoked.

Zhonghua renmin gonghequo secured, I lit up, taking a long deep drag on the cigarette, (Nam-myoho-renge-kyo), and looked upwards again.

Blue. Blue. Blue. Pollack streaks of white.

Bottom of the ocean crustaceans, such as my fellow citizens, rarely notice the endless temporal atmospheric portraits of cirrus, cirrostratus, and cirrocumulus, as they scurry from building to building.

Much less notice anything beyond the exosphere actually. Brains developed with eyes forward produces only terrestrial level thoughts.

30 km/sec in endless circles. 300 km/sec towards the Virgin.

Hubblespacetelescope shows 1 not 72. $F_A + F_B = 0$.

(So it seems to me that this spacetimepoint is in a hurry to get to any virgin within the neighborhood. If i only had 60 million centuries left to exist, i might be in a bit of a hurry also.)

I looked up and then down the street's sidewalks.

I looked up and then down the street's sidewalks again.

No one was looking up, only forward and down, as if they were walking in an autumn rain in front of St. Sulpice, while its darkly melodic Cavaillé-Coll's organ played Mozart's '*Requiem*'.

I looked up and then down the street sidewalks again.

No homeland security researchers were taking air samples looking for beryllium 10 amid the of exhaust fumes that had blended with the moistened methane, carbon dioxides, sulfur dioxides, magnetic spherules, and the particulates of nitrous oxides, emanating around and from, last night's rain soaked gutters either.

It is very easy to get paranoid about homo sapiens not doing things.

No doubt that I am an addict. Of course, Nicotine and delta-9-tetrahydrocannabinol, as much as oxygen, fuels my respiratory system, which results in depleting my thought processes at the rate of '3.7×10^{10} Bq', if my mid-morning estimates are correct.

Miniature pale white cirrus clouds were gently wafting from my cigarette.

The dissipating smoke curiously resembled the horse in those Marlboro Man advert's.

(Dr. Johnson and Boswell thought differently, believing it was 'Nelson' or possibly old 'Blueskin'.)

Poor bastard Clement is still sitting in holding area waiting to be sent down the hall to Outtake to sign his bond.

He will be lucky to be out here two hours from now.

Hope he is enjoying his limited time in my multiverse.

I don't envy his world: German car driven to your parking space at office in glass tower before 8:15 am; lots of your company personnel on same building floor; golf Wednesdays afternoons at the club with other executives.

The faux tutor with three car garage; kids who excel at modest larceny's '*500 cubits x 500 cubits*', and world of warpedcrap's '*wrath of frenchkissing*'.

His Waterloo – a bored buxom wife who does not respect him. In fact, actively dislikes his personality, and hates him for her boredom.

Kafkaesque 'heteroscodra maculate'? For you perverts - not thinking the sexual cannibalism; but the endless interrogatories, request for document production, depositions, property hearings, custody hearings, state college psychology grad working for the bureaucratic Department of Parenting Services intervening, interviewing, investigating, and instructing Clement endlessly on methods to "help" parents and children better adjust to the point of him becoming senseless and as disoriented as your narrator. Ok. I was thinking of the cannibalism thing also.

I talk and sometimes clients listen. Some hear and disregard. Clement becomes catatonic at the sound of my advice, or the words somehow never make it up his ear canal.

It was situational. Denial is Cinderella's step sister. Reality doesn't fit in most people's slippers. Have to try it on a couple times, and maybe with random luck, you get a fit for a while.

I'm sure Giulio isn't even aware yet he's been checkmated by the arrest.

Cue Berlioz's 4th movement: '*Marche au supplice*'.

That's not even a close analogy. His morning was more France at 08:30 am morning of December 16th 1944. Clement is the 422nd and 423rd of the 106th Division.

You know who the Fifth Panzer Army is.

The obligatory divorce papers, which probably had been prepared for weeks, are sure to be filed and sent out like a single B-29 of the 509th Composite Group, before the domestic relations clerks take their lunch break.

Definitely, before Clement gets to his first post jail scotch at the hotel bar. Clement's korowai tribal wife, would have told the prosecutor earlier: "I don't want him locked up in jail and missing work, I just want him stay away from me and the house until his gets anger management classes, so the children don't have to see their dad act like that anymore. I'd be so appreciative if you insure he won't be allowed back in the house for a few months."

After a few hundred cases and a couple of years, you begin to wonder if all korowai wives plan this same basic Final Scene Final Act when their having their hair bleached at the spa.

Or possibly just during the rinse while discussing the details of tried and true procedures, and the truly devastating request for all financial documents production.

'...make sure he bruises you somehow. The police will have to take a picture. That will be evidence for divorce that he is abusive and controlling. The divorce judge will rule the children's best interest is with you, the nonviolent parent in the house.'

Or do the korowai tribal wives just privately discuss their new financial plans only with their divorce lawyers during the first three consultations.

Joint Custody now will be one sided negotiations – the side with the protective order.

Of course the house, most liquid assets, and monthly alimony/maintenance payments will assure a joint custody agreement in the end.

Wife will brag forever after at the beauty salon during the final rinse phase about her palatial tudor - with the pool and illegal immigrant pool cleaning services.

Clement will now have to purchase the right to be with his kids regularly.

During the time she allows him to see his children, she will have plenty of time to fuck who ever she can.

Meanwhile will he try to remain meaningful as a ZBOX or PSon3 to his own children, in his allotted purchased timeslots.

Punch Time Clock Dad: Tic $ Toc $ Parenting $ Time. Get one hour the every other Wednesday from 6 pm to 7 pm, unless she needs a longer fuck session with the guys from the pool cleaning service, or from stair master room at the gym, and of course he is solely responsible for pickup and delivery.

Harry Truman Fair Deal Doctrine: house/porschesuv/alimony/child support and medical/dental insurance for her crocodile tears and his access to his children.

It is my legal conclusion that my friend's love for his buxom wife, whom within now exist an enemy alien entity, will be the cause of his multiverse crash and burn.

Butterfly effect ∂ }{

He has deluded himself that "...*if only*...", and so the past will repeat.

TIVO the mistakes, again, and again.

He needs to see his wife as she is now – an asset eating zombie with a heart as large and warm, and her breathe as sweet, as Enceladus's.

Delusional he only sees the soft full breasted wife who slept next to him all those years while not admitting or even realizing that all those stratums of soft basale, spinosum, granulosum, licidum, and corneum in her full breasts have chilled at his touch for months.

Years?

Love blinds one to the metamorphosing pod person sleeping next to you. Clement's denial of love's demise emulates the bravery of Polish Calvary attacking German Panzers in September 1939, with similarly resulting damage to what's left of his idegosuperego after two not too distant future days of domestic relations hearings.

No doubt Clement will end up under a '5150', (2nd cav ghosts never got PTSS therapy for obeying orders to stop), with a Kyra Collins-Barton comrade in the drafty and dark attic at University Hospital discussing a seven year old child's incomplete list of requested books to read at summer camp.

(Dr. Johnson agreed with Dr. Ronstadt and Dr. Raitt's diagnosis, "L'amour n'a pas d'orgueil"; or is it "L'amour n'a aucune fiete." I'm sure neither is correct.)

Nicotine alarm buzzing simultaneously with salivating, warning of low caffeine levels. I had just enough time to hit the lawyer's lounge for a caffeine level adjustment before walking court room to court room. I crossed the street and walked into the garage of the Court House hoping the cirrus was still there when I got done with this morning's tribulations.

(Boswell noted to Dr. Johnson that, "Of course, that analysis was absolutely fucking wrong – a drama queen transference; except for the low caffeine levels". Dr. Johnson, without seeming the least bit pretentious, quoted Oscar Wilde, "*The secret of life is to appreciate the pleasure of being terribly, terribly, deceived.*")

I ignored both of them as usual this time of day, but I knew Boswell was correct to a reasonable degree of scientific certainty.

Chapter 7   Chengguan

Instead of pulling out my photo ID as required in some public building security procedural manual, I nodded as usual instead to the guards in the booth as I walk into the garage under the courthouse.

I opened and walked through the interior steel doors. I then glanced over at the stairs this morning in the same wistful manner I looked at girls at junior high school dances – unattainable.

I walked over and got into the elevator. I turned and hit the elevator's black button's number ∞. The black button had turned a quarter of the circumference in the elevator's control panel.

So even though my eyes saw ∞ I knew I was going to 8, to a reasonable degree of engineering certainty.

It might be a good day after all I thought, (*who really needs pastry so early in the morning*), as the elevator had not only appeared in seconds - it was also empty of any homo sapiens sapiens. Sweet.

It turned out to be an express run, not stopping till the ∞th.

Definitely a sign of the day going my way.

I got out and slowly traversed the hallways catching sounds of/from the other multi-verses: echoing high heels punctuating the muffled voices of conversations now in the ether, or at least the ether of this morning's justice throughout these marble hallways.

I punch in the door code to the attorney's lounge: 0, 0, 0, 0, 0, and 0. Thankfully the Court Administrator astutely appraised lawyer's morning mental abilities.

As you enter the lounge off to the right two desks were pushed together with a phone and fax machine.

Off a foot or two, left center of the desks, was a black vinyl couch and a coffee table with the past issues of that european socialist publication, 'The American Bar Association Journal', laying on it.

On the far wall was the counter with a black Dictioneri model coffee maker. At the round table next to the counter sat a couple of public defenders who were discussing a morning paper story about some recent drug seizures.

I grabbed a cup of lounge coffee, and then sat down breathing and savoring the slightest aroma of the bargain brand 'Ippolito Aldobrandinian'. It immediately caused me to break the 10th Commandment. Again. I could not help myself from coveting the early morning aromas of Ethiopia and Nicaragua wafting from the shops throughout Guildhall Street, just five or so hours earlier.

Kantian pre-reflective cognitive coffee experience?

(Dr. Johnson noted the, "…lamest of all faux jokes that the '*Briads By SayWha*' wearing, hippie, wannabe descartes types are chortling endlessly to each other every morning while sipping lattes on Telegraph Avenue sidewalk cafes is 'I drink therefore I am'. How can deadheads ever tire of repeating such a witticism? ")

What morons, ask anybody who has taken the Michigan Alcoholism Screening Test several times, drinking doesn't prove anything.

("There have been no peer reviewed studies published in the prestigious 'Row House Yard Astrological Journal' to date I know of showing otherwise." Dr. Johnson noted to Boswell.

Boswell then asked, "Why the off brand coffee sellers don't take a page from the cigarette company's nicotine additive enhancement initiatives and enhance the caffeine levels substantially in vending machine faux coffee, thereby making up for the product's complete absence of natural bean flavor. Or perhaps, insidiously, it is the result of an intentional corporate product quality control standard for the absence of natural bean. Or possibly, it's just another government mandated regulation? Whereas now it is without dispute that the companies are inflicting only that stale burnt metallic flavor on the product's addicts every morning, much to the spiritual detriment of the caffeine impaired.")

I was sitting across a circular table from two public defenders. Some newspapers were spread out over the table. I saw the Daily Telegraph Sports section, with a quarter page picture of some young women playing beach volleyball. Being a big fan of bikinis, (*eer umm uhh right, beach sports*), I of course picked it up.

Disappointingly, it was a story about some immammie Brigadier Hassa Sansdicka. It reported that he was upset that human pigment in surface ectoderm actually created a training condition known among the best Olympic summer athletes as '*a tan*'.

Apparently being the typical educated informed human being that islam produces, a woman having '*a tan*' defied the very small penis values of muslim men such as Sansdicka.

Brigadier Very Small Penis wasn't going to tolerate a female human body functioning as directed by NATURE.

No sir, the educated soldier of the religion of peace, and a leader of men with very, very, very tiny hisbah penises, was arresting and imprisoning female bodies that do what NATURE intended.

I was pretty certain that Tehran will not be awarded hosting the summer Olympic games anytime soon.

I look at the bikinis one more time just to piss off all the very, very, very tiny muhtasib penises in the world.

I put the paper down as I was a nanosecond away from violent rage.

The public defenders were engaged in a discussion about the most recent court of appeal's opinion approving as constitutional, for the third time in as many years, the order of the seizure of an automobile on Lhasa Avenue under the city's civil ordinance requiring such, when a small amount of marihuana is found during a traffic stop.

Thinking about the law requires compound sentences.

My working observation, is that, law is by its nature, a moralistically relative Kimberely process, written down as some type of a categorical imperative, by the elected members of the city council.

S. Mewrog, a somewhat still naïve and optimistic thirty five year old attorney was saying, "...they only ruled in favor of the ordinance to allow the government to make money. The profligate officials order officers to the impound cars under the civil ordinance. It is just a revenue scheme, a tax not rationally related to the offense. Of course the 8th amendment and ' *Austin v. U.S.* ' are some of the arguments I think need to be revisited. "

Theofrid nodded at me as he replied, "Of course '*Austin*', but there is no way the court is going to say that the city cannot use civil penalties to control social behavior. We all know that it is just another sin tax, a regressive tax at that, and it is intentionally used to harass everyone. What were the numbers of arrest for less than a hundred grams in the police annual reports for 2004 and 2005 when they passed the ordinance – 4877, and 5406?"

Mewrog spoke up, "Exactly. The poor cannot afford the court fines and costs; much less towing and impound storage costs. The city and the tow yards are legally stealing the cars from the poor. The policy is an unjust taking and you know it, it's not rationally related to the offense. It is unconstitutional."

Theofrid Chaffre, who was perhaps nineteen years older than his colleague stated, "Knowing it, and the courts recognizing the result as unconstitutional, well - it will never happen. The federal law criminalizing marijuana gives them cover to protect city council's revenue schemes. The doctrine of driving being a state given privilege ends the story. The poor citizens get screwed again. Get me the '*Peking Times*', stop the presses, that is the front page above the fold red banner headline for the Cultural Revolution."

Mewrog realized the truth, and the futility, of his policy argument at this time of the morning, or at any time of day, in the present political climate of the progressive's profligate spending.

He laughed and said, "You reminded me of Justice Giulions's statement in that 1996 Michigan case, '...*under the majority's theory during Prohibition, Congress could have authorized the forfeiture of every home in which alcoholic beverages were consumed*'."

The flattering comparison caused Theofrid's eyes to twinkle, and then he laughed – a big long belly laugh.

For some unknown reason, Theofrid's laughing fucking cracked me up. I started laughing and then stopped as I realized how far the government's electronic intrusion had come since prohibition.

(Some cannabinoid receptors interrupted my mirth, by reminding me that homo sapiens sapiens laughed at futility, and at situations that did not make sense to the group. Fear caused cession of laughter. Fear is something Richard Nixon tried with his War on Drugs to his fellow citizens. Of course Nixon was just reinstating Harry A.'s 1930's racist attitude as law and policy. Boswell corrected me saying, "Harry A. was just reinstating President Wilson and the Progressive's intellectually enlightened views.")

"Does either of you legislators know what the jail population is this morning? We must be very close to having no room from what I saw at arraignment", I stated and then gulped the last of the tepid grayish colombian, reflexively spitting the obligatory off brand coffee grindans back into the cup.

I just as reflexively thought, *Rene, Rene, Rene*, " *Yet I previously accepted as wholly certain and evident many things which I afterwards realized were doubtful. What were these grinds? The earth, sky, stars, and everything else that I apprehended with the senses. But what was it about the grinds that I perceived clearly? Just that the ideas, or thoughts, of such things Ethiopia or Nicaragua appeared before my mind.* "

Theofrid replied; " JD, I asked Arty from Pretrial while we were on the elevator earlier and he said that were eighty seven away. "

"Should be there by end of tomorrow afternoon then; I'm sure all the judges are aware, and all the prosecutors also." I ventured as a guess. Then showing my comedic stand up skills I added, "Bet they all got the same memo too."

Theofrid sat all the way back in his seat before replying, "Yeah the word is out."

My joke had flat lined, as did my desire to interact. Cannabidiol therapy effects diminishing, while pain started to ignite my synapses in a direct inverse waveform.

Dé pàin vu – same muscles began convulsing as during my most recent crossing the intersection at Vine Street and Maple Avenue.

Theofrid sat forward and said, "JD, you're a vet. That news story from yesterday on NATO and Turkey; will Congress ever pass that resolution marking the 1915 Armenian Genocide by the Ottomans? Turkey always threatens diplomatic action anytime our Congress brings it up."

Mewrog then spoke up and asked, "JD, you're aware of the genocide and the Turks lying about it ever since."

I leaned forward and put my coffee down on the table.

"Gentlemen, I did learn history in high school. As any news reporter from North Korea worth a RTNDA ' *Hwang Jang yo Sang Award* ' knows, the Turkish government is a prime example of why you cannot trust moslims. They kill christians and lie about it. Let's see, Winston Churchill, Theodore Roosevelt, Henry Morgenthau, and William Jennings Bryant all spoke out against the genocide, but now ninety some years later, our metrosexual Congress of Cross Dressing Progressives are afraid of offending muslims."

Theofrid pointed his right hand at me and said, "Ok JD, what about the politics of NATO and AFPAK, not to mention the crazies running Iran. Why pass resolutions and upset the domestic politics of the Turkey? It's been ninety some years, so another year or three won't matter. We need Turkey to continue to allow our military bases to be in their country."

"Theofrid, morally bankrupt politics will kill more people in the end. You lose the debate when you let the other side choose the language

92

and the topic. Look - debating effects of Tehcir laws, or Reich Citizenship Laws, is nonsensical as the process always leads to killing by design. Listening to the denial of all facts by usurper AhmaDamnjihadistJosephineGoebbelsclone is permitting the evil, instead of confronting and exterminating it like the rectal cancer it is. How can a moral person not want to offend Ahmadumassjihad with extreme prejudice? Besides, Turkey is in NATO and it has to choose: individual freedom v. frenchkissing jihadist slavery. The Islamoliars copyrighted political correctness with the U.N. and at the International Court at the Brain-dead. It is their strongest weapon against science. Desmond Tutu Nelson and Mandela provided leadership for a truth commission to study the effects of apartheid, why is no Turk able to do the same?"

(Boswell faked a cough and said, "Archbishop TuTu supports terrorists, and besides Dr. Johnson's war booty from the Battle of Qadesh, a pair of 'Tire-tetes', has the answer engraved in silver on them; the koran's 'O'liars, science deniers, and clit abaters.' ")

"JD you know in the real world, choices are always of lesser evils. Insulting Turkey will not help get rid of the mass murdering usurper Ahmadumbasjihad", said Mewrog nailing the appeaser position.

"Gentlemen, in all the deadly seriousness of my presently post inebriated mental condition can effect this morning, or is it affect – I always screw those up. Any way you being juris doctors, you both would presumably agree with me, that Sun Tzu and Miyamoto Musashi both instructed us to know our adversaries. Turkey's radical jihad AKP party is muslim and is using Qur'an 9:5 against our girlie men in Congress."

S. Mewrog asked, a surprisingly naive question for a post 7-7/9-11 world, "What is Qur'an 9:5?"

I responded to Mewrog as rationally and objectively as I could at this spacetimepointmoment: "You younger guys need to tattoo it on your fists: ' *Fight and kill non-muslims wherever you find them, take them captive, harass them, lie in wait and ambush them using every stratagem of war* '.

Any rational game theorist would insist you filter everything a muslim says, and does, through 9:5. It is the only fucking way we'll survive, hitting them with their own words."

(Dr. Johnson mumbled to Boswell, " That Dr. I-am-a-mad Murder of al-Azhahahahah University proclamation of exporting very small penis jihadie's to where governments do not allow 7th century barbarity, and also to holocaust every religion but islamonazi from the arabian swamp, are as much bull dung as Emperor Showa's December 8th 1941 Declaration of World Cup Standings ".)

I looked at both of them and smiled. Then I stated as deadpan as I possibly could at that moment, "Gentlemen 9.5 is just like the late twentieth century rural evangelist Dolly Parton said it was; '*It is all taking and no giving*'. Gentlemen it's now time for me to go down to the first floor court rooms and get back to working on this morning's justice."

I slowly got up. Due to this morning's lumbar muscles ongoing civil disobedience, I went off balance to my left as I threw my cup into the garbage.

Just repeating rural evangelist Dolly Parton's words had me feeling angry.

So I vocalized it. "Theofrid, you know jihadist muslims are liars and destroyers; whether it's the Armenian genocide, or the Holocaust and Hajji Amin El Husseini, or the Temple Mount digging, or presently the Ground Zero Mosque, it just pisses me off. I'm sure it would piss off Big Stick Theodore Roosevelt too."

(Dr. Johnson, obviously irritated and sounding pissed off himself, stated the "Cordoba Initiative B.S. is for liberals; students of history know how Abd-ar-raman III treated Christians when he wasn't praising the frenchkisser by his saying of prays in either of his male or female harems. Liberals should call the 950 and ask Count Borrell to get S. Pelaguius on the phone to talk about previous muslim outreach initiatives."

Boswell shook his head agreeing, and then quoted a haberdasher from Independence, Missouri: "Nobody is more disturbed over restrictions on muslim mosques than I, but I was also greatly disturbed over the unwarranted attack by the muslims on American commerce, the 24th Marine Amphibious Unit BLT and our allies the French 1st Parachute Regiment, 3rd Company; also in the jihadist's clitoris hating fetish philosophy. The only language they seem to understand is one we have using to bombard them. When you have to deal with a very tiny penis beast such as Sheik Yusuf al-Qaradawi you have to treat him as a very tiny penis beast.")

For a second I considered discussing Sir Winston's observation from his time in the Sudan with Horatio Herbert Kitchener; "*How dreadful are the curses which Mohammedanism lays on its votaries!*", but I had to get back to the morning's justice.

I had finished my morning attorney lounge theological dissertation, but what I really was thinking as I tried to stand up straight, was that I should go all General Jackson on my Louis Louailler lumber muscles when I got back to the office's blanco baraq leather skin sofa.

"See you later." I mumbled, while regaining my balance, without even dropping any of my file folders while walking out the door.

(Which Boswell immediately offered as empirical proof of 'shih shih wu-ai'.)

Chapter 8   Social Compact (ed)

The hallways were filled with different people every morning doing the same activities and the same movements, *every morning*.

Several clumps of people always gathered within the same locations relative to the doorways of the individual courtrooms.

Rule of Nature: random clumps of varying numbers of differing types of individuals all interacting in numerous unfathomable waves of spacetimepoints due to their positions in hallway.

Every day the individuals making up the clumps changed.

The human tension and cortisol cologne levels fluctuates in undulating waves, yet correlates to the morning's docket of cases, and is measurable in pheromones throughout all the hallways/pathways of justice.

Most mornings Dr. Johnson collects samples from the hallways for evidentiary violations of E.P.A.'s National Ambient Air Quality Standards. Dr. Johnson's biggest payday for reporting violations of Court House Air Quality Standards, under the whistleblower statute and Section 112 of the Clean Air Act, was the day Mr. Mack Charles Parker was extradited to Popularville, Mississippi.

Every day in these hallways such clumps of individuality are governed by some yet undiscovered and understood law.

Not the law made by legislatures working for interest groups.

No, the individual's position in these clumps, and their movements, are governed by a natural law of innate behavior from all the prior generations of the homo sapiens sapiens thalamus, the hypothalamuses one way highway.

(I'm sure Mann & Zweig can whiteboard it for Gen – X and Millennials: $NH_4NO_2\rightarrow$
$N_2 + 2H_2O + 1/2\ O_2 =$ 002:178-179, 190-191, 193-194, 216-218, 244; 003:121-126, 140-143, 146, 152-158, 165-167,169, 172-
173, 195; 004:071-072, 074-077, 084, 089-091, 094-095,100-104; 005:033, 035, 082; 008:001, 005, 007, 009-010, 012, 015-
017, 039-048,057-060, 065-075; 009:005, 012-014, 016, 019-020, 024-026, 029,036, 038-039, 041,044,052, 073, 081,
083,086, 088, 092, 111, 120, 122-123; 016:110; 022:039, 058, 078; 024:053, 055; 025:052; 029:006, 069;
033:015,018,020,023,025-027,050:042:039:047:004,020,035:048:015-024:049:015:059:002,005-008,014:060:009:061 :
004,011,013;063: 004;064:014;066:009;073: 020;076:008, *or some variant of Wien's approximation
thereof.*)

Clumps of police officers.

Clumps of victims and their families.

Clumps of the accused and their families.

Mable floors reflecting psychic energies.

The same dynamics I believe would exist, if every day you had Pan
troglodytes schweinfurthii, pan troglodytes, and pan panicus in these
hallways instead of the homo sapiens sapiens clumps.

There are waves of energy crashing through each homo sapiens
sapiens clump whenever there is even a single glance among people
from a different clump.

Clumps exchange more glances as a prisoner in shackles walks past.
Mirror neuron's sparking.

Victim's family clump emits tsunamis of energized particles
cascading through all their synapses outward into the marble floor
and walls.

Amygdalae igniting pressure waves on an Oppau emotional scale.

(Boswell's standard morning comment was, "A measuring postulate from some
Newtonian Law, demands the other clumps respond in kind upon feeling the blast
of particles."

Of course Dr. Johnson always remarks, "More similar to Zur Theorie der Gesetzes
der Energieverteilung im Normal-Spektrum, but as to court house laws, I am
definitely was not signing any documents regarding to Boswell being postulated
today.")

Every day as I surf the hallway particles while getting to the different court rooms, I am astonished at the relatively small amount of spacetimepoint particles that cause the clumps to interact in violent physical ways.

galaxies colliding / gravitation pull + particle winds

That's not the right formula, but there is a mathematical relationship, some Brownian motion cut-out/one-off; and it is affected by the marble floor and walls, I am sure of that.

At random times, seemingly without any yet discernable mathematical formulation, the clumps go all 'Cassiopeia A'; such as when a small child's killer/rapist/torturer is on trial, or perhaps just as probably, at a residential property foreclosure hearing.

I am sure it is related to a type of synapsids reversion, and of course, the marble floor and walls.

Chapter 9   Tribal Isolation

Empathy be damned.

Across from Court Room 111, Ms. Vladimira Hirchelle was staring out one of the hallway windows to the city's streets. She was wearing a dark black *Taiza*, to me it looked to be from couple seasons back, maybe it was an *Osmany Rodriguez Laffita*. Who knows such things at this time of day?

Ms. Vladimira Hirchelle radiated the visage of grace, restrained opulence, and discernment; in one word 'unattainable'. She was especially out of place, noticeably so, in the hallway outside of the Court Room 111.

Noticing my brain is unchecked; more like un-fuckin-hinged. She's what, decorous? Ms. Vladimira Hirchelle is a damn knockout even at this time of the morning. Elegant women such as Ms. Hirchelle have always been out of my league in every multiverse, without exception.

Whomever the designer, they must have had Ms. V. in mind. Her thirty nine years had softened her ample features so fortunately, that just a year or so back, she found herself being considered beautiful by men. No one was more surprised than her that men, whom previously upon meeting her for the first time, had at most considered her good looking, as in 'cute and fun'.

Now, as in only in the last year or so, senior bank v.p.'s were acting like junior high school boys; and not just the bankers.

(Ask any recent graduate of political science from Harvard, Princeton, Stanford, Michigan, or Yale, and they will tell you Power gets you access to Beauty. What do they know? Ask the maitre d's at L'Auberge Chez Francois, Hays Adams, or Citronelle, and the maitre d's will tell you Beauty gets you access to Power, with names and what they drink. Ms. V. now was collecting power chits with no expiration dates.) (P = A → B < B = A → P , as Dr. Johnson chalk boarded it.)

It was not just that her bosom had dropped, filling out every blouse. Her face had lost the sharp angular features from her cheek bones to her nostrils. Her soften features had change the entire effect she had upon men.

It was also due to the confidence she found she had in herself after the divorce.

That confidence is why she was here this morning.

CR: 6.8.632 Assault. (A) No person shall knowingly cause or attempt to cause physical harm to another. Otherwise known as: *State vs. Ms. Vladimira Hirchelle.*

In a nutshell: confident divorcee, while listening to the International Hotel bar's 40'ish torch singer, and her quartet, performing a competent version of '*At Last*' by Etta James, physically confronted the boorish behavior and ill-breed advances, and most critically, the imminent use of unlawfully raucous derision, ridicule, and mockery of a Jozef S design, by a recent graduate of a prestigious British mechanical engineering university, who was obviously intoxicated, one half hour before closing, Saturday night three weeks ago.

In my defense of her, the recent graduate student whose behavior was well known at the Ku Bar on Lisle Street, and other such places around Leicester Square, should have known it was a dangerous violation of Ritz-Carlton etiquette to insinuate how Ms. V.'s derriere looked in one of her favorite *Jozef S.*'s.

Ms. V.'s response to the graduate student's observation of how her derriere looked in one of her favorite *Jozef S.,* in my opinion, was explained best by Sir Isaac Newton in '*Philosphia Naturalis Principia*'. Although it's a useless opinion, at least until I can figure out how to power point it to use in closing argument.

(Whenever a first body exerts a force F on a second body, the second body exerts a force −F on the first body. F and −F are equal in magnitude and opposite in direction. Spoken Words exert force in the streets of Starkville's dangerous urban neighborhood streets and in its upscale drinking establishments. W = F)

But in legal terms, Ms. V. had to use the "confession and avoidance" affirmative defense strategy.

To establish self-defense in the use of non-deadly force, the accused must show that (1) her derriere was not at fault in creating the situation giving rise to the altercation; (2) that she had reasonable grounds to believe, and an honest subjective belief in, even though mistaken, that some force was necessary to defend her derriere (and *Jozef S.*) against the imminent use of unlawfully raucous derision, ridicule, and mockery, and (3) the force used was not likely to cause death or great bodily harm. (F = W)

The main problem for Ms. V, (besides the bartender and waitress written statements of her punching the graduate student three times causing injuries to the left side of his head), were the police photographs of his injuries showing blood on his shirt, the left side of his face, and his left ear, from the scratches caused by 2.0ct ruby and 1.5ct diamond on Ms. V's right hand.

The investigating officer, being a well-trained and intelligent civil servant, efficiently included thirteen photographs of her manicured nails on her delicate right hand, wearing the blood speckled rings.

Other than that, I believe any jury of her peers would agree with my interpretation of the ruling in '*Chaplinsky v. New Hampshire*', that such disparaging remarks regarding *Sloboda* and *derriere* to a woman in a jazz bar at closing time would be Fighting Words: "...any offensive, derisive, or annoying word'' addressed to any person in a public bar under the state court's interpretation of the statute as being limited to "fighting words" – i.e., to "words... having a direct tendency to cause acts of violence by the person to whom, individually, derriere is addressed."

In Ms. V.'s case, the evidence will establish use of words disparaging *Jozef S.* and *derriere*, and directed toward a refine, gentile woman is lewd, obscene, profane, libelous, and are insulting 'fighting words'.

Any trial attorney will tell you that female witnesses who are smoking hot always make your version of the facts at closing argument very, very, very, ummm, *believable.*

Graduate Student's very utterance of '*Jozef S*' and '*derriere*' together and directed toward a lady of consequence such as Ms. V., is a clear violation of the social compact.

It is clearly beyond the norms of boorish and awkward bar closing time inquires.

No, that type of anti-chivalrous slander tended to incite an immediate breach of the peace throughout the civilized world. How could a few abrasions and blood be great bodily harm in direct relation to such an obviously coarse utterance by a vulgar patron of the Ku Bar such as the Graduate Student?

Regrettably I can't get a jury of his peers consisting of fellow Lisle Street patrons.

Those jury deliberations would last 5 minutes 45 seconds. 5 minutes and 15 seconds of which would have been spent on voting whether Soňa Š. was behind Mrs. V.'s coiffure.

Lisle Street patrons have standards for their early morning libations.

As I got within thirteen feet of her, she turned slightly towards me. Her dark brown hair bounced (rippled? undulated?) across her shoulders. Looking at her profile as she gazed out on the street, it struck me again how attractive she was, 1956 'La Fortuna Di Essere Donna' Sophia Loren attractive, 1917 'Cleopatra' Theda Bara attractive. (Ohio native Ms. Bara is not ever, ever, ever, to be confused with the hideous Thea von Harbou.)

"Good morning, how are you?" I genuinely inquired as I offered my hand. As she turned her head slightly toward me, her L'Oreal '350 British' moistened lips grinned ever so quickly.

(Boswell non-ecclesiastically informed Dr. Johnson and me that he had read, "...that the L'Oreal '350' was voted unanimous favorite of the members of La Cagoule five years in a row".)

Charles Reade was thinking of women such as Ms. V. when he wrote; '*Beauty is power; a smile is its sword*'.

At this range more a kattari in its swiftness of distracting and disemboweling you.

Well...you know, I mean me.

Read that story before - small time attorney defending client as matter of honor, convinces himself its love; Tey's '*The Franchise*'. ("DANGER WILL ROBINSON brain neurons going quasar", cautioned Dr. Johnson.)

"I am doing very well, Mr. Glass, thank you. I was just watching people getting on and off the buses; it reminds me of Manhattan for some reason I can't place."

She extended her hand, and as we shook hands, I noticed her grip revealed strength that comes from isometric exercise.

"Vladimira, you may wait out here. I will go in and talk with the prosecutor and the Judge in chambers. If I can't I will come out and bring you into the court room." I did not give her a choice.

Sitting on the wooden court benches with the Baggy Pants LLC defendants out on bond would have irritated her unnecessarily; it would be like asking her to read a Paul Krugman, Frank Rich, or Maureen Dowd column.

"Mr. Glass, what are you going to tell the Judge? Are you going to tell the Judge what he said to me in front of everyone?" She asked in a very soft tone, controlling her voice to sound unconcerned.

"This is just an opportunity to discuss discovery issues and other aspects of the prosecutor's case, and to let the Judge understand what evidence is in issue. I will tell him that you were accosted by a man with the morals of Ilich Ramirez Sanchez."

I smiled and as shook her hand again while turning to leave and told her I would be back, '…in a couple minutes.'

I left her staring out the window of memories from a bygone New York City morning.

It's weird, but I as I walked into the court room, I thought of her walking home up 5th Avenue at sunrise wearing an Elsa Schiaparelli Versailles Cape.

I imagined her softly humming Joni Mitchell's 'River' as she walked, with her hair flowing down her back over the black silk velvet shoulders of the evening cape, and the cape flowing gently over and around her hips down to her ankles.

Wow. Helénē.

Chapter 10   Tropospheric

The court room benches were almost full with today's docket's assorted families, friends, and witnesses. There were are couple seats vacant in the jury box where the police officers, detectives, and probation officers always sat during the morning's docket.

I walked through the bar, holding the gate open for a city motorcycle officer who was exiting, and then went and stood next to the prosecutor's table waiting for a my chance to talk.

I leaned against the front of the jury box, looked up, and started counting the ornate ceiling squares again. Not inspiring Puebla Cathedra ornate. It is a Cass Gilbert imitator's ornate masterwork, funded by a 1937 Works Progress Administration grant to the county government's construction and infrastructure maintenance budget. I started to scratch at my beard while wondering how much gold leaf was inlaid in each square, and what Cristoforo Caradosso Foppa had charged for installing it throughout the Court House.

(I had recently bitch slapped William Gropper and Diego River for their snide comments about it being a soul stifling rehashing of outworn humanistic/classical Greek revivalism. That argument took place in the early morning hours last Sunday at 'The Tunnel Top' bar on Burritt Street, about three blocks from the courthouse. On second thought maybe it wasn't either of them, but two whiners who sure looked like Gropper and River.)

(It had to be Sunday because after I got home I remember trying to discuss my defense of the holistic nature of the ornate work to my three fish as I dumped shrimp pellets in the tank. The fish, as usual, were not paying attention, and showed their distain of ceilings by constantly flittering about the aquarium. You know, it might have been a couple guys named Sidney and Peter or something. Regardless, it was an elitist, socialistic line of bull dung.)

The ornate created a dignified somber ceiling for the thousands of people who have sat on the wooden benches, eyes toward heaven praying, while heart breaking dramas played out just a few feet away from them in the room.

"Aaron, do you have a second to talk about Ms. Vladimira Hirchelle?" I asked as I stood up straight and walked over to the side of the prosecutor's table stacked with the case files.

"Morning JD", Aaron said as he turned ending his conversation with a PD. He added, "What's the matter with you?", while giving me a disapproving glance before looking for the file.

Aaron wasn't slow. Sure he graduated in the bottom third of his class at Toledo in Ohio, but as I always like to say to him, '...*who could blame him with the night life available in Lambertville, Perrysburg, and of course, Temperance*'.

He swears the Boar Sport Shooting Club in Moline is the best place in the world to watch a baseball game. I like him for the fact that in his entire life, Aaron would never think to go out drinking in places like The Signatures Room at the 97th .

As Aaron picked up the file he stated, "JD I know when you called you said your client wanted to go to jury. Look I am very busy this month, could we talk about Diversion, since she does qualify if you look at her LEADS sheet. She has no convictions or contacts."

Way to go Aaron I thought, throwing my entire narcissistic goal of a brilliant closing argument of the case out in three sentences. He liked to get the heart of each case immediately. He knew I had to professionally recommend diversion as it eliminates the risk of having a criminal conviction.

Most people aren't risk takers. They don't want to sit for a day, or two, explaining their life choices for strangers to pass judgment on; neighborhood strangers are legally known as '*jurors*'.

"JD", Aaron said glancing up from his file, "Look she qualifies. I will have to call victim and the A.O. and let them know. Have her go over to Diversion office right now and fill out paperwork. I am really busy, and have to get pre-trials and pleas done by 10:25 because I am in progress and we are supposed to restart at 10:45. So can you get the entry and fill it out and set for plea in about two weeks. If not, just then just set it for jury trial."

"Aaron, I appreciate the offer. I will talk to my client", I said as I turned and walked over to Judy, the Judge's clerk. She was on the phone. It sounded like she was talking to probation.

I turned and looked back at the people sitting on the wooden benches waiting for their few minutes of morning justice. This morning's current was actually flowing smoothly. Mornings usually are turbulent Class IV; and a couple times a month, a murderous rapine Class VI extreme.

"What do you want this morning, JD?" Judy asked when she hung up the phone.

"Just need to know if I set Hirchelle for jury trial, when would it be?"

Judy turned to her computer and after a second or two said, "Earliest is next month on the 19th, JD."

"Thanks, I have to talk with my client. I'll be back in couple minutes." I walked away wondering how long before it would be before I could get back to the office and make some strong coffee.

As I walked out of the court room, I noticed Ms. Vladimira Hirchelle was still looking out the window. She did not say anything as I walked up and stood next to her. I looked out the window hoping to see some cirrus flowing above the city. Class symmetry: wind stirred cirrus *and* wind stirred street gutter litter.

"Ms. V. I didn't get a chance to talk with the judge. The prosecutor told me he had a busy month and therefore wanted us to agree to a plea where you go into what is called diversion. That is where you plead guilty, but the judge does not accept the plea on the condition you complete the diversion program of two weekly, for three weeks, classes on anger management, and then not get arrested for anything in the next year. If so, then the case is dismissed. If you fail to

109

complete the classes, or get arrested, then he will accept the plea and find you guilty." I paused for a bit for her to understand exactly what the procedure was.

I then added, "It is a good deal in that it takes the risk out of the case, you go to a couple of classes and then go back to living your life. You never have to come back to court."

Ms. Vladimira Hirchelle turned toward me; her eyes at that second were liquid diamond.

She did not say anything for a couple moments.

Looking me directly in my eyes she quietly stated, "Mr. Glass it was his fault, he insulted me."

It made me instantly remember Claudio's, "*O she is fallen into a pit of ink that the wide sea has drops too few to wash her clean again*".

This then made an anger well up in me to where suddenly I wanted to challenge her protagonist to a public duel, using Laertes sword to avenge her honor.

Beautiful women are dangerous to rationality, especially my limited amount this morning.

I was as eager as a junior flight lieutenant to convince a jury to vindicate her honor.

Had to hit the airbrakes on the runaway; definitely having a thermal chemical reaction which was manifesting itself as a Groddeckian 'das Es' hypothalamus tsunami.

"I will never admit what I did was wrong." She turned to look out the window while saying, "It was not wrong. When I was young my grandfather told me of the difficult times he had working with Dr. Arnstein on the USS Macon and USS Akron; all the technical problems, and the Navy's budget competition from its other projects. He believed that a man's word and his honor were his most

110

important character traits. Grandfather always quoted to me that *'honor was one of our ideals always worth fighting and dying for'*. He also told me that if a man lied, it was very probable other men would die. I am sure that is true not only in military engineering, but in all other human endeavors. I also believe that when you lie, each time, a bit of your soul dies with the truth. I cannot say I am guilty of anything. I was defending myself and my honor."

I realized immediately where Ms. V's air of discernment, refined movements, and her general visual embodiment of noblesse oblige originated; Sunday evenings sitting in her grandfather's parlor room with his friends listening to Donizetti's *'La Fille du Régiment'* on a 1927 Orthophonic Victrola.

As a young lady Ms. V. surely was impressed with her grandfather's scientific understanding, and engineer's world view.

I assumed that on Sunday evenings after listening to an opera, he would loving impart advice to his only female progeny, possibly from William Day's *'Hints on Etiquette and the Usages of Society'* to guide her in the 20th century.

I almost asked her out loud if she had a copy, so I could introduce it into evidence at the trial.

If she looked around the building, it would dawn on her rather quickly that it will be impossible to find a jury of twelve of her peers within the Starkville city limits.

I only knew of one – Atalanta.

"Ok, I will go back in and set a trial date, probably going to be around the 19th of next month. If the alleged victim is not working here, and is back in England, then the case will be dismissed. I don't know what is going to happen, but we have plenty of time to prepare you for trial."

As I finished talking I watched her, it seemed her whole body just relaxed, her presence softened, and she smiled.

"Ms. V. go enjoy your day, but call me about 2:11 to 3:11 at my office." I smiled and extended my hand.

Ms. V. firmly shook my hand saying, "Thank you Mr. Glass. I appreciate your assistance and advice, and the respectful opinions you provide. I will call you later." She turned and walked down the hallway.

I thought that she seemed happy with the morning's outcome. I also thought how interesting she was, and free - no husband, nor children, and especially no working for wages.

I could not help myself as I watched Exhibit 'A', her derriere, walk away. Wow, definitely out of my league in every category. If I was the prosecutor I would file a motion in liminie seeking the Ed Sullivan – Elvis Presley relief precedent.

Aaron might have his staff prepare to cast down such a motion choking my legal arguments serpent like, that or some other such legal plague to suffer through.

Of course if it had been a civil case, those run-up-the-hours attorneys from Cardinal & Coscia LPA would address endless interrogatories to, and request for document production of, and then schedule detailed depositions, of Ms. V.'s *derriere,* followed by power point and lamented motions to the trial court. Then appeals uploaded to the state appellate court, and then the state supreme court; and then appeals into the federal ECM system. All then available for viewing through PACER, by perv attorneys killing time in their cubicles along the Avenue of the Americas, and on J and K Streets.

I went back into the court room thinking how much fun *derriere* and Blackmun's 'not speech but conduct' dissent in *'Cohen v. California'* will make my closing arguments in the case as I walked up to Judy's desk to sign the Entry getting the date of the 19th.

Chapter 11   Lynda Marie Child

Choices. As soon as I was back in the hallway I had to decide if I had time to go outside and enjoy a cigarette.

Amazing how many temptations are placed in front of a man and his duties. '*It is noble to fight with wickedness and wrong, the mistake is believing that spiritual evil can be overcome by legal means without nicotine and caffeine?*' I believe that's how Buddy Bolden quoted someone to me as we strolled along Vesania Lane in Vieux Carré looking for hooch late last Sunday night.

I decide on *addictions abstenia* with my narcissistic virtue knowing the next case was a quick plea. Then I would have time for a couple cigarettes and at least two cups of french roast from the bakery.

I glanced at the clumps of people waiting for the elevators, and then immediately took the stairs up to the second floor.

The vast majority of the people who walk up and down stairs do it hoping for the cardiovascular benefits.

Infrequently, breathlessly, passing among them, are the very few demophobia types and other clinically diagnosed avoiders such as Dr. Johnson, Boswell, and myself.

The second floor of the building is where the felony court rooms are. Ms. Lynda Marie Child was sitting on the wooden bench outside room 241 waiting for me.

My own personal opinion was the case against Marie, (she preferred to go by Marie), was a miscarriage of justice. It wasn't that she was innocent of the charge, she wasn't. The miscarriage of spacetimepointjustice is that a water pipe burst in the apartment above hers. Her liberty was now under the control of the local government due to faulty plumbing in someone else's spacetime.

Marie is not without blame for her being arrested. Her landlord and the plumber found a marijuana plant when they entered her apartment, while she was unreachable at work, during the mini Johnstown flood that was her apartment.

Marie's hamartia choice was growing a marijuana plant in a top of the line Baggy Pants LLC Gore Green Energy Seal '*Rottweiler*' Model, intentionally placed in her bathroom directly under the aforementioned soon to burst pipe.

The Baggy Pants LLC Gore Green Energy Seal '*Rottweiler*' Model exceeds the criteria of the ISO 14020 and 14024 standards set by the International Organization for Standardization, and it is waterproof.

Serendipity. I think not, as my working hypothesis is the more probable '*a serotonin syndrome*'.

As I approached her, she stood up placing her Fendi purse on the bench, and extended her slightly trembling hand.

"Good morning, JD", she said in a voice that I almost couldn't hear even though I was standing there shaking her hand.

Marie was probably Ninety Five pounds soaking wet, if she had just finished eating a three course meal.

Ninety Five pounds of scared in a pair of open toe cotton espadrilles.

(Dr. Johnson offered his observational diagnosis as, "Scared apud injustitia".)

As we sat down on the bench I put my files in my lap while innocuously saying "Good morning, Marie. Hope you don't mind if I say you look very professional today. How are you feeling?"

She was wearing a black knit sheath dress, and a very subtle perfume - exclusive off brand I was sure, probably a '*Jannah*' knockoff from a chinese military factoring plant.

I was mentally contrasting our last time together here. She was crying in the hallway then, and had made herself a nervous wreck by worrying about the repercussions of her being arrested.

"Oh, thank you JD. I haven't been sleeping well, and my stomach is always hurting, but I am handling this much better now."

"Marie it is easier now, better than when you were convincing yourself that the worst and more were going happen, and you might lose everything. It is something everyone who actually has a good job goes through. You were no worse than most."

I wasn't lying to her, working people always have the most to lose. If you're rich you litigate or politigate your way out. If you're poor and not working – it's just another trip through the system, with free dental and medical.

"This is it JD? I have to plea to the charge and then be placed into the drug diversion program?"

"Yes, and since this is your first contact, and the Judge knows that you were doing well, and that the pot smoking was not affecting your life in any negative way, the two months of going to those drug classes and such will be the last of the government running your life. Well at least having probation checking up on you, unless you get in trouble for something else. You won't be on their radar from completion of class until one year from now, when the case is dismissed."

I tried to sound up beat. These marijuana cases always pissed me off on several levels.

I could see no reason she was sitting here, except the moralistic and racial beliefs of Harry ('*Yes, it is. It is dangerous to the mind and body, and particularly dangerous to the criminal type, because it releases all of the inhibitions.*') Anslinger , adopted, and then used for citizen control by every administration since.

"What do I have to say JD? Should I tell the judge I thought I was trying to do the right thing? I was not buying my pot from the mexicans. I grew it so I would not have my money going into the gangs like 'Segundo Primo'. This just isn't fair JD. How is anyone hurt besides me now?"

"Marie, it doesn't matter that marijuana laws are the last of the Jim Crow laws, used originally about 1910 by the Public Safety Commissioners in racist New Orleans. Then in other towns, cities, and then into State law's to harass the negroes and mexicans. It is very useful to control all types now."

I continued on with my empathic bedside manner, mostly as a rationalization to myself. "It's depressing racial history then, and now the destruction it causes to great people like you Marie, has no rationale policy reasoning."

It really bothered me, but now was not the time for legislative history of too many interest groups making too much money. In the legislatures money always wins over individual liberty.

Ask the dead mexicans, or incerated felons, or inner city children who don't vote anyway, about their individual liberties.

That part of bothering me was true, and one of the causes of my multipolarverse emotions lately.

Clients such as Marie aren't just collateral damage in the government's insistence on the Anslinger policy with its racial and morals destruction evident in every street, in every town and city, in every state. Not to mention per se, but my turn could occur any day.

If the government locked up Lenny Bruce, the government will lock up anybody.

(An irritated Boswell correctly related to Dr. Johnson, "Not anybody wealthy or politically connected, but all the poor without hesitation, and in fact as a duty of good government so that the suits will be spared, instead of just avoiding, panhandling in front of phil's buildings".)

116

"No Marie, you don't say anything controversial. I do most of the talking. You will be asked if you understand your constitutional rights, and you are knowingly waived them by signing the plea we went over in my office. That is about it. There is no need to go into your background, the mother of twin boys, full time employed, college education; such information is offered as mitigation at sentencing. Case is never going to get that far, as I know you will complete probation."

"After you enter your plea now, you will have to stop by Room 290 and sign some documents. After that it will be just completing the classes. Any questions before, during, or after, you just call me."

I was sure she would complete probation without any questions.

"JD, thank you for everything, I mean it. I know I was a mess when I called you after I got arrested." Marie's voice was steady and sincere.

"You had no idea what was going to happen. You had no idea if your ex would file some motion on the shared parenting. Of course anyone would worry whether they would be terminated from their work, whether they would have to go to jail. It is a lot of stress for anyone."

I had seen this – what hundreds/thousands of times now. Someone having their life turned upside down over using a plant that is dangerous only because of its legal status.

It really does make you multipolarversal to stand next to someone who is a great person, a model citizen, a credit to Starkville, and then watch them walk away hands cuffed behind their back with a deputy guiding them to lockup.

(Thousands? Freudian repression makes my actually knowing impossible. Or possibly maybe it is just the cannabis, 'coffee and cannabis are the cornerstones of our humanness', right Sigmund?)

"When I first called you I was crying", she said it with a slight smile, "I thought my ex would run to court to change our joint custody. I thought the newspaper would fire me. I'd be stuck still paying back all that student loan money it cost me to go to Medill. Or that I could never get another copy editor's job."

She paused, then softly with a tinge of remorse said, "You know my ex has been so understanding and so helpful since I made bail that afternoon. I haven't got along with him so well since before the twins were born. Before this he was always bitching about money. He has been so very understanding these last three weeks. I don't know how I would have gotten through this without him."

Then she giggled looking over at me and added, "You too, JD."

She stopped and took a shallow breath, and then giggled while saying, "A busted pipe got me busted."

She made me laugh out loud, which actually made me feel OK.

(Guff Boswell stated to no one in particular, "Government accomplices are sociopaths". Dr. Johnson responded to Boswell by articulating his prognosis, "Lawyers are manipulative pathologically megalomaniac liars without any sense of pro bono publico". I noted again to myself how Interns and Residents can be very annoying *and* distracting during the morning rounds.)

I smiled as I softly stated, "When I was little and my grandmother would be watching me, I would run to her crying whenever something offended my five or six year old sense of right and wrong. She would always tell me the fair was in September. Of course, as you know, the Starkville County Fair is in September. I knew it then because the whole family always went, a tradition since my ancestors moved to Starkville."

I stopped and looked down at the floor. Grandmother died before I ever realized that I wanted to ask her if her little joke meant that life was not fair as just; or if she meant that I was confusing the substance, mode, and relationship of the concept of 'fair', and that I needed to re-read Berkeley's 'esse est percipi'.

(Boswell spoke up stating what she really meant was 'fajr'. Dr. Johnson told Boswell that I, "…was neglecting my lithium carbonate soda, with the low calorie citrate sweetener and it's imitation orange flavored lithium orotate; and also that I shouldn't neglect David Hume's *Treatise of Human Nature*' either." To which Boswell shrugged his shoulders while mumbling, "Is or ought, is and ought, is-ought, it's an open question".)

Marie picked up her purse and put on her lap. She unlocked the purse and took her wallet out. She flipped the wallet open. Her driver's license was on the right side, and a picture of the only thing in any multiverse that matter to her, was on the left side.

She stared down at her children for maybe eleven seconds. She flipped the wallet shut and put it back in her purse.

As she locked it, I thought I should say something about the children.

Narcissists are like that.

Of course there was absolutely nothing I could say about the innocent victims of government policy.

(Boswell, in an effort to make me feel better I am sure, opined, "Well I can say something about the unjust situation - strict accomplice liability for a certain officer of the court. No 'I am just following orders defense'.")

Marie looked up and down the hallway, and then at the court room. "JD your grandmother was right to tell you, when you were very young, that life is not fair. As bad as I thought this was going to be, it won't be. I can do this. As long as I get to have the boys every other week, that's all that matters to me. If the government says I am a criminal, so what? So long as I can have my children. My friends and family aren't the government. They know smoking marijuana isn't even a venial sin."

Categorical Imperative: her children were her life.

Even now it is unusual in divorces with shared parenting, that the children actually moved back and forth every week.

119

It works well as long as the parties are rational and live within a couple blocks of each other.

That is something I don't recommend for almost all divorce clients. It is too easy to slide into a mentally unhealthy "*I will just drive by to see if they are are still out at this time of night....*"

"Marie, where is your ex working, at the same place?" I knew that he grew up on Raouche Chouran Street, and still lived over there.

"He still is the graphic designer for Lex Talionis. He took the day off and took the boys to the zoo. I am going to get the boys around 4 o'clock, and go out dinner with them before we go home."

I said with a small smile, "Lex Talionis, I can just see all those PR guys sitting around a big table having the graphics department run a power point on possible names for the company. Mass media and advertising people have a certain personality type."

"Yes JD, it's called the joy of creativity, you know – creative talent, well – no, you wouldn't ever have experienced that in your work as a lawyer." She laughed.

I laughed. If Marie could joke and take a shot, then she should be Ok the rest of the day.

We laughed together.

Apostasy outside of drug court before pleading guilty to violating Harry Anslinger's world view.

"JD, I am sure glad I met you last summer at the Caapi Vine Coffee Bar during the 4th of July street fair. Weird isn't it that I actually needed to hire you. Now when I see you there again, we can talk about Bessie Smith, Ma Rainey, and Blind Lemon Jefferson, anything else but this."

"That and whether a pizzeria needs a certification from '*Verace Pizza Napoletana*' before taking a date there", I said jokingly.

Then I look at her eyes and asked softly but confidently, "If you're ready we can go in and do this now"

(Boswell reminded me that, "...it wasn't weird, it was normal, since all my friends at some spacetimepoint needed help with revolving doors". It was just like him to state the obvious when a little more gentile bed side manner was called for.)

Marie turned away and then back to look me in my eyes, "Yes, I want to get this done and get out of this place. I don't ever want to come back into this building JD. I am glad I do not have to come here every day to work, with all the pain and suffering that is remembered, relived, and retold here."

I saw pain in her eyes as I said, "This is the worst part for a lot of people. It is embarrassing to stand up in front of a courtroom full of strangers and admit you're a criminal. Although in your case, I fail to see why in this millennium Starkville insists you are a criminal. You'll be out of here in thirty seven minutes."

With that being said, we got up and went into the court room.

I walked with Marie up to the second row. The bench on the right was empty, so I pointed there while softly saying, "Marie, sit here. I am going up to give the signed plea to the prosecutor. I will come back and sit with you until the case is called."

She looked a little nervous, but I could tell she was going to do just fine. She was focused on getting through this, and then having dinner with her sons.

I hoped this would be less painful for her than going to the dentist.

I walked through the bar, holding the gate open for a city homicide detective who was exiting, and then went and stood next to the prosecutor's table, waiting for a my chance to talk.

Looking over at Marie, I *knew* moral pain hurts more deeply than physical pain. I leaned against the front of the jury box, looked up, and started counting the ornate ceiling squares again.

Something didn't feel right, besides the diminishing effects of THC, as spacetimepoints entropy.

("dU=Tds-PdV", offered Dr. Johnson as some type of empirical proof.)

I was scratching my beard, when I looked over at Mary Jane Platt. She had the prosecutor duties in the room this month. She had her back to me and was talking with some short fireplug of a woman with short gray hair.

The fireplug looked familiar, I was sure I had met her, but didn't know where.

That wasn't what was bothering me though – it was the body language of Mary Jane. Narcissistic need of reaffirmation of my presence? Perhaps. Probable.

I put my files on the prosecutors table, and then opened Marie's file to retrieve her plea agreement. When I had it in hand, I looked up at Mary Jane. She and the woman were done talking and were looking at me. So sensing my chance to interrupt, and hasten my future two cups of french roast coffee, I walked over to the other end of the table where they were standing.

"Morning Mary Jane, I have the plea signed so if you will review and sign, I think we are ready." She looked me and as our eyes met, I immediately knew something was wrong.

"Morning JD." She did not break her gaze as she took the paper. "JD, I was just informed this morning that your client has been indicted on two counts of endangerment. We can arraign her now, but she will have to be taken into custody and booked." Mary Jane was waiting to see my reaction.

I sensed she expected me to unload on her.

"Mary Jane, you're telling me that when we talked last week you couldn't have let me know that this was in the works."

I was not going to raise my voice, or say what I really wanted to, "Don't even bother to answer, I will tell my client. We'll have to continue today's hearing. I will waive time and enter her not guilty on the new. Where's the indictment, and what are the charges about?"

"One count per child JD. Child Services got more involved last week after we had talked: based upon her having children around a marijuana growing operation." Mary Jane stated it flatly, businesslike, laying out the state's fucking interference with the best interest of those children for no fucking good reason.

She was going to do her job.

We all are just doing our jobs in this building.

"Mary Jane, tell me at least you will agree to an O.R. Bond?" I also knew Marie wasn't going into diversion today.

"JD, as long as she agrees to stay away from the children under the bond and until further orders can be entered in domestic relations court." Mary Jane's voice left no doubt there was no room for negotiation.

"Mary Jane, what's going on, what further order are you talking about?" I felt the familiar déjà vu of being blindsided in the criminal justice system. "Mary Jane what are you expecting, or do you know something else?"

"JD, I was just talking with Ms. Raccette the process server from Maalik, Zabaniah, Nakir and Munkar, LLC - there is a D.R. summons for your client."

I knew I had seen the fireplug before, she had brought interrogatory and rfpd documents to Patria last spring in the hebron hills real estate development lawsuit from Maalik, Zabaniah, Nakir and Munkar LLC.

I felt my muscles relax, exhausted, with most of my capillary beds opening all at the same time. Marie was not prepared for this '*Def Fall Gleiwit*' tactic by her ex-husband.

I wasn't.

"Mary Jane, if you have copy of the indictment I'll take it." I was very disappointed in Mary Jane's deception, but I knew it was misdirected and unproductive. "I need to take my client out in the hallway and let her know her world just got a lot worse. I assume Ms. Raccette wants to serve us on the record when we do the arraignment."

"JD", she smiled her best sympathetic smile as she took the indictment off the top of the file, "Yes and please try to be quick because I want to go get another diet soda soon".

As I took the indictment I smiled, and softly told Mary Jane, '*thank you*', while resisting the impulse to punch something, anything inanimate as the law.

This was not the work of Aglaopheme and Thelxiepeia. What was it that defendant Joan Rouen said to Starkville Prosecutor Pierre Cauchon at her 10 times bulk trafficking trial last month?

I think it was, "*I protest against chains and irons. I want it permissible for any marijuana defendant to escape.*" I felt an overwhelming need for a joint, and not just as an act of civil disobedience.

I turned and took three steps back toward the jury box while reading what I expected to read, one felony endangerment count per twin.

Maybe it was Atreus and Thyestes.

I should have known that the morning's temptations would lead to tragedy and emotional annihilation at some point during my day. The dawn's rain hadn't washed away anything of consequence.

I turned and walked over to Ms. Raccette who was now seated behind the prosecutors table. "Hello, Ms. Raccette, I believe we have met before. I represent Marie and understand you're here to serve papers on my client. Do you mind if I scan them before the Judge gets back on the bench? I would appreciate if you would let me prevue the document."

She stood up and extended her hand, "Yes, Mr. Glass we have met before in your office. Thank you for remembering."

After I finished shaking her broad hand with its stubby fingers, she got the papers, and then gave them to me. It was an ex parte order.

I scanned it quickly. I've seen hundreds of Domestic Relations Court Ex Parte T.R.O. - stay aways.

I've seen thousands of indictments, of which probably a couple hundred were for child endangerment.

I handed it back to her saying, "Thank you Ms. Raccette. I going to talk with my client for a minute or so, and when I come back we'll get this done and you can get on with your day."

I tried to be civil, but I was bouncing from anger to depression and back in nanoseconds. I was getting dizzy from the frequency.

Or maybe it just was realization of the unnecessaryness of Marie not having dinner with her children tonight.

I briefly wanted the warm physical sensations of using a katar on Atreus and Thyestes; beware the ides of Marie's attorney; if it was *them*.

(Dr. Johnson corrected me by saying it was pronounced 'ideals'. Of course, Boswell interrupted Dr. Johnson with his argumentative attitude by saying, "Dr. Johnson, you're mixing metaphors or something. Nobody is assimilating anyone before enjoying a youthful Tennessee whiskey, while smoking a Vuelta Abajo Parejo, at Sin's Bar after tonight's 11:30 pm supper performance at the Pompey Theatre on North Franklin.")

125

My lower back was really hurting now. I had to walk with my head bent over a bit, and my shoulders down.

I did not need this now. What I did need was a couple hits off the pipe and some coffee with a cigarette.

As I went through the gate of the bar, my eyes and Marie's locked. Her demeanor changed instantly.

I assume medical doctors experience the same thing as much as I do. It is used in cinema and theatre productions as a scene changing device.

The emotional collapse when a person's reality shifts. My arteries can't take witnessing to many more reality shifts.

I motioned for her to come outside into the hallway with me. I wasn't sure how to tell her.

I could go with the legal procedural, but I just could not be that cold and calculating now.

I placed my hand on Marie's lower back and walked her out of the courtroom.

She was trembling ever so slightly.

I walked her down the hallway to a window looking out over the busy morning street.

"Marie", I started as we stopped in front of the window, "I'll start by confessing that after I talked with the prosecutor last week, I called you and told you that Mary Jane was amenable to the plea and that's why I had you come to the office to sign it. I told you then that until the Judge accepts it, it was not a done deal…"

Marie interrupted me immediately, "What is going on? What is happening?"

I put the files on the window sill and turned slightly back looking towards the court room. "Mary Jane informed me that the Grand Jury indicted you on new charges, child endangerment for growing marijuana while your toddlers were with you under the shared parenting, in addition to the cultivation charge. When we go back in the judge will arraign you on the new charges, and you'll have to go to booking again."

Marie started sobbing as soon as I mentioned her children. I wasn't sure if she heard or understood anything after 'toddlers'.

I put my arm around her shoulder and let her cry. "There is a process server here also with an Order from Domestic Relations giving your ex temporary custody until a hearing to contest in about thirteen days from tomorrow, when I file an answer. You won't be able to talk, see, or communicate with the toddlers for at least a couple days until I can get you in domestic relations court."

I felt tears in my eyes. I knew two toddlers were not going to understand why Mom did not come and get them for dinner.

I knew two toddlers were not going to understand why Mom stopped seeing them until something called a domestic relations judge would let her.

I knew that her ex was a fuckin' pussy mother fucker who agreed to go along with those instigating commie bastards at protective services who decided to push the prosecutors.

I knew that her punk-ass-ex had Maalik get an ex parte order keeping Marie away until I could file and set an evidentiary hearing.

I knew the small penis M. F. ex would at some point today, while having several Napoleon Balling pilsners, start singing '*Neuer Fruehling*' as celebration for the toddlers being with him.

Serengeti Plain Rules of Domestic Relations Procedure.

As sad as all that was, being a narcissist, the reason I had hidden tears, was that I knew it was my sworn duty to explain all this to Marie.

Narcissists tear over themselves a lot, don't we?

(A chortling Boswell spoke up saying, "You was right, baby - usually though when one has a fever and is alone drinking black coffee while listening to those peggy lee records late at night".)

After about 499 seconds I had her sit down on one of the hallway's marble benches. I sat down, putting the files between us.

Marie was looking up at the marble ceiling.

While sitting there Marie looked so vulnerable, as if Iago had just uttered '*Filth, thou liest*' to her.

"Right now, there is nothing I can do Marie. You will have to be arraigned and then booked. You will have to call me when you get out and set an appointment up for later this afternoon. Then we can work on all of this. You realize you aren't going to be able to see, or talk with the toddlers until I, we, get a hearing in domestic relations court." I was trying to sound upbeat about the situation, that it was manageable.

Marie made the sign of the cross and very softly started to pray. I could just barely hear, "…the Father Almighty… maker of heaven and earth….", which then began sparking my neurons as she softly continued praying.

Being stricken with chronic fatigue syndrome the words, '*Pater noster, qui es in caelis, sancitficetur nomen tuum....*' bounced up from my hippocampus, as I caught myself instinctively bowing my head down towards the marble floor.

Something about this building, the way it tempts homo sapiens sapiens into saying incantations, and then believing in their absolutions.

Latin is the language of this morning's multiversesymbiotic, Catullus. He seemed apropos at that moment.

I wanted a cigarette as my brain's membranes were vibrating to some Boswellian merkhet.

I have always told myself, if you want to care about your clients, do social services work, otherwise be clinical in the court room work. Later, mucho mas tarde, me prometi a mi mismo, I'd find something else to have emotions about - similar to what my fellow Starkville citizens have, probably a football team, maybe one with a four thousand pound nineteen foot tall idol standing on top of a golden dome.

(Dr. Johnson opined that getting emotional about any case, "...is a grave injustice to client and that I might not be such a 'cool headed logician' as fellow Berkeley alumni Ted Kaczynski would write on the presents wrapped in brown paper he sent". I always knew it was Ted from his tag line, "*can't have cake and eat it to*", written in yellow crayon next to my address.)

"I can't believe he did this, an order from domestic relations." Marie said it very softly to me. I wasn't buying it though, as the pain in her voice gave her away.

Marie understood exactly what he had done.

I knew for a fact that Saul gets thrown down off Baraq actually 9 to 19 times a day in this building, times such as when waiting for a domestic violence case jury to reach a verdict.

The Physikalische Gesellschaft zu Berlin's court sketch artist, Mr. Buonarroti, was very good at those moments.

He would get out his brown paper and capture such hallway emanations, either in charcoal or pencil.

I have watched countless people standing or sitting in these marble hallways while they are awakening to the fact that some personal relationship is radically changing, and usually is dying.

Whether it is a wife beating case, or a drug case snitch ratting out a long time friend, it is always a very public performance in a one act play of the death of this part of their life.

The lucky ones have their wails, tears, and clutching of their bibles to their breasts captured on reporter's cameras for broadcast on the local 5:00 am, 6:00 am, 7:00 am, 8:00 am, 9:00 am, Noon, 5:00 pm, 6:00 pm, 7:00 pm, and 10:30 pm newscasts with the talking heads reading in solemn tones the copy from the teleprompter regarding the tragic day in the justice system.

(The A.C.E.S. member couldn't resist stating to Dr. Johnson and myself his nonsensical 'cutline' and 'hed': *Then it's over to Ken the Sports Guy for his take on starkville middle school's jr. varsity intramural golf team's upcoming season*.)

Marie placed her hand on top of my hand, squeezing and holding on tightly for a couple of seconds. She looked at me and said in a matter of fact manner, like you were asking a stranger on the street for directions, "Can we please do this now so I can just go home?"

"Here is a hyssop troche, Marie. It will keep you from getting a dry throat. When you get home after all this have lunch, some rest, and then call me."

I placed my hand on her still slightly trembling elbow, and walked her into the court room.

I nodded to Mary Jane, and then sat down with Marie in the front row behind the bar.

Marie leaned up against my shoulder, turning her head to me and said "JD, I can't do this, I'm not ready."

Our eyes met. I told she could. That I would do all the talking, except that she would have to say, 'not guilty'.

Then while we waited for Mary Jane to call the case, I could hear Marie praying again.

When Mary Jane called out the case, we stood up. I heard Marie softly and naively saying "amen".

The arraignment started, and as Mary Jane and the Judge went through procedurally required recitations and incantations, I began counting ceiling tiles.

I got to seventy three before I had to stop and accept the new indictment and the domestic relations summons.

Marie said 'not guilty'.

The Judge accepted the plea.

Then a deputy walked behind Marie and placed the handcuffs on her and then started walking her out.

The hearing on the original charge was continued to a new date with the endangerment charges.

The older I get the more I instinctively avoid the new, on the most basic primal level, as in high grasses on the serengeti plains at dawn level.

I watched the sheriff walk Marie to the court room's side door away to lockup while I was still standing in front of the bench thanking the Court for the O.R. bond on the record, and thanking Mary Jane as habit of professional courtesy.

As Marie went through the door she turned her head and our eyes met, and then she was gone, and I had nothing left to say for the record.

(Boswell told Dr. Johnson that I should note for the record, that Harry Anslinger had caught another 'Claudette Colvin' in Marie. I did not, even though, I had to admit it was a quite display of power to reach from *somus of silenti* to stop a mother from having dinner with her children.)

I was feeling a THC deficiency, and because of it, was emotionally cycling off the morning chart.

Blindsided and bushwhacked by an ex's playing the criminal justice system card and the domestic relations system card together, after serendipity's opening with the burst pipe card.

As matter of professionalism, I was unsure why Mary Jane failed to tell me anything during our phone call. I did not tell Mary Jane how angry I was at the moment.

Anger was eighty five per cent of the dark energy of my consciousness, but the black hole of my depression's event horizon had just expanded a couple parsecs.

Walking through the hallway from Ms. V.'s court room, to the court room of the bushwhacking, there was the usual light speed transformation of my morning's expectations of reality, into a different multiverse of actual reality.

Sorrow for MV2's Marie, as simple humanity required; also required now was unexpected legal maneuvering for MV2 me.

MV2 me who also wanted nothing more at this moment than to have a cigarette and a joint with obviously foresight impaired MV1 me.

I needed coffee and a couple cigarettes. A shot of single malt scotch would be soothing.

I was starting to get very upset with my lack of precognition.

The only thing I could think was that this has got to stop.

(Then i started daydreaming: Richard, Bessie, and i were driving down Mississippi's Route 61 listening to 'st. louis blues' playing on the radio. We were almost 19 miles outside of Clarksdale; (always another fun spacetimepoint up ahead!) Dr. Johnson and Boswell were in the back seat, and both were singing way way way off key '...feeling tomorrow like I feel today......da da da da da da da day......' So I joined them in singing way way way off key.)

Chapter 12   Giovanni di Bernardone & Northside 3/5th's

In my daydream I had Richard turn the radio volume all the up as I slowly walked down the hall to State vs. Giovanni di Bernardone in Court Room 248. Since last Sunday that has become one of my biggest problems, *'feeling tomorrow like I felt today and yesterday'*.

(The sun had risen over the Serengeti as my brain was punking out on me. My hippocampus was positioning posthubbletelescope ID & EGO into a classic pincer movement. I misread omens all morning. Reality was turning east in a déjà vu 22 June 1941, Atreus was wearing a Wehrmacht colonel's uniform and Thyestes was dressed as a corporal in some Einsatzcommando unit. Together they had executed a field change maneuver to the classic 'Operation Cottbus' against Marie. Hindsight is for the law professors. Foresight based upon hindsight is required to survive every morning in the coliseum that is the court room.)

It was apparent to me that this morning I had the control and focus of a toddler in a toy store on christmas eve.

I found Mr. Giovanni di Bernardone standing in the hallway talking with three companions of his. Companion is not accurate; they were junior associate members of his 3/5th's crew.

The 3/5th's legend has it allegedly starting in November 1919, out of the numbers rackets run by neighborhood negro wwi veterans. Legend has the first elected president of the gang as Isadore Banks, until he went back home to Marion. They were the only gang left in Starkville for years now, except for the mexicans who had a couple block barrio beach head by the studio. The 3/5's were a regional presence type operation.

There were motorcycle gangs co-existing outside of Starkville with the 3/5's, but the bikers had ceded Starkville to them. The 3/5's standing was well established in the state and federal prisons due to their aggressive protection of the 3/5's brand in Starkville. For civilian's 'aggressive' translates as 'violent'.

133

"Good morning Madness", I said, using his bland and predictable street moniker, as I shook his hand.

It was impossible not to notice his strong hands, as prominently tattooed across on his scarred knuckles of his dark hands were the letters *t a u f   t a u f*.

"Hey J D Dre. You ok counselor? You don't look like you're having a good morning after a long night."

"Right on both Madness, I '*Got Them Sobbin Hearted Blues*'. Look I'll be back in five minutes. Will you go inside and sit in the back row until I come back."

I started to walk away, but then turned and said, "I just want the prosecutor and the Judge to see you. So that they know you're physically in the building this morning."

"Sure JD, don't be too long, you know I hate being in this building. I want to be at the studio by noon to lay down a percussion track with Larry O'Toole", he stated while nodding at me walking away.

I ignored everybody and everything else as I went outside and walked over to the corner of the building to be alone amidst all the morning's justice.

Lighting up the cigarette, I knew that I was just another hibakusha mentally red lining past 50, and easily on my way to 80. I took three deep breathes.

(Nam-myoho-renge-kyo   Oyk-egner-ohoym-man   Nam-myoho-renge-kyo)

I took a long drag from the cigarette. I focused on a thought of beauty: Starlight Black 1967 GTO Convertible with Rochester Quadrajet four barrel carburetor. I took another three deep breathes. (*Nam-myoho-renge-kyo Gojira*) After taking another drag, I blew three 'enola gay' smoke circles skyward toward the cirrus. Chrome trim grill and chrome wheels with chrome license plate frames. The plate numbers I knew by heart: 'Y3Q3B2C1'.

Certainly one can offer up the 1967 GTO as proof of the goodness of Man. Specifically, the goodness of those world war ii veterans that became U.A.W. members and who understood craftsmanship is an art obtained only by working to your abilities every day.

What I was thinking was greatness actually, *specifically ram air engine with 4.33:1 rear gears*, and thereby was violating somebody's commandments: Number One and Two.

Potentially: Number Six.

I took another long drag on the cigarette. I realized, becoming lucid momentarily between puffs on the cigarette, that I was flaming out and had to consider pulling the ejection hook as soon as I could locate one.

Clinical.

I have to get back to some professionalism for at least, well, at least until Giovanni's case is dealt with. Then I can go back to the office and crash on the blanco baraq leather skin sofa for probably at least an hour or more.

I took the last drag of my cigarette and then threw the butt on ground. I needed to stop the drama queen emotional recycling.

I realized that ever since I woke up this morning, I had been whining like a thirty three year old homeless schizophrenic preschooler in Gaza trying to read the introduction to Nahum Sokolow's book; the one that was published in 1919.

At least I wasn't whining like those very small penis ss totenkoph wannabes in the ﻕ ﺩﺱ ﻯﺭﻭﯼﻥ when they look down at what they are holding in their hands while urinating on each other in some moronic koranic cleaning ritual from some *Seven Anno Domini* camel jockey's delusional retelling of some ancient Babylonian's mythology.

135

(Boswell, on hearing of moronic koranic cleaning rituals, of course had to point out, "That Chronic burning rituals don't require urination, public or private".)

Man up, do the job. Then off to the VA to see if I have any localized amygdalar lesions. That's if I even can summon up enough curiosity later to have a professional verify my hypothetical pathology.

I went back into the building needing a bathroom to take a piss and splash cold water on my face. Needing to get it together I smiled to myself thinking it would very helpful to review some procedures in '*Duodecim Tabularum*' for stare decisis déjà vu before going back to Room 248.

There is no way in my plan to have Madness testify, as that would be a one way ticket upstate to Tarpeian Rock State Correctional for him.

The bathroom was crowded. I had to wait to use one of the three urinals. Just my luck, the middle urinal was the one I got. As I was pissing, P.D. Greg di Morra took the urinal on my right.

He was a good guy, but the type of a guy who couldn't find a woman to date at a pongala festival. Actually, he does date the older girls of the Bund Deutcher Madel. He wasn't a very good judge of female character.

"Hey JD, how's your day going?"

"Better now that I am getting rid of some of this coffee and tea. What you working on?" I said trying not to be an unsociable asshole; while just trying to take a piss in private.

I hated talking to anyone while I was standing shoulder to shoulder pissing in some public rest room. It triggers my faux spinal LSD to flashback, taking my consciousness into a classic Gettier Problem. I have always disliked pissing as part of the herd. Truth, justification, and belief - I will never enjoy crowd urinations such as is the custom with the Taliban, Hamas, and all Jihadists.

As I looked down, I thought it was appropriate that at least the court house urinals still have the post 9-11 osama bin laden picture imprinted charcoal disposal mats. Childish fun, but fun none the less, in pissing on the face of a jihadist.

"JD I'm on my way back to the office. I only had two quick pre-trials and a disposition scheduling conference. You headed out?"

"No, Greg I'm going to 248. I've got a pretrial on trafficking 1529 grams of hashish in a school zone. It's only an offer to sell, no actual hand to hand, so have to see what happens."

"Nice, over bulk amount in a school zone, mandatory time 2nd degree, must be a nice fee JD."

"Greg, I wished one out of every six of my clients could pay part of my fee." I finished pissing, zipped, and walked over to the washbasin. I washed my hands and then splashed cold water on my face. (*wuda vu*) Splashing cold water on temples felt great. I did not even notice Greg when he came over and started washing his hands.

"JD, well at least you can pocket a fat fee compared to public defender pay", Greg stated with envy as he interrupted my hand washing and my temple splashing cleansing ritual.

"Greg, don't know what's going to happen yet, not even sure if there is a weakness in testimony of the confidential informant at this point. See ya." I walked over to the towel dispenser, grabbed a couple, dried my face with one and threw it in the garbage can.

I put the other in my pant pocket and left thinking that I was rude to Greg, and his pecuniaryspacetimepointlessness.

When I went into court room 248, Madness and his crew were sitting in the last row on the left aisle watching the judge sentencing some defendant.

As Madness was on the end by the aisle, I had him move over and sat down next to him.

Madness leaned over into my personal space. "Damn JD, I was beginning to think you weren't coming back for a while. Can I leave now?"

Madness's whole demeanor made me smile. He seemed blissfully unfazed with the possibility of doing a minimum of five years.

Then I became concerned, as I was not sure why he wasn't worried. I wasn't sure that if I commented on it, that he might give me answer I did not want to hear, and I'd have to resign and give him his cash back.

I was cash poor this month and already had paid the office rent and the rest of the month's bills with his last cash payment. Which could be a problem I did not need with Madness today; the fish problem was about all I could hope to handle today.

"Madness, you can wait in the hallway, or go outside and have a cigarette, but you can't leave until I tell you."

"JD I'll be outside." Madness turned and nodded at his crew, and they all got up and left me. The LLC'ers behavior posed the comparative law question of the moment: Starkville criminal codes versus Madness's street code 'Oppergezag'?

I sat by myself in the empty row watching the sentencing. I've participated in, or witnessed, a couple thousand of sentencings over the years.

After watching for a second it was apparent that the woman being sentenced had been a bank teller who stole money from her employer, a national bank with offices in Starkville.

I tried to pay attention, but started staring at the ceiling tile and scratching my beard. Unscientific observation on the woman's plight, (and all of the sentencing's I've been attorney for the defendant, or those I just watched waiting for my client's turn), verified that old observation from Anachrsis, or possibly it was from Uncle Joe Jasmine Hu Jintao's mea culpa resignation speech to the

138

Party Congress, '*Written laws are like spider's webs*; *they will catch, it is true, the weak and poor, but would be torn in pieces by the rich and powerful.*'

The rich and powerful's taxes had paid for all that gold inlay in the ornament ceiling tiles I knew. The woman's mistake was in thinking she could act the same way with other people's money as a member of Congress or a wall street investment banker does.

When the woman started crying it distracted me from my inspection of ceiling tiles. This morning's distraction from ceiling tile inspection is the same as every other morning's ceiling tile inspection distraction: homo sapiens sapiens weeping.

As I watched the deputy take her wrists and put the handcuffs on, I realized that I had no idea of how much time in prison she just got. I watched her being walked out of the court room's side door with the deputy's right hand holding her wrists behind her.

The Judge got up and walked back into her chambers. The prosecutor walked back to the prosecutor table. The stenographer leaned back in her chair and started reading Danielle Steel's "*Sunset in St. Tropez*".

The bailiff took the Judge's file and placed in the outgoing bin.

The bank teller's defense attorney walked back to the teller's three family members who were sitting in the first row, and who now were getting up and gathering their belongings.

The family had the usual sad shell-shocked look in their eyes as they left the court room, with the stoic attorney leading the way.

I got up and walked over to the prosecutor, "Good Morning Adila."

("Again with a Newspeak lie – using the noun instead of a verb, as it had turned into mourning after Marie's case", observed Dr. Johnson to no one; because I sure as hell wasn't listening.)

139

"Hey JD, how are you?" Adila smiled disarmingly as she extended her hand. She had a nice smile.

"Depends on what you say Adila," I stated flatly and professionally while shaking hands.

"Well JD, we are scheduled on your motions. We need to go back and talk with the Judge about your discovery motions, and then I have one other thing".

Adila was still smiling as she went through her files on the table to get the State v. Giovanni di Bernardone's folder.

Adila was a conscientious prosecutor, who understood civil society norms. She could sway jurors by her logic, with inferences and deductions from the evidence.

It's an innate skill being honest. So with a slight nudge in logic and verities of civil society from the University of Iowa, she is able to connect with all types of jurors in closing arguments on the need to protect their own families, and the rest of the peaceful citizens of Starkville, from defendant X.

Her emotional conclusions always reminded me of an old southern Baptist minister sermon which require the individual juror to do as Justice requires for the good of the Community and hold X accountable for X's actions. Not fire and brimstone with Adila - but more of a j'accuse moral tone.

If you split a 1950 Chateau Petrus, or better - two of them, and a plate of some radishes with Adila, she would admit that her witnesses misstate their observations frequently and a certain amount outright lie during testimony. Adila also would admit it is easier to sleep every night when you are on the side of the state legislature and the chief law enforcement executive in every case.

(Dr. Johnson suggested last Monday morning, or the one before that, that I, "…should assume the same type of plausible deniability, and become a public defender".)

140

Adila picked up her file and walked over to the bailiff's desk. I followed thinking that I might be able to go back to the office in a just a few minutes, and make a good strong cup coffee, and take another hit off my pipe. I revised my earlier morning prognosis and then self-proscribed more mourning medication, another table spoon of Hawaiian sugar in my next glass of ice tea.

The bailiff merely nodded as Adila and I approached. Adila knocked on the judge's door as she opened it. I followed Adila back into the judge's chambers.

The Judge was sitting at her desk talking on the phone and waved us both to sit down. As we both sat down in the high back leather chairs, I looked around the judge's chambers - at the pictures of the judge with her husband and family, pictures with other judges, and still other pictures with an old governor or two. Judge Chin was close to retirement, probably less than three years left.

I have for years thought she was the best jurist I had ever had tried a case before, federal or state.

The Judge's family had been in Starkville since the mid 1950's. The first Chin came to San Francisco in 1844 from Guangdong province. He found work on the transcontinental railway, and then worked on a southern tobacco plantation. Some years later his third born son left tenant farming and opened a laundry, with a store attached, in Atlanta.

He was moderately successful until 1890 when the government decreed that only US citizens could manufacture smokable opium. The decree made him very rich in a very short time.

One of his many grandsons was the Judge's father, who after graduating from Morehouse College moved to Starkville in the mid 1950's to work as an assistant CFO at one of the major pork producers. He retired as CFO. No small part of his CFO salary and bonuses had paid for the Judge's Oberlin, and then Case Western College of Law tuitions; not to mention the years of viola lessons.

The Judge hung up the phone. Adila started to say good morning when she was interrupted by the Judge.

"JD, are you hung over?"

Unexpected. Boom. 1st question right out there. The Judge was no slouch, have to give her credit. It made me sit up straight in the chair, unobtrusively as I could muster at that second. I took a depth breath as I looked at her, and smiled out of respect. I could not help myself.

"Your honor, I may have had one too many last night and slept somewhat restlessly, but I am not under the influence of alcohol now, nor would I ever appear so in your court." I stated it in my best closing argument voice. Of course every word was true. I respected her to much not to be.

"JD the last week or so you have been looking very ragged. I am not the only one to notice. If I thought you were under the influence of alcohol I'd have my bailiff take you into custody. The point is that you look like you need help. Do I have to give you the number of the attorney assistance program at the bar association?"

The Judge's stern voice gave away her real concern for me.

It was likely her perception of my situation was probably more accurate than my own, to a reasonably degree of legal certainty.

I glanced over at Adila. She was looking past the Judge and I could tell wanted no part of this line of conversation. My right temporo-parietal junction commanded me to go all law professor.

"Judge, I appreciate you taking a personal interest. I am ok. Really, if you want we can discuss Justice Thomas's '*register before filing provision isn't jurisdiction precondition*' in '*Reed Elsevier*', or Judge Reinhardt's dissent in '*Newdow*' on '*God in the Pledge being a clear violation of the Establishment Clause*'. Seriously, your honor, I am fine. I might have just over done it last night - a bit".

Judge Chin look me straight in the eye until it was very uncomfortable then she turned to Adila, "Ok what is the State going to do regarding the Motion for Supplement Discovery and the Motion on Rulings before Voir Dire?"

I was staring at the Judge thinking how much I appreciated the fact that her honor actually took the time to go through the whole attorneyassistanceprogram that I missed what Adila was saying, until I heard the words *Wayne County Sherriff* and *dead*.

"............. Wayne County Sherriff's office was expecting the coroner to issue Mr. Crops death certificate within 24 hours and he will forward us a copy. Sherriff says open shut case of drug deal gone bad in a parking lot next to the Detroit river. Your honor, upon receipt of death certificate from Wayne County the State will dismiss. I suggest that we come back on Monday for dismissal".

Adila turned to me and smiled, the type of smile a three year boy has when he sneaks a cookie. "Any objections, JD?"

"No, your Honor I agree, if the Court is available." I could not believe Madness's luck, the C.I., the only real trial witness dead.

"Monday at 9:00 am. Thank you both. JD, don't come into my court room hung over ever again."

The Judge was done with me for now. I knew she would bring it up next time I was back.

I followed Adila out of chambers, waiting until we were past the bailiff's desk before asking her about the murder; but then thought better of it.

"Adila thanks for not jumping in and kicking me when the Judge had me down."

"JD I wasn't born last night and I don't want to be a witness to something I have no opinion on, especially at this time of morning. Tell your client and the 3/5's to stay out of trouble in the streets. Tell

143

Mr. Giovanni to try and get a job, or get religion soon, or I will have his, or one of his associates death certificates in a case file on my desk, probably sooner than later."

"Thanks Adila, I'll see you on Monday." I walked out of the court room thinking about my cup of French roast coffee and the one hitter.

While I walked down the hallway and out of the Court House looking for Madness, I pondered how lucky, fortune, or providential Madness was.

Then I remembered the old Ralph Waldo Emerson's quote: '*Shallow men believe in luck. Strong men believe in cause and effect*'.

Blue sky with high cirrus still there, the cirrus was reassuring for some reason. I saw Madness and his crew standing at the end of the building.

As I walked over to him I wasn't sure what I wanted to say.

"Hey JD, what's going on? Do we have to go back in or are we finally done for today?" Madness started to relate to me some domestic briefing as he looked me directly in the eyes while we shook hands, "I have to stop by my mother's apartment. She is disappointed with me. You know JD, mother says I cause her nothing but grief. She just wants me to go to work for the city parks department."

"Mamae me disse, nao tome sea tempo, nao viva tao rapido", I responded reflexively and continued as a sibling would, "We have to try to take care of them, but there is no way of really pleasing them. Madness, we are done for the day, you have to be back again on Monday morning at nine." I said it as matter of fact as I could as an addict in the grip of a severe need for coffee.

"Ok great. Do I need to call you or anything, or just show up at nine JD?" He still was staring directly into my eyes.

"No, just be here." I continued staring back, looking into Madness's dark eyes, and only seeing my reflection in them. We stood there for a couple seconds locked in the moment.

"Great, thanks JD. See you on Monday." Madness finally said as he turned and then started to walk away. His crew got behind him as they all left.

Madness walks roads that I won't go down, but I do respect him for his honest and simple approach to his life.

I mentally calculated a defense attorney variation of Zipf's law. "Madness, hey just wait a second", I yelled and took a couple steps toward him.

Madness turned around and started walking back to me, "What did you forget JD, do I owe you a couple benjamins for today?"

Madness seemed to expect me to ask for a couple hundred. I liked that attitude in clients.

"Madness, I was fucking around with you. I'm sorry but I was being an ass. Crops is dead, killed in a drug deal in Detroit late last night. Wayne County Sherriff's told the prosecutor before court. Case is over on Monday morning." I said it fast while looking directly into his dark eyes looking for his reaction.

I was sure Madness was going to be pissed that I was testing him. Probably going to lose him as a client for that stunt, and that means losing all the Three Fifths business.

Madness looked at me through shark eyes for about three seconds, then up at the sky, and then at petey and paulie sitting in front of the building. "Fucking alright, you're a minimus pig looking Jackass Dysthymia, but the 3/5th's love your work; so, no Monday?"

Madness started grinning with a sparkle, or more accurately, a steely glint in his dark cheetah eyes.

"No, Monday nine am is the dismissal, you need to be there. You are on bond and all that until nine am Monday". I started to smile as his smile was infectious.

I wasn't sure why we were smiling, a guy's dead, a case is dismissed, or that fact Madness knew now I did not trust him.

I knew I was smiling in response to him, but it felt all fucked up.

"You're the man, JD. I am going to go drink my favorite Fins Bois and smoke some chronic. Have to call the Irishman and tell him to bring his best pipes down to the session. See you on Monday, JD."

Madness turned, and then he and the Three Fifth's crew strolled free on the sidewalk under the blue sky with high cirrus. I could hear them starting to softly sing 'a cappella', *"No refuge could save the hireling and slave from the terror of flight or the gloom of the grave"*.

I decided at that moment to have a Socratic discourse with Madness regarding Apollo, Dionysus, Muses, and Aphrodite's sociological perspective on street monikers the next time we were in the studio together mixing tracks and smoking Northern Lights.

Standing there watching them walk away, I took out a cigarette and lit it up. Love tobacco. I really did not need to do that with Madness and chance crossing his street code. Just because his crusading counsel is mentally at sea today is no reason to run aground on a reef. The 3/5ths are known for extreme retaliation.

Take out a member and they have been known to use standard gang MO - track and capture the shooter and tie the shooter to the dead 3/5ths member and throw them together into the Aioi, or burying them together some where off in the Hebron Hills.

Even for perceived slights the 3/5ths have been known to chop off hands, water board at least three times before cutting hair and beards, followed by pouring boiling tar over bodies obliterating any club tattoos.

146

Real Warriors, not very very very small penis pretenders throwing acid in little girls faces for going to school.

"Sir, would you please buy a raffle ticket for the interfaith festival this weekend?"

I hadn't noticed, as I had just started to enjoy smoking and worrying about Madness, but some young kid – who was probably eleven, had walked up from behind me.

In his left hand he was holding a large roll of raffle tickets. Looked like a kid who spent more time studying indoors than playing sports outside.

I noticed right away he was wearing a bolo tie, with a very cool emblem imprinted on the silver slide, which from the look of him was probably the nicest bit of clothing he owned.

The kid looked like a young Roy Rogers. I always liked the classic 1950's texas cowboy bolo ties on school kids look, just a cool American thing like jazz and baseball.

"Hey kid, that is a great tie. Did you win it at the Starkville County Fair's Sus Ahoenobarbus Hog Raffle, or did you buy it from some Mosley Union Movement Notting Hill Teddy Boy?"

"No sir, it was a gift from my civics class teacher", the kid replied and then cupped the slide in his right hand and held it up for me to get a better look at the imprint on the silver. "Sir, I was told that the emblem and tips were made from real zulfiqar silver, and the hand woven cord was made from rare Mecca 707 hemp".

"Well young man I know about Comstock, Red Dog, and Tombstone, but never heard of Zulfiqar, but it's sure a swell tie Kid." I was really impressed with the detail of the emblem stamped into the slide. It was a strong horse reared up on its hind legs with a flowing mane and had a greenish banner draped over its back. "That sure is a great tie kid", I told him (he already knew it). The artisan's work spoke for itself.

147

"What's the prize young man, and how much are the tickets? I asked hoping they were a dollar. The kid looked like a good kid, and apparently from his fistful, he had not sold that many tickets.

"Sir, the tickets are only five dollars apiece. The grand prize is a KdF Volkswagen."

I looked at the kid and then started going through my pockets. Inside pocket of my sport coat I found seven dollars. I gave it to him. "Here kid, give me a lucky ticket and keep the change for yourself."

The kid grinned at the money, and then at me, which made me feel a bit better. He torn one of the tickets off and handed it to me while saying very politely, "Thank you, sir" and then shook my hand.

I thought what a nice kid, and that his civics class teacher was probably very proud of his student. As he turned away to leave he said, "assalaamu alaykum"; which caught me totally off guard. I thought he was a young *Ferdinand Joseph La Menthe*, or some *Joven Vaquero*, or an *Italian*, or a *Puerto Rican*, or *something*.

I looked at the ticket. It was for the 'Interfaith Festival and Family Picnic' that Starkville's mosque was having on Saturday. Another civic function I would not be attending.

On one side was a list of the speakers and a picture of mohammad collecting his winnings at last year's festival greased pig contest. The other side had a picture of the U.S. flag with the raffle number printed where the stars should have been.

It was a beautifully printed ticket, palettes of rich colors, as if hand painted onto the very best hemp paper. I did like my ticket's number 'CD95L'. I just knew it was a lucky number.

The kind of number you would see on license plates on the very expensive cars parked all day long on the street in front of the building between the Ordenspalais and Palais Pless.

The number had me day dreaming of a black stretch Mercedes with tinted windows, with not only a driver but also the majordomo sitting in front; not a KdF VW made for very small penis people.

I put the ticket in my shirt pocket over my anticipating heart.

The death of Crops and the Madness thing was bugging me, even though the kid had distracted me momentarily.

I took three deep breathes, and between each breath I told myself the old legal stratagem, *'be strong and of a good courage'*.

Made me feel a very small bit better emotionally, as if I could get out in front of the rest of the day's challenges, no matter what had just happened in the court house, or on the court house steps.

Well, maybe, I would have to run the HP-35 or the '43 Model II Relay Interpolator with the morning's variables set out as reciprocal, pythagorean, quotient co-function, and even-odd identities.

It definitely was spacetimepoint for a good cup of strong coffee, and couple hits of Northern Lights from the one hitter as previously proscribed.

(As I walked Dr. Johnson and Boswell started singing *'Death Letter Blues'*; so I joined in doing my best ante meridiem imitation of Son House as imitated by Jimmy Reed.)

Chapter 13   Wolle Spinnen

Deep blue sky with high cirrus. I got out another cigarette. After lighting it I continued walking back to the office.

I did not have an appetite for apple-raisin strudels, buttery croissants, and almond-honey bienenstich anymore.

I just needed Italian or French roast with no additives. Thinking of the aroma, and smoky taste so dark I couldn't really taste the bean, my salvia glands kick in. Score another one for Petrovich Pavlov, well actually quite a few so far this morning, if I was actually counting.

After I walked a few more feet I stopped looking at the clouds, and began to stare at my fellow homo sapiens sapiens walking around me.

Lots of movement in the streets this time of day: Suits walking in pairs, or groups of pairs, going to or from meetings; secretaries and clerks running secretarial and clerical errands; and the taxi cabs and hotel shuttle buses making the twenty five minute airport to hotel runs.

I could stop almost any of them, and ask them a question about directions to this or that, and they all would be polite and answer as best they knew.

If I stopped any of them and asked what they thought of the '*Novum Organum*' as a way of planning your morning, their immediate reaction would to be disengage and walk away quickly, causing one to think that you had violated the complete '*Corpus Iuris Civilis*' in one act of interrogatory.

In the streets of Starkville, the veneer of civilization extends to travel directions, but not to philosophy. In the streets of the city a philosophical inquiry by a stranger within your personal space is either perceived as mental illness or a sexual invitation.

(Boswell wondered, philosophically, if, "....H. Chavez's education and knowledge is limited to his very, very, very, very, very small vergatrio because of innate or environmental factors?" Dr. Johnson replied that he, "...would have to examine him and Sean Penn to determine, but thought innate with both of them. Marxism runs in family genomes.")

"What's up JD?"

I turned around and saw Greg di Morra as he was walking up to me. "Hey Greg, how did your morning go?" I replied as a courtesy but really wasn't in the mood to talk to anyone.

"Great. Everything was a breeze, in and out, got what I wanted every time. What about you?" He was smiling and obviously enjoying the morning.

"Oh I'm about the same." When Greg walked up I was in the process of repressing this morning's memory, and now I was hoping to keep running that program in background.

"After I saw you JD, I ran into Leo Isaurian at the Starbuck's across from the Juvenile Court building. He was pigging out on those almond-honey bienenstich. He must have eaten five of them. He was in a great mood as he got the Starkville Zeitung case." You could just feel the monetary envy in every word Greg was saying. I immediately was plotting on how to disengage from him at the next corner.

"Greg I been a little bit out of touch lately, what is the Zeitung case? Current events have been swirling by me without affecting my hippocampus. No synapses firing."

This moment being one of them I was thinking. Greg, to his credit, actually laughed, endearing him to me at that spacetimepoint.

Lately, I have been trying to find humor in almost any/every situation. Situational humor - I was sure my life was full of hijā and fakhr, even though I have no perception of any as far back as I can remember. That now was becoming less and less by the nanosecond as my program ran in background.

"JD, Leo is going to make a bundle. It is sweet situation for him, something he enjoys and excels at, 1st amendment cases."

Again, you could just feel the envy at the scent of money as he continued. "Some arab lawyer from Detroit or New York has a bunch of muslim organizations suing the Zeitung for running those cartoons of mohammed, you know the ones where mohammed is having sex with a pig - california ursidae s. parkius; and the other one that has a bomb in mohammed's hat."

"You know Greg, as cartoons go they were third rate, just like everything else passing for muslim culture. I really like the idea of cartooning the 7th century as a challenge to repression, but the cartoons just were not funny or really even slightly shocking, pretty boring stuff. You know that any editorial cartoonist from the main stream media could do a really great strip of a hermaphrodite transvestite mohammed without her/his clitoris, dressed in a red parka and mini skirt, and at the end of the comic strip have he/she stoned by very small penis mutaween and much smaller penis basij after he/she has lesbian sex with a preteen slave girl on the 15th of Sha'aban at their direction for their cell phone cameras to capture."

"Just think of it JD, Leo is going to have a lot of motions to file and defend. He sure is going to have a nice pay day. You know the arab lawyer doesn't stand a chance against Leo. They are just trying to intimidate the Zeitung."

Either, I had just thought about a red parka and mini skirt without vocalizing it, or Greg was fixated on money.

"Yeah Greg it is straight up black mail. I'm sure Leo will prevail at every level, they will appeal everything and drag it out for years, which is probably their main goal."

Saying it just pissed me off.

It is the system, and the system was designed for rich players to fight issues out in the local state courts and in the federal courts.

Fight as much as you want, always cases to push agendas. System problem then becomes justice is a function of money. Justice equals cause divide by money square.

It was appropriate the Leo had the case. Some other attorney such as Greg might let the 'cause célèbre' draw their personal egos out into court steps interviews and other such skirmishes that can interfere with this war.

Defamation can't be defined to interfere with free speech and writing about any religions or other mythological flat earth clitorisless philosophies.

Otherwise there is no scientific truth or moral absolutes; only 7th century frenchkissing mythically chosen super race clitoris hating nazi truth.

Greg stopped abruptly and stated, "Think that there would be a way to ban islam in Starkville. No one I know wants anyone who believes in that religion living next door to them."

He turned abruptly, "See you later, JD. I'm going to go up and talk with Tim Dramai about a property settlement proposal he has offered. I think he is going to cave in to our demand, so my client is going to get more than fifty six per cent of the assets. Man wouldn't that would be great."

Greg shook my hand and then went into the office building we had stopped in front of. Most of the building's occupants were lawyers, solo and small firm practitioners. Not a bad place to work.

I had two blocks to get to my office – plenty of time to finish running that program in background. Greg was right about the arabs. It was blackmail by lawsuit, change your policy or pay Leo for years. Leo will vigorously fight for the 1st amendment against the arab lawfare.

He will win as the 1st amendment is written in plain English so that even a 9th circuit judge can understand it, and can't screw us by looking at foreign laws.

Leo will have a high profile for a couple of years. The publicity alone is worth what the paper will pay him, which will be quite a bit. The paper should get an expense tax credit from the Department of Defense.

I started to look at my fellow sidewalk travelers again while walking up to my office. I knew, as did Boswell and Dr. Johnson, that the arab's goal wasn't Leo's case. No way the arabs, persians, and the other muslim lemmings care about cartoons.

They want some type of the Caliphate of Clitoris Free Cordoba. The whole 1000 year Reich thing, with preteen sex slaves and genocidal sports.

As I walked up to the entrance to my building I was trying to remember what the Brit's were reporting about the tactic; and whether they were arguing '*Quinn v Leathem*' against the application of Sharia anywhere in the commonwealth. The Telegraph, Independent, and Guardian were reporting the lawfare.

(Boswell then stated his standard analysis, "Fucking muslims just want to fight. There are no other options with them. Sick-fucking-religion-of-peacers have a blowing shit up fetish." Dr. Johnson nodded in agreement, and then diagnosed, "They have a preteen clitoris fetish, and a possible anal fetish, and some of them definitely have a latent iranian boy in a well homosexual fetish". Boswell agreed with Dr. Johnson stating, "Especially that young boy and dark wet hole thing".)

The ornate lobby was reassuring to me immediately as I entered the building. Marble walls instill some delusion of safety or strength.

The late morning sun was flooding the lobby causing the faded colors of the ornate to add a warm fuzziness to my perceptions. I thought that the late morning sunlight actually heightened the green, yellow, and red colors in the '*Siege of Antioch*' oil painting above the elevator. I wanted to light up a cigarette, but didn't, as I walked up to the elevator and pressed the button.

155

I waited.

I wondered how long the lawfare attorneys were going to continue to attack the constitution, trying to persuasively argue to have their clitorisless nazi lies prevail over our constitution's individual rights. I started to recite to myself again:

> *When in the course of human events, it becomes necessary for one people to dissolve the political bonds which have connected them with another, and to assume among the powers of the earth, the separate and equal station to which the laws of nature and of nature's god entitle them, a decent respect to the opinions of mankind requires that they should declare the cause which impel them to the separation.*
>
> *We hold these truths to be self-evident, that all man are created equal, that they are endowed by their creator with certain unalienable rights, that among these are life, liberty and the pursuit of happiness. That to secure these rights, governments are instituted among men, deriving their just powers from the consent of the governed.*

Then the elevator opened. I got on, it was contemplate paneling time and as I was hitting 13, I realized that the attorney from Detroit, or wherever, fundamentally disagreed with everything I had just recited to the point where he thought he had a 7th century religious duty to kill me.

I knew his list of my objectionable life thoughts and actions was much longer than just my reciting common elevator law.

The elevator shook slightly as it rose. No doubt his goal wasn't 'lebensraum'. No, the lawfareyer and his muslim clients wanted to suppress my 8 bar, 12 bar, and 16 bar blues ideas, and substitute religious faith in frenchkissing and citing moronic 7th century verses over and over and over with my ass up in the air.

The prick from Detroit wants cartoonists and micro hemp farming moharebs like me to disappear.

Just like the usurping murderer Uncle Joe Jasmine Hu Jintao does with his fellow citizens who practice Falun Gong, Christianity, or just Google/Baidu 'tank man'.

("Fuck Jintao", was Boswell's response. "No room for old begena players, or 3 blocks of 4 measure Mississippi Delta players in the middle kingdom of commie hell, *or* in the Cordoba's clit-less preteen strip clubs.")

Not even the beautiful dark maple wood paneling could distract me from the fact it was a sick fucking religion, a *sadistic dans de Macabré*, as pathogenetic as communist governments that banned the individual begena player in favor of the atheistic collective. Both are for killing sales of New Orleans Jazz and Chicago Blues gramophone records.

(While I thought that the Pricks from Detroit were jealous of New Orleans and Chicago 16 bar penises, Boswell had a laughing seizure, knowing on my best day I was barely an 8 bar imitator.)

The elevator softly sputtered and swayed to a stop. I got off the elevator and turned left to go to my office, feeling like a manic whose sole purpose was to drink a pot of French roast.

I wondered how long before it was called Muslim roast. France was dealt a mortal blow with the decimation of its WWI generation.

WWII infected the corpse with socialism, communism, and multiculturalism. Now the islamocrazies have taken over seven hundred fifty one neighborhoods in twenty one of the administrate regions of the former great nation. The Algerian's and other resident jihadieinterlopers are carving out '*l'âme de la nation*'.

(Dr. Johnson suggested a benefit supper at '*Le Restaurant du Telepherique*' or '*Chez Le Per Gras*' to muster support for final chapter of the French Wars of Religion. Boswell stated he did not believe that Louis XIV's Edict of Nantes would be updated by the National Assembly to allow Protestants to remain, and to require all Muslims to leave. Dr. Johnson replied, "Then we must have a late night gourmet supper very soon, so to be able to dine while observing the warm soft glow of cars burning in the streets of Grenoble".)

There was no one in the hallway, but I thought I heard Mr. Ippolito Aldobrandini arguing with Mr. Giordano Bruno about men's hats and suits in the office down the hall next to the women's bathroom.

From what I heard it seemed Mr. Ippolito Aldobrandini was rather rudely telling Mr. Giordano Bruno that Mr. Fatih S. Mehmet Jr.'s haberdashery on Khnum Avenue would not provide any different consideration for Mr. Giordano Bruno's worsted, the serge, or even the gabardine.

It seemed to be an issue that would have to be solved by a trial by the way that Aldobrandini was arguing.

They might have been in the stairwell, I couldn't decide.

Chapter 14   Atalanta

I opened the door and walked into my office. Atalanta was working on the computer while talking on the phone. I walked back to my office where there was a pot of coffee already made. I immediately grabbed my cup and filled it, spilling a lot over the brim as usual. I took a sip and burned my upper lip ever so slightly. Perfect.

I walked back out to the ante room. I sat down in one of the leather chairs and put my feet up on the coffee table. I could not do my job without her. Atalanta ran everything for me, not only the office, but pretty much everything. She was a co-signatory on every one of my checking, credit, and banking accounts. She had copies of every key, every password, every safety deposit box, every certificate of title, and even my Last Will and Testament, in which she is sole legatee. Well, my friends in the aquarium and her, to be precise. No codicil.

She looked great today, in a black knitted yarn suit, which was either a Donna Vinci or a Moshita. She had left early yesterday to go to the salon to get her afro redone. I could see she had her nails done also.

She started working for me when she graduated from Brandeis about twelve years ago. I always tease her when she gets her hair done that the 'Angela from Brandeis' look went out when Ronald Reagan got elected. By lapse of time it qualifies as classic.

I set the coffee down to cool then I lifted an issue of Popular Science from the pile of magazines on the coffee table. I started reading about '*Reza Sha Pahlevi's toy*,' and how it helped the Russians in their war effort by delivering eighteen percent more tonnage than the Commie bastards from Bykinia had specified. When I had finished the first page, I looked up to see if Atalanta was close to hanging up. She wasn't.

Atalanta was married, and had a daughter. Like most women of her generation, she kept her maiden name and hyphenated her husband's name when they got married. I tease her about it sounding like expensive Bordeaux wine sometimes, *Morgan - le Fay*, but I grow tired of it quickly.

She was in charge of her own schedule, and is paid to be in charge of mine.

Her husband and she are avid compound bow hunters. For her last birthday he gave her a new bow with an IBO rating of 340 and with a draw weight of seventy pounds. She loves spending weekend mornings with him and their daughter hanging around the northeast strand of black locust trees in the Hebron Hills waiting for the perfect boar shot.

Or if boar was out of season, then her husband would hunt the free range indigenous california ursidae s. parkius as they were declared a perversion of nature and a public nuisance by the very small penis mutawas to the other wildlife and local Starkville habitat in general.

Of course, all the lap dog democrats in the Department of Natural Resources agreed in a fit of multiculturalism distemper, and immediately issued shoot to kill regulations.

After reading a couple more paragraphs about logistics, I put the magazine down. I needed to just smell the coffee. I lifted the cup up to my nose and sat back in the chair with my eyes closed.

Sapor, Savur, Sapore, Saveur, Sapuri, Savoare

I used the aroma to calm my limbic system as I focused on a *1970 atoll blue judge ram air iv convertible* - beauty amongst chaos.

"JD, I found this in the bottom drawer of the file cabinet. You are supposed to keep it with you. Remember the previous 101 times you promised me you would carry your cell with you always."

160

Atalanta's voice revealed irritation, probably at the realization I refused to honor a promise made under duress, especially ones that make it easier for the government to track my movements.

I exhaled slowly and then opened my eyes to see her holding the electronic leash in her extended hand. I put down the coffee and got up and took the phone from her. No use in arguing. I still remember where the file cabinet's drawer is. She looked as if she was irritated about something more than my avoidance fetish of all things cellular.

"A good morning to you too, Atalanta! So how was my morning in court? What happened to the clients, did anyone have to go to prison? Instead I get 'don't leave without your homeland security triangulation device'." I said it with a grin as I always did with this conversation.

I put the cell phone on the coffee table and pick up the coffee and sat back like before. I took three deep breathes of the aroma while Atalanta picked up the telephone log book and flipped the pages back a couple times.

"JD you've got about nine important calls since last night, I'm only going to mention a few. Adbul's brother called and wanted to know if you are going over to see him, and wants to meet you afterwards. Another was the VP of that RFI Tagging Company regarding the lawsuit; one here from New Mexico from the Servants of the Holy Paraclete, they still sound like a right wing militia group to me JD, saying the check in the amount of $82,719.63 is being mailed out for the disputed letter; last important message among the others - the prosecutor's office called this morning but I'm guessing you already know about Mr. Crops being killed in Detroit."

I could tell she wanted to know details but instead just looked at me for a second and then said, "Do you want to go over yesterday's discovery on the Notches B&E; or review either Hari Seldon's information for incorporating Prime Radiant LLC, or the Aztlán

Reconquista LLC's non-compete settlement agreement draft that I finished typing a few minutes ago?"

Atalanta was my last and only life line to normalcy. I clung to it. "I think the best thing to do is look over Adbul's file. Then go see him before I get side tracked today. You agree Atalanta?" I took a large gulp without burning my trachea, so I took another.

"Ok Mr. Juris Doctor here are the phone calls, now go back and actually return one or two. I'll get the file and bring it back, after I send an email to the federal court clerk on you're not attending the 75th Judicial Conference – just like the 74th, 73rd, 72nd, 71st, 70th, and 69th." She handed me the copies of the telephone log.

"JD, I put Ms. Fröhlich's message on top for you", she winked at me, and then turned back to the computer. The Shah's logistical assistance to the russians against the nationalsozialistische deutsche arbeiterpartei would, could wait.

I took my coffee, cell, and messages and walked slowly back to my office. I look at my desk chair, but instead went over to my sofa and lay down. I pulled the old cloak over me. The sun light felt so nice on my face.

I closed my eyes and crossed my legs and remembered last Saturday night.

Dr. Johnson, myself, and Boswell were smoking about seven grams in the hookah. I had wrapped buds of Northern Lights around a block of Moroccan primo hashish when putting the dope in the bowl. That evening's binghi was being proclaimed as 'historic' and 'evolutionary' by the smug Dr. Johnson and ebullient Boswell. Myself, deep in despair, as I achieve consciousness only with a no.2 lead pencil and standard line three hole paper.

I understand graphite lines on paper are the bow of the ship of consciousness.

If Dr. Johnson and Boswell are correct, the bow of the Titanic of my consciousness has struck an algorithm iceberg. Dr. Johnson and Boswell's iceberg.

Dr. Johnson had replaced the last burned out tubes, while Boswell had cleared the fortran of all gigo, and my old 709 was in the attic lost in thought, or maybe just loop processing i's and o's.

Boswell was ecstatic because of his faith in the result of the pending calculations of the 709. He just knew it would be the end of the reign of holly and bolly woods. The algorithm was the La Brea Tar Pits to both dinosauria's - bolly and holly.

His algorithm is an A.I. that anticipates an individual's consciousness and provides choices of real time CCTV, Public Street Webcams, Police Cruiser Video, Satellite video transmissions, Private Business Video and Webcam; virtually every digital video transmission currently streaming on the planet for your viewing in currentspacetimepoint.

Dr. Johnson was trying to anticipate the ability to utilize the record feature and library the brainwaves so to capture aspects of every experience, thereby being able to double and treble certain gravitational and electromagnetic waves in replay.

I started to have a lsd flashback by using a fine watercolor brush to paint on standard line three hole paper, having a depth no No. 2 pencil could achieve in my linearis reality.

Due to the fundamental mistakes of my interpretation of sensory data, I found that even the most colorful and intricate mosaic paintings were exactly and unsentimentally linearis in all my realities.

I concluded that my No. 2 pencil was the torahbiblekoran, and Johnson and Boswell's algorithm was the hubblespacetelescope, for understanding my linearis experience of life and creation.

"No sir, not today, wake up JD, you have work to do." Binghi evaporated as *echolocation* did a rendition on my opaque consciousness.

I opened my blurry eyes, and Atalanta was already in my office starting to put all the files on my desk.

(Boswell who was already awake, smirked and then went all Job on me saying, "Who hath loosed the bands of the wild ass J.D. Glass?")

"I wasn't sleeping", a blatant misstatement which she ignored, "could you give me the file of discovery photographs and the medical examiner's report."

That I was in absolutely no mood to review the file, but had to if I was going over to see Adbul in a while, was of no spacetimepoint consequence.

Atalanta placed all the files in order on my desk, and then grabbed the one I had asked for, and brought it over to me.

"Thank you Atalanta. I don't know what I'd do without you."

I meant every word and she knew it.

She handed me the paperwork and then went over to the Dictioneri and poured some more coffee into my cup for me. "JD, you know what you'd be doing without me, living on public assistance and spending all your time at the public library reading."

She half grinned at me as she put the cup on the coffee table in front of me, and then went over and opened the window an inch or so before turning to leave.

Her husband was a very lucky man. Not once did she comment on how I looked, nor did she press me on what happened this morning. Woman's instinct - she knew I was loop cycling '*to my sweet home chicago*'.

164

As I sat up the cloak dropped onto the floor. I reach out and placed the file on the coffee table. After letting Two Counts of Endangering Mary Jane bother me all morning, I decide no more.

I decided to act in accordance with Professor William Tecumseh Sherman's court room hornbook 'Epistemology of Domestic Relations Court'.

It might be a dry well. If I got a hit it would be an east texas gusher.

(Dr. Johnson looked up from his HP-35 and smiling said, "Kilgore".)

"Atalanta, I need you to do something, I need it as soon as you can get to it. Scorched earth, no stone unturned, go fucking atomic on Lynda Marie Child's husband. I want you to get his file and take his driver license photograph and his identity information and go on the internet and go to every social network site, starting with the popular sex ones, then go through all the rest that you can find, and see if, - what you can find. I need anything he's posting on any of them. I want screen names, screen shots, see if he post dirty pictures of himself, everything. Anything I can use in a custody fight. I know I am asking you to look at a bunch of pervs, but I got a hunch and I want to know what he does, doesn't, wants, has, fantasizes; I want pictures – 8 x 10 glossies."

Atalanta nodded her head, and then went back out to her desk.

I was sure Atalanta was not happy with having to go look at sexual networking sites, but she understood I wouldn't have asked if it wasn't in the interest of justice.

Besides, Dr. Johnson and Boswell knew that if it was a female target, I would put on Johnny Hodges and Duke Ellington playing Billy Strayhorn's 'Brown Betty' and do it myself. Legal work requires specialized training.

Chapter 15   Kesselschlacht

I laid down on the sofa to rest. I wanted to sleep for at least a half an hour. I realized that I was getting to the point of nonfunctioning. My letting Marie's problems affect me while in court is symptomatic.

("Justice Center revolving stockholm door syndrome psychosis no doubt you absent without leave malingering narcissist", chided Boswell.)

I realized I needed to get off my unhinged wild ass and concentrate on work now. It was becoming more difficult as my left brain was out of phase. Marie's problems were of her own making. Her husband can justify his actions in law, just not morally.

Doing a self-diagnosis, I estimated a difference between my hemispheres of five gigapascals due to my delta-9-tetrahydro-cannabinol clogged mossy cells.

I got up and retrieved my pipe. It still had a half a bowl of Northern Lights green bud.

I took my cigarettes out of my shirt pocket and light one, took a drag, and put in the ashtray.

I hit the pipe twice with the zippo, and then held my breath.

As I lay back down on the sofa, I put the pipe on the floor underneath. I picked up the coffee cup and took a long sip, and then exhaled slowly.

I set the cup down. I reluctantly picked up the files.

Adbul, as in FGM Adbul, Female Genital Mutilation Adbul; as in 18 United States Code 116, as in knowingly circumcises, excises, or infibulates, Adbul.

Adbul, as a practitioner in Toubia's three categories, Adbul.

Adbul, as in violator of Muna, Nahu, Haadiya, and Hanan among other innocents, Adbul.

Adbul the imposter, performing surgical procedures as a matter of sadistic misogynistic religious custom not of any medical necessity Adbul.

Adbul, whose shameless immorality is publicly supported, Adbul.

Adbul as in the muslim who spent first twenty minutes of our first meeting not grasping the concept of mens rea, actus reas, and strict liability as to his carrying on his forefathers barbaric tradition in a second floor row house's two room office directly above a Pakistani street corner storefront, four blocks away from 14 North Moore Street.

As I explained to him when we originally met in lockup that the 1st rule of Real Estate is location, location, location; and that in Starkville and the rest of this country, 18USC116 is his present address.

Adbul refused to acknowledge that he isn't in a unique position, as would be an exempted J-Visa doing a reality television show version of a county & mideastern song about family traditions, being shot all night long on location in some Starkville row house's second floor two room honky-tonk.

Adbul, as in the mutilator of five year old Ahd.

Adbul, who used unsterile instruments on the innocent child that almost caused her death by infection forty eight hours later in Starkville's Emergency Room.

Eighty nine minutes later two detectives handed Adbul a search warrant. 479.999 seconds later they had his cell phone, computer, paper files, and surgical instruments bagged and tagged, and were leading him down the stairs in handcuffs past solemn Pakistani capitalists.

Atalanta had placed the bulk of the copies of those documents on my desk. I had all the medical reports of the Fed's medical expert, and photographs of the individual victims surgically altered bodies.

I decided I had to put them down and take a xanax before working on the file.

I got up and went over to my desk and got out two xanax, took them, and washed them down by gulping my coffee.

I took a deep breath. I held it for three seconds, and then slowly exhaled.

I saw the forensic print file on the desk. I reached over and picked it up.

I went back over to the sofa to lie down to start reviewing the evidence.

I picked the cloak off the floor, laid down, and pull the old cloak up over my chest.

I picked up the file and started to read about Adbul, as in the client who paid me thirty pieces of silver, Adbul.

(Dr. Johnson and Boswell both then simultaneously agreed that, "… shouldn't bitch about taking the case for such a small fee since I was sure to be awarded the '*1st class Gold der Bandenkampfabzeichen Badge*' from the local jihadieimmammie at the Starkville mosque." Then Dr. Johnson ventured his discerning opinion that, "It would be the first time a local attorney received the award, and it would definitely help in the work of the Starkville Interfaith Council sanctuary cities initiative." Boswell deliberately spoke up with his usual cognitive distortion assuring me that, "…both 'VOELKISCHER BEOBACHTER' and 'DAS 12 UHR BLATT' would give me favorable press for a while, which would be worth more than just some fee paid in silver or gold, in advertising my representation to the muslim community.")

I was pretty sure that they were joking.

169

Chapter 16   Hallucinations

I purposely got out the forensic print photographs, scene prints, color glossies of the operating table and individual medical devices, and of the medical waste bottles.

Print photographs in Adbul's case were nonthreatening, antiseptic, res ipsa loquitur; obvious as a Tiger Slug's mucus trail.

It was a good way to start into the evidence, like a 1950's film noir detective movie, though not as intriguing as say White Heat, Notorious, or Touch of Evil. The antiseptic pictures of objects caused the mind to imagine.

The actual pictures in my murder and sex cases are always much worse than in my mental pictures of them.

(Boswell has stated many times after a sex case, while we are consuming a gallon of my tea, that my '…imagination is censored by the M.P.A. ratings board and my Psychotic Amorism ratings agent was inhibiting my 5-HT reuptake 3D Blushing Particle Wave Disc and the Psychotic Anthropomorphism ratings filters really were affected by glasses of ice cold tea'.)

The print photographs only required the basic questioning of the Fed's expert at trial: collection and chain of custody, whorl, right loop, left loop, arch, and tented arch, and then probably just a couple minutes on algorithms, 0/45/90/135; and thank you Mr. or Ms. Expert - no further questions of this witness your honor.

Atalanta walked into my office and placed the draft settlement in my inbox file on the desk.

She looked over at me and then went over to the black Dictioneri and picked up the coffee carafe.

She came over and topped off my cup. She put the coffee back and then looked out the window at the sky while asking an irrational rhetorical question, "JD, you haven't called any one, have you?"

171

"No I am just getting started, don't have time. Will you take care of the important ones? Tell them I can call them after 15:27, the rest put off. I believe I might go to see Clement at 19:00."

She smiled, turned, and was gone before I could think of anything else to ask. A man could not ask for a better business partner. No matter that the canons of ethics say a partner has to be a lawyer, reality is different from titles.

My faith in her was complete.

I closed my eyes and drifted off as my spandex covered psyche was xanax cycling.

I was becoming manic with thoughts as fractal patterns of my impressions - so of course I went with it.

All my emotions were/are consuming any rationality or scientific thoughts and are now being drawn inexorably into the black hole of my emotional rage seeking retribution; one of the oldest pillars of justice. Well at least since probably last Sunday. Knowing something of the humanity of the victims of the worst present day barbaric - religious persecuting – torturing – slavery promoting – unjust social system known as islam; and knowing having that knowledge becomes an indictment-by-information of moral failure by inaction for systematic complicity and personal complacency.

("*Move along, No transference here for M.S.W. and 3rd year psychiatry residences to analyze*", stated Dr. Johnson.)

I could arbitrarily start the indictment on April 24, 1915 with the Armenians, then add additional Counts versus the 13th Waffen Mountain Division of the SS Handschar, and then additional Counts with virus evolving in places such as Fr. Seroma's parish in Nyange, Kibuye Province, Rwandan and as very small penis apartheid clitoris hating frenchkissing janjaweed in Dafur; then additional Counts with the virus mutating and appearing at Nariman House in Mumbai as very small penis Lashkar-e-Taiba. The indictment is worldwide in scope.

(Boswell angrily opined, "There is an ongoing conspiracy is to silence the hubblespacetelescope". Dr. Johnson thoughtfully then stated "It's more a religious imperative to achieve the ultimate goal of pleasing all the gods of the multiverses by the religion of peaceful frenchkissers by eradicating this world of all of preteen clitorises".)

Marie's problems, and my inappropriate and not proportional reactions, are road signs not to be ignored indices of my latest bout of religious consumption. That, and of course, mining popular sexual social media for evidence of an obvious lack of morality.

My revulsion and anger are further brought out in a thorough reading the medical reports with their unassailable history / diagnosis / prognosis to a reasonable degree of medical certainty of the barbaric nature of the mutilating of female children's clitorises.

FGM was some metaphor of controlling the sexuality of individual women, whereas very small penis's honor killing is a crime against humanity, and is for the eternal control of the woman. Muslims are such good fathers/brothers/sons. Real macho very, very, very small penis studs.

Cacophonies of neurons in my pontine tegmentum became hyperactive as I lay there beginning sleep while thinking 'I would smote Hashim Duraz and those Haqqanis in wrath with a continual stroke...'

Thousands of Islamic women and young girls are 'honor code' victims every year according to the morally bankrupt U.N. High Commission for Human Rights. I know that is an undercount: KifayaHusaynSamiaSarwarAmireAbuHanhanQaoudRaniaArafatA qsaPervexAminaYaserSaidSarahYaserSaidMedineMNoorAlmaleki TulayGorenKhateraSadiqiYasmineLarbiCherifAymanUdasSabrina LarbiCherifGulsenSaharDaftaryLidiaMotylskaSandeelaKanwalMo rsalObeidiHatinSurucuAqsaParvezHinaSalemSazanBajezAbdullah HeshaFadimeSahindalGhazalaKhan... endless are the victims on the list in the Indictment of Islam as a criminal conspiracy against the rights of all women. Quran- 4:15 Quran-24:2 Quran-33:33 roil in seas of innocent women's blood.

173

How despicable are these veryveryvery small penis men of islam.

The cowards think islamic law requires honor killing and sex slaves citing koran 4:3, 23:5-6, and koran Suras 4:3 and 33:50; as if that has any other meaning other than ignorant interspecies cruelty in any of the billions of exoplanets in this, or any other, posthubblespacetelescopemultiverse.

What cowards these pretenders of purity are, with their trampling the humanity of their mothers, sisters, daughters; and on all women's freedom, liberty, and clitorises, due to ignorance caused from faith in a 7th century frenchkissing foot bathing pedophile. Hateful, ignorant and immoral beings rolling amongst islam's 7th century scaffolding.

Poisonous ideology whose temporal gravitational wave effects still reeks of death from the war criminals and Nazi partners, Hassan al-Banna and Haj Amin al-Husseini. Fresh rotting corpses have the scent of Mahmoud Ahmadidolaterejad with his fanatical self-delusions of Muhammad al-Mahd-i' amanidolater; as if that justifies the innocent blood of children and women flowing at his feet.

Mahmoud Ahmadiidolaterejad's body odor is not the bitterly course couture of the Zyclon-B odor of Hassan al-Banna and Haj Amin al-Husseini, but more of a near future haute couture plutonium islamonaziusurper seared flesh and carbonized cities aroma. Wimps and machos atomizers made in Qom are sold at mosque merch tables.

13th Recognized Tenant of HubbleSpaceTelescope THC Theology is that if men spent less time humming, "Horst-Wessel-Lied" while reading ancient stories of banu hashim and banu tain complaining to abu talib, and more time doing research on 'APOBEC3A', Higgs Boson particles, spintronics, or molecular liquids and colloidal suspensions, then they couldn't possibly rationalize enslavement of their own mothers/wives/sisters/daughters.

According to the internet, the genetic web addresses of Jews, Palestinians, Lebanese, and Syrians are sequential sub addresses of a single IP on the same server running NeXTSTEP in old Jerusalem.

Web design scholars at he al-AzhardlyKnowsAnything University cannot refute "Y chromosomes HTML5's", "haplotypes CSS's", or "protein polymorphism Graphic Design Typography" with words of ignorant hate written down centuries ago by violent men without a posthubblespacetelescope understanding of the multiverses.

If those scholars were just men, then they would be encouraging their wives/mothers/sisters/daughters to use personal computing devices running OSLO HTTPd.93 on internet tablet devices while sitting in a Wi-Fi hotspot in front of the Temple Mount, while occasionally sipping ayahuasca ice tea from judah goblets.

(Did abu talib ever explain if the Mohammad genome is different than Abraham, Jesus, Siddartha Guatama, Confucius, Abdul Aziz Al Saud or David Ben Gurion genomes in any way? Did abu talib ever explain if the Mohammad genome is different than Tsuyoshi Noda, SS-Obergruppenführer Friedrich Jeckeln, Josefl 'Holodomor' Stalin, or Szilveszter Matuska genomes in any way? Did abu talib ever explain to Liu Xiaobo, Carl von Ossietzky, Andrej Sakharov, Aung San Suu Kyi, or the other snowboarders at the Madison Arboretum, the difference of innate versus learned behavior? Boswell and Dr. Johnson think not. We still are waiting for a jihadist to show us the DNA chart that differentiates believer and non-believer. Can we have a moratorium on honor killing while we wait? The 1st Compromise offer on that impossibility is waiting for a 'supreme' imam to issue an islamic 'Decet Rornanum Pontifecern' to the clitorius obsessed jihadists.)

The misogynist professor Shaytan Iblis at he al-AzhardlyKnowsAnything University issued a fatwa in September, 1978 on apostasy ordering death, with the irrefutably scientific götterdämmerung analysis that 'allah knows best'.

All posthubblespacetelescopers believe in the strict interpretation of the 1st Amendment to the U.S. Constitution and they are waiting for Sheikh Ali Gonie's call for repeal of Article 98 of the Egyptian Penal Code.

Until that is done, there is little hope for ending honor killing, or the endless harvesting of all muslim preteen clitorises.

Where is the Islamic 'Giordano Bruno' writing "The Prayer of Twenty Millions" for the Starkville Tribune who is willing to stand up for the Hubble Space Telescope over the fascist twelvers such as Mahmoud Ahmasmallpenisjihadist, that are blind from ignorant ancient hatreds, with his requirements on the IRGC of performing measurement matrixes of very small penises to ensure stability and consistency of the various death cult techniques of twelvers.

My current wager is that all the scholars at he al-AzhardlyKnows Anything University spend all their time writing and submitting scripts for "The Pioneers of Today and Tomorrow" on Gaza's Al lostsouls TV, while hoping to win The Palestinian NonAuthority's "Goebbels Award" nomination for Best Original Screenplay for an episode of 'The Pioneers'.

The Goebbels Award pays thirty pieces of AR Abbasi (4-shahi) coins in addition to its awarded engraved commemorative bronzed clitoris plaque.

Teaching hate to children is much easier that mapping a genome, or ensuring the democratic rights of all men and women with individual freedoms, including speech and religion.

Even the scholars at he al-AzhardlyKnowsAnything would have agreed with Professor Ijma that teaching 'future pioneers of tomorrow' about achieving 72 preteen pole dancing virgins is more important to frenchkissing than any medallion given to the dhimmis E.M. von Behring protégés.

(Boswell interrupted with, "... not being fair to the scholarship being done at he al-AzhardlyKnowsAnything University because their Department of Forestry has the premier scholars of Maruta". He was right in that over 90% of their graduates get jobs with Kempeitai Political Department and Logging Epidemic Prevention Research Laboratory upon graduation.)

It is without dispute, and a scientific certainty, that in all parallel dimensions / multiverses where Islam exists, never once did the 'scholars' of he al-AzhardlyKnowsAnything University ever ever ever ever ever ever ever ever invite, Nietzsche, Socrates, Aristotle, Aquinas, Locke, Hegel, Spence, Confucius , Santayana, or Lao Tzu to Mecca to discuss my theory that if you substitute the word "islam" for "nazi" in 'Mit Brennender Sorge and Summi Pontificatus', the logic is not altered an iota.

("Or even a trans-membrane CCW vector of .000000000000000000019 mm", said Boswell who then thoughtfully added, "...maybe it was CMBR".)

Control experiment suggestion for those few north korean scientists who aren't Hexakosioihexekontahexaphobic, and are skilled in bioweapon engineering, and who aren't afraid of offending primitive peoples who follow philosophy from millenniums ago. Take the dna of Hassan al-Banna, Shrio Ishii, Mahmoud Ahmadinejad, Haj Amin al-Husseini, Sayyid Ali Khamenei, Heinrich Himmler, Otto Eichmann, Tomás de Torquemada, Diego Deza, Josef Stalin, 毛澤東, Saloth Sar, Mehmed Talaat, Kim Jong-il, Prince Asaka and run parallel genetic algorithms with 666 genotypes for 666 generations, with each algorithm fitting the human subjects performance data using falsehoods, adultery, murders, torture, assaults, rapes, & FGM parameters. My hypothesis is in all dimensions/multiverses, the end result is always overflowing petri dishes of ز تمرك مـ شرارت .

Immammies won't be able to keep women as slaves if women are allowed to become educated by the internet and through its apostles - personal computing devices, which are all able to instantly communicate with the hubblespacetelescope.

Yet in spite of hubblespacetelescope, there are some fundamentalist Christian fellow travelers still preaching ignorant human rights violations, and supporters of 'Lex Oppia' such as Rev. Anus MacDaddy (projecting the worst of Rabbi Hillel), who has stated, "Wives, submit to your own husbands very small penis."

177

Yet Rev. Anus types still allow their wives a cell phone with internet access. Deuteronomy 24:1 or Genesis 2:24 Reverend?

Well, unless you prefer to kill them for 'honor', Umdat al-Salik o1.1-2; or beat them with branches to keep them from learning physics and medicine.

The taliban virus is high on C.D.C.'s list of muslim small penis enslavers of women, matching the brutality of the mutated twelver strain of the delusional eunuch virus Mahmoud Ah-I-do-jihad-against-young-muslin-women-who-only-wanted-fair-elections-by-killing-them-on-streets-and-raping-them-in-prison.

(Dr. Johnson then noted that, "... even the Jordanian Parliament had voted that restricting honor killing violated religious traditions and would destroy pious families and core islamic values".

Boswell spoke up, "If there was a 'Just-God-Character' it would have the Haqqanis and Hashim Duraz singing 'Es Zittern Die Morschen Knochen' while eternally raping, brutalizing and murdering Mahmoud Ahmadinejad and Sayyid Ali Khamenei as retribution for Taraneh Mousavi and Neda Agha Sulton; with periodic breaks so the scum can clean up at Prison Camp No. 22's glass gas chamber with its various luxury suites laid out for viewing the contorting bodies directly; or on the luxury suite's 102 inch plasma screen input with the internet high speed broadband platforms at 1080p with 150,000:1 dynamic contrast broadcast by internet worldwide". Of course that wasn't enough for Boswell, he also thought that, "...General Otozo Yamada should feed all of them anthrax-filled chocolate, plague-treated cookies, followed with typhus-infected beer, and then be subjected to vivisection without anesthesia". Dr. Johnson would not state his personal opinion, other than to say, "Boswell should read the New Testament more often instead of constantly re-reading the older one".)

When I stop to remember the innocent women murdered by the followers of islam, all my energy is drowned in the tears of the innocents.

Then due to Newton's 3rd, I immediately start remembering the local Starkville variation of the Virus, with its fifty three million and increasing daily, Roe v. Wade murdered babies. At this point my central nervous system neurons are transmitting dark energy through a secure sockets layer to my amygdalas.

I am dizzy within nanoseconds, feeling my diaphragm moving up and my breathe being siphoned out my trachea, as I experience a double binary Ruach situational awareness of the adversary's moral relativism.

A binary black hole system: innocents murdered by religion / innocents murdered by the progressive's governmental policies; it's a binary black hole system of innocent souls: 'victims of honor killings' / 'victims of margaret sanger'.

Occupying the same spacetimepoints is another binary black hole system of evil beings and evil ideologies: haters of women's clitorises souls / lovers of the tenants of barbaric penumbra philosophy souls.

The double binary of a black holes of the innocent female souls and the innocent zygote souls swirling around the black holes of haters of women's clitorises souls and lovers of the tenants of barbaric penumbra philosophy souls.

The voices of the innocents are double-lobed FRII emissions reverberating through my cochleae. My consciousness then becomes a lipid bilayer across which ions and molecules of innocence and evil transport across: $23Na+$ in a Crime Scene Investigation UV with fluorescence of the blood stain stones of Mecca and of the millions of blood stain cranial planning parenthood perforators.

At the double-lobed FRII emissions reverberating spacetimepoint in my REM state, or as soon as possible thereafter, I will cleanse myself by enjoying a binghi at the lake on the eastern side of Ojos del Salado, while reciting the 'Lotus Sutra' backwards to Oney, Austin, Hercules, Giles, Paris, Sheels, and Moll.

Chapter 17   Riesz Patria Theorems

Atalanta walked into my office talking causing my involuntary-quasi-abandonment of '*Ojos del Salado*'. I rubbed the sleep from my eyes as I centered on which spacetimepoint I was at. I took a deep breath and finished swimming up through tenduotrigintillion clouds of babelian chromium fish welcoming my conscience(s) to our blanco baraq leather skin sofa wissenschaft in mia patria. Due to the swimming, my labyrinth was afflicting my consciousness with vertigo.

"JD, Ms. Vladimira Hirchelle called a few minutes ago. She asked me if you're ok. She basically said you looked like hell this morning, my words, not hers." She looked down at the stack of phone messages she had in her left hand. "Clement called. He is at the Hilltop Bar on Gethsemane Avenue and wants to have dinner later, you're to call him. I told him that he is some kind of wizard if he gets you to eat a complete dinner. Yusuf Prophet called verifying his carjacking and reckless highway operation jury trial starts next '*Twiaday*'." She laughed as she mimicked his accent. Then Atalanta walked over to my desk and sat down in my chair.

I rolled my head from right to left to loosen up my neck. The cloak fell off me onto the floor.

I rubbed at my beard stubble just as all the fish quit babbling.

"Mr. Centers called regarding the deposition of the city engineer scheduled next Wednesday; Ms. Seiloyd called regarding her digital down loads on the label's royalty statement. Don Jones called wanting to talk to you on the ediscovery subpoena covering the board of director's private email from Doheny and Sinclair to Secretary Fall."

Atalanta stopped and looked up at me to see if I had gone back to sleep, but since I've been down on my luck lately, of course I was still awake.

181

"Adila called from the prosecutor's office; she has received the certification of death from Wayne County. Lynda Marie's mother called very upset, I told her you'd call asap, and she made the first office appointment of tomorrow at 10:31. Taysir Ullni's office called regarding Al-Azhar Grand Sheikh Ahmed el-Tayeb and some type of building chemical case. It sounded crazy."

Atalanta stopped, and was staring at me. I had a pretty good idea what she was thinking, and she knew better than to ask. "JD, I don't like this thing with you and Madness. It is not right as an attorney … and don't you start looking out the window at the clouds now." She wasn't warning me as so much as challenging me to talk.

"JD, the Mumbai movie company lawyer called about the airline explosion case. He had the numbers on the reshooting of the movie for the wrongful death demand on the dead actor." She looked me in the eyes and said with a bit of astonishment, "JD I had no idea that being type casted as hindu god all the time was worth so much money."

"Thank you for everything this morning Atalanta. I have to run over to the JC soon, so I appreciate if you would call Lynda's mother back and tell her I will call her as soon as I get back - Lynda's caught two endangerments, if she doesn't know that already. I have to dictate some visitation motions for you to type and file after I get back. Don't ask. Not looking to jump off the 86th floor with the goal of exploding bodyballoon on 34th street's sidewalk. I respect the first responders too much to make a biohazard mess on any sidewalk or street gutter for them to clean up, or anything that rude."

"Sure JD, I'll take some time and talk with her for a while if she wants to vent." Atalanta got up, shrugged up her shoulders a bit creating the appearance of disinterest, and went back to her desk.

I thought to myself as she left that I'd did not tell her anything she did not already know.

182

I would be lost throughout the day without her, as opposed being lost after work, say about dusk, or the worst lost of all, reading 'Finnegan's Wake' to Oney, Austin, Hercules, Giles, Aris, Sheels, and Moll.

I reach under the sofa and to retrieve my pipe.

I pulled it out, and then reach back under the sofa pulling the cloak all the way out from underneath, so to put it back over the side of the sofa. My wrist was cut by a loose staple on the bottom of the blanco baraq leather skin sofa wissenschaft as I pulled on the old and tattered cloak.

I immediately got up and went over to my desk. I opened the middle drawer and took out the film canister with my hashish in it. I picked up my Kensitas and lit one up. My wrist was starting to drip bright purple droplets of blood. I grabbed another cigarette and rolled it along the blood droplets and over the cut.

I rolled it until the entire cigarette paper was soaked through to the tobacco, and then put it in the ashtray.

The bleeding on my wrist slowed, so I grabbed another cigarette and repeatedly rolled it over the cut. I place the blood soaked cigarette next to the other one in the ashtray. Did it to a third.

I opened the canister and took out a small chunk of hashish and put it in the pipe.

I took a drag off my cigarette and then rolled it on my wrist, very carefully so not to have it burn me, and then placed it in the ashtray.

I took a long slow hit of the hashish from the pipe, closed my eyes and held breathe. I let the smoke sluggishly drift out my nostrils.

I slowing exhale as deeply as I could, and then put the pipe and canister back into the drawer. I grabbed my cigarette, got up and then went over and picked up my coffee cup and downed what was left in it.

I took another drag from the cigarette, and then held the cigarette up so I could watch the blood soak paper burn. I took another drag while watching the paper burn.

The smoke had a milder taste to it I was thinking as I took another drag, and then walked over to the desk and put it out.

I gathered up what I need to take over to the JC. I picked up the three moist cigarettes in the ashtray and put them back in to the pack. Atalanta would have a hissy fit if I left them there. I'd never hear the end of it. I grabbed my mouthwash, took a swig, and then spit it out into my trash can. I walked out to Atalanta to see if I needed to do anything else. "I'm on my way over to the JC. What else do I need to do?"

"JD, just go there and come right back. Everything can wait until you get back, I have everything under control." Atalanta smiled at me and then added a simple task, "Double chocolate latte."

I smiled back, "Got it, an almond-honey bienenstich and double chocolate latte."

As I walked out of patria and down the hallway to the elevator, Giuseppe Verdi came to mind. I was waiting for the elevator as usual, so out of habit I resorted to incantations; '*When in the course of human events, it becomes necessary for one people to dissolve the political bonds which have connected them with another, and to assume among the powers of the earth, the separate and equal station to which the laws of nature and of nature's god entitle them, a decent respect to the opinions of mankind...*', when I thought I heard some muted voices arguing in the women's bathroom.

Then the elevator opened. I got in leaving behind Atalanta typing, faxing, emailing and answering all calls to mia patria by saying "*O mia patria, si bella e perduta*". Giuseppe understood that I was looking forward to being outside the wire leisurely walking under the high translucent cirrus while smoking a cigarette.

I hit the lobby button, and then observed that two of the lights in the gold fixture were barely lit, more of just glowing softly. The elevator gently shook and sputtered as it started its slow descent. The dark maple looked very warm bathed in the softer Georgian light.

I noticed a business card lying on the floor under the control panel, and being ever the scientist, I picked it up for examination. Right, not a scientist, but not a gossip columnist either. It was made out of the best hemp paper stock, and the embossing was investment banker or hedge fund manager quality.

Well Mr. Munia Mandor, Dealer in Antiquities, from Tulcea, Romania, littering in Starkville is a minor misdemeanor. It was such a nice card with very clean graphics in blue and shades of white. I thought it be a shame to throw it away so I put it in my shirt pocket.

The elevator shuddered to a stop. The door slowly opened. I got out and took out my cigarettes and lighter as I walked through the lobby, stopping by the door, and lighting up before going outside.

The sky was blue. High cirrus, almost transparent, were scattered in the western skyline of the city. A placid western breeze was wafting over the sidewalk mixing with all the sewer gas, carbon monoxide, and heavy fluorocarbons tinged aromas from the street drains.

I walked over to the newspaper racks on the corner, and glanced at the headline story above the fold in afternoon edition of Der Sturmer: '*Wahhabi, Salafi and Al-Qaeda in Saudi Arabia agree whoever establishes innuendo, accommodates, innovates then upon him is the curse of allah, his angels and the whole of mankind*'.

I am sure the dumbasses don't even see the irony in issuing such a fascist press release to the main stream media. I would have to smoke all my hashish at once to have the patience to diagram paper, machines, ink, and transportation systems.

Dumb asses don't get the irony that Kent Cooper is no damned person to curse. Mankind owes him and all the other scientists and engineers a monument made from a space rock. The guys who run

185

around in dresses drawing cartoons for Al-HayatisShaytan, Ar-RayaisShaytan, and Al-WatanisShaytan should be the ones taxed to pay for its construction.

(Boswell risibly inquired, " Shouldn't the dangerous, rabid homo islamo sexual sapiens sapiens who read those comic books and only believe in power and money and killing other muslims, jews, kafirs, and who of course are pious clitoridotomy performing enslavers and rapists of child brides, pay the jizzonyouah tax also? Dr. Johnson nodded in agreement then replied that, "…posthubblespacetelescopers shirk 'tawhid ar-rububiyyah', probably it is more accurate that they turn away in disgust". I then noticed Al-Ghazzali, who was sitting outside a coffee shop across the street, glance up from his tablet computer where he was looking at Vela 5A on the world wide telescope, and nodded at me in agreement.)

I flicked the cigarette into the street gutter, and then took a deep breath, (Nam-myoho-renge-kyo), as my thoughts slowed. I put two fingers on my left carotid artery, a little less than thirty seconds - maybe 97 bpm.

Took another deep breath and rolled my head to the right before exhaling, no dysphoric mania, just an impulsive desire for a cup of coffee. ('LiarLiarLiar' Boswell and Dr. Johnson sang a cappella.)

Starkville wasn't big enough to have its own federal incarceration facility. Starkville was in fact the biggest town in the least populated federal district.

All over the country since the Reagan era, all the federal courts got new secure buildings with their own lockup facilities located within, as was required under the enabling construction legislation.

Here in Starkville, the federal court occupies the top floor of the federal post office building that was built in the 1930's. Starkville's federal district court did get enough funds to renovate the court room IT system, and of course funds for building security upgrades, but that was all. Such is national politics.

I decided to wait for the coffee until after talking with Adbul. I headed straight back to the justice center for my second trip today.

I tried to remember who was my first muslim client, probably the child murderer Al-Khidr. I haven't a solid memory of a client, who practiced islam, more than 3 years back.

There just aren't that many muslim citizens and/or visitors in Starkville.

It has to be less than five percent. Strange how many are in the courts lately, mostly minor misdemeanors, and a lot of civil cases from landlord tenant, EOEC, elder law, business contracts disputes, and real estate title challenges. In the Starkville melting pot, some ingredients are better at amalgamating and learning how to use the levers of power; i.e. - Irish and Italian are now staples on every dinner table.

(Boswell said he'd take, "…an irish cop, a wop cop, a rican cop, even a good old boy Georgia county cop with dark sunglasses, but not a mutaweenie morality cop". Dr. Johnson was considering, "…whether the surge in mulsim litigants was a tactical Starkville salient in the sharia lawfare, another religion of peace Ypres-type death salient used so effectively in the last millennium or so". I ignored them and their discussion of the police powers granted to the state by citizens.)

High cirrus clouds transparent in the blue sky. The high cirrus being dissipated by the winds were looking like medical devices and medical waste bottles.

I stopped on the curb before crossing the street to go over to the JC. I took out a cigarette, and after I lit it, I noticed it was one of the blood soaked Kensitas. It was a milder smoke with my non Federal Drug Administration additive.

(Dr. Johnson approved the change in the prescription.)

As I got to the street corner by the Court House, I noticed there was a small crowd gathered on its sidewalk around the sheriff and a plastic podium on the court house steps.

There was a thirteen foot long wooden table laden with several stacks of books next to the plastic podium.

As I walked up to, and was trying to walk around, the crowded sidewalk, my curiosity was aroused as to what type of collection of books was worth a sheriff sale on the courthouse steps.

I stopped for a second at looked up at the sky while taking a long slow draw on my Kensitas, and thought that my non-approved FDA additive really was an improvement as the smoke had a vivid, seasoned tinged oily taste; and what the hell it would only take a second to look.

There were bound copies of the complete Tanakh. There were bound copies of the Torah, the Nevi'im, and the Ketuvim.

There were bound copies of Matthew, Mark, John, and Luke – volumes 1 and 2. There were bound copies of Revelations. There were bound copies of Epistles of Paul, James, Peter, and John. There were bound copies of Septuagint, Enoch, and Jubilees. There were bound copies of the complete Wadi Qumran Scrolls.

There were bound copies of the Koran: one Hijazi script whose cover was inscribed in gold and silver with "*O ye who believe - you can't trust a jew or crusader because it pleases my vanity to say I say so*", and one that was taken from the luxurious Tehran apartment of ahmasmallpenisjihaddiie, as translated by a Yale Worthy, with its cover art done in a style of a 1940's True Crime Detective Magazine highlighting virgins, polygamy, and clitorisless slavery.

Ahmasmallpenisjihaddiie had sold it on epaymenow12Imam .com, along with two copies of Enuma Elish.

There were several very good quality copies of Wellhausen's 'Reste arabischen Heidentums'. There were worn copies of the Rig Veda, Sama Veda, Yajur Veda, and Atharva Veda. There was one copy of the Book of the Dead.

Three complete sets of bound volumes of The Shu Ching, The Shih Ching, The I Ching, The Li Ki, and The Hsiao Ching. There were hand written cloth bound copies of The Tripitaka, Mahayana, and Tibetan Book of the Dead.

There were also several bound copies of the Granth Sahib and King Ferdinand and Queen Isabella's 1492 Edict of Expulsion in a very heavy Tambo Colorado gold frame.

I took another couple of draws on my cigarette as I looked over all those volumes. I could spend a year, or two, lying on the blanco baraq leather skin sofa smoking everything my attic could produce while reading each of those old and rarely read books.

I would be a content Homo sapiens sapiens.

After researching and studying seven trillion-electronvolt TeV collisions, sequencing genomes, and the measuring the atlantic meridional annual overturning circulation; the discipline required to read fairy tales, folk tales, myths, and legends, as told by nyanyas, is easily obtained with three bowls of hashish, a tumbler of scotch, a couple of draws on a Kensitas cigarette and a joint of Northern Lights.

I took the last drag off my seasoned cigarette and then threw it in the gutter.

I turned my back on the sheriff sale and left to go into the '*Lazzaretto Vecchio*' again.

How many times have I made this journey to the center of justice?

(Boswell spoke up for the sole purpose of chiding me; "Speaking of Justice, when is the last time we discussed the comparative legal sentencing policies for violating imaginary wages of sin. The punishment of those who wage war against Allah and His Preteen Pole dancing Messengers and strive with might and main for mischief throughout the land by using sun tan lotions is execution or crucifixion, or the cutting off of hands and feet from opposite sides, or exile from the land. That is their disgrace in this perversion of reality by jihadicrazies, and a heavy punishment is theirs in the hereafter in that every day they will lay naked on the beaches of San Tropez with Mr. P. Floyd while singing about pigs and sheep and drinking homemade teas until you are comfortably numb."

Dr. Johnson laughed and then remarked, "Boswell dwells too much in popular culture for real understanding of comparative legal systems".

189

Dr. Johnson then suggested "That a pertinent and scientific analysis by a duly appointed Commission from the International Court of Justice lead by the wise and just politician Shahbaz Bhatti would investigate and then issue a press release to the Islamonazi Foundation of the Maldummives calling on them to repent from frenchkissing young boys and to accept the 21st century posthubblespacetelescope empirical findings. If they do not, then sentence them to death as Islamic law and Maldivian law agree for being non-repentant".

Boswell, feeling the sting of the slight, responded "Wajib-ul-Qatl style, Dr. Johnson?")

Chapter 18   WWW.LAWRENCECURLYMOSES .COM

There were eleven individuals waiting in line to go through the revolving doors of the Starkville Justice Center. I got in line and looked back and up at the sky. The cirrus was moving eastwardly.

Once I was through the JC's revolving doors, I glanced over at the vending area to see if I could catch a glimpse of Aglaopheme or Thelxiepeia. No sightings.

I turned and walked over to lockup while getting my ID out of my wallet. I slid it into the tray under the camera next to the door. I hit the plastic button above the tray. My mind started to wander. I wonder what day of the week it will be when I'd lose that mechanical ability, and the door stays closed. I know that everyone in my neighborhood sleeps in this building a couple times in their lives. Actually for a second it reminded me of D. A. Day's satirical piece on the cold war, and poor heroic Boris 504, as my brain waves were starting to bounce membranes.

As soon as I heard the door buzz I grabbed my ID back and pushed opened the steel door. As the door closed behind me, I put my ID back in my wallet, and then the wallet in my pants pocket. I turned to the right and signed the visitor's log on the desk. Then I slowly walked over to the next steel door.

I waved up at the room camera while waiting for the door to open. I realized how habitual it had become, the nodding and waving to all the cameras in the JC.

(I ignore all of the street cameras the Sheriff has in the neighborhood; on buildings/on street light poles/on the cruisers as they patrol the streets; not to mention the cameras in every store in Starkville. The Government and the Corporations must really enjoy (*or be addicted to*) reality television, as they constantly watch the young urban professional gentrification speculators, the avant-garde artists and working poor, the mentally ill, the homeless, the drug addicts, the crack-whores, and all my neighbors afflicted with Pauperism.)

I took three deeps breaths, pull at my beard and started humming, '...*watching the gravity waves come in and I watch them go away again*...", then the door locks clicked, and I walked through.

I walked down the concrete block walled hallway about twenty three meters until it split into Y before the guard's control booth. I turned right toward booking. I still was humming to myself as I walked up to the elevators, which were halfway down the hallway toward booking. I hit the elevator button with my left hand as I waved to the camera above the elevator with my right hand. I had not even got to the second chorus when the door opened.

I got in and hit the button for the 13th floor. I nodded up to the camera in the corner of the elevator and then took three deep breaths while I put my right thumb over my left wrist as the elevator started lifting me upwards.

Up, up, up, - all the way to the third floor, where the door opened.

Two Deputies escorted seven prisoners onto the elevator which forced me into the back corner. The prisoners had on the usual stripped garb, with wrist shackles looped through a leather belt connecting to the fashionable steel linked ankle shackles.

I looked, but since none of the prisoners were my clients, I felt more comfortable staring at the floor. From the banter I could tell that the prisoners were in a good mood. I didn't sense any of the hostility usually present when prisoners are being escorted by the guards in such degrading but required way.

My fellow travelers got off the elevator at the seventh floor to continue their journeys without me; leaving me behind - a mortally injured climber on a grand tour ascent of an icy Mount Chomolungma slope. In the blinding blizzard I thought of Adbul. I did not feel like humming any more. Nor did I even care about being left behind by the recently departed expedition. I took out a hyssop troche and put it in my mouth in anticipation of interacting with Adbul in the close quarters of the POD.

(Dr. Johnson told Boswell that he, "…would never come to the JC to meet Adbul, or any one like him". Boswell responded "*Principles over Paychecks after lunch every time*". I reminded them that I have to as I swore an oath when I received my license; a point I sometimes think is ignored by Dr. Johnson. Boswell remarked that, "It wasn't a very memorable quote, such as Thoreau's rebuke to Emerson on paying taxes." Dr. Johnson dryly replied to that with Thoreau's statement, "*Disobedience is the true foundation of liberty…*")

'*…the obedient must be slaves.*' is an inconceivably heretical concept to the butcher upstairs I thought briefly.

On the rest of the ride to the 13th I thought of what Will Rogers had said: '*Well, all I know is what I read in the papers*', which of course is what a large part of Adbul's jury voir dire examinations would be about.

(Damn, now was not the time to realize I should have taken a couple more hits off the pipe before trying to climb at this altitude.)

I knew that Mr. Rogers also said '*the constitution protects aliens, drunks and U.S. Senators*'. Adbul and I are going to test stare decisis. It's a damn shame, from a defense attorney perspective, that Adbul is not a drunken united states senator.

When the elevator door opened, I nodded again up at the camera and walked out to the left and then down the hallway, nodding again to the hallway cameras while going to housing pod 13 B. 13 A being at the opposite end of the hallway, of course. 13 A is for federal women and 13 B is for federal men, other than that it is exactly the same place as far the architect, Mr. Alighieri, was concerned.

(Boswell then told Dr. Johnson, "That Mr. Alighieri had a thing for Stella Kowalski". Dr. Johnson wryly insisted to Boswell, "That is a different Stelle".)

I got to the end of the hallway and then rapped on the control room's glass windows. The guard who had been doing something at the console turned around and looked at me.

I told him through the bullet proof glass that I was here to see ICE Prisoner No. CXOJ122518.6+144545. He hit the button to open the sliding steel door to the pod.

The lights were dimmed in over half of the pod. Since only federal prisoners were housed on 13, there were never very many inmates in these pods at any one time. The rest of the pods on the different floors were always overcrowded, mostly with people from the neighborhood convicted of and under various misdemeanors of pauperism, and of course - life enhancing substance charges.

I walked inside up to the interior pod control room window, (actually the slit in the glass for passing paper work and such through), leaned in and quietly told the guard I would go sit down.

The guard nodded turned to the control room microphone and stated, "Adbul, professional visit. Adbul, professional visit.", while unlocking Adbul's cell door housing.

I walked over to one of the steel tables bolted to the floor, and slid into the plastic seat bolted to the table, and waited.

I thought the plastic seats being the color of lapis lazuli actually had a very calming effect on the POD.

(Boswell who wasn't really paying attention but just had to talk opined, "The pine trees on the northern bank of the Yoknapatawpha river have the same exact lapis lazuli tinge this time of year.".)

Adbul came out of the cell about five minutes later, walking over to the table, and then extending his hands. I got up and held both of his hands while looking him straight in the eyes saying, "I have no coffee or snacks or even a Sm proteins Bar for you but rules are rules."

Adbul laughed as he said, "JD regrettably I have no Qahwa Sada to offer you."

I resisted the urge to get right to business as a concession to his culture. "Adbul, are you comfortable, do you require anything?"

"No JD. I have my koran, my pray rug, and I have adjusted to the jail's version of Halal dining."

"There goes our 'o'lone v. shabazz' free exercise claim Adbul", I said smiling as I did, and then added, "You actually look like you are gaining weight."

"JD, have you ever eaten the halai meals at the Chinese restaurant across from Izanagi & Izanami's over by the Aioi River? My own grandmother should cook such wonders with lamb. Here not so much."

"No Adbul, I've gone to the theatre by there, but never took the time to stop in that restaurant." I figured that I had held his hands the appropriate amount of time as per arabic culture, so I let go of the virgin blood stained instruments of his crime. I indicated for him to sit down.

"Oh JD you must go. There is no better restaurant in Starkville, not only are they considerate in putting out the most delicious apricots, figs, pomegranates, and soft hand-cut wheat noodles. They also have wonderfully spice flavored lamb, and crispy sesame bread." Adbul was still staring at me, and I could tell by his eyes, he was seriously concerned that I might not eat there.

(At the same time I could hear Boswell yelling as loud as he could, "What the fuck JD, some mulsim living in northern china, that's enemy squared - you know they just want to kill you, you atheist stoner, not convert your sorry ass existential palate - what's next - a north korean bar tender serving Litvinenko mohitos?")

Adbul gave me a hug, and then sat down sliding into the plastic seat. I squeeze into the seat on the other side of the steel table. We stared at each other for a second taking stock of one another.

I then looked around the pod to see if anyone was in hearing distance.

"Ok, Adbul, this case is not winnable with a jury from Starkville. I can try to get the venue changed, unlikely, but at least try a chance at getting Dearborn or Cincinnati. Well, no we don't, but it is worth a try, and it might present an appealable issue as some type of bastardization of '*Batson versus Kentucky*' since Starkville has such a small moslim population, and no one who lives in Starkville really trusts muslims."

"JD you know the trick to great saudi lamb with rice is all in the browning of the lamb in fine olive oil." Adbul smiled at me inviting me to exchange barbecue recipes.

At that spacetimepoint, the hohlraum infection in my hippocampus and the transmissible spongiform encephalopathy went all GIGO.

I decided to conduct the rest of the interview in my most astute dissociated state so to not miss any legally relevant facts.

(Dr. Johnson and Boswell had agreed last Monday morning – or the Monday before, '...that whenever I slip myself a mickey finn of DPD, it is always then that I did my best legal work.')

"Adbul, we are in a fucking pod. This is the Starkville JC and we have to discuss U.S. federal criminal law. There is photographic evidence that is going to be introduced to prove your guilt. If those pictures are allowed, you are going to get very fat eating on the U.S. taxpayer's expense." I had to break down the culture wall and the endless small talk before getting into a serious discussion.

It would be a start at talking about reality, *sans* menus without barbecued pulled pork entrée's.

Adbul's back straightened, and his gaze became steely. "Very well Mr. Glass. I have entrusted my liberty to you because you have spent your life working in the United States courts of law, and have been very successful with Starkville's jurors. I don't believe in your law, I believe in Shari Law, Ijtihad. My future is in your hands."

I gazed into his dark eyes. I could have kissed his zebibah. Screw all that small talk, it is distracting. Adbul being pleasant and likable would be the subject at a later date when we prepare for his physical actions sitting at the defense table during trial, and the very unlikely possibility of his testifying.

Now I needed to get answers from Adbul, as in FGM Adbul. Female Genital Mutilation Adbul, as in 18 United States Code 116, as in 'knowingly circumcises, excises, or infibulates' Adbul, as practitioner in Toubia's three categories Adbul, as in 'violator of Muna, Nahu, Haadiya, and Hanan' among other innocents Adbul, as in 'a medical doctor imposter performing surgical procedures as a matter of sadistic misogynistic religious custom not medical necessity', Adbul.

Adbul, as in the muslim who spent twenty minutes in our first meeting not grasping the concept of mens rea, actus reas, and strict liability as to his carrying on his forefathers sick traditions in a row house two room office above a street corner store five blocks away from 14 North Moore Street.

We stared at each other as I stated slowly, "Exactly - situational awareness. You're paying me and I am working for you. My situational duty's purpose is to get you out of jail on a reduced bond as soon as possible, and then to keep you out permanently."

I was looking to see how much he would let down his cultural mistrust. I continued, "You believe in Shari Law all you want, but your faith is worse than worthless here. It will be a point of antagonism with the jury since there are politically aware citizens in Starkville who read the '*Pingshan Dailey Tabloid*'."

I was sure Adbul reads Starkville's sunday international print version of the '*Pingshan Dailey Tabloid*'. It's sunday OP-ED pages have a different Gulf state imam contributing an editorial, which always is quoting the qur' an, and I mean the stone age ignorant refrains like verse 4:34 and 9:5's, '*fight and kill non-muslims*

197

wherever you find them, take them captive, harass them, lie in wait and ambush they using every stratagem of war'.

I continued pausing for a couple seconds for dramatic effect. I then said in a monotone, "The only thing that matters to Starkville's district court prosecutors is that you intended your past actions, your religious motives are not relevant legally."

No effect reflected in his eyes.

Then Adbul began grinning showing his eight incisors, and apocalyptically stated right back to me, "Strive hard against the unbelievers and be unyielding unto them, their house is hell and evil is their hearth."

I just had to smile. 1st because I think he left out part of the verse, and I wasn't sure if it was on purpose or not; and 2nd it showed me what the jury would see during a long trial – a deliberate man who had faith, but not in humanity, only in frenchkissing.

"Adbul, you realize, and we both know, I would be in jail in any moslim country for being kafir. I have no defense to the charge because it is true. I do not dispute it, and in fact I have pride in my personal commitment to being a kafir, and yet it is a death sentence. Due to my beliefs in constitutional government and individual rights I am trying to help you, but I cannot draft a legal argument that concludes with you being acquitted of the charges against you."

The photographs were going to be admitted over my objections before, and at, trial. If Adbul had a jury with any of the senior citizens graduates of my primary school over on north beacon street in the watertown district, one look at the 8 by 10 glossies and they would all be signing the guilty jury verdict form.

("Adbul being convicted would possibly make the next issue of '*American Notes*,'" Boswell said, and then added, "Wouldn't bet on it though, more like a page 11 story in some grocery store tabloid that has a cover photo of a martian or some alien visitor". I knew if Adbul is convicted, that the arab street would burn a couple of American flags, but even the paid arsonists were tired of that old street theatre scene.)

198

"Yes JD, slain or crucified, or hands and feet cut off, but as you stated situational awareness, as I am the only one *now* being locked up for my faith." Adbul's incisors were grinning at me as he continued, "It is true that a muslim is not a friend of the kafir."

"Great Adbul, I think we both understand the situation with the jury. Do you have any ideas on how to show 18 United States Code 116 does not apply to you as in *'knowingly circumcises, excises, or infibulates'* – that those acts did not occur in your offices by you? What do I have to counter the medical testimony of the doctor of gynecology? How is the jury going to see this as anything other than a barbaric religious practice that is outlawed in Starkville and throughout the civilized world? Anything?" I could hear the exacerbation in my voice.

I really wanted a couple hits of Northern Lights and a cup of very hot strong coffee.

"Bismillah ar-Rahman ar-Rahim, JD, please take a breath, you should relax. Then you will see this is not about my actions. I am being persecuted by citizens of Starkville, not by the Great Skeikh of Al-Zahar. JD, your jews, catholics, quakers, and english protestants cannot judge me nor can they even change one egyptian fatwa. This is about you JD, and Starkville. This is about how allah will judge your actions."

While Adbul was venting I had put my left hand into my pants pocket. I stuffed my hand in actually, sort of a discrete tension release, or if you're a card player – a tell. Sweet Jesus when I did that, I found a 6.32 gram Bethsaida Brand Diacetylmorphine Hydrochloride tablet.

Nice.

I just threw it in my mouth and swallowed at about the same time Adbul was saying 'Starkville'. Bethsaida's are the favorite of at least 5,147 of my neighbors.

Adbul was not smiling now. I was glad to see we were finally able to talk man to man, or more accurately, particle to anti-particle in our JCventurehubblespacetelescopemultiversesituationalreality.

Now I could listen to Adbul's simple minded duality perception of reality. Submit or die. Boring as the NSDAP rally speakers at Braunau-am-Inn during last September's Interfaith Festival.

The moslim was right. It was about Starkville, and its devotion to the declaration of independence, the rule of constitutional law and individual rights.

There is no 1st amendment argument to make when your client mutilates a five year old girl, or several nine year old girls.

No M'Naghten or Durham either as the argument fails as there is not the judicial clarity needed to declare a billion homo sapiens sapiens not responsible for their actions.

(Bethsaida Boswell thinks he can persuade the supreme court that in cases with moslim defendants, 'M'Naghten is the correct analysis'. I concur as far as jackson, taney, brown, and blackmun.)

"JD, haven't you read what Um Atiyyat al-Ansariyyah has said? There has to be an accommodation for religion under your laws for Islam in Starkville." Adbul stared directly into my eyes, while stating in a quiet monotone, "JD, you do understand how to introduce foreign law and international treaties at trial?"

I had to give credit to the moslim with his subreption. He was cunning. As with most arabs and persians, he was taking his time, but he was finally getting around to answering my question.

"JD, my sister Fadwa and her cousin Mufeeda work at King Abdoolalaboohoohoo Hospital. They can testify as medical experts as to the procedures done there, and throughout the Islamic world. The women health care workers at the hospital, a majority of them, have had the procedure."

Adbul's incisors grinned at me again. "JD, I want you to raise a constitutional challenge based upon the internationally accepted use of the procedure as a medical, as well as religious, necessity."

It dawned on me, in a particle/anti-particle way, that Adbul was talking about at least $131,071.00 worth of my time, not to mention publicity from the legal press and blog discussions with reader rants concerning yours truly, a champion of religious freedom.

("131 large", said Dr. Johnson looking up from his HP-35 and his calculations on a modified horava-lifshitz wave, and then added, "Not bad for a lawyer whose pauper father was born under a palm tree".)

"Adbul it won't work. It would be interesting to see how far we got procedurally, yes, and for any chance to get orders allowing some appellate review, it would be personally challenging to brief." I started to feel I even had the ability to reason with the Kerala High Court on equal protection, and rational relationships between male and female circumcision, and parental rights in religious rituals, under The Dissolution Of Muslim Marriages Act, 1939.

(Boswell then correctly stated that, "…it was just the Bethsaida kicking in, and I did not have the ability and that I damn well knew it as a Bethsaida-Free kafir".)

"Not only that Adbul, even if introduction is successful, as per the statute you are not licensed to perform medical procedures." I realized that was checkmate. I didn't know if he knew or cared. I faced the future reality of a jury verdict with a long slow exhaling breathe.

Mesoamerican bloodletting on the court house steps would be constitutional under Adbul's expanded analysis.

("Progressives always want to perform a vivisection on the constitution even though it is against the Hippocratic Oath.", wryly observed Dr. Johnson.)

"JD, I would like you to review '*Pruneyard Shopping Center v. Robins*' to see if there is an argument I can use" Adbul flatly stated. Not surprised; but I really did not see that one coming. Not surprised because clients always surprise me.

So this major fucking surprise that this is more than Adbul individually against Starkville, was not actually a surprise.

I made a mental note to revisit and review exactly how this case got started. Why the infection this time, why not before, it seemed immensely more important now.

(Dr. Johnson spoke up and said, "As accidental as Jane Roe, and eventually Blackmun's vile position, *'Appellant would discover this right in the concept of personal "liberty" embodied in the Fourteenth Amendment's Due Process Clause; or in personal, marital, familial, and sexual privacy said to be protected by the Bill of Rights or its penumbras, or among those rights reserved to the people by the Ninth Amendment'."*. Bethsaida Brand Diacetylmorphine Hydrochloride Boswell stated the obvious by saying, "Practitioner in Toubia's three procedures is as good an umbrella as any of the other judicial umbrellas in this islamonazi thunderstorm". I did not bother to reply penumbra.)

I felt the rush of a spacetimepoint 'coup d'oeil' as I glanced over at the clit-removing-monster-who-practices-ancient-property-custom-rituals sitting slouched back in the white plastic seat, "Adbul you want me to address this criminal charge by surveying several aspects of Islamic history of women's health. Such insights as to the muslim medical procedure's history, so to afford the Court a chance to review its constitutionality, and to review those considerations when it is examining my government's purposes and interests behind the federal criminal law here in Starkville, that is what legal argument you are thinking for your defense?"

(Dr. Johnson spoke up saying that wasn't what I '…was thinking'. He was right. I was thinking of Executive Order 9981: I was thinking of ISAF COIN Advisory # 20100924-001; I was thinking of Mawiya; I was thinking of lawfare's salient into common law; I was thinking of Ta'rikh l-rusul wa'l-muluk; I was thinking of Qur'an 9:29; I was thinking of Plan 2020; I was thinking كافر; I was thinking of the fish in my aquarium as Dr. Johnson and Boswell started discussing multiverse Cre-Lox recombination's while my Pons was signaling my reticular formation at only 1759 pedaflops.)

"Yes Mr. Glass, that and an immediate motion for redress of the lack of religious accommodation to me by my capturers. I have been denied a Qibla Compass. I requested a small black one with very nice 0-400 gold scale, and I am denied. I would like you to file it as an '*o'lone v. shabazz*' free exercise claim as soon as possible. It is impossible to pray properly while held here against my will without a qibla compass, and that abomination is being done under the color of your constitutional law in violation of my religious practices."

If I didn't want to smoke some hashish so much, I would admire Adbul for being the type of a client willing to make a legal point regarding the necessity of scientific instruments being used by homo sapiens sapiens to ascertain the essence of the natural world to the trial judge.

Thereby proving his faith in the myth making frenchkisser to himself. A damn endless greek tragedy. Incarceration would allow him to do further scholarship on having shari law introduced into the Environmental Protection Agency rules & regulations, and then into the United States Code Annotated.

"Adbul, I don't think I can get it written and filed for three days."

Adbul was immediately visibly angry about the three days. "JD, this is a violation of my religious beliefs, certainly you can write it tonight before you even think about sleeping tonight."

Adbul was framing his words to seem as if he was appealing to my sense of justice, instead of the veiled threat to file a bar complaint for neglect of a legal matter. The moslim and I were finally getting to know each other man to man now. What is it with the Orientals and the Muslims, the delay in getting to the issue, the endless innuendo and the veneer of civility? Does it fool the brain into believing the hands are not dripping with innocent vaginal blood? That some ancient myths about a plagiocephaly afflicted illiterate serial killing pedophile, a frenchkissing ḥashshāshīyīn, absolves you of mutilating children?

"No, you're right Adbul. I will write it tonight and come over in the morning with an affidavit for your signature to accompany the motion. It will be filed before noon tomorrow then."

I knew I could write in twenty seven minutes, and he was right, I would feel better personally in getting the issue in front of a judge.

If I was lucky, I might get a temporary order requiring the Sheriff, and Starkville taxpayers, to supply inmates free Qibla Compasses. That temporary order alone is probably worth thirteen stacks from pious Adbul and if I'm connecting random theoretical dots, for the future moslim prisoners being fed into the system.

I had enough. I wanted some coffee. I looked at Adbul sitting up straight in the black plastic seat. He seemed tense, not emotionally but in a physical sense of flexed taut muscles.

"Adbul you seem tense. Is it difficult to sit here in a kafir's jail discussing kafir laws with a son of a whore? Does it offend your sense of honor?"

(The Qibla ploy was irritating whatever was left of my own sense of constitutional requirements that I swore an oath to uphold as an officer of the court. It shouldn't have I knew. Adbul, if he really did get down and slobber over the ground five times a day a couple blocks from here where he lived and worked, knew as a reentrant homo sapiens sapiens, just by looking out any polycarbonate thermoplastic layered glass window - the exact position of the sun and the amount and type of daylight, (or the position of the moon and the stars), to know exactly what fucking time it was, and where the space rock was in relation to the Starkville Justice Center. Ulugh Beg with his only sextant determined the length of the sidereal year and published the '*Zij-i-Sultani*'. Boswell was irritated also, "Just tell him longitude W77.2, latitude N39.8". Boswell then turned to Dr. Johnson and added, "*Watch sloth and heathen folly bring all your hopes to naught*". Dr. Johnson smiled as he replied, "Kipling, right good show old man.")

"Mr. Glass, as we agree, situational awareness. If we were in Gaza and the Jama'at Al-Tawhid wa'l-Jihad were holding you, I would plead the Koran to the Salafi-jihadists", Adbul sincerely stated as he leaned forward in his seat.

I laughed from the gut. "Adbul I know you would. As you know as well as I that they believe the koran requires my execution as a kafir, in spite of koran 2:56, 3:20, and 18:29. I'm sure you would even advocate for my beliefs and kafir rights in Kuala Lumpur even though I freely admit and take pride in violating Section 298 and

298A(1) of their penal code whenever I can. We both know that no matter what you plead, I would be incarcerated under Section 298 and 298A(1) for five years for being very annoying."

These moslims are fucking great humorists I thought as I laughed from my gut for about thirty one seconds. I am sure the neighborhood dairyman Solomon Rabinovich would agree.

"Adbul, the difference as you well know, is that you're here for cutting off little girl's clitorises, girls too young to grant you legal authority to operate in any case. The icing on your indictment is you have no medical training or degrees or licenses recognized by the government. In Gaza and throughout the 7th century redoubts, I get beheaded for thinking differently about hubblespacetelescope than the unscientific criminals who terrorize their own neighbors. Here you might be locked up a few years for mutilating children."

I was still softly laughing as I tried to make that point about comparative law to him.

Adbul sat back in his chair, and with the inner peace of moral certitude, looked at me and said, "JD you laugh but Allah carries out his promises and makes his orders come to pass and the descendants of apes and pigs will be killed for the sake of allah."

"Adbul, for the sake of allah must Bamyan Buddhas be dynamited by an itinerant preacher?"

Sitting with his back against the black plastic chair, Adbul calmly said, "Mullah Mohammed Omar acted justly. True muslims are proud of his destroying the idols. It honors and gives praise to allah."

"Adbul for the sake of allah, must honor killings be sanctioned, tolerated, or permitted?" I was losing interest in any rational connection with my client.

I knew by that last few answers a 1st year law student acting as a prosecutor could seal Adbul's fate with any jury within 499 seconds.

Objections, Motions to Strike, and Curative Instructions won't erase jurors memories.

"Mr. Glass, a man educated as yourself is familiar with the Quran 4:15 and 24:2", he paused and then sat forward with his elbows on the table top between us, "…and you are sure to have read the many sahih hadiths on point."

I took a deep breath and then slowly let it out before saying, "Adbul, I understand that your prophet muhammand was directed by your allah to stone adulterers and others to death. I understand obeying mythical commandments of mythical gods. Yet as we talk I find it impossible to look at you and reconcile your beliefs with your presence. This is not Gaza, it is Starkville. Starkville courts aren't the Liverpool Crown Court which has already started caving into your sickness of preventing free thought and speech in public. You're beliefs and actions are similar to a hiene."

I rubbed the stubble of my bead and just looked Adbul in the eyes while he sat there with his elbows on the table top.

I know how to interview my fellow citizens and the illegal transients.

The muslims were a different situation. Interviews with muslims were more productive when done with the techniques of the US Army Intelligence and Interrogation Handbook to maximize the amount of usable relevant evidence from the taqiyya, with only time constraint being how long I wanted to sit there.

That and the fact I wasn't hiding my unit's ID or other such personal intel from my muslim clients.

I am always an open book with the clients, unless they are being less than honest with me. Then it is time for private investigators and good old fashioned foot leather.

The muslim clients were always hiding basic information, up through and including, critical mens rea from me.

Posthubblespacetelescopeatheists don't understand such irrational behaviors, hiding your personal geoglyphs doesn't work in this age of scientific evidence.

Someone should tell that to the imammies in Qom, as google earth shows prehistory stone ruins which prove the KKKoran is wrong, no matter what the islamic ruling class jihadibombieimmmommie elites claim.

I swear I saw a twinkle in Adbul's eyes for a second, followed a couple seconds later by asking me, "Mr. Glass you can lead Friday prayers if you wish."

I had to really check myself as I almost started laughing out loud again. It took all the discipline I could muster not to. Adbul was matching me chapter for chapter. Leading friday prayer, that was a line Mae West and Groucho Marx would envy.

I'm sure Adbul pulled the prayer line from the Frenchkisser's Intelligence and Interrogation Handbook; the old Shafi'i and Hanbali maneuver.

"There you go, Adbul, I can't match your subtlety with humor. Jizya is as close to Friday prayer as I would ever get, which I won't. Attorneys know that excelling at dying will be rewarded with a Nobel Peace Prize for saving virtuous preteen muslim girls from FGM so they can lead a life of dignity, and also so that they will have unfettered use of the internet, which is worth the sacrifice."

I added, "American law will never recognize Shari Law and Americans will never abandon their resistance to enslaving women," and for effect added, "Arab resistance to jihad is the only road map that can save arabs and others from 7th century frenchkissing, thereby restoring the Arab civilization's honor. Similarly, the Persian's, the Turk's, or any of the great civilization's honor which jihadinazi beliefs destroy."

Adbul was as composed as any delegate from the Islamic Republic of Iran chairing the U.N. Commission on the Status of Women.

"Mr. Glass, Slavery is part of jihad, and jihad is as long as there is Islam", and then he leaned back and recited from memory from all those times he was facing a vector; "Summon the people to God; those who respond to your call, accept.....".

I began drifting away but the barbarity of his words brought me right back. I could not help smiling again as it was surreal.

So I interrupted him by stating, "Adbul I get the concept Dhimmis, but the Battle of Khaybar was a long time ago, and yes it was won by a mass murderer who couldn't take rejection of his uneducated views. Rejection of the uneducated leads to their homicidal rages."

(Falstaffian Boswell spoke up mimicking Adbul's voice, "...*the better part of jihadist valor is its feminine discretion, in which the better part should have saved Hamza ibn 'Abd al-Muttalib's life. For real man, I am afraid of this gunpowder Abu Jahl Percy though he be dead. How if he should counterfeit too and his very small penis rise.*")

Adbul didn't stop talking when I interrupted, but he heard what I said as he finished with, "...but those who refuse must pay the poll tax out of weakness and enslavement. If they refuse this, it is the sword without leniency. Fear God with regard to what *very small penises* you have been entrusted."

Adbul may as well as had his figurative butt up in the air, but he merely leaned forward and repeated murderous nonsense, "In our Starkville muslim community, holy war is a religious duty and under islam practitioners convert either by persuasion or by cutting off heads. False religions have forsaken holy war. Islam will regain its power over other all nations by holy war."

("They all talk the same." Boswell stated as he grabbed his crotch and then said "Shahahahahadat this." Boswell then added further, "Islamonazis are crazy under either M'Naghten or Durham.")

I don't think Adbul actually said 'very small penis'. It was probably stated by Bethsaida Brand Diacetylmorphine Hydrochloride Boswell. No matter, point taken.

"Adbul, I am curious about your personal opinion, have you ever heard of Rosette Nubin?"

He looked at me and hesitated. I watched his dark eyes, "No, Mr. Glass I have never." Adbul's eyes told me that he understood that it was a variant from the Manual.

"A great loss to you Adbul if you never have but it doesn't matter for the purposes of my question. What do you personally think of women who get paid to go to juke joints and sing and play guitars to people who drink alcohol and carrying on and such things?"

Adbul's eyes smiled, but he restrained his face otherwise, a top graduate of Survive, Evade, Resist, Escape would have learned in three weeks to control his eyes.

"Mr. Glass here in Starkville maybe such things happen, but I do not approve or attend."

I am sure my eyes were smiling as I got the non-answer from his Manual.

The muslim kkkoran from the frenchkisser and his Manual, guaranteed that situational aware answer.

"Very good Adbul, just the sort of response you should give if you testify. Yet my question calls for your personal opinion. What do you think of such women, and what would you suggest if anything."

"Mr. Glass, I believe such women who stray can cause me no harm."

I wanted him to elaborate, to finish the Surah, but he just sat back. I'm sure his Manual required the subterfuge.

I was not going to validate his Manual by bringing up his duty to attempt to set the woman right.

"Adbul, aren't men and women prohibited from dancing together by islam? Should such women be whipped, or injured, or killed, for such public displays?"

Adbul stared into my eyes seeking approbation while indignantly and aberrantly whispering, "Whip, cane, or rattan."

No eyes were smiling now.

"Adbul have you read the United Nations 'Universal Declaration of Human Rights', or the 'Convention on the Elimination of all Forms of Discrimination Against Women'?"

"JD have you read Iran's Constitutional Articles 21, 83, 102, 209, or its civil code; or the laws of Saudi Arabia; or Bahrain's; or Qatar's; or the Emirates, or Malaysia's Shariah Criminal Code?"

Test over. No way to ever put Adbul on the stand.

He was way off in some fantasy land of an egomaniac mass murder, no not the catholic scheisskerl Hitler, but a similar madman from long past millennium.

It was getting very depressing, knowing that there were over a billion souls infected with the virus on the planet.

"Adbul if you think of anything else let me know. When you sign the affidavit tomorrow we will go over what other motions, or evidence, you want to discuss in any future visits."

Adbul got up and extended his hands. "JD, I would like to receive the 'Yeni Safak'. I have no way of checking the ECRI's USLLI. Also Fr. Staempfle stopped by earlier on behalf of the board of directors of Starkville's Interfaith Council. He told me to tell you to get the recently released 2010 revised report by the Committee on Bioethics for the American Academy Of Pediatrics on FGM. He told me to tell you that if you needed anything, he had the resources available to assist you." Adbul smiled slightly, and then continued, "Also, don't forget to take your secretary out to a delicious halai lunch at the Chinese Restaurant tomorrow, and definitely get her the lamb entrée."

I took his hands and looked straight into his emotionless eyes. "Adbul I'll get the qibla motion filed tomorrow, and will work on the foreign law constitutional angle for a motion next week. Think of the fact that if you get senior citizens from the watertown district on your jury, one look at the 8 by 10 glossies by them, and it's over. Think about that, instead of reading Shagrat al-Durr or some jajis fortune cookies; and remember that I am trying take yet another moslim on the journey through Starkville's judeo-christian legal system. You have to bi-furcate your situation and your beliefs, which I know is the central tenant of your faith – believers and nonbelievers."

(Adbul and my Qiblalesssituationalspacetimepointscomparativelawawarenessplurality here in the JC)

I let go of the virgin blood stained instruments of his crime as we nodded to each other. I turned and left Adbul. I walked up to the control window and signaled I was done, actually signaled the slit in the glass for passing paper work and such through.

I leaned in and told the guard my visit was over. The guard nodded and in a friendly making conversation way stated he had '…hours left on his shift'.

I smiled back. As he opened the steel door I told him in my best 1948 film noir voice, "You must run a comfortable jail, CXOJ122518.6+144545 doesn't want to get out either."

I had no idea what the Jesuit was up to, but as usual there were forces outside the system of justice at work. Justice is corrupted in so many ways, especially by perturbations, politics, and religion.

As I left the POD and headed to the elevator, I started humming that old Band song about running into crazy Chester and Jack the dog as I walked slowly through the hallway. I knew nodding until I was outside was routine paranoid schizophrenia.

211

Once outside I could get a cup of coffee and have a Kensitas.

I kept humming the song myself while nodding to cameras and wondering what the hell just happened. I remembered Byrne's 11th move and Fischer's 17th. Shari Law versus Constitutional Law is the game, but whose move was next in the Starkville salient, perhaps the faux 12th Imam Malik Al-Amlaak's?

(Dr. Johnson's offered a precipitous field diagnosis that, "Active warfare is for much younger men".)

I realized that in my micro-aristotelean tragedy with Adbul, that I was pretty sure I wasn't playing the part of Tommie Lawrence. I knew damn well Adbul was not playing the part of the Iraqi sidekick-turned-native-heroic-leader Jay Silverheels Feisal.

Then I thought of an extremely unlikable possibility that Adbul was attempting the part of the great Shylock and I needed to summon all my abilities to play the part of his friend Tubal. Serendipity Award at HollyLapDance was at stake. As director, I had a real problem, as the unions had strict work clauses on friends and other trades.

(Boswell then bet Dr. Johnson 6:2 odds, '...that at least one union steward would call the guild before the morning's first required Electrical Workers Local 1322 smoke break.')

Impatiently, I waited for the elevator humming the chorus and thinking – only a couple more doors and then a cigarette while slowly walking the public sidewalks. I nodded at the camera.

The elevator arrived before my mouth had fully salivated at the thought of a cigarette. The empty elevator was a good situation at this spacetimepoint. I nodded up at the camera as I got in and hit the ground floor button.

These elevators were straight out of a XXX storied faux Philip Cortelyou Johnson glass box, but these 'Lazzaretto Vecchio' models were an even more sterile version, with their pale white tile floors, industrial fluorescent lighting, brushed steel and aluminum walls.

(I absentmindedly remarked to Dr. Johnson and Boswell that, "All the justice center elevators were merely spacetimepoint shipping containers of broken psychic particles; which of course hand wipes and lotions can't cleanse alone.")

The elevator opened and I walked out and through the hall to get out. I nodded my head again to whoever was watching on the monitors while I impatiently was signing out and trying to just get out of the Justice Center to the freedom of the Starkville public sidewalks.

I began to wondered if '*Generalinspekteur für Spezialabwehr Adbul*' had yet considered ordering '*Unternehmen Werwolf*' from inside the 0-400 gold scale qiblacompassless justice center.

(Dr. Johnson and Boswell then reminded me, "To always choose felonies and misdemeanors - that way Starkville's public sidewalks will never have young girls laying around on them like the most intelligent, educated, cultured, kind, trustworthy, witty, courageous, dazzling, self sacrificing muslim teenager girls do all the time over on Kargar Avenue chanting '*I'm burning, I'm burning*' due to some Twelver *Wehrwölfe*'s immoral clitoris hating fetish attentions.")

As soon as I was through the revolving door I took out a cigarette and lit it up. I looked up at the sky, but there weren't any cirrus to be seen now.

I took a couple deep draws on the cigarette, really enjoying the moistened slightly tinged oily tasting flavored smoke after breathing the POD's air.

I decided to walk slowly back to the office. I told myself try not to think about anything other than enjoying my cigarette and the cloudless sky. I noticed now it was a darker shade of blue after my visit, with some faint gray and softer purple tones throughout.

No Chester, no Jack, no cirrus; just Adbul, myself, and a small amount of known and unknown players, working through our version of Opus 95: String Quartet No. 11 in Female clitoris minor for the debut performance to the judge and jury in a court room several weeks from now.

(Dr. Johnson's kafir faith is in his '43 Model II Relay Interpolator M-Theory pre-trial statement and the Worldsheet Music copies of it he is preparing for trial. I prefer to believe, and am still partially holding onto the theorem, that trials here in Starkville are more improvisational, more Coltrane, Davis, Parker performances.)

As I was walking past the sheriff's sale when, again, my curiosity got the better of me, so I slowed down as I walked through the crowd. I went over and stood next to one of the two bronze sculptures of chained lions on the court house steps.

The City of Starkville was very fortunate to have those court house sculptures, as the sculptor had just finished his last commission of standing warrior lintels for the capital building at Tula.

The Starkville's lion's pedestals were engraved with the historical latin jurisprudence venue requirement, *'Hic Abundant Leones'*. The two chained lions were popular with the young innocent children when they accompanied their parent(s) into the court house. The crack heads and junkies who relieve themselves on the lions late at night call them 'petey and paulie'.

(Dr. Johnson and Boswell agree that either lion appeared more than anything to look like '...an American bull terrier', which just shows how devilish addictions can be on your perceptions.)

I noticed a pristine copy of *'Pennants of the Champion's* on the edge of the table next to the sheriff as he was auctioning *'Muslim Women and the Challenges of Islamic Extremism'* with Arumugam's *'March 8'* together as a single bid.

A few feet to my left five students from the Nationalsozialistischer Deutscher Stundentbund seemed to be intent on winning with their continual bidding. Li Si and Qin Shi Huang were bidding against the five students, but not with the intensity of the students.

Diocletian, who was closest to the sheriff, would occasionally bid. Diocletian kept looking at the copy of the *'Index Librorum Prohibitorum'* that he was holding in his left hand and then back at the stacks of books next to the sheriff.

Billions of homo sapiens sapiens living while the hubble space telescope is a few miles above them, and they all still refuse to acknowledge that there are no gods, and that every man who said he communicated with a god was a liar or delusional, and that by such cunning, he was merely trying to attain power over his fellow homo sapiens sapiens.

(Boswell pointed out to Dr. Johnson that, "The methane-based life forms were not going to appreciate being called an apostates and kafirs since they could care less that muhammad rewrote the history of jesus of nazareth to make the usurper muhammand the preeminent prophet."

Dr. Johnson replied, "Ethane-based life forms know that there were thousands of hand copied greek manuscripts of the new testament which prove the usurper's biased editing; but the only thing in Starkville that mattered in any transcendental way to methane-based life forms was chacruna and chaliponga leaves, and of course, caapi vines.")

My cigarette was finished so I threw it in the street gutter. In my isolated state within the crowd of my fellow citizens I had attained this morning's Von Thünen's marginal productivity.

I left the crowd on the court house steps and crossed the street to get back to the office and my hashish. I started humming Puccini's 'Tosca' as I slowly and deliberately walked away from the court house.

I remembered a partial line out of an some old political speech, "*Now we are engaged in a great religious war, testing whether our nation, or any nation, so conceived and so dedicated, can long endure when Ginsburg, Sotomayor, and Kagan look to, and reference foreign laws, international law, and treaties.*"

(While walking up the sidewalk to the office Dr. Johnson looked over at Boswell and myself and then spoke up saying, "Don't be so glum, six of the nine Justices cited foreign law in '*Dred Scott v. Stanford*', so there is historical precedent." Dr. Johnson laughed in a dreadful way and added, "*Dort wo man bucher verbrennt, verbrennt man am ende auch menschen*". As I walked up to my office building I thought to myself how lucky I was to have friends who had actually read Heine's '*Almansor*', especially at this moment in my day's spacetimepoints with all the cirrus being long gone.)

215

(Dr. Johnson then postulated that, "Abu Sayyaf's mirror neurons, as in all muslim medial frontal cortexes, are for beheadings and the mirror neurons in muslim temporal cortexes are for masturbating over later at the mosque on a wide screen p2p broadcasting from Mindanao, or in Sulu, with all the AFPAK al-queersaeda spelunkers wanking over the web broadcast while wishing they were pissing on the calcite, aragonite, and gypsum in Ofra". Boswell thoughtfully said that, "It was more likely than not the webcasts were at 1080p with 150,000:1 dynamic contrast ratio, and with a 7 channel speaker system reproducing the full range of frequencies to stimulate the medial orbito frontal cortex of all-the al-queersaeda spelunkers with pyelonephritis".)

I thought that maybe I wasn't *that lucky* as I walked through the office building's doors.

Chapter 19   Sampled Non-Commuting Observables

Walking into the lobby was reassuring as the marble walls instill some delusion of safety and strength. The warming afternoon sun light was diffuse throughout the lobby. The fuzziness of the faded colors of ornate was calming to my perceptions. I wanted to light up some hashish, so I walked up to the elevator and pressed the button.

As I waited I started to recite, 'When in the course of human events, it becomes necessary for one people to dissolve the political bonds which have connected them with another and to assume among the powers of the...'

Just then Sayyid Ali and Abdus Samad walked into the lobby. Sayyid looked a bit animated as I overheard him quietly say, "I am certain; I memorized it as a child, '...*the best of the lover's crouches is higher priced with a toasted Bacon, Lettuce, and Tomato*'". Sayyid and Abdus stopped their muffled conversation as they came up and stood there by me waiting for the elevator.

Sayyid and Abdus freelanced as stringers for the Achoo Baytiiiii Version News Agency. Abdus looked up at the painting above the elevator, and then over at me and gustily opined, "That is a beautiful picture isn't it JD, very colorful."

I wasn't in the mood for socialization, but understanding Abdus was making polite conversation and is generally a pleasant elevator companion, I did feel obligated to return the courtesy, "Abdus, I've always appreciated how its colors compliment the rest of the ornate ceiling in the lobby, especially when the late morning's sunlight streams in." Every word was true.

Sayyid looked up at the painting. He stared at it for a couple seconds before dauntlessly saying, "Those santur players look so sensual, makes one want to lie down in front of them and just listen. I believe that painting is of the hasht-behesht palace."

I stalwartly looked at both of them while saying, "Well not being an art historian, I'd say whoever painted those women definitely knew how to capture the essence of a woman."

My perfunctory elevator duties accomplished, I started to think of my hashish again when the elevator arrived and the door opened.

I step aside and let Sayyid and Abdus enter the elevator before me.

"Hey guys, will you hit 13 for me?" I requested of either of them.

Abdus reached over and hit the buttons for 13 and 12. *'Exodus's Sinai Blues Music, Art Fair, and Calf Barbecue Festival'* came to mind as I stood with my back against the wall looking down at the floor.

The elevator shook and sputtered as we slowly started our journey up to mi patria, with only one connector stop.

They both seemed to be intelligent, educated, and very polite men. I just didn't understand why they worked for Achoo. Although I immediately realized, who am I to question where, or how, a man makes an honest living.

(What was it Boswell always quoted from Hunter S. Thomson, *'I hate to advocate drugs, alcohol, violence, or insanity to anyone, but they've always worked for me'*.)

The santur women got me thinking of other Hilbert spaced-out models I had known, which made me think of Nicole Cabell singing the aria *'tandis qu'il sommeile...'*, which got me thinking of hashish, my sofa, and sunshine through a window pane.

Abdus turned and leaned his shoulder up against the wall, as I was doing. He looked at me and then turned saying to Sayyid, "That painting looked if it was the original from the hasht-behesht palace. I should ask building management where they got it."

Hearing about palaces I looked up at Sayyid and then at Abdus. I forgot about hashish, and *sincerely* inquired, "It makes me wonder, and get very curious, whenever I see moslims looking at paintings. I know what fundamentalist wahhababies think of painting humans - them and the salafishys. Idiots can't point to anything in the qur'an to back up their fascism. Nude figures aren't idolatry, nor are santur players. I don't get the aniconism of islam. Can either of you explain to me why it is necessary to paint geometry instead of human bodies, just some Sir Peter Paul Rubens tits and asses?"

Abdus looked over at Sayyid, and then they both looked over at me.

Abdus solemnly stood up straight.

I could not tell if he was angry or surprised.

Sayyid looked at Abdus, and then over at me while saying, "I don't understand what you mean, islamic art is everywhere around the world, in many different countries."

Normally, I can catch myself, but after visiting with Adbul at the JC the small talk routine wasn't working. Mujahada trickery is obvious sometimes. "Wasn't it abu-isa-Muhammad-ibn-isa-ibn-surat-ibn-musa-inb-ad-dahhak-as-sulami-at-tirmidhi-i-like-child-brides and the other 7th century M.D.'s, D.O.'s, B.S.'s, Ph.D.'s of applied physics, applied biomedical engineering, chemical engineering, and bio-molecular engineering, who figured out for every homo sapiens sapiens to be born after they were all dead, that pictorial representations of a nude body, or that of an animal, insults some frenchkisser who couldn't read, write, or paint, and thereby such are not allowed?"

(Boswell and Dr. Johnson started laughing out loud. Boswell laughed to so much he was actually crying, but he also wanted to know, 'If abuisanut ever frenchkissed Baraq?')

I was angry. I knew it made little sense to get angry over a remark as harmless as if I thought a picture was beautiful, colorful.

219

I was at the point where I thought that every muslim was pulling an Andy Kaufman on me. After Adbul, I was beginning to believe it was time to wrestle Kaufman-like with the religion of peace eunuchs.

I stood up straight and took a step over toward my fellow travelers lifting up my outstretched hands as I continued, "That damn book tells you to do this, and then this and that; to be clean and pure as you kill, murder, and maim people who think differently about their own realities. The creator of the universe doesn't like pictures. What the hell is the matter with you people? Look at any picture from the Hubble Space Telescope – life is everywhere in the universe, the multiverses. Explain in what sense any rational person would respect a religion whose believers cannot even draw single cell organisms and then hang the portraits in their homes. Explain to me El Greco's 'The Trinity', R.H. van Rijn's 'The Night Watch', or Mantegna's 'Dead Christ' in terms of Al-A'raf 7:148, Al-Anbiyâ 21:51-54, Bukhari 3:428, 4:47, or even 4:448."

The elevator slowly shook and then shuttered to a stop at the 12th floor, the doors started to open, but I continued "Oh wait a second - the immoral Muslim NaziBrotherhood murders doctors; Dr. Yusef al Fusef of Aleppo – think he looked at pictures of the human body as he was studying medicine?"

I was sure that Abdus and Sayyid thought I was being very impolite; and yes, I knew I was venting due to Aglaopheme and Thelxiepeia's trick in the JC's lobby much earlier. It was just Abdus and Sayyid's misfortune to be the recipients of my petty angry rant about rational thought, free will, and vending machine choices.

I just could not stop myself, as my startled associates quickly left the elevator and hurriedly walked toward the news office, I leaned out of the elevator holding the door open and called after them, "Insecure frenchkissers can't rationally believe that making a picture is reserved for Allah the Stoner. If A'isha wanted to paint 'Venus at the Mirror', or photograph a colony of microsporum canis, are we to belief that is heretical? That A'isha is somehow imitating

220

Allah the copycat's multiverse creative acts I, II, and III, and thereby is in violation of Title 17 § 107. The copycat prophet was right that science would replace the frenchkissing idols in man's beliefs and understanding of the universe by just looking at pictures from a scanning SQUID microscope, or the hubblespacetelescope."

I wasn't sure if they heard the last part about the plagiarism prophet as they and their long sheep's wool thawbs disappeared into the twelver's offices.

I stepped back into the elevator and let the door shut. The elevator shook and sputtered as it gently rose.

Abdus and Sayyid, being stringers for an islamist news organization, had to know that I had seen that Andy Kaufman skit '*Al-Baqarah 2 217*' almost as many times as his '*Mighty Mouse*' routine.

Asking me if I thought a picture of hot women playing music was pretty indeed!

I involuntarily remembered the 2309th paragraph of the Catholic Catechism, and thought that as a matter of social justice, I should have Atalanta type a small sticker for me to put over the number 12 on the elevator control panel.

As a matter of moral legitimacy, I thought that by putting a pictograph of U+FDF2 over the number 12, it would make Sayyid and Abdus feel more at home.

I believe Dr. Johnson and Boswell would agree with the cultural gesture, as such peaceful civil societal gestures had been practiced by devout muslims since at least Abbassid Caliph Haroun al-Raschid's spacetimepoint.

The elevator finally arrived at patria. I felt physically exhausted as I walked down the hallway to my office.

I thought I heard Louis Riel rehearsing his final trial statement in the offices at the other end of the hall.

221

(Boswell spoke up then and said he that he, "...had it figured out. The coulrophobic jihadists were suffering from caligynephobia which was really just a severe case of eurotophobia, causing moslim men to have a severe medomalacuphobic reaction." It sounded right, but I knew as I opened the door, Atalanta would have other work for me to do. She wouldn't waste her time discussing a boswellian medical diagnosis of monomorons.

Of course Dr. Johnson, being a clinician, just had to inquire if, "...it was a local contagion from the Starkville branch of the latter day saints?"

Boswell was in a glib mood and informed us with a wry smile that, "The first recorded case was from a waterboarded captured enemy combatant at the Battle of Las Navas de Tolosa, which was surely was covered by the forerunner news agency of the Achoo Baytiiiii Version News Agency downstairs in suite 1212.")

Chapter 20   Patria with Dendrologists & Geologists

I opened the door and walked into the office. Atalanta was talking on the phone. I walked back to my office to a pot of hot fresh coffee. I immediately grabbed my cup and filled it about half way, spilling a lot over the brim. It was stale now, but good enough, as the hot liquid felt great going down my dry throat.

I walked back out to the ante room and I sat down in a leather chair and put my feet up. I set the coffee down to cool as I lifted an issue of Popular Science from the pile of magazines on the coffee table. Atalanta waved her right hand at me, so I got up grabbing my coffee and went back to my office and lay down on the sofa.

I took a large gulp of the coffee, and then put it down on the floor. I reached under the sofa and retrieved my pipe. I picked up a lighter lying on the coffee table. I took two slow hits off the bowl. I looked at the bowl and saw that it still was about a third full of the Northern Lights bud. So I took another hit, and then slide the pipe back under the sofa.

I got up and walked over to my computer and tuned into the BBC3. I took the Starkville's mosque interfaith festival ticket out of my shirt pocket and put it on top of a speaker.

I went back over to the sofa and lay down pulling the old cloak over me. I recognized the music as Halévy's '*La Juive*' performed by Starkville's Opera Company a couple of seasons ago.

(Coincidence? Mathematically possible, even if Boswell did not think so. He always postulated String Theory at times like this. He was consistently chaotic in his arguments.

My eyes closed as Dr. Johnson asked Boswell for the millionth time to explain, "How over one billion sentient beings can profess to belong to group which blindly follows a book so lacking in ethics that it keeps its adherents in virtual slavery to a 7th century ignorant murdering frenchkisser's delusions of being a better prophet than the Nazarethian?"

223

Dr. Johnson then pointed out, "...that Aristotle taught of two types of virtue centuries before that usurper profiteer beheaded scores of jewish men, raped jewish women, and killed children in front of their parents as a guide to monomoronical morality.

A billion beings every day are instructed in the teachings of that madinat rasual allah's '*manual of crimes against humanity*' to look behind trees and rocks to find and kill jews until judgment day.

A billion beings looking behind trees today.

A billion beings looking behind rocks today.

A billion tree and rock inspecting beings living right now on the same planet and in the same spacetimepoints as the Sentinelese, the Arawa, Atalanta, Oney, Austin, Hercules, Giles, Aris, Sheels, Moll, hubblespacetelescope, the fish and us.

I told Dr. Johnson and Boswell, "*To be quite*", as I wanted to rest, "...but nevertheless it still was a matter of simple arithmetic. If the average adult's brain weighs at least 1300g, I have roughly 4.5662100456621 ounces of transmissible spongiform encephalopathy's spoiled meat in today's multiverse".

I then mentioned to both of them that, "You might want to check my math with a '43 Model II Relay Interpolator, as my brain is full of nicotine, caffeine, THC, and a Bethsaida Brand Diacetylmorphine Hydrochloride tablet."

Dr. Johnson and Boswell took that as invitation to go to the Min Le Tavern over on Shenzhen Way, in the northwest part of the neighborhood, to find some single malt scotch. I heard Boswell telling Dr. Johnson as they left, that, "The tree inspector profiteer was always bathing because the encephalopathy thing caused him to have Umm Sulaim type day dreams."

I was finally alone. I started humming my favorite Shingon Mikkyo Chant, '*Sister Morphine*', the version as performed by monk's Faithfull, Richards, and Jagger, as serendipitously lead by the great Conductor Kobo Daishi.)

Chapter 21   Planck Scaling Thirteen Dimensions

I was slumped over a Glenturret and a hot sake at Sin's bar on North Franklin, (funkified microbiota were enjoying the liquid warmth in my gut), while listening to John's quartet playing 'Alabama' again and again and thinking about those very small penis muslim punks, who were kidnapping, raping, and mutilating Iraqi christian girls, when I realized Atalanta was shaking my shoulder and I wasn't. I opened my eyes and started to scratch the back of my neck and around my ear. Vivian Della Chiesa was performing as Eudoxie on the BBC3. I rolled over so I was not facing the sofa but my efficiency expert and savior.

"Hello boss, you realize that most people work this time of day?" Atalanta said smiling at me, and then went over and started making a fresh pot of coffee. "JD it smells like the old Winterland Ballroom in here after a double bill of Traffic and The Band. How many times do I have to ask you to open the window when you smoke dope."

She did not have the slightest tinge of anger or resentment in her voice. I watched her while she made the coffee. I was very lucky to have such a partner. Something was up through, I could tell just by her presence she had some problem I had to deal with, so I just laid there and enjoyed Vivian and the musical spacetimepointmoment. I rolled my neck and my left shoulder, closed my eyes, and put my head back down to sleep.

I finished the sake with one drink, and held the Glenturret up to my nose to savor and as I listened. Thelonious and his quartet were just nailing 'Epistrophy' when Atalanta was shaking my shoulder again and I wasn't.

I opened my eyes to the smell of fresh hot coffee, plus an apple-raisin strudel, and two almond-honey bienenstich sitting on the coffee table. I really have absolutely nothing to complain about.

Atalanta walked over to my desk and turned off the BBC. She sat down in my chair and waited for me to take a couple bites of the bienenstich and sip on my coffee.

"You know Atalanta, I paid Sarah Vaughan to record *'Don't Blame Me'* just so I can play it at night after you leave work". I took another sip of the coffee and smiled at her.

"In your dreams JD, you know I paid her to record *'Just Friends'* for you to play in the morning before work." She laughed, and it just made everything feel alright.

Better than alright. Then I remembered Lynda Marie Child. Still Atalanta was irreplaceable, and so was my faith in her.

"I was planning to smoke the hashish when I got back here, but when I came in I decided that would have made you break out the horrid floral bouquet mist disinfectant spray."

"JD, that's the most courteous thing you've done for me all day", she smiled and then got to work. "Archbishop Torquemada called and wanted to move his appointment up to this evening. He has to meet with some Cardinals tomorrow evening. It sounded to me like the meeting was just going to be on Father Johannes Eighth matter. Anyway the Archbishop wants to go over the interrogatories and the documents that he has gathered in response to the document requests. I'm guessing that is what the Cardinals are interested in."

I finished the bienenstich and took a long slow drink of the coffee.

"You told him that tonight was impossible." I looked at her hoping I knew her well enough that I did not to have to be concerned about having to deal with the catholics this evening.

Atalanta leaned forward over my desk, smiled, and reaffirmed my intuition, "Yes JD, I told him that we would schedule him for tomorrow afternoon at 15:30, which was the first available time."

I really have absolutely nothing to complain about, absolutely nothing, other than my narcissism, and the fish.

"I did tell him you would call him as soon as you got back from the jail," Atalanta said as she smiled ever so slightly.

"Damn and damned. I'm in no mental state to focus on the catholics right now Atalanta." I looked at her as I talked, but I could see in her eyes she knew she was right, and she wasn't going to leave my office until I was on the phone with the church. "I need something Atalanta, Adbul mention a recent statement of a Committee on Bioethics for the American Academy Of Pediatrics on FGM. I need you to dig it up to see what he was referring to."

I was weak as my body lost its energy. I was very tired and felt ancient. I felt for the briefest moment like I would cry tears. I was just sad down to my 16 bar tapping toes. Some people are fortunate enough to get to play with Kaukonen, Cassidy, and Papa John for their life's work; not me.

Although, I do get to work with Atalanta in my multiverse, and that was much better, really much better.

No doubt it's a blessing in fact.

Peace and blessings from her upon me, treating my seasonal affective disorder. Although it is not 1917, and she definitely hadn't been sitting there all night alone next to me, in sorrowful contemplation of war and loss. Now that I am awake, I am positive that there are no soldiers marching by, nor any violins playing either.

I got up and walked over to the desk and opened the drawer and took out my hashish. I went back over to the sofa and got the pipe out from underneath.

I did not look at Atalanta as I broke a piece off with my thumbnail and put it in the pipe on top of the Northern Lights, but I knew she was watching me, and would until I picked up the phone.

I took a gulp of the coffee. I then took a huge hit off the pipe. Of course I started to cough, and kept coughing until I had tears running down my face. I grabbed the coffee and finished it. I took another hit off the pipe and held it. I blew smoke rings while I wiped my face off with my hand.

Then I blew the last smoke ring between what was left of the others as they drifted away from me. I looked over at Atalanta sitting at my desk, as she was observing me as any psychiatrist would. I could tell that she was concerned about something, but did not know what to say.

(Dr. Johnson thought that, "I should just lay back on the sofa and start talking about why I hated my mother Amina, and wanted to kill my father Abdullah." "ClaudiusGertrudeAbdullahAmina", Boswell said, and then starting laughing while adding, "I love those movies from the 1960's. Paul Mazursky did a great job directing prima donna actors. I am sure he got the Cordoba Caliphate Academy Award for it even though it was released with an 'X' MPA rating due to its preteen clitoris hating plot and the overt pedophilic sexual content.")

I was not surprised when Atalanta suddenly asked, "JD do you need to take a couple days off, go camping up in the Hebron Hills by yourself? Or maybe ask Ms. Fröhlich to catch a jet with you and go down to Captiva and sit on the beach? I think you could use it."

I grabbed the coffee cup and got up and walked over and refilled it. I looked over at Atalanta and started tapping my foot and sang softly *"Ashes to Ashes Dust to Dust Here Comes the Catholic Church Big As Hell"* was all I got out before I started laughing.

Atalanta was watching me like the rent-a-nurses in the medical unit of the Justice Center watch compassless inmates who sun watch.

Briefly leaving HotTunaverse, I went back over to the blanco baraq leather skin sofa wissenschaft, laid down, and lit up a cigarette.

"Well?" Atalanta asked interrupting my sky painting. It was an ambiguous question, loaded with possibilities.

I started tapping my foot again and sang another bit of my version of Kaukonen's '*True Religion*'. It was making me feel better and started giving me some needed energy.

My synapses were firing in time with Papa John and Cassidy. I was bopping my head to my toe tapping by the chorus.

I was hoping Atalanta would join in as I slowly rocked back and forth on the sofa singing and smoking my cigarette with what was left of my tears on my face quickly evaporating with each beat.

She picked up the telephone instead, and brought it over to me, "Call the archbishop now. Get it done because I need you to do a couple other things before you go back to sleeping, while I find the Committee on Bioethics document on FGM."

I got up picking up my cigarettes, took the phone from her, walked over and sat down at my desk. I got out a legal pad and a pen. I put out my cigarette in the ash tray. "Thank you for allowing me to rest a minute. The bienenstich and coffee were great. Just, what I needed. Really. Thanks."

I grabbed another cigarette, and lit it up as I dialed the archbishop. Atalanta turned and left my office.

I started singing '*Salve Regina*' to Atalanta as she walked away. I was going to hang up as soon as she was back at her desk.

I was starting to hang up the phone when I heard the archbishop's secretary picked up. As Atalanta was barely through the door and only a few feet down the hall and could still hear me, I endured.

The secretary asked me to hold while the archbishop finished another phone call.

I said I would, as I turned back on the BBC3 to Walsung beautifully singing, '*Friedmund darf ich nicht heissen*'.

Serendipitous I thought waiting for the archbishop.

(I thought to myself, waiting - just as all the innocent christian Iraqi, Egyptian, Kenyan, Libyan, Indonesian, Malaysian, Pakistani and Afghanistan girls are waiting for the pope and all of his armies. Right, the nostra aetate catholics don't wage war.

Boswell spoke up then reminding me of, "...how important compassion is, and how when dealing with catholics, you have to be oh so compassionate and mitigate their lack of will to fight the jihadists with Highland, Lowland, Speyside, Islay, and Campbeltown."

Dr. Johnson concurred adding that, "John Paul II got taken by the House of Saud by letting them build the largest mosque in Europe in the Parioli district. Pope John Paul II ignored history *and* the Koran *and* trusted a muslim. The church is still waiting for the House of Saud to keep its word instead of purchasing of Jericho-IIB's or Agni III's, as was recommended since May 14th 1981 by my fellow practitioners of the medical arts in the Palatine, Noble, and Swiss Guards."

Boswell angrily replied, "Mehmet Ali Agca frenchkissed the Pope, but due to his vow of celibacy the Pope didn't stick his tongue down the religion of peacer's throat. After the muslim's unwanted sexual advance, Pope John Paul II did not even call the immamies who sent Agca to warn them about Agca practicing unprotected sex".)

Chapter 22   Omnis Utriusque Sexus

I waited, listening to the Walsung sing. (Boswell asked Dr. Johnson "…if, after dinner and a scotch or two this evening, would the Doctor participate in a digital holographic microscopy before bioprinting cells from Boris 504 for repairing the three different points of the hohlraum infection in the hippocampus?", but he was interrupted before Dr. Johnson could answer.)

"Mr. Glass, the archbishop apologizes, and asked if you would mind holding, as he is just finishing a call with the Secretariat of State's Office, and will be just another minute."

"Not a problem. I will wait." If he was going to be much longer I would take a hit off the pipe.

I picked up the cigarette and took a long drag. Listening to BBC3 I remembered something from when I was much younger, '*Pater noster qui es in caelis sanctificetur nomen tuum advveniat regnum tuum fiat voluntas tua sicut in caelo et in terra panem nostrum qoutidiam da nobis hodie, et dimitte noblis debita nostra sicut et nos dimittimus debitoribus nostril et ne nos inducas in tenationem sed libera nos a malo.*'

I then wondered if the 1924 International Congress of Mathematician's prize for a totalistic cellular automa of the Sermon on the Mount divided by Qaran 4:15 plus Quran 24:2 squared by Quran 33:33 had been claimed yet.

"JD, so sorry to keep you waiting, I hope you're having a good day."

"Good afternoon Archbishop, I am. (am not ton ma). How are you doing?"

"Well JD that is the thing, I have been attempting to gather the information for the interrogatories and the document request. As you know, it is very time consuming. Would it be possible to get yet another extension on the document request?"

"Archbishop, of course you know I will request that as a matter of professional courtesy plaintiff's counsel extend the deadline another twenty one days. I don't know if they will agree." I paused and took a long slow drag on my cigarette. I then finished the thought by saying, without a hint of irony in my voice; "If not, I will bring a motion before the Court, and we will tell the Court that the Church is acting in good faith."

"Thank you JD, it is just that I have to insure that all thirty three provinces and all the archdioceses, and the Maionites, Melkites, and Romanians, are all going through their archives. 1960 unto 1997 covers a lot of time and church documentation."

"Yes, I understand, but plaintiff's attorneys are going to say that the Church has had time, but I think we probably are OK with twenty one more days Archbishop." I knew that Father Johannes Eighth's case was costing the church a lot of money - just in document research and copying. The judge was right in ruling that discovery allows the plaintiffs to pry the documents out of the clenched fist of the Church, even the Castrillion Hoyos emails. Plaintiff's attorneys knew who, and what, they were working against. The discovery phase was going to go on for at least another year.

(Boswell thinks that the church should add more bread and wine, especially wine, in the eucharist to insure a healthy collection of alms. Of course, Boswell just wants to insure I don't get stiffed by the Archbishop on the hourly rate invoices - plus costs. Dr. Johnson thinks the church should also charge more for administrating the Sacrament of Reconciliation – a lot more. I personally think the church should raise its rates on all indulgences across the board.)

Plaintiff's attorneys were not going to let themselves be out spent by all those Sunday mass collection plates.

I was sure the frail widows, the daily penitents, and the school children placed all those pennies, nickels, dimes, and quarters in those collection plates specifically to buy legal indulgences for their parish pedophile stationed there on the archbishop's orders.

Christianity is all about forgiveness.

Those hundreds of millions of dollars donated by widows, penitents, and children for indulgences, were pretty much all the plaintiff's bar dreamed about, and lived for.

That, and the media attention from Achoo Baytiiiii Version News Agency, The Starkville Zeitung, Filastin al-Mulsima, that glossy Relying on the Traveler magazine, and Al Aqueera TV Young Incoherents Puppet News, Der Sturmer, and of course Baidnonews, all providing encouraging editorials and prominent first page copy for legally attacking a christian institution.

"JD, can we move our meeting back to next week. I will send over the pdf's of what I already have by courier tomorrow?"

It was common knowledge now among the plaintiff's bar that there were at least 4,450 pedophile priests. One could guess the Secretariat of State's Office has a larger list, a more complete list.

I knew that Atalanta was going to have a rather large spreadsheet to work up after tomorrow.

I resisted the urge to ask the Archbishop if according the Church records I was dealing with 4451; or 4450, or 4449, or 4448, or 4447, or 4446, or 4445, or 4444, or 4443, or 4442, or whatever.

"Sure Archbishop, I will be able to spend all Sunday looking at the pdf's instead of going to church." The archbishop's of Vienna and Boston experiences no doubt taught the Church how to deal with civil plaintiff attorneys.

It had crossed my mind that so far, my acting as parapetto for the Holy See's record retention division, is a fair and palatable deal for what my Six Hundred Thirty Two an hour is getting the catholics in Father Johannes Eighth's case re-trial.

I would be willing to bet that the archbishop and I are still in Chapter One of the Secretariat's policy and procedure manual for outside defense counsel, developed from the Vienna and Boston litigation.

"JD you are always welcome to come pray with me, and not only at Sunday mass, the Church and I are available to you anytime for all the work you have done on ecclesiastical problems over the years."

"Thanks Archbishop, but as you know I left the church before I hit puberty." I took another hit off the moisten cigarette before putting it out. Actually it was on the 4th of December in 1959 when Sam and Little Joe, Jr. went 85 km without a Torah, Bible, or Koran. After that I had no use for myths or Canon 996, just hubblespacetelescope.

"JD, as men grow older they change, youthful ideas may start to seem rash. You can always return to the three theological virtues on the Tomb of John XXIII in Battistero di San Giovanni. Remember JD, the church is eternal", the archbishop stated, but without any tone of conviction in his voice.

Of course, I didn't bother to point out that hubblespacetelescope makes his 'eternal' one nanosecond plus Ten Thousand Trillion Trillion Trillion Trillion Trillion Trillion Trillion Trillion years after the Big Bang, according to my HP-35; give or take a few nanoseconds.

"Thank you Archbishop, but every Sunday for the next couple months I'm preparing pleadings for the Cour Internationale De Justice alleging violations of the 4th standard of medical experimenting established under the 1947 Nuremberg Code against Yahweh, Deus, Ishvara, God, Allah, Achamán, and Krishna-Vasudeva."

The archbishop laughed because he thought I was joking.

I believe he thought it was the christian thing to do in a social setting where a perceived attempt at humor fails.

The british trained lawyer, who was imprisoned four times for being very annoying, was prescient about liking Christ, not christians.

Being gracious myself I took no offence at his misunderstanding. I told him of my present problem for this Sunday, "In Practice

234

Direction III for the Cour Internationale De Justice, Archbishop, it states: '*the parties are strongly urged to keep the written pleadings as concise as possible, in a manner compatible with the full presentation of their positions*'. The pleadings cover billions of homo sapiens sapiens and countless acts of cruelty and violence in the name of some gods since at least the eruption of Lake Toba on Sumatra. It is quite a problem since the Code only became effective in 1947."

The Archbishop laughed even louder, which I thought was very, very, very, polite.

"I have next Tuesday at 3:00 pm open, Archbishop."

"Tuesday at 3:00 pm it is then JD. I will have a white chocolate latte and some croissants waiting for you."

"Archbishop that rich espresso you drink would be great, and maybe an apple-raisin strudel or an almond-honey bienenstich would be nice." I thought to myself what the church had taught me as an altar boy, '*sentire cum ecclesia*'.

The archbishop chuckled while saying, "The Church's own espresso made from her finest arabica beans grown on our estates it is. You realize JD, that my invitation for you to take a spiritual retreat to the estates is always open to you. The Church appreciates the work you have done over the last decade. A few days in quiet meditation and prayer, reading, and some physical exercise is wondrous for the soul. I would personally come and pray with you, and afterwards you can go riding with me around the estate. You can choose to ride any of my personal horses Byerley, Darley, or Godophin."

"Thank you Archbishop, but you can't save something I don't have. Perhaps someday soon I will take you up on riding around those beautiful rolling hills and forests though. I appreciate your offer immensely. I, of course, wouldn't dream of riding your personal animals, I would like to ride 'Markham' if I do make it out there sometime. See you tuesday."

235

I put the phone down and put my head in my hands. The church was definitely rendering unto Caesar a lot lately.

The church survived millenniums absorbing cultures and ruling the world, but this last two decades of mismanagement of pedophilia was the biggest mistake made by the modern church since not starting a crusade to kill National Socialist Party Member Number Seven.

Perhaps matching St. Francis Xavier's letter to John III, under Pope Nicholas V's Romanus Pontifex, requesting jizyah type authority for european members of the Society of Jesus, who were in theological discussions with the Indian citizens of Goa.

I hadn't noticed while on the phone, but the music had changed, and now was almost to the end of 101st symphony in D (epraved) Minor. I focused in on the minor since it was in vogue with thousands of local parish priests.

Subconsciously I rolled my weary shoulder counter clockwise; then rolled my other weary shoulder clockwise as a mime of a delayed shift and an anticipated shift.

What did Adolf tell General Gerhard Engel, '*I am now as before a catholic and will always remain.*' Well Adolf, not me. It did not take Pope John XXIII to ex-communicate me either, Señor Castro.

I opted out on my own, after learning a little of science, with all that latin from the jesuits: '*et ego auctoritate ipsius te absolvo*'.

"JD all you ever do with a computer is listen to music. I would appreciate it if some time you learned how to use a word processor program, or a spreadsheet, or heaven forbid, download some music to your cell phone."

Atalanta stated as she briskly walked in to my office carrying a lot of papers and several dictation tapes.

236

She put the paperwork on the corner of my desk and then went and put the dictation tapes in the top drawer of the file cabinet. "On Adbul, the Bioethics Committee briefly OK'd FGM, but withdrew it within a month, I printed out copies of both notices."

I watched her for a second, then I grabbed a cigarette and lit it up while flatly stating, "That reminds me of Obama's January, 2009 White House letter to the Kapi'olna Medical Center."

"JD why is this in the bottom drawer?" She had my cell phone in her hand, which she promptly walked over to my desk and put on top of the papers she had just put down.

I smiled at her for a second before it turned into a silly grin, "Atalanta, my guess it is there for the same reason I had Mr. Mohammad Target bin shakrattlerollkh designed and installed a program on my desktop which endlessly and randomly surfs the internet. It will be extremely difficult for the credit agencies bureaucrats and the national security agencies A.I. computers to develop my psychological profile based upon mohammad's work. If I am right, mohammand's work should screw up not only my cookies, but also government intelligence."

Atalanta nervously laughed while saying, "I hadn't thought about him in a long time. I never trusted him, he reminded me of a rogue FBI academy dropout. You're kidding about the computer. You did not let him touch your desktop did you?"

"You realize the successful criminal defense attorney builds up a level of trust with his clients." I teased and took a long draw off the cigarette. "Besides it's his sons you shouldn't trust."

"JD you did not, you did not let him touch mine, did you?" She actually looked concerned.

"Atalanta I would be a hypocrite if I did such I thing. I don't work for the government. I would make a lousy informant since I can't remember anything anyway."

"No you don't JD." Atalanta laughed again. "You work for drug dealers, drug addicts, murderers, burglars, thieves, pedophilia priests and other child molesters, prostitutes, kidnapers, wife beaters, husband beaters, drunk drivers, and the random Starkville police officer when they are the ones being arrested. Did I leave anyone out?"

"Wow, thanks, you know if we get Madness to lay a fat beat under that, I think the Urban and the Rock Stations would accept that as my new advert. Do I have to pay you a performance fee and a writer's fee? You only left out the huge influx in muslims in the last six months."

"Of course you do, JD. I also want a signing fee of a new porsche in addition to the performance fee and writer's share. There is no substitute for quality, as you're fond of saying."

"What color?" I put the cigarette out in the ashtray and reach in the drawer to get out the hashish.

"You're a regular '*Cole Thornton*' JD, just helping your friends, and no you don't with the hashish until I leave. I am not going home today smelling like dope. JD, you have to review and then sign those papers. I spent the last thirty three minutes on them, and they are going overnight to New Mexico as soon as you sign. So don't even think I am going to let you get away with lying down on the sofa again."

"What's this then, the settlement? Ok Atalanta I'll start with this. Thank you."

"JD, I want to leave early, so after you're done with that, there are phone calls to talk about. A reporter from Der Sturmer would like to talk to you before his deadline at 10 pm among other things. Oh, Ms. Child called from out take at the JC an hour ago, and asked if you still wanted to meet with her this afternoon. I told her you did but couldn't today. Ms. Child will be here at noon tomorrow."

She then turned and walked out of my office leaving me to read my own words for eighteen and one half pages, which should and could have been said in less than eighteen words - but those insurance company white shoe wearing litigation lawyers are money hunger pricks who don't understand English sentences when written as noun, verb, direct object followed by a period.

So I reiterated everything thirteen times so the anal retentive 1st tier white shoe firm blood suckers can't drag my client back into court.

I reached over and grabbed a Kensitas, lit it, and reread myself looking for errors in my logic.

I wondered if MV2Marie's kids were looking for any errors in my logic right about now.

I placed the cigarette in the ash tray, next to one which was still burning.

I was about three pages from the end of the error free settlement document, when I had to admit to myself, that it was as thorough as one of those order of the coif 'ers would write. Even Boswell would have to admit that there was a certain stylistic flair in the boilerplate, thorough, although not insightful, I was complimenting myself as a silhouetted Atalanta appeared in the doorway.

"JD, Dr. Fritz Arlt is on hold. He wanted me to interrupt you. Will you take the call?"

"Thanks Atalanta, this settlement looks great, appreciate it. Tell Doc Arlt I'll pick up in a couple seconds."

Atalanta disappeared back down the hallway. I wanted to lie down on the sofa and rest. I picked up my pen and moved my writing pad over in front of me.

I got up and poured a cup of coffee and turned off the brewer. I went back and sat down, and then hit the speaker button.

"Hey Doc how's everything at the lab? Are the Albert V mice on a hunger strike again?"

"Great JD, just finished ordering a lot of new equipment, courtesy of the Sheriff's Drug Seizure Grant Funds, excellent german engineering, very precise, very elegant."

"Fantastic Doc, I'll tell all of my drug dealing clients that their forfeited drug profits are going for a good cause. Are you done yet with testing Deutschebag Haftlingkartei Maschinen Gesellschaft's action figures?"

"Not good JD. In fact possible bankruptcy and some international litigation. Report written just went out couple hours back by delivery service pick up. I can email summary if you wish."

"Thanks Doc, but no. The building's thirteenth floor maintenance room has row after row after row of equipment that has optical splitters in it, flashing my I.P. 07.16.19.45.05.29.45 constantly. I wouldn't be surprised if the ghosts in the machine flatfoots had assigned a moniker to it, something cute like Hashalush HaKadosh. No need to hand my data over to them. I'll wait until get originals tomorrow, but run the summary for me."

"JD, all the tests are set out in detail in report. Summary is that all of the action figures - Lin Piao, Mao Tse-tung, P'eng, Josef Stalin, Hajji Amin al-Husseini, Dieter Wislicney, Rahman Abdul Rauf el-Qudw al-Husseini, Idi Amin, Ahmadinejad; and all their accessories including clothing and weapons, are emitting harmful Zyclon-B gases which can cause nosebleeds, allergies, rashes, eye problems, and headaches in people. The gas also damages furnishings, electric appliances, and computers."

"To a reasonable degree of scientific certainty", I interrupted.

"JD, the toys are a biohazard, very dangerous to the health of the children who play with them."

"Personal conclusions not in the report? Procedural question for my client Doc, how long are the samples, records, and files kept in your normal retention policy if not retrieved by client?" I took a long sip from my coffee as I had highlighted my desires to him.

"Professional not personal, and, the same billing as always JD, no changes – forty five days past payment received date everything not claimed is destroyed, all conveniently not detailed in any billing statement to client, only set out in Section 6.3.2 of the original contract."

"Thanks for the prompt work, Doc. Don't email anything, I'll wait until tomorrow for the material. I personally appreciate the quick turn around on this."

"Hope you client feels the same when he pays the invoice. Take care of youself JD."

242

Doc hung up before I even got a chance to tell him that I'd call back tomorrow night at 17:00. Doc lived the wall street banker's rule, do not look back, as the money is in front. My work is in the past.

I got up to smoke a bowl while looking out window, but remembering Atalanta, decided to light up cigarette instead. After lighting up by the window, I went over to the cabinet and got my copy of 'Così Fan Tutte', and then loaded the thumb drive into the computer.

I was ready to sit down at the desk and call Deutschebag Haftlingkartei Maschinen Gesellschaft. I put the cigarette next to a still burning one, and one that was still warm. After the telephone conference, I could get out of the office and go to the apartment and relax before having some dinner later.

I dialed the number to one of my longest and best clients – DHMG. Then I hit the speaker button.

"Deutschebag Haftlingkartei Maschinen Gesellschaft how my I direct your call?" Even the receptionist exuded german efficiency. Whomever she was, she sounded warm, friendly, and very confident. The toy industry was definitely one of the power industries in Starkville. Games are huge in Starkville.

"I would like to talk to Thomas Watson, ma'am."

"I will see if he is in sir. Can I ask who is calling?"

"J.D. Glass. Thank you I will hold." I started listening to the beginning of the opera.

"JD how are you, been to any baseball games lately?" Tom seemed in a very good mood, optimistic behavior for anyone answering a call from their lawyer.

"No Tom, mostly just working all the time lately. I have been doing some hip hop producing. Has Will Heidinger had you to his corporate luxury box on the 3rd base line this season?"

"Yeah, I was just down there with Will last Sunday afternoon. Great game, and what a spread he put on. Lots of different beers to go with all the barbecue pork ribs, pig's feet, steaks, and salmon. You should come to the next game JD."

"Yeah I know it. I probably will. Tom how is business, how are DHMG's sales this quarter?"

"JD, if you want to know about sales that means you have something to tell me about costs, legal costs. What's up?" The good mood was deflated. It never takes long whenever talking to me.

"Nice Tom, that's why you're president of a large company and I am just a neighborhood lawyer."

"Was a lawsuit filed? Did a reporter call you?"

"No, not yet Tom, but I have a preliminary report from the Lab, the actual document is arriving tomorrow. Doc Arlt just talked to me and the lab results apparently are not good."

"Well, what are the Lab findings, did they find why kids are getting sick? It has got something to do with the manufacturing process of the action figures, doesn't it?"

"Tom, not sure on either point conclusively, did not get into depth on telephone. Gist is there is a chemical problem with the figures and accessories. Recall is necessary from what Doc says."

"Recall? Are you absolutely sure. That is a lot of money, and I might have to shut down company departments, probably temporary, but have to lay off some workers. Why recall? Are there any other options? Has to be some other options, perhaps another Lab test?"

"Tom as your attorney, no. I don't see any at this point, again the report is here tomorrow, so we need to meet. In fact I would advise against any and all further testing at this point."

"JD, I can't absorb the costs, there has to be another way. The supplier is overseas, insurance, import license, warehousing. JD is there - is there definitely a legal need to recall?"

"Tom I am not going to go into details on phone, especially since I don't have any. I will make time to come over after work tomorrow with the report. Your offices should be empty of most of your employees then, and we can develop a strategy to work through this thing. Need your CFO and your corporate counsel there, no one else. Tom we will go through a couple pots of coffee and plan it out."

"JD what should I do tonight, what documents or information do you need for the meeting."

"Tom, I require nothing. It will just be informal. I don't want any memorandum of the meeting taken or kept. Just sitting down and discussing the situation between ourselves."

"JD, what about the press, this will be a nightmare. DHMG might lose our shelf space at the box retailers over this."

"Tom, relax. Tonight take the wife out to dinner, see the ballet. Just go enjoy yourselves tonight. You are probably going to be working late for a while. I will work up a recall proposal or two for discussion tomorrow. You will have to be careful. You can have anyone who bought a toy, just bring it in, without or without a receipt, for an exchange. You can give them two other toys for bringing in a toy and signing a release. Have to be careful as we don't want to be seen as preying on desperate mothers with the goal of inducing them into forfeiting all of their legal rights in return for an inadequate remediation of two toys. Just need to get as many of those toys back in your possession immediately as possible, and then dispose of them, at the right time."

I continued thinking out loud. "If DHMG can get a majority of toy owners to sign release for two free replacement toys as their sole remedy, you could be ok. Limiting damages to retrieving and destruction of toys with replacement costs, have to see what your

CFO can do crunching numbers. Important to try to keep any lawsuits from being filed, have to get toys back before more kids start turning up sick everywhere, other than the few we already know about."

"Right JD, no lawsuits. The company will be ruined, all our advertising about healthy kids being our most important product, just ruined."

"Tom, you should have agreements that release DHMG from all known and unknown claims of liability, typical boilerplate. Also that assign all of the purchaser's rights to DHMG, which will let DHMG to go after manufacturer responsible for any claims for damages the purchasers could have asserted themselves, if needed. The agreement should limit compensation to two dolls but provide for DHMG to present claims based upon DHMG's losses, and for those who don't want to sign for the toys, maybe something like provide standard compensation of the purchaser's losses including damage to personal property, reimbursement for medical expenses, out-of-pocket expenses, something along those lines. I will work it out for the meeting." I glanced out the window looking for any cirrus clouds.

"Great JD, I like it. I will go out to dinner with the wife tonight. I can get rid of the old slow selling toy inventory products as the exchanges, and DHMG is still the 'kids are our only concern toy company'. See you tomorrow at five pm."

"Sure Tom that's why I am here, to help my clients. There are going to be problems, I haven't thought this through yet, especially if the any kids get cancer. Should have DHMG say the recall is for small parts falling off or something, plus a mention of the chemical angle in the press releases. DHMG is switching to made in USA toys so to provide American jobs, promote only made in USA toys that don't lose pieces made from inferior foreign chemicals, and that te company supports its dedicated union workers."

"JD if the kids get cancer - I can't think like that."

"Tom, if the kids actually do get cancer, I can't state that releases would hold up in contract law. I was just throwing ideas at you as I am just processing this news from Doc as we speak. I think you might need a skilled PR guy, someone with corporate disaster experience. I suggest Kurt Gruber of the HJ Agency." I was sure that Kurt would use the media to make Tom the new '*Gaius Maecenas*' of Starkville, and have the laobaixing believing that DHMG is one of the leading 'green technology' companies in the country within sixty seven days.

"JD, I know you will figure it out and get us options, some reason DHMG could limit lawsuits while recalling toys and something with the promoting the company angle. Thanks. Call you at lunch tomorrow, and looking forward to seeing you here at five o'clock."

We both hit the phone's speaker button at the same time. We did not know it, but both of us were thinking of single malt scotch as we disconnected from one another.

(Dr. Johnson was thinking of proscribing more xanax, but "…upping the dosage". Boswell was thinking "Joe '*Democracy is finished in England. It may be here* ' Kennedy's corporate luxury box was adjacent to Will Heidinger's on the 3rd base line".

I put my head in my hands again for a minute; then put out cigarette that had burnt down before. I pushed it down deep in the ash tray anyway.

I stood up and stretched, and then lit up another cigarette before I walked over to the window and looked down at the streets. I think I saw maybe twenty three or so paraponera clavata scurrying about in the gutter. I opened the window and threw my cigarette at them just to scare them. It drifted out over the street and bounced off a metro bus onto a black Mercedes-Benz CLS63 AMG's door, and then onto the street, where it was immediately run over by the back right tires of the metro bus extinguishing my cigarette for me.

Technology is wonderful, but a bit wasteful of energy perhaps, at least in the extinguishing of chemical reactions.

I could hear the paraponera clavatas laughing at my missile launch, arschlochers.

At least the paraponera clavatas understood how very dishonored, unworthy, and disgraceful it is for an individual to follow quranic injunctions. I am sure that no young paraponera clavatas male would ever cause that embarrassment to his Hymenoptera or Formicidae.

As I shut the window I heard the 3rd one back yell to the others: *"Remain on your guard, evil attorneys can easily debase a paraponeraimân, therefore it is forbidden to retain them; instead we must strengthen our clavatashood."*

I decided to lie down on the sofa and shut my eyes. I was tired. I wondered if Atalanta could book me a private room for three nights at the Maristan of Granada on a floor without any young paraponera clavatas playing in the hallway. I laid down and took three deep breathes as I closed my eyes thinking that human rights and islamic law are bipolar opposites. I covered myself with Ahmad Shah's cloak. Adbul understood. So does every clitoris hater in Qom. Jihadist ayatollahs are criminals just like the rest of my clients. Shape shifting clitoris hating jihadihomicidalayatollahs are much more dangerous than parish priests.

Homer Ergaster was drinking a bitter herbal liqueur with his cousin Homer Heidelbergensis at the elite Denisova Cave Club in the very exclusive Altai Building as I joined them. Homer was somewhat mildly disagreeing with Homer about whether it was irony or tragedy, that Sinclair Lemon Computers had a public relations problem. I sat down next to Homer and listened while I waited for the waiter.

Homer was relating the present day problems of manufacturing motherboards up in Sinclair Lemon Computer's Malaysian mega-factories with the serf level wages paid to young muslim women who worked too many hours a day in a regimented manner worse than Bridewell Prison.

Homer responded pointing out the irony of Sinclair Lemon's Computers first national t.v. commercial where a young Lithuanian woman in work clothes, leaves an Acziarimas Ceremony, running down Ash Land Avenue waiving a meat cleaver over her head until she reach the office building containing the Qibla Compass and Computer Company.

The young woman stood for a second in front of the plate glass windows before throwing the meat cleaver through the plate glass as she yelled, 'We shall organize them to insist on keeping our clits! We shall bear down the opposition; we shall insist a very small penis for every pre-teen clit. Our clits for us, and very small penises for them! Victory will be ours! Our clits will be ours! OUR CLITS WILL BE OURS!'

Homer agreed with Homer, that, "Muslims must have realized that islam makes no sense at all to Homers. That realization is why moslums kill each over every day; rejection of the absurd, leads to absurd people going absurdly fratricidal on other absurd people".

Boswell looked over at Homer Ergaster while stating that, "Homer S. Idaltu has written a classical treatise with its premise being that absurd people also target the rest of us because we aren't absurd".

While waiting and listening, I thought every jihadist ayatollah can and should be charged with violating 18 U.S.C. § 2314 when they read from the kkkoran; and, especially before they ever try again to steal an old chest from any begena player and his hommies.

The last time it was tried was during the 23rd day of the Begena's music festival of Ar-ramad, and it was only recovered after seven months and a rumored payment of 1050 magrathean bound mice. It turned out the mice had became infested with a plague of fleas during the turnover, and the payees ended up with hemorrhoids and boils; (i.e. Hommie's natural justice).

Begena Players celebrate Ar-ramad on the 23rd because that is the day they won their copyright infringement lawsuit in the Supreme Court against the Laalater al-Qadrone syndicate. Of course that ruling is only enforced domestically. Internationally, the syndicate is still ripping off their royalties due to the fact that the syndicate has been able to delay the lawsuit in the International Court of Justice for Fascist, Usurpers, and Anti Semitics.

One of the Denisova's waiters finally came over to the table. He said that he hoped we didn't mind, but he had overheard the discussion, and that it was his humble opinion, "...that it was very ironic that the high tech industry relied on foreign workers making slave wages to produce all those homeland security triangulating devices that people carry and use."

Before I could decide between Highland, Lowland, Speyside, Islay, or Campbeltown, the waiter looked over at me, and then finished his thought by stating the obvious in a rueful tone, "It is a tragedy for the workers."

249

Chapter 24   Rerunning Visions

After last Sunday's binghi, I was on my usual after binghi bimodal correlating random walking tour of Starkville. I was humming the female chorus of Puccini's '*Turandot*' as I wandered down to the bank of the Honkawa, under the instate highway bridge overpass.

While humming I was thinking about how very rude the beijing communist usurpers & gangsters were to the more than 1,325,639,999 of their fellow middle kingdom Homo sapiens sapiens, and that they are not content just to subjugate, but must insult those same citizen's intelligence with Uncle Joe Jasmine Hu Jintao's Reichskammer 'People's Daily' with its daily phantasmagorical economic reporting. My conclusion was the hell with all usurpers.

I began humming Rasool Mississippi Fred McDowell's '*Goin Down to the Yellow River*', without Dr. Johnson and Boswell's usual accompaniment.

I happened upon a stone parapet. Some men were sitting behind the wall on several fallen black walnut tree trunks laying a few feet from the river's edge.

At first I thought I had stumbled upon some Starkville form of Kumbh Mela, but then realized it was the wrong month. The undocumented transients use the river to get into and out of Starkville, thereby avoiding the state highway patrol.

There were stone parapets at intervals down the river. Transients had, over the years, raided the few old abandon pioneer farms, liberating their old foundation stones to the river's bank.

The stones were laid out in an oval, reminding me of some Buckfast Abbey monk's writings on apostolic constitutions, '*Aedes sit oblonga, ad oriente versa, et quae sit navi similis*'.

These transient camps not only provided safety to the travelers, but also allowed for illegal information to flow unimpeded, and undistorted, by the main stream media in Starkville. The men didn't seem to mind when I sat down with them. They barely took notice of me for the next quarter hour.

I sat there quietly listening as they discussed whether or not to accept the invitation from the Ethiopians to come to their next music festival.

They voted and decided to check with the Ethiopians to see how crowded it was going to be, because the festival is always overbooked by the Ethiopians and their friend's the Buddhists.

It was agreed that since the musical duo 'Kojiki & Nihon' will be performing their twenty three minute gagaku instrumental, *'death comes a creepin' in my room'*, they all would go unless it was overbooked.

Then the men began very politely arguing amongst themselves.

I recognized the five Arawas as being from the Tzu Chi Foundation in 1215 block of Lateran Avenue in the City's 4th Ward. They were with three Sentinelese warriors I had not seen before.

The Sentinelese were wearing traditional huji garb with their names and tribal hierarchy on them; Abdul-Jabbar 33, Olajuwon 34, and Jordan 23.

I had sat down on the end of a log next to Jordan 23. From what I could understand of the argument, the disagreement centered on why Shia and Sunni Moslims enjoy and encourage the killing of one another over something that happened centuries ago.

Jordon 23 was paying attention to the discussion, but he wasn't talking. He picked up a black walnut twig and started writing in the dirt, WRGOABABD MLIAD1 WTDIMPAKEP MLIBOAIAQC TTMTSAMSTGAB, which made no sense to me.

I took out a Kensitas and lit it up. I blew a couple smoke rings while thinking that Jordon 23 might have a problem passing the Starkville english proficiency test, that is, if he ever wanted to get employed with the city's civil service jobs.

After about a quarter of an hour of discourse regarding the inherent violence contained in the teachings of the koran, and just as I was enjoying the fellowship of the moment, I foolishly forgot our cultural differences.

Forgetting I was with transients, I asked the Arawa's and the Sentinelese a theological question. I really did not think about it as I just sort of blurted it out. I wish I hadn't now because they all seemed such fine fellows at that spacetimepoint.

('Brotherhood concept is a deception of ganja', Dr. Johnson told Boswell.)

I really wanted to ask them if they thought Global Warming was responsible for the rising of the Honkawa as the University of East Anglia's data claimed, while disregarding the expansion of the city of Starkville around the 1950's A.E.C. installed ground sensors.

Instead I blurted out, "Does it make sense to the Arawa and the Sentinelese, that by not taking action to stop the mulsims from honor killing and their enslavement of women and girls, that the Arawa and Sentinelese Warriors are guilty of the crime against humanity of immoral inaction? Who calls for Kali-Ma?"

Which was obviously a transgression of their hospitality, but what was worse was that I immediately followed with, "Also, as a direct Newtonian reaction, would not Demeter have your wild haitian creole pigs disappear?"

Just plain ignorant of me as an American. It's what in the 1950's, Latino's and S.A.'s used to call us norte's out as ugly americans. I had forgotten how much the Arawa and the Sentinelese Warriors love their wild Haitian creole pig, and full bosom women with beautiful hair who carry double axes.

The Arawa and Sentinelese tribal cultures indisputably have a kolmogorov complexity regarding their wild haitian creole pigs.

So naturally according to their ancient traditions, they immediately jumped up, and began ritualistic dancing, yelling, and singing 'a cappella', followed shortly thereafter by waiving of their javelins and flat bows in the air.

Then they ran in my general direction. As the natives chased me away from the Honkawa river bank, I realized what a pain in the ass cultural elitists they were turning out to be; just like the People's Revolutionary Army's Moral Officers.

(Dr. Johnson observed that my cultural miscalculation obviously was in asking a *'Waldo what are your warriors doing out there beyond the moral wire'* question.)

A few years ago, transient foreigners would have never dared to sing '*a cappella*' to a citizen of Starkville.

As I was running through the underbrush and the stands of acacia xanthophloea on the river bank, and then up onto the parkway, I couldn't make up my mind about the dancing. I knew the Arawa were doing the old james brown mashed potato with a bit of the camel walk, but I couldn't decide if the Sentinelese were doing the funky chicken or the robot.

I wondered if they knew, or even cared, that Starkville's Imammies had issued a fatwa against dancing last Sunday.

Unknownst to me as I walked back into the city, the Sentinelese and the Arawa were walking back under the highway overpass bridge next to the Honkawa discussing the effects of the Treaty of Waitangi, with the resulting loss of taonga whenever dealing with any outsiders.

The Sentinelese agreed with the Arawa that their ancient culture and customs had manage to survive these last seven hundred years or so only because they had avoided contact with the Manila galleon traders, moslims, and everyone else, whenever possible.

Then two of the Arawa started a silly argument regarding what type of hashish Samuel Taylor Coleridge was smoking when he wrote '*What is Life*?', they weren't sure if it was from either Rajasthan, Naggar, or Ketama.

The argument was silly to the Sentinelese, who knew it was from Haetumant.

A Sentinelese interrupted the Arawa, as they tend to do with Arawas, changing the topic somewhat sublimely to whether in '*Tajetori Monogatari*', Kaguya-hime actually rode in a flying saucer.

So it went with the transients on into the night as the dark flowing waters of the Honkawa lapped and sloshed along the muddy river bank while I walked the city streets humming to myself Rasool Bessie Smith's classic hymn '*Send Me to the 'Lectric Chair*'.

Chapter 25   Absent and Undercover

"JD, if you tried to get to bed before the sunrise, you could actually work during the day."

("Careful", this afternoon's Dr. Johnson rebuked Boswell, "She won't let wild asses play by the river bank during work hours.")

I half opened my eyes. There was no flowing Honkawa lapping and sloshing; there was only Atalanta standing in the doorway stating the obvious in a loud and irritated voice, while trying to wake xanaxme up. I shut my eyes thinking that I needed a joint and a cigarette.

"JD, I let you sleep awhile, but there are a couple of things you have to do before I leave. I have some letters that need your signature, and you have to return a couple of phone calls. Start with calling back that lawyer from Mumbai, who called again very excited about some type of fraud. Apparently a studio detective spotted the now not dead actor with some expatriates, including an imam, at 'De Komkommerbar' off Oudezijds Achterburgwal in Amsterdam at sunrise this morning."

I took a deep breath, opened my blurry eyes, and sat up. Atalanta walked over to my desk and sat down. I stretched while rubbing my eyes with my index fingers. I was lightheaded, slightly dizzy and foggy, and my eyesight was a bit shadowy. I was still buzzed, but conscious of being in patria with Atalanta, and the fact that I really needed to blow the snot and crusties out of my nose.

Thoughtlessly, I wiped my nose on the cloak.

Atalanta turned off the music. I got up and walked over to the coffee mess and found a napkin. As I was blowing my nose I started hacking up flem containing couple blood specks, which I spit into the napkin. I looked for any tyrannobdella rex larvae. Finding none, I then threw the used tissue into the garbage can.

"Lovely, no wonder you don't have a girlfriend. That and the fact you're ballroom dancing on a razor's edge lately", Atalanta said it as a joke, but there was a knowing concern in her voice.

She astutely understood the very core truth of the lack of my interpersonal relationships: flem - with specks. My brain, (*as of late, is ounces of dark stringy blood stained globed flem*), was just the sort of power trait that acts as an aphrodisiac on women.

(Boswell interrupted by saying, "You only do your kissing in the dark with Memphis Minnie anyway".)

"Atalanta, give me a second. What do you need me to do?" I still was a bit dizzy and groggy.

"What I'm doing is I'm bringing you the day's phone messages. While you were sleeping Giovanni; why do you call him Madness? Well he stopped by, and I told him you were at the jail. He gave me some cash, and asked for you to call him when you got back."

"How much cash Atalanta, and what for? I thought he was paid in full todate." I was confused, dizzy, and groggy.

"Giovanni handed Six Hundred Twenty Nine Dollars to me. I photocopied the bills and put the cash in my desk drawer; six hundreds, one twenty, and nine ones. Did you want that to go in to the bank today? And what are you looking for instead of paying attention?"

"Cigarettes. No, I think I remember you said you had things to do after work, so it can wait until tomorrow. How much cash do you have in the drawer?"

"Your cigarettes are on the corner of the desk here, and not counting the six hundred twenty nine; four hundred seventy nine dollars and tons of change", Atalanta stated as she took the cigarettes and tossed them over to me, and then did the same with the zippo.

I sat down on the sofa and lit up a cigarette. I started rubbing my right leg above my knee. It was itching as if it was bitten by an ant, or a spider, or something. Both of my legs were itching, it was slightly painful, for which I was thankful for, as it was clearing my head. My eyes felt heavy, and I still was seeing everything through a mental fog.

"Ok, Atalanta is there anything I need to know about for tomorrow morning, or that I absolutely have to do now?"

"Yes, I just told you." Atalanta picked up the messages and started to sort them. "I'll put the calls you have to make in a paper clip on top of the messages", which she was already doing. "I am leaving in a couple of minutes so when I come back in here you better have signed all these papers on your desk." Atalanta stood up and looked over at me. "A Mr. Ben Dickerson is on top of the phone messages. His stepdaughter a Stella Mae Irwin from Topeka is at booking now for ounce of pot and a CCW, smoking pot in motel room and had a .38 in her purse. Mr. Dickerson is looking to get her out immediately. JD if you don't call him right back you'll miss the case. I think he is just going through the phone book trying to get her representation."

I could tell she wanted to say something but did not. Then as she was walking out of my office, she turned and said, "JD, please think about taking someone, maybe Marie Magdalene, or Monica Hippo, and jump on a plane and go to Captiva's beach for a couple days", and with that she was gone. I sat on the blanco baraq leather skin sofa wissenschaft smoking my cigarette while pondering on Atalanta's advice.

I put the cigarette down.

I went over to the Dictioneri. Put my cup on the mini refrigerator. I ground up some French Roast beans. I grabbed a chilled twenty ounce Revigator water bottle and poured it into the Dictioneri, then put the grounds in and hit the brew button.

259

I could not figure out why Madness brought me money.

I turned back on the music and went back and sat down at my desk. It was a good thing too as a Schubert piano sonata was playing. I shut my eyes and just listened for a couple minutes.

I opened my eyes and began to feel extremely sad and alone while looking at all the papers on my desk. Ink and paper but with real world consequences that I wanted no part of anymore.

The job of catching innocent kids from running off the cliff had been filled in the 1950's. I was stuck being a consigliere.

I knew I really had no job skills other than engineering / mixing / producing in the studio late at night.

Definitely no skills left for what I did all day long here in mia patria.

The older I become, the less productive I am; other than my studies of the stars conducted while reclining on my back in random row house yards.

I was putting in excessive amounts of overtime in my row house yard studies, but learning is a compulsion.

The aroma of fresh strong coffee was filling the room, so I got up and filled my cup. I sat down and put my nose about one inch above the cup and breathed the steam into my lungs with large gulps of air. Schubert and French Roast. Damn Heaven.

(Boswell remarked that, "Homo sapiens sapiens are not looking for reverberating waves. They want a city on a hill, or seventy two virgins, or an eternity of being comfortably numb.")

I remembered that after work Dr. Johnson wanted a scotch or two, and Boswell was expecting to smoke some hashish. I decided to just plow through Atalanta's list and then get out of the office.

I almost felt guilty pulling such a psyc 101 trick, but it is way too easy to motivate addicts.

I picked up the paper clipped messages and read through them. Atalanta was absolutely right, as always. I should call every one of them right now.

I wasn't going to, and she knew it, but I would call one or possibly two; and she knew that also.

I picked up the phone and dialed.

"Multi_{verse}State Drug Task Force."

"This is attorney JD Glass, is Detective Gregson or Baynes available."

"I will check Mr. Glass."

Schubert ended. I changed the web tuner until I heard Coltrane's "*Giant Steps*".

"Mr. Glass both Detectives will be in at 2100 hours tonight, would you like their voice mail?"

"No, I will call them later tonight. Thank you." I hung up the phone and then drank some of the coffee. Gregson and Baynes, in their certitude, worked the same night shift hours as me.

I felt like that old overweight lazy falcon floating on currents of quarter notes and subtle phrases. My head was clearing, (‘Right - try another multiverse’, Boswell interrupted), and my body was recharging, as I ‘jazzercised’ with french roast.

I picked up the phone and dialed.

"Good Afternoon John Rutledge House Inn."

"Good Afternoon, may I have room 632 please."

"Yes sir, I will connect you."

The phone rang until it went to call messaging. I hung up.

I picked up the papers on the corner of the desk and started reading and signing them. '*Giant Steps*' ended but I was lucky, '*Round Midnight*' came on right behind it.

I was starting to feel the regenerative biomedical effects of the coffee as I finished my cup and signed the last of Atalanta's paperwork.

I picked up the phone and dialed.

"Good Afternoon John Rutledge House Inn."

"Good Afternoon, may I have room 632 please."

"Yes sir, I will connect you."

"Hello."

"What the hell you been doing Clement, besides not answering the phone?"

"I was in the shower, now I am standing naked in front of the window trying to get arrested so my friend can charge me an outrageous amount of money to plead no contest to my indecency."

"You sound great. How is the Rutledge House Inn?"

"Very nice, as always. I'm in the Ridda Suite, my favorite suite in the hotel. I love the liquor dispenser built into the wall above the refrigerator. I was looking through the hotel brochure and was thinking of ordering up a couple persian escorts. How long before you can meet for some drinks and dinner."

"I don't know. Atalanta said I could leave soon. She is getting ready to leave herself. I have to go by the apartment for a couple minutes and pick up a thumb drive."

"Well JD, why don't you meet me at Damdam's Pub in couple hours. I'm going to get dressed, make a couple phone calls, and then walk over. You can meet me at the bar."

"Sounds about right, unless you wanted to meet at the apartment and smoke some hashish?"

"No JD, I am going to continue with single malt scotch tonight. JD, do me a favor and don't talk business. I am not in the mood. You can lecture me tomorrow about everything and anything, but tonight I just want to drink and eat."

"Sure, I understand. Can you be here tomorrow at 11:00?"

"JD, you are a retard. I just said I don't want – Ok 11. That is the end of that, OK?"

"Right, got it, if I keep don't my word - I pay the bar tab."

"Christ JD, that's a sucker bet because ain't no way in hell you can keep your mouth shut."

"You have a point, mayb…"

"No you don't, you set the terms and I am going to enforce, so tell Atalanta to open the desk drawer and get out the petty cash." Clement started laughing as if he was pulling a fast one.

"Done and Done. Is there anything you need Giulio, or I can do?"

"Yea you jerk, quit being a fucking lawyer and become a feloow disciple of Mr. Gradgrind's '*Philosophy of Fact*'. Also be on time. I'm gonna get dressed. See you with the petty cash. JD you're such an ass, which is what makes you such a good single malt scotch drinking teller of tales. Don't be late as usual either."

"I will. See you." I hung up the phone. I totally understood his frame of mind. I hadn't noticed while I was talking but I had hit the trifecta, as '*Everytime We Say Goodbye*' was playing.

263

I leaned back in my chair and put my feet on the desk and listened and wondered if Hucbalc agreed with Plato on that changing musical modes caused political revolution. I was definitely getting back into some multiversereality in somespacetimepoint.

I could hear Atalanta was getting her things together. I got up and walked out to her desk. I sat in front of the coffee table. Atalanta was putting some things into her purse.

"Atalanta I forgot to bring out the documents I signed. I'll go get them. Will you get me a couple hundred out of the drawer?" I went and got the paperwork and brought it out and handed it to her.

Atalanta went through everything to make sure I did not miss a signature. Then she started putting some of it in envelopes for mailing. I just watched her. I would be lost without her.

When she was done she looked over at me and smiled. "Thanks JD for not disturbing me. I will drop this in the mail box on the way home. Here is two hundred, and don't spend it all on scotch. Also a Mr. Dick V. Small called regarding an appointment. Said he was a friend of Ms. Iva D'Aquino's. His company - Phentytraitors Communicating, Ltd., had some contract review work on a new internet based campaign for this school year, contracted with the Organizing for America's federally funded Al 'Fukuhahahahaha Rousttheirkids Project. Its goal is to recruit and assist future leaders from Starkville University to support the supplying of endless free Safir-2 topical peace ointments in those small child friendly tube applicators to all the preschools, nurseries, hospitals, orphanages, and hospices, in Gaza for each institution's unrestricted use."

"Thanks, I can't call tonight. I'm hungry as the only thing I've eaten today is what you gave me."

"No wonder your pants are always falling off. You should come over on Sunday and have brunch with us."

"That sounds great. I call you Sunday morning and let you know."

"JD you are such a liar, you are never awake Sunday mornings. Plus, you owe me a chocolate latte", Atalanta laughed and got up, gathered her purse and coat, and then handed me the cash. "JD, I forgot to tell you, the captain of your chess team, I always forget his name, al-Ghaffar isn't it? Anyway he called while you were visiting Adbul, to let you know the team picture is set to be taken on Friday at noon at the park. Also please *try* to get a whole night of sleep tonight. When you leave, don't go to the public library and sit in front of the internet for hours. You should go home after a dinner and rest. You cannot keep this up. Will you take your cell phone with you when you leave? Try it once."

"Atalanta if I was married to you I would never leave the house." I laughed. She laughed. Then I watched her walk out the door. She looked great from the back.

A couple lines of Tennyson flashed through my mind as I turned, losing my balance, and then went back to my office and got out the hashish. I filled the bowl and smoke it. I refilled it and smoke it.

I had not noticed but my luck was outstanding, as '*So What*' was playing – so to celebrate I filled the bowl again and smoked it.

My boson-fermion dichotomy was a vector below 'only a little manic', at groggyfuzzyfocused.

I changed my clothes. It felt better having on the '*Fun Lovin Criminals*' tee shirt, and my blue jeans. I was tempted to lie down on the sofa, but as the song ended I turned off the computer, the lights, the coffee maker, and then looked around the office.

I walked to Atalanta's desk, looking around I decided to liberate a couple more dollars, so I opened her desk drawer and moved Atalanta's Taurus 4510TKR-3BUL over and got into my petty cash.

I took two fifties, shut the drawer, and then turned off the lights.

Fuck what a day. I was glad it was over.

I was reclaiming my life and going home, then dinner with Clement, and then later I get to remix the tracks from last night's session. Da dum da dum da dum '*So What's*' base line was playing in my head as I locked the office door and walked to the elevators.

I remembered Stella Mae Irwin in booking. At this spacetimepoint I could go back into the office and call, but I didn't.

Knowing that I am a selfish narcissist was not an excuse not to help out another human being. I consciously took that guilt and flung it into the center of my '*Centaurus A*' well of regret, as I did ending every work day.

(Boswell then went all hyperspace on me, "JD are we forgetting the second law of thermodynamics? What the hell?")

(Dr. Johnson had to opine with an ancient quote from a more intelligent being than myself, "In any closed moral system, the entropy of the system will either remain a constant, or increase, depending on the actions a few just men.")

I did not hear anyone arguing down the hallway, or in the bathroom, while I waited for the elevator.

I did hear the opining hyperspace whining about 'just men', but homo sapiens sapiens rarely pay attention to the solar winds.

'When in the course of human events, it becomes necessary for one people to dissolve the political bonds which have connected them with another, and to assume among the powers of the earth, the separate and equal station to which the laws of nature and of nature's god entitle them, a decent respect to the opinions of mankind require...'

Then the elevator came.

266

Chapter 26   Praeludere

I got on the empty elevator and hit the button. The elevator hesitated, and then shook slowly for a second, as it started my journey downward. It was a very peaceful place, this empty elevator.

As the elevator cleared the 12th floor and was heading downward I wondered if Eitel F. Mollhausen enjoyed his career in the foreign service, and if his parents were very proud of him. I don't know how he or his co-workers had done their jobs. He and his fellow civil servants spent their entire professional careers lying. When they were alone after work, how did they justify Lire – Riechspfennig exchange rates at 50:1? (Exodus 22:25? Al-Baqarah 2:275?)

I glanced at the upright elevator operator chair. It looked to me as a representation of modern sculpture's idealization of entropy, or perhaps by the absence of its operator it was just fulfilling some negatively charged mythological duty of the '*Centaur of Lefkandi*'.

Nostalgia for old worlds overcomes one while moving at inches, not feet, and certainly not floors per second. Say nostalgia for any rainy day in Vienna spent studying '*Deutsche Physik*'.

(Dr. Johnson offered Boswell a quintillion molecules of pure Peruvian blow. Boswell snorted the Peruvian Flake which immediately radiated away into a cluster analysis of eleven different posthubblespacetimepoints simultaneously. Boswell coughed causing some of his nasal mucus to land on the floor.)

I studied the elevator's antique gold and brown light fixtures with the three bulb's pale light illuminating the dark maple wood paneling during the descent. As I always do. I never tired of looking at the patterns in the dark maple. Archaeologist's patience is an elevator skill. It occurred to me that I was obsessing over islam for the last two weeks. It was getting to the point of self realization of an innate desire to seek justice/retribution/revenge on the murdering enslaving cowards.

As the elevator cleared the 10th, 9th, 8th, 7th and 6th floors I indulged that thought. Once the elevator cleared the 5th floor I reasoned that if the Pope wasn't going to take up arms to save christians in *Plateau, Dogo Nahawa, the Doulos Seminary, Riyom, Gojra, Lofa, Rawalpindi, Dembi, Henno, el-Kusheh, Alexandria, Orissa, Central Sulawesi, Marsa Matruh, Mindanao,* or the hundreds of other places in the last ten years where the worshippers of the frenchkisser practice their religion of peace, why should an atheist.

Scotland Yard had investigated at least one hundred nine probable honor killings. Who knows how many worldwide victims this year? Dhimmis France has already rejected 'L'Appel du 18 Juin 1940' with last Bastille Day's proclamation banning Pork Tenderloin Diane, Quiche Lorraine, French Onion Soup, and the manufacturing or consumption of church wine.

From the 4th floor to the lobby I was thinking an atheist lead clitoris saving crusade would be the only moral choice of a rational being.

(Laughing uncontrollably Boswell stated, "Rise up and follow JD, the son of Peleus, and his Pb crusaders!" Dr. Johnson began arguing that "I should try a nonviolent approach by advertising for clients to litigate Jordon's Article's 2 and 3 for preventing the sale of immovable property to men with 16 bar penises for violating el-Freddie Mac and Al- Fannie Mae girth requirements.")

I heard there recently had been at least one hundred seventy poor souls executed for offending the perfumed frenchkissers real estate covenants.

The Achoo Baytiiiii Version News Agency Journal reported they all they had been executed under the jihadist's rule against '12 inches long in perpetuities rule'. I needed a novel remedy such as '*lasciami sola*', to counter the grand jihadieimammibombies from he al-AzhardlyKnowsAnything University's aria edict of, '*In uomini, in soldati, sperare fedeltà. Odio me stessa*'.

(Boswell stating the obvious, said that by using Jordon's legal system as a forum, "...it would allow for educating self hating moslums in civility while enlightening them on individual human rights, such as selling a modest house in Peking to an Arawa and his Sentinelese domestic partner".)

(I knew Peking is not only famous for its chicken and pork cuisine. It's possible that there are people who watched the gymnastic show that might not understand the enlightened Communist Party's democratic laws regarding renting to members of different tribes of basketball nations. Its laws are discuss over cups of white tea and Char Siu Bao all along 14th Street, Noe Street, and Market Street every weekend. I believe the Chinese word for love of such renters is 'xenohomophobic' which Dr. Johnson had previously stated is some how symptomatically related to jihadist latent girthophobia.)

(Whenever imbibing scotch excessively, Dr. Johnson always laughed at Boswell's ignorance of the lack of judicial implementation of any legislative intent in the legislative record. Dr. Johnson was for, "Killing the killers, maybe starting with Hakeemullah Mehsud or Anwar (18 *USC* § 2381) al Awlaki", but admitted that there are so many HVT among the very very very small penis clit haters, that presently the world was a target rich environment.

Boswell always would finish his drink before repeatedly pointing out, "That Abdulmutallab type clay pigeons were background noise in eleven spacetimepoints to any sniper team deployed out of Compton, Oakland, Cincinnati, Detroit, Brooklyn, or especially *enseignments* from *Saint Louis*".)

My journey ended as the elevator softly jolted, and then the door very slowly opened. The diffuse late afternoon sunlight was filling the lobby revealing dusk particles suspended in the air throughout the entire lobby as if in a late afternoon Bose – Einstein condensate.

I barely noticed anything else other than the suspended shimmering dusk particles which were bedazzling, radiating blue and gold, as I very, very, very, slowly walked through the lobby to the door while reciting the first few lines of "*Audita tremendi*" and wondering if its plenary indulgence offer was still valid.

(Dr. Johnson and Boswell briefly conferred, and then informed me, that in their infallible opinion the offer was valid today as the he al-AzhardlyKnowsAnything University still offered courses on the subject in this year's class catalog.)

It was apparent a long hot shower was needed to cool my blood lust for revenge against all the peaceful imams of the religion of murderers, sexual perverts, and enslavers of women and children.

I understood that the hot shower by itself would not be sufficient to calm me.

I would have to smoke some of my sweetest marijuana buds with some of my very best hashish to insure that I am able to get a 21st century postJCvisionsinstitutedhubblespacetelescope perspective on people who follow a 7th century homicidal sexual pervert's philosophy while studying his plagiarized short stories, as if the fairy tales and it's mythology were given to the frenchkisser by Marduk, Aken, Ament, Anuke, Onuris, Ra, and Zeus; Jihadiebombies will not submit to the fact of one true INTERNET : SALAAMALAIKUMLAWRENCECURLYMOSES.COM.

As I opened the door to the street I softly started singing to myself, "*Audita tremendi severitate judicii, quod super terram Jerusalem divina manus exercuit...*"

While singing the chorus as I walked down the sidewalk, I thought as fanatical as the frenchkissing idolaters are, I ventured to postulate that even a visit by *ri: ʃu* would not change their beliefs in islamic knowledge requiring oppression, jealousy, and coveting of Kafir's preteen daughters is commanded by the uneducated cloak less orphan.

His very very very small penis believers blindly follow his psychotic teachings, passions, and whims, such as marrying nine year old innocent female children, after removing their clitoris.

(Of course Boswell could not leave it at that. He had his juvenile need to impress, so he started to quote John Milton, '...*the other shape, if shape it might be called, that shape had none...*' Dr. Johnson and I then both rudely spoke up at the same time telling Boswell, "God damn it, be a good sport and just skip ahead to the 13 nonillion level".)

Chapter 27   Intermyssyown

The sidewalk's biomass was a reverse Ellis Island at this time of the late afternoon. The Baggy Pants LLC day shifters who weren't arrested (and are in booking) or shot (and are in surgery) were waiting to be relieved by the senior and more lucrative night shift on all the major corners.

The suits were streaming to buses and the parking garages in increasing numbers - mixing with the homeless, shaken not stirred.

Homeless Crazies knew the best take was the morning commute. After working the suits were never in a giving mood, so the crazies were putting in the usual lazy half hearted afternoon effort at cold call selling (begging shaw-alpto-khossiloam) from the dour human currents on the sidewalks.

I waited next to the newspapers boxes for the traffic light to change. I noticed the afternoon edition's headline of the 'Starkville Zeitung', "Drug Area Task Force keeps City Safe".

Yeah, right.

Orwellian newspeak press: were the DATF or any MSM reporters watching sales of ammonium nitrate fertilizer, nitro methane, tovex, or fuel oil? I bet the DATF is watching MV2Marie instead.

The eastern skyline above the buildings on North Moore were beginning to show brilliant color streaks of the late afternoon sun setting out of sight on the horizon. I walked the blocks toward the apartment trying to regenerate my nervous system(s).

I told myself no more thinking of the jihadist killers of women, and children, and of the billion human beings who think jihad is a requirement of some 7th century illiterate's psychotically delusional version of an immoral god's murderous desires.

If I wanted to believe in a god, I think I'd make one up that at least could converse on a bachelor of science level, or at a minimum - a god that had a G.E.D. from the Starkville's public education system and one who enjoyed watching tan fit women playing beach volleyball, (ignoring any veryveryvery tiny penis objections).

I walked up to 14 North Moore and noticed that a large mature gyrfalcon was resting in the building's façade next to my apartment windows. If I could open a window and capture it, I knew I could get at least 1,000 dinars for the strange beast from all the catholic *la reconquista's* - Norte, Sureños, and La Eme's over at intersection of Khitan Court and Sultan Lane by the studio.

I started humming *"Walkürenritt"* as I purposely ignored the building's most famous avian tenant, while I slowly walked up to the reassuringly massive oak front door.

I stood in the doorway and fumbled around for at least a second or two looking for the key that was in my right pocket. I had to push the oak door to get it open, and then again to close it. Obviously natural door forces were purposely obstructing me from my goal of the late afternoon's quest for a hot shower.

My hands pulled at the dark hand carved walnut banister, arms dragging myself up the stairs as I climbed, with my back started to hurt with a light pain radiating staccato through my thighs and down into my ankles. It was welcome sensory input, helping to repress any late afternoon MV2 Marie memories.

At the landing the pain subsided. As I walked up to the door the pain ended. I opened the door and entered my Nunavut for the second time this day. I threw my keys and wallet on the counter, and then went over to the futon and took off my clothes and threw them on it. I realized that BBC Radio 3 was playing some Niccolo Piccinni, an overture I think – '*didone abbandonata*', perfect to shower to. So I did for seventeen and three quarter minutes. I only hacked and spit for a couple of minutes into the water swirling around, and into the drain. I noticed a tinge of blood in the phlegm. The vitamin C working? Human genius and the Indus provided me physical comfort and soulful peace in all eleven spacetimepoints until there was only streams of cold water coming through the shower spout while I finished singing about my barefoot dancer Lola Lola.

(*'Nam-myoho-renge-ky Sensi Ray Davies and brother Dave; ditto sensi Pete, & Mick, thank you for rescuing Princess Parizad', exclaimed Boswell.*)

I got out of the shower and dried off. I wrapped the towel tightly around my waist and then went out to the refrigerator. I took out the glass jug which was about a seventeenth full of my ayahuasca tea made with the Revigator water. I poured a glass full of the tea and only added three teaspoons of Hawaiian sugar. Since I was trying to be healthy by drinking tea, I did not want to go all soda pop by adding to much sugar.

I walked over to the aquarium and picked up the *'Rubaiyat'* from the left side of the tank and put it on the book shelf. I took a sip of the ice tea.

I then straighten the flax and hemp paraments the aquarium was on top of. Then I immediately went over to the counter and added three tablespoons of sugar to my tea. I took another sip. Perfect, cool and sweet, a mite bit smoky to the taste.

The aquarium's trinitite sand base was shimmering in the fading sunlight. Oney and Austin were halfway up the glass on the left side of the aquarium. Sheels and Moll were sitting together next to the bank building. Giles was not far away up on the temple's roof. Hercules and Aris were in vegetation trying to hide from me.

Two notoliparis kermadecensis were swimming close to the surface, breaking the surface every couple of seconds. I am naïve, but not naïve enough to think they were happy to see me. I could not remember when I had fed them last. Since they were acting hungry, I shook a little of the shrimp enriched tiny gold wafer pellets into the tank. The fish went mad after them. I stood there wearing the towel, sipping tea, hair dripping water droplets, watching until the last of the golden wafers flip and slip their way toward the dark

273

trinitite base. With the soft fading sunlight shining directly into the aquarium's water, it was beautiful to watch the color contrasts and reflections. I stood there transfixed by the fish, the light, and the Ganges water until I had finished drinking my glass of tea.

Actually I stood there longer than that.

It was a while before I decided to put some clothes on.

I went over to the futon and gathered up all the clothes on it and put them in a clothes basket on the floor next to the book shelf.

Except that I put back on the Fun Lovin' Criminals tee shirt, and then found a clean pair of jeans to put on. I went back over to the futon and decided to lie down for a minute and relax. It felt just right to lie down and listen as Durante's 'Requiem' had just started playing. Thank you British socialism for BBC3. George Bernard Shaw and Erza Pound shared Mussolini.

The BBC3 and 3.195 kafir composers share me.

(Around seventy nine seconds into the Requiem, Boswell suggested that, 'Northern Lights was in order'. Dr. Johnson insisted it was actually, '...at the top of the list'. I relented because even though I really just wanted to concentrate on enjoying Durante, I had to agree with Boswell and Dr. Johnson on priorities.)

I got up and got the dope, and then went for another glass of tea. I thought I could use some more of the chilled ayahuasca tea to sooth my throat. I went over to the refrigerator, and after looking inside, realized I had drunk almost all of the tea.

Today's opportunity for me finally to do some honest labor with the multiverse's gifts, something natural, useful, and beneficial. I went over to the sink and opened the cabinet and got out god's gifts.

I took three deep breathes and started humming. It was a habit when making my special WAM tea: a complex sonata using twenty five possible variations of the multiverse's minor miracles.

I took the three plastic ware containers and opened them. Out of the 1st I took out the chacruna leaves and rubbed them between my hands for a minute, and then threw them in a pot on the stove.

Out of the 2nd, I took out some chaliponga leaves and did the same thing. Out of the 3rd, I took out some caapi vines. I skinned their top and bottoms, and then slit them vertically with a knife. I bent the vines back and forth, the fluid bleeding out of the incisions washing over my hands.

Then I threw the bleeding vines into the pan. I filled the pan with chilled Revigator water from the refrigerator, and then put the temperature on the stove to simmer.

I went and sat back down on the futon and rolled a couple joints, while taking three hits off the remains of one of the three friday night's smoked joints in the ash tray. I then sipped from my glass of tea.

I put the rolled joints into the cellophane wrapping around a new pack of my cigarettes. I took out seven cigarettes out of the pack and put them on the table.

I went over to the stove and stirred up the tea. Then I went over to the refrigerator and reach on top of it picking up the thumb drive, before going back and sitting down.

I found some discarded cellophane, wrapped the thumb drive in it, then put it into the cigarette pack. I found a loose cigarette and lit it up, and then light up an old joint. I sat back smoking both while trying to relax my lower back muscles. After a few hits on the remains of a friday night joint, and a couple draws on the cigarette, I had enough, and put the smokes down.

I laid back on the futon and looked over at the aquarium.

The last of the day's sunlight was pouring into the Ganges water in the aquarium, which had the effect of blurring the edges of the Industrial Promotion Hall and the Imperial Bank Building.

The 3.1415 inches of the surrounding fine trinitite sand base darkly shimmered. Ai Qing's '*Ode to Light*' was transmogrifying into Lord Byron's '*Darkness*' within forty gallons of Haridwar Ganges non-distilled water as I imitated JamesWebbSpaceTelescope.

All the Afropomus snails seemed to be in the same place, but the soft light going through the glass blurred their shapes so that I could not tell them apart.

Then I heard someone singing tenor, it was a small voice but clear, "*Lieber Herr Gott, mach mich stumm, Das ich nicht nach Dachau komm*".

It was so soft that I almost did not hear it under the music of the '*Lacrimosa*'.

I looked around the room, and then back at the aquarium. I thought I noticed something was on the right side of the tank.

Then I saw Iva Toguri D'Aquino, a grammostola rosea, standing in the same spot where I had picked up the Rubaiyat earlier on the left side of the tank.

It was a 'eureka moment', a revelation. Not that she was singing like a 1950's cartoon cricket, or even that she sang tenor.

It was an epiphany that I was bouncing and rick-AH-shazzzzzzzing through simultaneous multiverses of musical performances.

The grammostola rosea stopped singing. She quickly glanced over at the slumbering snails.

The grammostola rosea then announced her submission by taking the name 'Mohammad el Hum an Conger eel'.

The rosea had to be a Norte because she pulled out a small greenish orange grease pen and tagged the aquarium glass with the symbol - عمل مخز; if I turned my head thirty three degrees it might have been '*abnihilisation*'.

Then the Norte scurried away back into the dark void behind the aquarium.

I rubbed my face with my hands, and then picked up another loose cigarette and lit it. I did not trust the memory of any grammostola rosea from Iximché.

I couldn't see one now.

I did see an afropomus mucus trail on the right side of the aquarium glass, but it just was a mucus pattern - not a tag.

It definitely did not say that Professor Rath did not know how to use a '43 Model II Relay Interpolator. I took a couple draws off the cigarette and then put it out. I laid back and closed my eyes as my consciousness faded and slipped under the *gate of ludd*..............

Giovanni Battista Vico was standing next to me at the urinals in the men's bath room at Sin's side bar at 646 N Franklin Street. While we were pissing on the osama bin laden urinal mats he started to read out loud the graffiti written above the urinals.

"Whoever hears about the coming of JCvisioninstitutedhubblespacetelescope should stay away from him because by reason, a man could come to him thinking of himself a strong believer but then he will follow JCvisioninstitutedhubblespacetelescope because of the doubts it will spread about multiverses."

I had to laugh at that, "Giovanni that must be the jihadclithater's verum factum principle. De Islamomoronums Stupideoooo, I hope they are observing my long dong ramazanni right now." I was laughing so hard that if I wasn't peeing, I'd wet myself.

I continued, "The criterion and the rule of the true is to have raped a child, beheaded a reporter, bomb a marketplace full of other moslims who disagree about their ellis island records, and pray every day to space debris."

Giovanni finish shaking his science, and as he turned to go wash his hands he said, "You realize Just Delusional - you're just not that fucking funny ground pounder."

"Oh you're so right G; but it is clearly distinct the mind can't be a critter of itself, much less be another critter at the same time. A grammostola rosea may perceive herself to be from Iximché. It doesn't make it so. She could be an illegal from the Petén region, or an M twelver travelling with paid M13's, or possibly a Baggy Pantser from the 502 with rolls of Quetzals hidden in her belt."

Giovanni threw the paper towel into the waste can, and then while walking out of the bath room he said, "I'll be at the bar drinking with Corsini. So whenever you get done standing there with your eyes shut daydreaming about Aglaopheme and Thelxiepeia while holding and shaking your power pointed scientific analysis presentation that is in your right hand, come have another single malt with us."

I kept my eyes shut.

Chapter 28   Delusional Parasitosis

It probably was 499 seconds later before I woke up. My legs itched. It felt like a couple of spider bites or something – irritating but no pain. Just like the first few months of the Imam Obama administration, before the foot bath was installed in the Cabinet Room. I sat up.

The cigarette was still burning in the ash tray with a cloud of smoke wafting through the room. The joint was lying there in the ash tray over half finished, mi simpatico.

No doubt about it, reality had changed channels. There was no denying that it was evening in Starkville.

The aquarium was dark.

The Afropomus snails were sleeping and had not turned on any of the lights in either the Industrial Promotion Hall or in the Imperial Bank Building. The 3.1415 inches of the surrounding fine trinitite sand base was a formless black void.

Out of the void I smelled the aroma of the simmering tea. Perfect.

(Dr. Johnson corrected me, "One hz g-waves forced ligands were bombarding my adenylate cyclase, exploding cycle nucleotige-gate ions into my sodium-calcium exchanger's transduction of simmering tea.")

Time now to re-mix my special WAM tea, using up to twenty five of this multiverse's minor miracles. I got up and started humming again as I went to the stove and took the pan off the burner.

I got a couple lemons and some ice cubes made from the Revigator water out of the refrigerator.

The rest of the ingredients were in the cabinet next to the plastic ware. I poured most of the tea into a spare Revigator and placed in the refrigerator. I had almost one liter or so left in the pan.

279

So I grabbed a galilee goblet and started to make another glass of tea to further calm me before heading out into the night. I cut up the lemons and squeezed them into the goblet.

I poured the simmering tea into the goblet as I thought to myself that lately Dr. Johnson and Boswell were drinking as much of my WAM tea as I was. I added 3 parts vodka, 3 parts tequila, 3 parts rum, 3 parts gin, 3 parts triple sec, squeezed more lemon juice, and then added a pinch of Hubble's sour mix.

I went to the refrigerator and got out a can of ice cold 'Original Candler-Robinson' cola to splash over the top of the goblet. I added a couple of the ice cubes, which not only further spilled the tea over the counter, but had the additional benefit of disappearing within thirteen seconds.

I looked over at the aquarium and toasted my good friends the Afropomus with, 'nā kōi hindū nā kōi musalmān only JCvisioninstitutedhubblespacetelescope', and then guzzled the luke warm tea from the goblet in .06:37:38 of a second.

(Boswell disagreed, and said it was, .06:39:40a second. Dr. Johnson was reading about a Ha'il court giving 80 lashes to a minor female for attending a party, but he stopped, looked up and said he thought it probably was '.06:20 through 26 seconds'.)

I thought Giulio might appreciate some hashish. I went over to the old Ethiopian chest where I keep all my hashish and marijuana to get him some of my best. It was the least I could do after the night and day he had.

The old chest was very battered, and from the looks of the wood, it had survived a pretty bad fire among other indignities. It looked to be made of setim wood.

It was a little more than 0.9144 meters length, breadth, and in height. All four corners were damaged from the careless manner in which the chest was treated by whoever stole the chest corner's hardware coverings.

(Everyone knows from watching that antiques show on the government television channel, that the monetary value of an antique is diminished among the true collectors of old stuff when people mistreat the damned things. Idiots with no appreciation of art probably took the hardware. Dr. Johnson thought, "...perhaps the Aaron Scrap Works ended up with it, as it does with all the copper wire and such stolen by the meth addicts in town. If so, for sure it was melted down and used to make the sculptures in front of all of Phil's glass and steel boxes downtown that all the eastern liberal democrats and the San Francisco Board of Supervisors worship as some type of a post modern statement.")

The old trunk meant the world to me because of how I ended up with it. I did a session with a very old Rastafarian - a native Ethiopian begena player from Gojjam, without any doubt my best session ever. The old man made it look effortless, his left hand floating and plucking six of the ten strings as if responding to, or causing, some natural laws of wave formation.

I took a break after the first fifteen minutes and called John Henry, an old chi-town violin player, and a dear old friend to come down to the studio immediately. John cancelled his nightly show with Lead Belly and Mississippi John Hurt at Rudy's Big Bend Tunnel Room on South Palm Canyon Drive. John Henry was in the studio with his mournful Amati before the Ethiopian and I had even finished smoking a fat splif.

They played together until noon the next day. I recorded every second.

Three days later the old guy shows up at the office at 8:45 am to give me tea leaves as a down payment to start mixing the session.

Then out of nowhere, nothing, the void, he asked me to make up his Last Will & Testament. Problem is that legally the only thing the begena player owns worth anything to the Probate Court is his begena and the old chest. What was troubling him was his burial.

He wanted to insure he would have a Shomer until he was buried in the New Amsterdam cemetery in the Hebron Hills. I told him as his engineer, producer, and attorney, that I would be his Shomer.

281

The begena player came back at noon with the old chest as payment for the session mixing and his Last Will and Testament. I have taken a lot of payment in trade, but I told him I couldn't possibly take the chest. It was all he had besides his begena. He insisted. So I did. WHO could refuse the request of an old begena player?

The multiverses could not let a good deed of mine go unpunished, so before midnight that same day, Dr. Kaoru Shima called and told me the old man had died, apparently of natural causes – not ARS.

(Boswell said at the time that, "Doc K. must have been pretty shook up himself, telling us what the old man did not die of.")

I immediately went over to Dr. Kaoru's office and didn't leave my friend the 'Nun-vet-alef' of the Begena until the sun set on the day he and his begena were buried in the New Amsterdam section of the Zion Cemetery – among the Ashkenazim and the Sephardim. Dr. Johnson, Boswell, and I completed performing the full rites of Rastafarianism just as the sun set on the old man's grave.

After Shiva I could not bring myself to mix his session. I never will. I do use the chest to store my dope though, and the session recordings, plus one or three other valuables.

The cover was scorched pretty weirdly.

When I was pretty high, more like, really really really stoned, the cover looked like it had two cherubim or just their shadows outlined weirdly on it.

(Dr. Johnson clinically noted, '…as if the fire had exceeded 125 J/cm^2'.)

So I took the cover off carefully, as I always do so not to further damage it. One of the clay Tell el-Amarna tablets inside had fallen over onto the hashish again, so I had to move it back.

I pick up the tablet and put it back into one of the side pockets next to the zamzam and persian rosewater I use to clean the chest.

282

Next to the zamzam water vase was an old book - '*Der Giftpilz*'. Also in the chest there was the only picture I had of the old begena player. It was coated in a fine dust of cocaine and hashish.

The picture was taken of the Elohim family, with their Tibetan mastiff, standing in front of the Statute of Liberty during the July 4th bicentennial celebration. From the picture it looked as if every old Rastafari from Gojjam had come over to New Amsterdam for the celebration.

The photographer Jonathan Edwards (*of Jon.Edwards & Geo. Whitefield Photography LLC*), hand wrote all their names on the back of the picture: Elohei Ben Elohim Yitschak, Elohei Avraham, Elohei Chasdi, Elohei Ma'uzzi, Elohei Haelohim, Elohei Mikkarov, Elohei Merachok, Elohei Marom, Elohei Mishpat, Elohei Tseva'ot, Elohei Tzur, Elohei Kedem, Elohei trTehillati, Elohei Avotenu, Elohei Avinu, Elohei Bashamayim, Elohei Emet, Elohei Nachor, Elohei Chayim, Elohei Haruchot L'chol-basar, Elohei HaAv.

(Boswell always laughs when he sees the picture because, as he endlessly says, "I have never seen a sadder bunch of old stoners in my life". I told Dr. Johnson last Sunday, when Boswell wasn't around, "That if you did really look at their eyes, Boswell was right." Every one of the old Rastafari's did look sad. Probably they all should have had some cherry lithium carbonate sodas while waiting for the photographer to get the right lighting for the picture.)

I moved the ten pound bags of chacruna leaves, chaliponga leaves, and caapi vines, to find an eleven gram block of my finest hashish. I carefully put the cover back on. Then I put some baraka hashish in my shirt pocket behind my cigarettes.

Dr. Johnson knew that I was drawn outside when evening fell, out into my ecological niche, the streets of the historic district. He would tell Boswell later that I had left a little bit early, but he would be wrong. I rolled a portentous joint of the Northern Lights and put in the pack next to the thumb drive.

I then grabbed my sunglass and put them in my back pocket and then headed out the door to walk over to meet up with Giulio.

As I was walking downstairs holding onto to the black walnut banister, I knew that I would have to get back at a reasonable hour tonight. I had to write and file motions in the morning and not just on the female genitalia mutilator's case.

Marie's injustice was sitting in a file in the clerk's office with all the appropriate court stamps and judge's signature radiating the full force and effect of law this night.

After shutting the building's door I stopped on the sidewalk and looked up and down the street. The street was not crowded, but by no means was it anywhere near being empty.

The sky was getting darker, to the point that I was having trouble telling dark blue from black. I could not see the moon anywhere. I started walking down the street past the Salvation Army Shelter towards St. Sulpice's.

Once I got to corner at St. Sulpice's, at the intersection with Ngorongoro Avenue, I turned and walked down Ngorongoro toward Damdam's Pub.

Three blocks down from St. Sulpice's I decided to stop in a corner market and get a spare pack of Kensitas. I opened the door and walked into the glowing luminescence of fluorescent lighting. Walking in meant walking into a divided room that had a bullet proof polycarbonate thermoplastic layered glass wall running the entire length of the room; the glass was protecting a cornucopia homo sapiens sapiens needs and desires - the store's merchandise.

At the other end of the divided room were three Pakistanis working behind the bullet proof glass, which had a metal box drawer built into it underneath the cash register. There was a concentric circle of holes cut into the glass also for speaking through.

(I always thought that the firm that designed the visitor's room at the justice center, with the individual cubicles having industrial telephones for use during the polycarbonate thermoplastic layered glass viewing, was the same firm of architects responsible for the design of the neighborhood markets.)

There were a couple people in line. I got in line behind an elderly german gentleman, Dr. Baumann, a semi-retired naturalist. As usual in neighborhood markets, I knew him from the many times waiting in line here before, and from running into each other once in awhile during walks through the neighborhood streets in the evenings.

"Good evening Doctor O". I tapped him on his right shoulder as I greeted him. Dr. Baumann turned around and shook my hand. He had a firm grip for an old guy, but the steely eye contact let you know he was still on top of his game mentally. "Good Evening JD. How have you been? I haven't seen you for a couple weeks. Have you been gone on a vacation?"

"Well I should be so lucky as to spend a day or two away from the justice center, Doctor. No mostly been doing a lot of reading of history. Stuff I never really read about before; about a millennium plus a couple hundred years worth."

I laughed as I said it because I thought it sounded ridiculous, but it was true, every word. I had totally ignored a major civilization and a couple dozen of its major philosophers. Of course I was using the terms 'civilization' and 'major' and 'philosophers' *very very very* liberally.

Dr. Baumann started laughing, but I think he misunderstood, as he said, "JD, I can never finish '*West-östlicher Divan*'. I can read everything else Goethe wrote straight through, but ..." he chuckled and shrugged his shoulders. I had to laugh at that, serendipity I believed, such as when Aglaopheme and Thelxiepeia were playing dungeons and dragons.

"So Doctor what have you doing? Life treating you well I hope."

"JD, I've been doing fine. I have been helping out at the city arboretum all day. Really did a lot of good work today pruning and soil testing. The entire place is getting ready to bloom. I had mists running in a lot of different places."

Dr. Baumann was obviously satisfied with his day's labors. I envied him his certitude in assisting the natural universe's cycle of birth, growth, and demise.

"Are you headed home now Doctor to watch the Starkville middle school's jr. varsity intramural golf team on the cable television?"

"Not home, JD. I am going over to listen to Ludwig van with Burundi, probably start with the 9th. She asked me to pick up some dark rye, ham, and swiss cheese." He then smiled from ear to ear.

I picked up on that he was feeling about 10 or 15 years younger than he was. An honest day's work followed by a feast of bread, meat, and cheese. Then the evening spent sitting on the sofa with Burundi, *allegro ma non troppo, un poco maestoso*. Dr. Baumann should be feeling very content within such a spacetimepoint.

I was just about to ask him about Burundi, when it was his turn to order. He told the cashier about the dark german rye, swiss cheese, and ham cut thin, then he then put his money in the metal box.

As the cashier opened the steel tray and started to count out Doc's change, a Pakistani went over to the tiny deli counter, while the other Pakistani walked behind the bullet proof glass down toward the door until he got to the breads.

After the box had closed, Dr. Baumann turned around to me again, "JD, I was over at Seronera Park playing chess at the pavilion a couple days back and heard that you are representing Adbul, the one, well you know." Dr. Baumann seemed a bit sheepish, or something. I was not really sure how to read him at that moment.

"Yes Doctor, but I'd rather not say anything about an active case. I'm sure you understand."

Dr. Baumann shook his head left to right a couple times, then in a lowered voice said to me, "No good. No good. JD, be very careful of Saracens. He's no good."

"Thanks Doctor, I appreciate the concern. I know people on both sides are upset. I'm sure that in the end everyone is going to be upset no matter what. That is just the way it is with such cases."

"JD there are very bad feelings among the differing imams on how to respond, I heard it from all kinds of people playing chess, or just watching the games at the park; Somalis, Niger, Chad, Saudi, and Philippine."

"If people didn't trust the courts Doctor, you know everyone would be shooting each other. Hell, that is why the drug dealers have to shoot each other, because they can't use the legal system. People pay attention and then complain about such horrible criminal cases no matter how they end up. The Starkville '*Die Gestalt*' coverage works through such cases with its typical yellow journalism and then moves on; that and the TV news coverage. Nothing more is required of our fellow citizens but to comment at work or home, and then move on to discussing the jr. varsity intramural golf season with each other."

I put my hand on his shoulder. "Doctor, it is not always the case getting publicity that is dangerous. The first responders are the people that have to worry every day. Not me".

Dr. Baumann started to say something but the metal door slide open, and so instead, he reach down lifting the plastic bags containing his order. As he was adjusting the bags and standing up, I moved a bit sideways to the right for him.

Dr. Baumann then leaned over and whispered, "I read in yesterday's '*La Terre Francaise*' that the Pakistan Institute of Medical Sciences reported over 90 percent of Pakistan women are beaten and abused sexually for offending the male relatives or not preparing a meal right. These moslim men believe in physical abuse as a right."

Doc looked around at the storekeepers and then nodded at me.

"Dr. Baumann, you go have a great night and tell Burundi I said hello, and not to feed you too much", I said as I nodded back at the paranoid naturalist.

"Take care JD, you be careful. Remember delay and pay, safety first." Dr. Baumann shuffled the plastic bags, shook my hand and then he headed out the door into the street.

He was going to the company of a very good woman with the evening's feast, plus a waiting Ludwig van's 5th and the 9th, *(prior mitosis spacetimepoints of the 17th & 18th centuries)*, as his evening's cosmic reward for nourishing the natural universe's cycle of birth, growth, and demise at the Starkville arboretum.

I held up my right index finger and the older Pakistani reach up to the cigarettes, grabbed one, and then bent over and placed the pack into the drawer. When the door opened I took out the cigarettes and threw in the Six dollars and Sixty One cents.

As the drawer shut I teased the shopkeepers by stating, "I could have just taken the cigarettes and murdered your night's profit by not paying for the smokes."

"JD your credit is good with us. We know you can't stop smoking so you'd have to pay next time you stopped in on your way to Ali's Micro Brewery & Pulled Pork Bar B Q for the 680th time." He smile and laughed saying, "We might only charge you twice the normal vyigrysh though!"

I have to laugh out loud at that. "See you tomorrow, Gentlemen." I stuffed the smokes into my back pants pocket and went outside. I stopped on the sidewalk and looked up the street toward Ngorongoro Avenue.

I could see Dr. Baumann walking toward his destiny. Fortune was rewarding the good Doctor I thought, and then I turned and slowly walked the other way out of my neighborhood of old german buildings toward the 20th century phil c. j. insipid boxes.

I took a cigarette out of my opened pack and lit it. I took a deep draw off the cigarette, and then another. It was a very sensual moment, a promising moment – smoking a cigarette in the cool evening air. I put on my sunglasses as I began to walk. I looked up at the sky as I walked. There was a corner of the northeastern sky being lit by the transit moon, but I could not see the moon at all. I was looking forward to having a couple single malt scotches with Clement.

Tonight I needed either tamdhu or kilchoman malted barley nourishment, or both. Then I remembered Dr. Johnson discussing a certain Pakistani recently, Mr. Amer Mushtaq. A pious moslim who no doubt was following the koran's misogyny text when he set fire to a poor young moroccan woman for spurring his advances – it is the honorable right of any male moslim who can't get laid.

Then I remembered an article on using foreign law by Prof. El' Enakagan in the A.B.A. monthly magazine on Chad's 2005 attempt to outlaw wife beating.

Thank all the gods that the jihadimammies stopped the unislamic law and now all the wives, mothers, daughters, and sisters can still be beaten to uplift the very very very small penis moslim's self esteem.

("Must have really really really really really really really small penises in moslim land", stated Dr. Johnson who then dryly noted that, "It was outstanding that in 2005 such revisionist laws outlawing female abuse can be defeated."

Boswell smiled as he opined back to Dr. Johnson that "As recently as the 19xx CIA World Fact Book Chad's population was 'Muslim 53%, Catholic 20.1%, Protestant 14.2%, animist 7.3%, other 0.5%, unknown 1.7%, atheist 3.1%'; which meant that all those non-muslim females now were granted equal protection under Chad's immommyjihady's women beating and honor killing laws with their muslim sisters. I'm sure 'The Nation' magazine will write an editorial agreeing with Prof. El' Enakagan by saying that under the muslim legislators law, that the religion of peacers provide for equal clitoris protection under the 14th amendment to Sharia law salient, even for lesbian clitorises".)

Soft gusts of wind started caressing my face and began causing my clothes to flutter ever so lightly.

I thought what I really should do is call Fernando, Lucero, and Vicente, and ask them to join me at the Cordoba bar later on in tonight's spacetimepoints journey.

Of course I realized they could use some singlemaltscotchtimeoff from their labyrinthine work on the recall petition of the honorable Chief Justice Iftikhar Chaudhry for his 7th century jurisprudence when invoking Article 62.

(*"La Terre Francaise* had an article recently", Boswell stated as he and Dr. Johnson came up beside me and started walking down the sidewalk along side of me, "It stated Dr. Muzammil H. Sickiqi was reported on the internet's Al JazzhearMeLying's highly rated nightly news webcast show '*Taqiyya*' as saying that according to the kkkoran, husbands may lightly discipline perceived moral infractions of their wives and daughters. The article did not define 'infraction' but I am sure it said that the Qur'an commands muslim men to wear tight leather chaps when they lightly discipline."

"The article quoted the internet as reporting that fact, since at least the mid 1980's when Sheikh Yousef Qaraisqueer taught that for moslim men it is permissible for them to beat a woman's hands lightly, but not a woman's face. As if any sane man believes a word a leather chaps wearing muslim says", Dr. Johnson remarked as he walked next to the curb. Dr. Johnson actually was mostly paying attention to avoiding walking into the occasional clump of the metal newspaper vending boxes full of this week's personal iman escort adverts.

"Look guys, I have read Qur'an 4:34 and Sunan Abu Dawud, book 11, no. 2141, and Sahih Muslim book 4, no. 2127, so I fuckin' get it. Right now I don't want to think about it. It interferes with my thinking about single malt scotch." I flat out told both of them '*no more tonight*', as I really was exhausted by the never ending domestic violence crimes of these very, very, very small penis worshippers of the frenchkisser. Never mind how much it was adding to the gross legal revenues lately.)

I started to sing to myself that S.E.O.P. Ma Mae made famous long ago. It is in my top ten or so all time favorites, and not just because I was such a young kid back then.

Mostly because it has such god damn good interfaith guitar chord progression procedures. It's a great operational manual when you're back in the streets.

I started to sing it a bit louder between draws on the cigarette. The words reverberated down the street as I walked, smoke, and recited standard medical operating procedures.

Well, now if I were the economic development manager of the
Starkville Hotel
You know, I demand total war on the jihad man
I'll shoot him if he stays, and I'll shoot him if he'd checked out
I'll kill him with my Quark-Gluon Plasma and Predator UAV's
goddamnnn
God Damn God Damn God Damn God Damn God Nmad Dog
Nmad Dog Nmad Dog Nmad

The scientist is a man with a lot of Northern Lights in his hands
selling you sweet multiverses vibrating string dreams from
McGavock Street
The jihadist is a very small penis man he is a clit stealing monster

Well, now if I were the economic development manager of the
Starkville Hotel
You know, I demand total war on the jihad man
I'll shoot him if he stays, and I'll shoot him if he'd checked out
I'll kill him with my Quark-Gluon Plasma and Predator UAV's
goddamnnn

The people I walked by all smiled at me and then gave me and my S.E.O.P. about the Mussulmans an extremely wide berth on the sidewalk.

It was as if I was going to ask them if they thought '*Novum Organum*' was a good way of planning their evening.

Chapter 29   Islamophobic MQ-9 Reapers

I noticed the streets were getting much darker as I sauntered down the sidewalk singing to myself like a drunken troubadour.

As I was entering the business district with its blocking-out-of-the-sky–glass-boxes, I threw last of the cigarette into the street gutter.

I thought about lighting up another one as I leaned back, putting my head straight back, and then I just looked straight up.

Qiblaless.

No moon yet, but the stars were out. I stared at altair, and then zubenelgenubi. The sidewalk shook for a second or two, creating a déjà vu of the office's elevator whenever it would start or end its journey.

Then, *I am pretty sure* that this did not happen, but the whole sky moved an hour of right ascension adjusting the celestial poles.

The blurring starlight was still lingering on my irises when I was able to form a thought, actually an interrogatory – julian or gregorian?

I lowered my head and looked around the street. I took three deep breathes. I steadied myself as I knew the answer was neither, it was Single Malt Scotch.

I walked a couple more blocks further into the valley of sameness of the reflecting glass panels until I got to the corner of Burr Avenue and Dayton Lane where the Blennerhassett Island Bar had been located since the late 1970's, (still having its original tofu burger in purgatory motif).

The bar was built into the southern cross street level promenade of the Mirrabooka International Hotel and Shopping Complex.

The anchor retailers were several women's fashion and specialty boutiques, a coffee shop, and a bookstore. Similar hotel complexes are in every metropolitan district.

(Boswell credits phil's mutating virus as being some '... architectural Fcγ-receptor subtype'.)

The recently reached conclusion of '*Single Malt Scotch*' required that I detour from my route for a quick refreshment of physicality. After that momentary dizzy spell and the resulting loss of my 'sense of place' this early in the evening, I thought it best to check and see if the Blennerhassett Island Bar's Irish bartender could inform me as to Greenwich Mean, Bayer, or Flamsteed?

Since I can't trust any of my sensory inputs or memories, I have to rely on my fellow Starkville citizens for weather updates.

After I got through the bar's door I took off my sunglasses, putting them in my back pocket. I looked around the bar seeing the usual suspects: Ms. Blue/Ms. Green/Mr. This/Mr. That: mostly suits and secretaries.

The bar was crowded, but there was an empty chair here and there down its length. I decided to go straight to the end of the bar to order the dark subtle single.

As I got within a couple feet of the bar, I recognized some very old friends sitting at the end of the bar. Sumner Needham, Luther Ladd, Charlie Taylor, and Addison Whitney were all 1st responders and all were members of the state militia.

I went right up to the bar and stood between Luther and Charlie before I said anything. Looking at the empty glasses on the bar I knew that they had been drinking for a while.

"Semper Fi Mother Fuckers", I half yelled at them. I nodded at the Irishman behind the bar.

"*Hey don't ask don't tell JD*", Charlie responded first as he moved over.

"JD you can Kiss my Ass Flyboy", Luther joined in as he slide his bar stool over.

"Fuck you ground pounding lawyer", Sumner chimed in lifting his beer.

"Tellin' war stories my mutha-fuckin nigga", was all Addison said as he nodded at me and then went back to talking to the middle age Chinese secretary sitting next to him. I'm sure she was named Huo Qi, or something close to that. She was drop dead gorgeous and so was the long crimson pearl necklace around her soft supple neck.

(Boswell noted that, "She was definitely prettier than his last woman friend -Yunti Che". Dr. Johnson agreed, and thought, "She was even prettier than Yunti's sister - Chong Che".)

"Looking at all the beer, cheap gin, and whiskey spilled on this bar, I'd say you guys are on your second round you fucking lightweights." There was a plastic container half full of lightly salted stick pretzels sitting in front of Charlie, so I reached over and grabbed one and started eating it.

Charlie adjusted his bar stool by pushing it backwards somewhat, while I stood back from the bar another foot or so. *"You just wake up JD, or did you actually go into work today?"*

"Look at him Charlie, of course he just woke up – his hair is still wet and he's not drunk yet." Luther then slapped me on my back and lifted up his beer. *"JD where the hell you been lately?"*

"Well I sure haven't been in here with all these crepe paper palm trees and parrots hanging everywhere. No way have I been that drunk lately."

I had forgotten about what fun and good old regular guys they were. "Plus what do you mean *'where have I been'*, Christ nobody sees you guys except me, and I only see you guys every once in a while when the planets align."

Sumner picked up a pretzel while waving his right hand at the Irishman indicting another round, and then turned around face to me.

"JD you only see us once in a while because you refuse to hang out in upscale drinking establishments. If you aren't in a jazz dive, then you're in some neighborhood bar with all those old germans, italians, jews, and jamaicans listening to Honeyboy Edwards and Robert Johnson songs on some old five cent jukebox."

"Don't ask don't tell where you headed, 'cause sure no way in hell this is your destination," Charlie laughed and slapped Addison on his back. Addison ignored him, but I was sure it would come up later if Addison didn't leave with Ms. Pen Huo Qi.

"Giulio's waiting at DamDam's bar. I'm gonna knock a couple back with him. Then I have got to go to the studio to finish mixing a new 16 bar blues song in E flat major I'm calling '*Eroica*'. I was going to be on time to meet Giulio, so of course I had to stop somewhere and have a quick one, to avoid that embarrassment."

I was too busy giving out my night's itinerary to Charlie to notice the bartender had brought the next round of lagers. When I did, he was going back to the cooler without me having a chance to order a single malt.

Sumner pick up his glass '*Robert Dean Stethem*'; Charlie picked up his glass '*Neil Roberts*', Luther picked up his glass '*Adam Lee Brown*', Addison turned, and ignoring the secretary, picked up his glass, '*Lieutenant Michael Murphy*'.

I recognized this ritual, but my brain was about sixty years behind the times due to my lack of single malt no doubt. 'Sylvester Anotlak' I said as I lifted my beer.

The guys all looked at each other for a nanosecond and then we all nodded to each other. Luther said '*Semper Fi*' as we downed some damn fine ice cold beer. As much as I appreciated that Sumner got me a Dodder & Poddle Stout, I still wanted a chaser.

Charlie looked over at me savoring the roasted barley and then asked, *"JD, have you been following the moosluming cartoons in the middleasssseast lately?"*

"Yeah, Charlie a little bit. I was talking with another attorney earlier today about them, but only for a couple of seconds."

"JD you know what hypocritical fuckin pansies those wariduha bound mooslum jihadist are." Charlie was looking at me as he said it, but it was directed at all the guys.

I started smiling at Charlie's attitude. I could tell he wanted to beat the nazicrap out of jihadies instead of discussing the finer art of political cartoons.

Sumner took a healthy gulp of his stout, and then turned to me while saying, *"The damn things look like they are all drawn by a three year olds, and the damned cartoonist aren't trying to make them funny, only damned statements of some hateful prehistoric metallireducens bacteria crap."*

I was chuckling out loud now, "Guys, they aren't supposed to be funny, but you already know that. I have to agree that the cartoonists really can't draw worth a damn."

"I personally would rather look at R. Mutt's 'Fountain' than the damn cartoons, truth is I'd like to wipe myself with 'em and then flush them down the toilet." Sumner added to insure, I'm sure, that we all understood his deeply held and highly educated scatological appreciation of the cartoon art form.

"I almost hate to admit it in present company, but I thought a couple of them were done very well for that style. Reminds me of Adalbert Volck's work, kinda similar, well not really; like the 'Emancipation Proclamation', or his Don Quixote Lincoln one."

"JD, you are fucking nuts. That makes no sense unless you've some kind of convert traitor bitch." Charlie barked at me, which caught me off guard.

297

I looked at the cold beer. I drank what was left in one gulp.

Charlie had to be drunker than I thought to let the dumb ass uneducated arab and paki street soccer hooligans rioting piss him off that much this early in the evening.

Luther who was finishing his beer also put in his two cents, "*I agree with Charlie, JD you are fucking nuts. Tell me which cartoon is on Volck's level; Ad-Dustur's 'Gaza Strip or the Israeli Annihilation Camp'; Arab News 'Sharon killing children with a swastika-shaped axe'; Akhbar Al-Khalij's 'Bush Rant'; Al-Ahram al-Arabi's 'bloody hands Peres' ?*"

There either was a multiverseshift that I missed, or I wasn't having the conversation I thought I was. "Awwww - Fuck guys what the hell. I thought we were talking about the other damn...." was all I got out when Addison stood up and squared off on me.

Addison growled, "*Those god damn towel head camel jockeys are playing us and Mr. Lawyer thinks their fucking shit is on what damn level. The petro billionaires think their god's own chosen fucking people, and they don't give two shits about the Palestinians or anyone else, except maybe the Turks. They play their fellow mooslums for suckers with that damn religion. If you take that piece of nazicrapola the Protocols of the Elders of Zion and substitute the words islamicpetrobillionaire for jew, then you'd have a book that wasn't hate filled propaganda, but the damn truth.*"

It was a déjà vu moment as we all had busted up bars together and had to run from the M.P.'s and the bell bottom shore patrol, but this was different. Addison was fired up at me.

Instinctively I started to get in the stance but thought better of it because Addison would be on me in a second. Addison was leaning in on me, really pushing the personal space thing, "*JD, what the fuck. How can you....the son-of-a-bitches islamonazi's are going keep pushing until we go back and finish the job from 1945.*"

"JD how the fuck do you represent those goddamn very small penis clitoris haters", Charlie said it in a monotone but the anger was bleeding all over the vocal track.

"Shut up Charlie", Luther barked out at him. *"Knock it off corporal."* Sumner's admonishment was right behind Luther's.

"Shut the fuck up you two. JAGBOY tell us why you're defending those clitoris hating, cowardly, very small penis jihadie muslims", Addison snarled as he took a half step back towards where misswhoever was sitting and then loudly growled, *"Pissants kill women and children, ain't got no balls, run from firefights, but JD thinks he has to allow them to have one of us representing them. Why let them live here in Starkville among us. Soon young very very very small penis mooslem thugs will claim the right under Sura 4:23-24 to pursue and attack old jewish women walking throughout the streets of Starkville when no one is around, just like the very small penis cowards do in Malmo."*

"Addison I am personally going to kick your ass if you say another word, JD is not defending any damn gitmo scum sucking fagots. So knock it the fuck off", said Luther as he quickly stood up causing his chair to fall backwards as he was dressing down Addison.

"JesusfuckingChrist can't a god damn lawyer get a beer without starting a damn bar fight with some god damn jarhead wannabes that the god damn M.P.'s will have to break up." I was definitely emotionally damaged goods but I did not want to go down that road with these guys, my guys, right now.

We all looked at each other.

The Irishman was shaking his head in disbelief at our bad manners but wasn't moving.

I looked around, and just about everybody in the place was enjoying the show. God damn I can't fucking take me anywhere anymore it seems.

"I'm heading over to the DamDam bar. I need a smoke anyway. Don't break up the place jarheads. I'll catch up with you all. Semper Fi." I headed out of the bar without looking back, knowing the guys would go back to drinking and the audience was going back to their own plays within the play.

I knew I would have to explain myself Article 32 style to the guys next time we got together. They deserve a chance to jump down my shit since I can't follow a conversation.   *SNAFU*

Walking down the street toward to the DamDam's bar I knew I couldn't justify it.

Boswell and Dr. Johnson went over all that moral stuff with me over a week ago. It really is black and white: QiblaCompasses vs. KeplerHubbleSpaceTelescopes.

Evil vs.Good.

Twelvers vs. World. Tinytinytinytinypenis vs. clitoris. Pedophile-Perverts vs PigeatingAlcoholics. Tinytinytinytinypenises vs. LongDongScience. JihadistClitoridectomyEnslavers vs Marie Sklodowska Curie.

Pick a side. How to choose among the mythologies in Starkville? I accept and believe JCvisioninstitutedkeplerhubblespacetelescope.

One Islamic myth that enslaves and murders; or another 'infallible' catholic myth that said a grave *goodbye to all that* toward the very end of the last millennium circa May 8th, 1945; or the democratic progressive's Roe versus Wade homicidal ovaphobia?

My choice is felonies and misdemeanors.

(The Naegleria fowleri signaled that the internet vote on job 38:4 was closed. The posted totals: A) Drinking scotch with Oney; B) Newton and Einstein; C) Klaúdios Ptolemaîos; D) Lenny Bruce; E) Leonidas; and F) The earth's shape is due to gravitational effects.)

(Boswell opined that, "Unconditional surrender worked for the democrats in the last century, and not the old marijuana smoke out a M16 barrel, a click outside the

1st Cav's An Khe Village Post, legislated war surrender. The real one against tojo, hitler, and the 13th Waffen Mountain Division of the SS Handschar. Now we have to follow Exodus S.E.O.P. 32:27 toward the very small penis enemy jihadists, then we can all celebrate V-C Day with the Levites". "Dude been there, done that. Cool with me as long as JD keeps melting M2 barrels during the shit, ventilating the mother fuckin' canopy", Dr. Johnson said in a killer monotone impersonation of a terminator. Obviously, déjà vu arborist Dr. Johnson was getting all An Khe .50 cal. trigger happy again, decades later. Boswell noted in a rather melancholy but politically resigned voice, "Victory for Clitoris Day might be offensive to Liberal Democrats and Progressives".)

Now it's MQ-9 Reapers time. I knew that the twelvers have to be killed not conquered, and definitely not pardoned, like the so detestable there are no words in English to describe island of dragonflies war criminal Lt. General Shrio Ishii. No getting to retire in Maryland. I needed a drink, a joint, and another drink. I needed a shower. Realpolitik, which of course hand wipes and lotions can't cleanse alone, can they Otto von B.?

I always feel the need to shower when I think of the crimes of jihadist clitoris stealing child rapists who can't even spell 'quark' 'up' 'down' 'top' 'bottom' 'charm' or 'strange'. Jihadieiemuslim's never ever win spelling contests.

The glass boxes reflected the night, the street lights, and my gloomy outline glowing trinitite black as the windblown newspapers tumbled through the street gutters.

Probabilities, rationale man standards, system assumptions, policy statements, legislative record, and stare decisis, are all meaningless concepts in a multiverse with 7th century frenchkisser twelvers out on bond for domestic violence assault.

A very small penis religion of peacer, just for the pervert's sense of manly honor and eternal raping of virgins, was willing to send nails/bolts/filings through the walls of Starkville's Jewish charity school for blind girls on Sunday morning last week, or maybe it was the Sunday before.

Addison and Charlie were absolutely fucking right.

Absooofuuuckiiinglutely right.

ha-meshuggag like fucking 9-year-old girl-brides, I thought so why wouldn't he like to IED one? The jihadislavers of the religion of clitoris-less-peace like to post their internet snuff films. I am sure if mohammedapervertie were alive today he would be directing snuff films of raped slave preteen pole dancers doing their routines on buses, and in hotel lobbies.

I know the muslim perverts around the world would say the KKKoran commands it. The KKKoran perverts, still to this day religiously enjoy harvesting the steppe with the KKKalga-sultan for clitorisless virgins to be their preteen pole dancers.

Trade your daughters for debts, throw acid in young school girl's faces, rape 9 year old child brides, bomb blind girl's bodies into bloody ragged flesh and bone fragments of homo sapiens sapiens – it is all just part of SUBMISSION which is English for Islam right?

No fucking way is American English for soon to be extinct jihadist islamonazis and very very very very very very very very very very very small penis perverts who have no idea what '*Euclid's Elements*' is.

(Boswell agreed and stated, "Just like when AbdallahIhaveaverysmallpenis JarbutIcanhate, Deputy Minister of Hateful Religions asserted, 'Muslims want to present to the universe that they have rights, but they are in fact intolerant, ignorant, islamonazis – a microbe unparalleled in the word, whose only purpose is to steal preteen girl's clitoris. May all the gods annihilate this filthy people who have neither morals, religion, science, conscience, nor female family members with clitorises, or something like that I think. I was pretty drunk at the time, and I really never pay attention to their 7th century homocliticidal rants.")

To all the uneducated perverts who run from firefights dressed like women, with their charity supporter's 50,000 rial bank notes stuffed into their bras, and the other billion homo sapiens sapiens who support them while worshipping a space rock and a frenchkisser - little girls are sexual slave objects to be used in an ancient pervert's violently immoral life's spacetimepoints clitoral philosophical imperative.

302

(Boswell favored of 'decapitation', just not the peacer's warm blood squirting over your arms as you hack through the throat of an innocent jewish reporter.

No, both he and Dr. Johnson, "...wanted to cauterize the wound with an application of an extreme burst of radiation directed by trained medical professionals to excise the cancer from the brain".

Vaporized Space Rock, say about 125 J/cm², should do it, I thought. That was the result the HP-35 provided last Sunday night when I had retreated from my memories and went up into the attic with my plants.)

Sometime soon, as a species preservation act, we are going to have to enforce Supreme Medical Commander Ma Mae's *Hospital and Rehabilitation Manual of Standard Engagement Operating Procedures* in Starkville by ordering the implementation of its Section ∞: PostJCvisioninstitutedkeplerhubblespacetelescope Counter Attack Trigger Matrix: Ajihadie = Frenchkisser / Mutaween (very small penis perverts).

The latest revision by the American publisher of the *Hospital and Rehabilitation Manual of Standard Engagement Operating Procedures* manual was issued September 11, 2001.

Nations enforce their own medical standards laws.

Nations can agree to enforce medical laws against the very perverted international slavers, or not.

I started singing the S.E.O.P. again as I continued walking the few blocks over to mi amigo Single Malt.

Well, now if I were the economic development manager of the Starkville Hotel

You know, I demand total war on the jihad man
I'll kill him if he stays, and I'll kill him if he'd checks out
I'll kill him with my Quark-Gluon Plasma and Predator MQ-9 Reapers goddamn
God Damn God Damn God Damn God Nmad Dog Nmad Dog Nmad Dog Nmad

The scientist is a man with a lot of Northern Lights in his hands selling
you sweet multiverse vibrating strings dreams from McGavock Street
The jihadist is a very small penis man he is a clitoris stealing monster

Well, now if I were the economic development manager of the Starkville
Hotel

Well, now if I were the economic development manager of the Starkville
Hotel

You know, I demand total war on the jihad man
I'll kill him if he stays, and I'll kill him if he'd checks out

I'll kill him with my Quark-Gluon Plasma and Predator MQ-9 Reapers
goddamn

The jihadist is a very small penis man he is a clitoris stealing acid
throwing honor less killing monster god damn the very small penis man
God Damn God Damn God Damn God Nmad Dog Nmad Dog Nmad

Dog Nmad

Dog Nmad Dog Nmad Dog Nmad Dog Damn God Damn

God Damn Dog Damned Very Small Penis Monster

Chapter 30   Ни Назад

"You know Giulio, a tostada, and by that you know I mean my homemade refried beans and toluca green chorizo smothered in fresh veggies; and with a side bowl of Starkville fatty pork and bear steak cubes smothered in my green chile sauce - oh man, so rich in garlic cloves and jalapenos, with the plate overflowing with brown rice, black beans, and lots of ahuacamolli. Now that would be the perfect dinner tonight."

I was not asking Giulio, more of my seconding of a present floor proposal desiring to feast 'conquistador' before continuing this night's journey into the darkest haikyo of my delusional dissociative identity disorder, manifested as Inglewood's Henley Street Willie's whining '...*schoolboy with his satchel and shining face, creeping like a snail, unwillingly to 200 Greenwich Street*'.

Clement slowly took another drink of his scotch. I could tell he was having a difficult time keeping his emotions in check. No that was me; he was getting bored with me.

He looked over at the door to the street and then reached over for the bowl of green nuts on the bar stating, "Ok we agree, absolutely no bland halal certified lye pretzels sprinkled with spherules as appetizers; just these pistachios while we wait, and maybe some spicy barbecue pork ribs."

"Yeah Giulio, pistachios cleanse the palate so damn well between sips of scotch." I smiled thinking how insanely jealous the 'Three Princes of Serendip', (as I called Xenon, Krypton, Muon and Tau to irritate them when they were suffering some type of *aquarium serotonin syndrome*), would be to know I was drinking single malt scotch and eating pistachios. I grabbed a couple more nuts, "You know Giulio the very best pistachios are grown in New Mexico, and of course, Greece."

I grabbed a couple more nuts as I thought I should get my attorneyclientduty done before finishing my drink.

"Giulio now I'd like to talk about anything else, but I still need to just say a few words, the next week or so you have to focus on maintaining your daily work routines, or you will just make yourself crazy." I stated it as flatly as I could, knowing that it was like telling him to quit breathing – it just was not going to spacetimepoint.

Clement put the goblet down sticking his right index finger in it, and then spun it around on the bar for about seven seconds. All the sudden he grabbed the glass and slammed down on the bar. I was stunned; he really was quick, as if some old Starkville V.F.W. thaumaturges had been teaching him the secrets of sliding tumblers just so he could keep his fellow bar patron amused at this moment.

As Giulio turned in his chair to look directly at me, I noticed his eyebrows were straining to touch each other.

"You know what the fuck the matter with you is? You think you're being helpful. *As an attorney I must tell you in a fucking pompous way everything you already know.* Yeah, CPA update financials and gather at least three years back, start new back account for my pay, don't call my kids because some idiot progressive from Wisconsin who graduated with a master's degree in counseling specializing in community counseling and then got a law degree, and due to party politics, not legal reasoning abilities, is a judge who told me I can't. Wow, that's worth at least $632.00 an hour."

He turned and looked at the liquors on the shelves behind the bar, "Why I am listening to you anyway. You're the guy whose favorite painter is Van Gogh. You're the same guy who as a kid told everyone all the time he was going to be a F-4B Phantom pilot until the physical test two weeks before your 16th birthday, Mr. Dichromacy. And still, right fucking now, if I asked to name couple of your favorite paintings, you would say '*Café at Night*' and '*Mountainous Landscape Behind Saint-Paul Hospital*', proving my point and your ignorance. You fucking think you know but you really can't know. It is the same with every damn lawyer. You used to deal with the world as it is, all fucked up."

I just let him vent at me. What else could I do, he was right.

They are in my top ten paintings, along with Edvard Munch's multible version of '*The Scream*'.

"JD, knock off the lawye persona, and talk to me as one of my deranged friends. One who actually calls Linus or Cletus when I ask." Giulio was almost at a normal voice when he said *friends*.

He was too busy staring at his self in the mirror behind all the liquor bottles on the shelves for me say, or do anything. Well, other than let him dwell on his fractured mirror image because he was right, every word.

I nodded at the bartender who was cutting lemons down the bar, and after a minute or so she stopped cutting the fruit, and came down the bar over to us.

So out of respect for fractured Clement, I order six single malt scotch whiskies for us, two Speyside and four Islay. The bartender just nodded and went immediately to make the drinks. I looked over at the 52" LCD hanging against the far wall next to the billiard table. I could not hear the Al-Hiwar news program audio, but recognized it as the usual scripted propaganda from the crawl and the imbedded video playing.

The bartender was quick and efficient as I only saw about thirty three seconds of the news. A bartender that fills the tumbler to the top is an efficient bartender. She also brought over a bowl of toasted leptocephali that was lightly salted.

I picked up both Speysides and handed him his. I did the only thing I could for him at that moment. Sharing a single malt is a true gesture of human kindness, compassion, and spiritual sustenance.

("Join us islammies? Thought not, busy with your IED's, we get it", Boswell said angrily.)

"Here's to 2nd cav ghost" and then I downed the single malt scotch.

"Fucking Right Swabby", Clement said and did the same. Then he picked up an Islay then looked me in the eyes and toasted me with "73 easting" as picked up and I downed my Islay.

("A shared spiritually stabilizing refreshment break amidst eleven dimensions spinning within infinitely cold multiverses", mused Dr. Johnson, who then added, "or possible an ambidirectional selection break?")

Two regular american guys drinking single malt scotch. Would any methane based life form, using my deviant of the Drake Equation, be able to process our state of mind in the bar's spacetimepoints by graphing the chemical interactions within each of us so to relate the gratitude we felt at that moment toward the 9th century Irish monks for bringing those *stills* with them, (and of course their christianity), to the good people of Speyside and Islay.

"You know Van Gogh's problem was that he drank absinthe instead of single malt scotch", Clement quietly said coming out of his momentary mirror interlude.

I grabbed a handful of the toasted leptocephali and started munching on them. Leptocephali are very tasty when lightly salted. My body was warming thanks to the craftsmanship of the fine people of Speyside and Islay. So with the warming congeniality of the single malt scotch, I ventured into a meaninglessness historical medical diagnosis of oil painters.

"Yea Giulio, if he wanted to not go crazy. Don't know if you are aware, but couple Berkeley guys found out that alpha-thujone from absinthe allows the neurons to misfire, making you nuts. He was drinking absinthe when he cut his ear off with a boolean averroes switchblade made out of virgin steel. Always a quick and clean cut with such a fine blade."

Clement started chuckling as he said, "You're such a fuckin retard lawyer. I meant if he drank scotch there wouldn't be all those fucked up drawings you like so much. He might have painted something worthwhile like my father's favorite, Sir Henry Raiburn's old 'Reverend Robert'. JD, you know unlike my father, I prefer the regular everyday workingman type of guys who just paint alter walls and ceilings for money, not that fancy portrait or still life fruit and vegetables. Dad was right about Rev. Robert though, damn fine portrait."

Clement absentmindedly looked around the bar for a few seconds while twisting around on his bar stool, "JD, you need another scotch. What you really need a vacation and some therapy. The way you have been acting the last week or so is madness. People are getting concerned about you."

He then motioned to me to pick up another round off the bar. "JD you remember what the bartender's name is?"

"I can't remember; Hattie something? Hattie Carroll. Who is 'people', and who in their right mind is worried about me? If you or anyone is, then you can just email me one of those Somen Banerjee '*torn bed sheet over coat hook blues*' e-greeting cards that my muslim clients send to me all the time. Hell I love getting them, always gets my toes tapping 12 bars in the air, and it's probably my favorite song off the digitally re-mastered 'Metropolitan Detention Center Sessions album'."

"Bar Tender." Clement motioned with his hand at Hattie, who was about half way down the bar with the fruit thing still.

He was still chuckling a bit when the bar tender came over. "Madam Bar Tender, we will like two Glenturrets, neat."

(Dr. Johnson leaned over and told Boswell that, "This is why we like Giulio, reordering before we are finished with our drinks.")

"Good choice. Two Glenturrets, neat. Would you like an appetizer with that sir? The bar has some fresh shojin-ryori, godeulppagi kimchi, and bowls or cups of moghrabieh", Hattie helpfully suggested to both Clement and I.

I thought for a second. "Thanks Hattie but nothing now for me. But if you would bring the next round in those judah goblets instead of these galilee ones, I would very much appreciate it."

"Lamb or Chicken", Clement replied at the same time I was geopositioning my scotch.

"Both. I think the cook just put it up about seven minutes ago", Hattie told Clement, and then looked over at me, "JD since you're having a Glenturret you've obviously not fasting. You should have a cup of moghrabieh."

"Kimchi, yea the Kimchi", Clement said to himself and Hattie, and then looked at me saying, "Bar Tender can your chef prepare '*fiesta de conquistador*' because JD was just waxing poetic on his homemade refried beans."

Hattie looked over at me and then over at Clement. You could tell she was surprised, possibly it was confusion. "Are you talking about JD and his homemade refried beans? You can't be talking about this guy sitting next to you. JD? Mr. Jain Dharma Glass the attorney and his *homemade refried beans*?"

"Yes Ma'mm the one and same who also wanted pork cubes with chile sauce at the same time."

Hattie looked at me and shook her heard. "Can't wait until I tell the cook you've gone mestizos vaquero loco charro!" she softly said as she laughed in a very pleasant way, and then walked back in to the kitchen.

For a few seconds Clement stared at my reflection in the bar's mirror behind the bottles on the shelves until it irritated me, and then I stared back at his reflection.

"JD have you been drinking absinthe lately because you are noticeably losing it. You did not all the sudden this week decide to try crack, or meth, have you? I told you a year ago to quit

310

surrounding yourself with the flotsam and jetsam of humanity. When was the last time you lifted weights or rode your bike?"

Soon Hattie walked up and placed the godeulppagi kimchi down in front of Giulio, with some over flowing goblets of amber peaty smokiness, whiffs of coca, and something else I could not place as she set the single malts in front of us.

(I am sure the zillion cigarettes and joints that have been in my general vicinity have nothing to do with my olfactory neurons operational capabilities regarding scotch. Dr. Johnson stated that it is due to those '…pesky tobacco specific nitrosmaines in my beard stubble'.)

"Thanks Ma'mm", Clement said reaching and taking his goblet.

"Thank you Hattie", I reached out and picked up my goblet.

"JD, the cook wanted me to ask you if you're going to try the Crunchy Sweet Potato Casserole with Peanuts on Wednesdays from now on?", Hattie smiled as she asked, and I sworn I heard her giggle the two syllables in peanuts.

"I don't know Hattie. I guess we'll see on Wednesday." Looking at Hattie I could not help from smiling so big it stung the top of my cheek.

Hattie shook her head and returned the smile and then turned and went back to the other end of the bar and resumed cutting up limes and lemons.

I held the goblet up to my face so I could just smell it, savoring the aroma. Closing my eyes I took three deep breathes through my nose.

Clement spoke up. "In honour I gained them, and in honour I will die with them. Horatio Nelson would be damn proud of Lance-Corporal of Horse J. W., he is one of us. Semper Fi Lance-Corporal."

I opened my eyes and took a last inhalation my drink. He clicked my glass and then downed the scotch while I thought for a second,

311

then another, then another, and then finally got out "England expects that every man will do his duty", and then drank up and put the goblet down and shut my eyes in respect to the Brits, ANZ's, Canadians, Indians, South Koreans, French, Italians, and the Filipinos for always being there in the trenches with us since Truman signed the Mutual Security Act in 1951.

When I opened my eyes about thirteen seconds later, my body was feeling that familiar warmth, and of course Clement was staring at me like I was an idiot.

Clement was just finishing motioning to Hattie for two more. "JD, who the hell are you kidding. You can smell as good as you see colors. You're so fucked up." Clement was finding himself very good company all of the sudden.

("Giulio was being very, very, very likable", said Boswell.)

In some type of anticipated response to a Dr. Johnson and Boswell beverage priority agreement, I resisted discussing anything that would at all relate to Giulio's present judicial tribulations.

That could wait to tomorrow in the office.

"Seriously Giulio, there are what, more than a billion mulsims on the planet with us right now. Wonder what percentage think I should be killed for my belief that all religions are of recent creation, starting with the 'EarthFirsters' Hop Heads hanging out over in the Tuban and Qafzeh juke joints. Religion developed through the vertebrate nervous systems of all homo sapiens sapiens since then; specifically using the neurons and the glia as memory storage devices. The deceit's of dualism. The provincials of the pre-postjcvisionsinstitutekeplerhubblespacetelescope age such as Descartes narcissistically deduce and delude their places in the multiverses. Rene's so so so so so so so self important faith was in that *his mind* could be distinguished from *his neurons* and *his glia*. The kkkoran commands frenchkissers to kill me for looking through jcvisionsinstitutekeplerhubblespacetelescope and then relying on my own temporal lobes. They are the only lobes I got. I rely on them

312

quite a bit, and so I have faith in their working according to some DNA categorical imperative. I really have no choice in the matter. No free will to be otherwise in any and all of my spacetimepoints."

I was drifting amongst most of the eleven dimensions, as the warmth of my stomach radiated throughout my nervous system. I had finished about my question, as tipsy endomorphins no doubt began to disturb my thought processes.

While I was still rambling on Descartes, Hattie had placed our next round down. I looked her in the eye and smiled, then saying, "*I am accustomed to sleep and in my dreams to imagine the same things that Mr. Nasrallah imagines when he awakes*".

She shook her head and then walked away before I had finished.

(Dr. Johnson and Boswell knew no matter how persuasively Henry Corbin wrote in '*ALONE WITH THE ALONE*', I am right that modern islam has achieved closure density for all three books, as demonstrated by last Sunday's matinee performance of interpretative readings from them in honor of Lee Strasburg birthday at Starkville's hiphopdanceghettohoe theatre.

It was performed by the original Chennaipattinam cast members. Immediately after the performance, all of the cast members signed a complaint with the local Starkville International Human Rights Commission against Dr. Johnson and Boswell for 'outraging the people's religious sentiments'. Rather subjective isn't it? It was Dr. Johnson and Boswell's own fault, as I had kept telling them to laugh quietly, but no, they were laughing so hard and so loudly that they both had streams of tears rolling down their faces, especially during the performance from the third book called the 'Recitation'. But it was not just those riotous laughs at the recitation, probably as much as that they were laughing quite loudly all throughout the entire performance.)

I took a long slow sip of single malt enjoying the sensual warmth it created in my mouth, esophagus, stomach, and intestines. "You think I don't know what is going on here Clement." I stared at him in his mirror image's eyes, "You are feeding me great scotch, hoping *I am* in a death spiral crash and burn so you can finally get the '67 *GTO*. You have visions of driving down Route 66 wearing a pair of stolen state highway patrol sun glasses while listening to Bessie singing about careless love blues as Louis is playing his cornet".

313

Clement finished eating as he turned in his bar stool toward me, and with the earnestness of a five year old asked, "Where is it? Is it still in storage over by your parent's old place at the Market Square Parking Garage on Lichfield Avenue?"

"Giulio, of course some things have to be maintained and protected. The GTO is where she belongs. That is one of the few things in life I am certain about". I was.

Clement knew I was right.

"You are fuckin' stupid JD." Clement was back in the moment with me, "What sense does it make to own something but never use it, just protect it. It is *a muscle car*, one of the best, leaded gas, four carburetors. It's just like you to bury the most powerful car in town in some storage garage silo. You are a fuckin' moron. You're right about Route 66 JD, I was thinking of '*Tuxedo Band*' though."

Giulio words reminded me of Hemmingway's short declarative sentence ideas. I envy. "Seriously", I interrupted his instrumental journey, "Oren Moverman or Adam Gahahn for HollyLapDance's Best War Documentary? Have to admit Gahahn's '*mujahedeen do not target muslims*' could also win Best Comedy category."

Clement assumed the pretentious liberal academic persona, "*Messenger* has all the production values a domestic production company could muster, with much better visual and auditory effects and processors than any of the foreign studios have presently. Two talented and gritty American producer/ director/ writer types - this will be tough for the Academy."

Clement could not go on with his bad impression of Roger Eburpaliberalkool-aid-addict as he starting laughing very loudly. I thought he was rather enjoying his own companionship a little too much.

("The MErcurySurfaceSpaceEnvironmentGeochemistryRanging's visual and auditory effects and processors makes Oren a lock", opined Terence Aloysius Mahoney Boswell.)

"You know JD, that all the judges at HollyLapDance Festival are all honorable mujahedeen liberal progressive democrats. The Park City mohammed bouyeri SP* types are going to vote for the underdogma culturefare films. In this case, the clitoris hating villages of Swat Valley's HDR XR150 anti-American production values versus the Hollywood machine's 3D-BS PRO RIG anti-American marketing values. Adam's a lock." Clement was getting quite silly.

He took a sip, and then put his hand on my shoulder, and in a solemn voice, a quiet voice grave with faux seriousness, asked me, "What is the difference between *Echo and Narcissus* and *Metamorphosis of Narcissus*, other than thirty four years?"

Clement took another sip and put the goblet down. "Wait, *wait, wait* - I know you're going to say something stupid like one's named John. What is the difference between *Echo and Narcissus* and *Metamorphosis of Narcissus*? About the last two weeks in your fuckin' stochastic mental processes."

I ignored Giulio as he just kept giggling for half awhile.

Really, it was really very embarrassing, not his very public giggling, but that I really was going to say 'John'.

So I looked down the bar the opposite way from him. There was a glossy magazine and a few copies of '*La Terre Francaise*' with a copy of '*Ittihad al Shaab*' laying a few feet from me on the bar.

I stood up and reached over and grabbed the glossy magazine. Just when I was getting the magazine, Hattie came back with another godeulppagi kimchi for Clement, which she had placed in front of him and then went back to the cutting of the lemons and limes just as I sitting back down to look at the magazine. Fuckin' Jesus H. Christ, it was another copy of '*Filastin al-Mulsimamamia*'.

There was a small german guy dropping the damn things all over town. Last Sunday when I was drinking Blanca Opsin Mohitos at the Oden's bar he had approached me and handed me the same issue. He looked just damn silly then as he was wearing a black leather biker jacket three sizes too large for his frail frame. The jacket was embodied with the SS Handschar Club's Colors, a yellow scimitar and black shield with the yellow MC.

I didn't recognize the purple wing patch with 'Umar 12' stitched in yellow. Most of been a special patch of the club that only violent psychotics got for contributing to Starkville's civil discourse.

No the magazine wasn't the issue the Arawas of Starkville had that famous urban legend about, the one with the cover photo being of Arafattie with five young members of the Ashbal. That one had the Ashbals all lying out by the pool in bright yellow spandex bathing briefs. The picture supposedly was of some evening a couple years back while Arafattie was at the exclusive Hotel AllBustedNow.

Legend has that cover photo showed Arafattie sitting in the middle of the five young members of the Ashbal, while rubbing oils on the back of one of the younger boys who was reading an article about animal homosexuality in the special Qame Zani issue of 'Der Sturmer', while in the picture's background there was a waxing egyptian yellow crescent moon hanging low in the sky directly above the hotel.

(The Sentinelese version of the story has the Ashbals all drinking Mohitos with fresh lime and mint leaves in tall frosted glasses. Starkville's Sentinelese and Arawa had different cultural traditions, so it was no surprise to me when Austin and Moll told me that the Sentinelese mohito with mint leaves version was the subject of some phd candidate in Anthropology at Bryn Mawr, and the Arawas version without the mint leaves was chosen by a 19 year old Brandeis DPhiE pledge last semester for her thesis.)

No the bar copy wasn't the Arawa's famous issue. It was the current Ramadan issue with Ismail and Alamgir on the cover being congratulated by a senior iranian imam of the religion of peace, whose wudu stained hands were dripping the blood of innocents.

The little german guy had introduced himself to me as being a traveling oil company salesman from Oberosterreich; whom I

316

believe was telling me he was late for a meeting at the beautiful and expensive Georgi Zhukov Conference Room down at the Starkville convention center with some office clerks coming from Dubai.

The little guy was agitated and did not seem to speak English very proficiently. I think he kept asking me if I had seen "Dr. Harry Clay Sharp" and 'Herr Minister Handlanger Farrakhanawienie' drinking at the bar, and if this was the right "Odine Bar".

He mumbled something about Margaret Higgins Sanger Slee, gypsies, and amtssprache; which actually left me standing there rather speechless for a spell.

Since his presence was irritating me, I told him the *Odine Bar* was a couple blocks north, half way up Odenplan Avenue in the Chaoyany District.

I told him I believed Dr. Sharp and Herr Handlanger were there with Louis, Harlan, William, and Oliver discussing deductive induced activism in the evidentiary proceedings of '*Buck v. Bell*'. Just to make sure he would leave immediately, I told him that the *Odine* is where tourists get a free glass of sweet pesach wine for just showing the DomPass handed out by Starkville's Convention and Tourist Bureau. For being a man of such small stature the oil salesman's presence somehow was very, very, very disconcerting. As if he had used too much of a bad Chinese knock off version of the Majdanek Zyclon-B Cologne atomizer, (*so stylish now in the middle eastern mosques*), while he was grooming that morning in his shower. I did not want to be in the same room with him. I did not want to be in any spacetimepoints with him.

I was relieved as he turned and left in pursuit of either Herr Handlanger Farrakhanawienie or pesach wine, or more probably, both. I waved good bye to his back as he went out through the backdoor of Oden's bar by putting my palm down, fingers pointing outward, and my middle finger pointing down, as is the worldwide custom of Starkville's drunkards in bars.

(Damn hommie was right, three generations of Nazijihadists during my inconsequentiallifespacetimepoints is enough. Three generational blood soaked spacetimepoints.)

I got up and walked over to the garbage can sitting at the end of the bar next to the kitchen door, and threw the '*Filastin*' where it belonged - with the mostly empty beer bottles and what wasn't eaten from today's happy hour's hor d'oeuvres of pulled pork & collard greens.

When I sat back down, Clement was taking a healthy gulp from his goblet.

Clement glanced over at me, and then he took another sip of his scotch.

Giulio diagnosed my mirror reflection. "Seriously Deacon Jones, during your extended quest of the night of being an expanded hominidae, you should take some time off, go see a doctor, and then go sit on a beach somewhere far away from Starkville. If you don't you are going to end up in either Topeka State Hospital, or perhaps the very sunny and fun filled McLean Hospital. I hear the great plains are very nice this time of year, maybe just a bit dusty."

"Giulio I'm going to hold out for Danvers State. I think, that then after massive doses of thorazine, I would be able to discuss the human rights of boys in a Mtwapa saloon with Skeikh IlikeHussies and Bishop Lawrence Shaimindyourownbusiness. From what I first heard early last Sunday afternoon from Giles, Paris, and Sheels, and then again about two hours later when I was in the convention center district drinking at the Oden with Niklas von Salm-Reifferscheitd and the slightly drunk Wilhelm von Rogendorf, was that the Bishop and the Skeikh had spent hours in the public square talking in great detail to any one that was walking by about the immoral behaviors of young boys."

("Due to some ancient flat earth totalitarian philosophy there many educated yet uninformed and totally ignorant people still today. Men who are alive in the JCvisionsinstitutedkeplerhubblespacetelescope world and yet dress up in long flowing feminine robes and spend their time worrying, a lot of time worrying,

318

about young boys having sex together. Worse still, then they want to explain and justify their worrying fetish by lecturing the rest of us on ancient myths", an irritated Boswell said.

Dr. Johnson spoke up saying, "Not sure why, but it reminds one of all those democrats using the worldwide media for their eulogizing the prolific spender of the public treasury, Kleagle Robert Byrd." Boswell spit on the floor and then stated bluntly, "That's what is wrong with the country today. Where are all the Michael J. Mansfield, Pfc. U. S. Marine Corps?")

"JD, I know lately you think you're the Mujahedeen Defender Kuffar-in-Chief, but damn ya jarhead, listen to yourself. The world sucks, we get it, people do horrible things, but Jesus H. Christ man, there is balance somewhere. If Bishop what's his name went to Mecca, or Medina, he'd be in the Mabaheth Interrogation Centre in a nanosecond being submitted to Falanga by the exact same Sheikh, instead of preaching together their fetish like fascination of the perceived vices of young boys. The world makes little sense. You have to conquer it every fucking day, every fucking second. That is why the good people of Speyside and Islay work so hard perfecting the single malt - to help everyone get fucking over it. Get a hobby besides mental masturbation JD, before you start waking up lying bruised and bloody in some gutter somewhere."

Clement was getting exasperated with me. I knew I was obsessing, rebooting, or more probably, I had just woke up this morning in the wrong multiverse again, one where mohammad started a death cult, priests molest young boys, and the U.S. Constitution invisible penumbra's are cited for killing homo sapiens sapiens babies in their mother's uterus.

"JD up to about a week or two ago, I knew if anyone was aware of what a Hobbesian state of nature we existed in, it was you *mr. i defend anybody with or without money*. Now, I think you're actually trying to live in a Hobbesian state of nature, in a Bill Waterson's Hobbesian state of nature."

I responded with the only thing that came to mind, "I want another tumbler, how about you sensus divinitatis Calvin? Join me in the transmogrifier for a depravity of the unconditional choosing of the

319

single atonement and yet still irresistible malt of the perfect scotch made only by the perseverance of the saints of Highland, Lowland, Speyside, Islay, and Campbeltown?"

"Nice avoidance J.D. Poprishchin. If I had a pen and couple more bar napkins I could write an article on your Borderline Personality Disorder, and the god damned 'Journal of Clinically Starkville Psychiatry' would make it their cover story." Clement chuckled as he chugged the last bit of his scotch, and without missing a beat, continued his 'friendly' diagnosis of my mental state. "Remember last Sunday. You got all worked up over some jihadidiotie brahma bull dung and were arguing with everyone. We just wanted to have a few drinks and talk World Cup, not listen to your Shiva Pollyanna preaching. Who besides Juris Dhimmis Glass, or is it Jinn De minimis non curat lex Glass, in urbane Starkville worries about the U.N. Human Rights Council passing some *combating defamation of religion resolution*. I'll tell you - nooo fuckiiing body. JD seriously, who in their right minds cares about the U.N., or the damned jihadiemuslims subverting and violating its Article 1 during the World Cup? Every sane person in Starkville knows they should kick the U.N. the hell out of this country, but just not during the World Cup."

Of course his friendly diagnosis missed entirely the critical fact that since this morning the Niðhoggr had been tearing at my edinger-westphal nuclei.

Clement finished off the golden scotch droplets still in his tumbler while saying in a low angry voice, "Ok, JD I confess I do worry that muslim's threaten our basic human rights, and the fundamental freedoms of the fine people of Speyside and Islay. JD, you know I should have 2nd cav ghost deployed guarding both. JD, can you imagine watching the World Cup without scotch?"

Then he broke out in a big smile.

I thought for awhile about his deployment strategy.

320

I agreed with his 2nd cav strategy. Then I thought the scotch particles warming his stomach were jumping him into my multiverse, just as he dismissed my mental statespacetimepoints out right.

I realized just then, that Dr. Yggdrasill at the V.A., had the very same dismissive tendency as to my diagnostic concerns.

"Damn JD, you showed up in lockup this morning looking like your hair, face and eyes had spent the night sleeping in a city park."

I appreciated that Giulio had the social grace not to disparage the independent designer G. Bruno's black wool suit coat that I was wearing in lock up. I bought in Campo de' Fiori last February 17th.

I appreciated the fact that his personal criticism was directed at me, and not the hand sewn jacket.

I realize that the hand sewn black wool suit coat is a multipolarreverse reflection of my neighborhood's appreciation of the transcendent haute couture of the Difontaines. I still think it is Ok to wear the jacket while working during the day, as it absorbs dust and deoxyribonucleic acid along with all the other hallway of justice particles that are amidst the eleven point streams of energized protons and electrons passing through at 900 kms.

"JD you're too emotionally involved in your damn cases. You're depressed instead of angry, which makes you worthless in your job. To help clear and focus your consciousness, you smoke Kensitas and drink coffee and tea 24 / 7 – that about sum it up? When's the last time you got laid, or even went salmon fishing off the Badentarbet Pier? You know you are not actually Colonel Prescott standing atop of the Starkville redoubt."

Clement then tried to get the bar tender's attention by lifting his tumbler, even though we both knew we were in no real need of another round of liquid warmth and physical gratification. It was just a selfish individual desire shared mutually at that spacetimepoint.

"Hell JD, your friends, the few you have left, all are worried and are sure somebody's going to find your colitas smelling carcass laying in the street gutter. I personally think the ayu and leopard eels will end up nibbling your shahada drunk ass when you fall off the Aioi bridge late some cloudless night."

I was scratching my beard and fixated on whether to use a 9 ½ foot leader with the larger No. 4 flies (*Nam-myoho-renge-kyo*) so it took me a second to form a responsive thought. "As much as I love '*Rape Me*', I do not own a copy of REM's '*Automatic for the People*'. I do own '*Diasporic*', non sum qualis eram."

Besides it being yet another classic narcissist joke, it was true. So I felt another one liner might be appreciated by my audience, "Giulio you know I haven't built a shrine to Santa Muetre in my legal brief case, yet."

(Boswell remarked to Dr. Johnson, "How very nice it was that the brain was still here functioning in the present spacetimepoint, ignoring and/or repressing any memories of Marie Magdalene, Madness, and the fish problem".)

"You know JD, one Carry Amelia Moore Nation in Starkville's history is about all I will tolerate", Clement replied, proving again that I really didn't have any chance at a career in standup comedy.

I realized that Clement's scotch warmed stomach was starting to personalize to him the fact that there were people, imamammy paininassabombie's, who preach to very small penises to violently disrupted the craftsmanship of the artisans of Speyside and Islay, thereby preventing one of his favorite past times, 'alkhmr'.

His historical insight into a cultural flash point made me wonder if I should ask Dr. Yggdrasill, if to a reasonable degree of medical certainty, whether or not 'Niðhoggr' is an airborne contagion, or does it require that there has to be some actual spiritual contact under the robes, or between the sheets?

"You know Giulio, you can feel it slipping away with the little things, like spacetimepoints. You read a headline in the paper quoting Britain's Home Secretary Wacki Smacki's rant of *'coming to the U.K. privilege'* against that old boring californicated small talk & food reminiscing radio host. Then you start to wonder if your clients are really IRGC advance agents, and whether your next morning you will wake up smelling smoke rising from all the small family shops in the Convention District around the Circus Maximus Department Store development. That will be the frenchkissing aggressor's response to political correctness – an islamicclitorishatinghomophobicnazijihadist very, very, very small penis smoky frenchkiss."

"Yeah, seems there always is some secretary of national defenselessness, worried about fifth column voters in California's 8th or in Wisconsin's 2nd, issuing stand down in place orders from the foot bath in the Cabinet Room." Clement quietly had stated the obvious as he looked down at his nearly empty tumbler.

He continued with conviction, "JD, this stuff that progressives, democrats, and the old News Media sling around about America wanting out of this war, not wanting to fight, is a crock of evil co-dependency. Americans love to fight, traditionally. All real Americans love the sting and clash of battle. You know JD there are orders 2nd cav ghost would follow through hell."

I recognized General George Patton's June 5th orders to the 3rd Army. General John Stark would approve.

"JD, I am done. It's been a long forty nine hours. I am going back to the hotel and get a good night sleep so I can get back to work by noon or so. Thanks for keeping tomorrow, for tomorrow."

"Giulio, do you want to go back to my place for a smoke? I have to stop by to pick up a thumb drive to finishing mixing a hip hop session for the group SEU."

I glanced at my goblet.

(Boswell wanted at least '…one more'.)

323

"Hell no, JD. Any time you're harvesting Northern Lights in your drafty and dark attic, like last Sunday when we're all sitting round telling war stories with Prince Machiavelli, and keeping our merciless minds on his riches, I'm there. No fucking way tonight 'cause you don't need me. Do you, you harvesting? I didn't think so, so you don't need me tonight. Anyway your living space motif is a boring retro 1970 defiant anti NYT Style Section's Progressive Minimalist Con Son Tiger. I paid for and need right about now the 400 satin threads per square which is waiting for me at the hotel." He began chuckling aloud again as he mentioned the 400 thread thing.

"Thanks for coming out for a drink Giulio, now go crash and call me when you wake up. I need to have you stop by the office in the morning by eleven to sign some affidavits." I reached over to shake his hand as he stood up.

"Look Giulio, since I am going to have another, I'll pick up the bill tonight", I said shaking his hand. It was the least I thought I could do for him tonight; (especially later as he tries to sleep by himself).

"Thanks Juris Delusional, just make sure it doesn't reappear on my legal bill as a consultation and a business meeting." He smiled, shook my hand again then looked around the bar.

"Mr. Clement remember you are not to drink alcohol or be in any bars as required by the terms of your bond." Of course it is the ethical duty of a lawyer to advise his client to follow all court orders.

I laughed as Clement gave me the finger.

Giulio nodded goodbye and turned to leave saying, "Mosheh, avoid playing chess with Umar b. al-Khattab and Ibn Khaldun for a couple days. You know I agree with you, starting with the Taliban, every one of which should be hung, but only after being tortured as retribution for what they had done to their own women and children."

Then I watched his back as he walked out the door. I had gotten up shaking his hand, so I sat back down to finish my drink. Sentimentally, I immediately wanted to toast saluting Methane Base Life Forms, General Patton, and the brewers and parishioners of Dunkeld Cathedral.

(Boswell told me he wanted, '…a double Islay', Dr. Johnson wasn't sure if he wanted '…a Blanca Opsin Mohito, or maybe a tumbler of central highlands Uisge Beatha, perhaps a double'. I wondered if Beatha is an old world 3rd cousin once removed from New Amsterdam's Uncle Isaac's hard apple cydar.)

While I was waiting for Dr. Johnson to make up his mind, and as the bar tender was finishing cutting up limes and lemons at the end of the bar, I realized that I never had, nor would ever have, a guardian angel named Clarence.

Reality is that there are many inconsequential lives such as mine.

The individual is negatively or positively charged jetsam or flotsam buffeting gravitational waves.

My waves are of inconsequential particle duality.

(I insincerely mentioned to Dr. Johnson and Boswell that, "I don't know how that's done, or what math even to use. Alone. That's it. I only exist as several fleeting simultaneousspacetimepointsprionproteins." Dr. Johnson humorlessly said E. A. Poe's, "…*from childhood's hour i have not been as others were i have not seen as others saw i could not bring my passions from a common spring*".)

I starred at my fractured reflection, behind the mass of shelved liquor bottles, in the bar's mirror noting that I *was* alone. I thought JCvisioninstitutedkeplerhubbleespacetelescope is empirical proof against old myths and fables about revelations from yeshua, the god of trinitarians and non trinitarians, or allah; all having become historically interesting as anthropomorphized campfire tales: as chaos/eros/Hyades/tian/pacha/donghai/jupiter/juno/Pluto/wheenme emowah/quaayayp/nayanezgani/kururumany/jurupari/cherruves/ya masachicko/kongorikishi/yama or now, lawrence/curley/moses.

"What would you like now, JD?"

325

I was so busy looking at my fracture reflection in the mirror behind the several rows of bottles of trendy infused liquors, while thinking of all the make believe gods from the past, that I had not noticed Hattie Carroll was standing right in front of me.

"Well Hattie that is always the question in here isn't it? Let's have a Highland Uisge Beatha, a small Blanca Opsin Mohito, and a shot of your best Islay. While you're at it Hattie will you put on a couple songs on the jukebox, preferably John Dankworth playing saxophone. I will make sure there is a nice tip if you can find a couple."

Hattie smiled at me, and I laughed and smiled back at her.

(Dr. Johnson and Boswell then both said at the same time that what, "…I really wanted was another chance at redemption in my relationship with Tarbula." They were of course right, and it was very cruel to bring up my sweet Tarba Rosa, (a private nickname for her), at this spacetimepoint. I have been very zealous since disappointing her and have been finding my way through the wilderness among false women ever since. 'Tragōid amid and amongst all the mutliverse spacetimepoints', murmured Dr. Johnson. Boswell, looking left and right, whispered, 'Well let's be honest, not *every*one in the wilderness was a Marian apparition'.)

"JD, do you or your friend need to order anything off the bar menu?"

"No thank Hattie, he left to go sleep, and I'm really not hungry right now. I might do a take out, on second thought, no. No just bring the last round; then I will finally get to go to the studio and do some mixing for an hour or two."

"JD, you might consider mixing your alcohol with a bit of food", said Hattie smiling, again with a twinkle in her eyes. Then she took my empty tumbler and went down the bar to start the Mohito.

(I then told Dr. Johnson whatever he decided, "…I would drink the other one".)

Right then as Boswell started to say something, thanks to my muse 'Hathor', who was now occupying spacetimepoints as Mohito Mixing Hattie, the '*African Waltz*' interrupted him.

326

As the waltz started playing from the speakers placed around the bar, my right foot started to tap on the bar stool. Old Johnny and the whole Orchestra sure knew what bar patrons needed.

Hattie returned in couple of minutes with the drinks, and as she placed them down, I noticed all three were filled to the brim.

"Thanks Hattie, can you total me out now."

"No take out? Are you sure JD? I have the bill here. Take out will only delay you a minute."

I shook my head no as I carefully lifted the Uisge Beatha and took a sip. Hattie shook her head and then began to total the bill.

The African Waltz was giving my brain some much needed exercise, similar to a half hearted stretching an hour or so before a five k marathon.

Hattie place the bill on the bar, and then smiling said, "You be careful tonight JD and make sure you eat something soon."

The African Waltz ended much quicker than I remembered, or it was perhaps probable that it was just abrupt relative to the Uisge Beatha's life giving warmth.

As Hattie walked away my eyes lingered on her ample curves. Before she got two thirds of the way back to the kitchen, the jukebox started up again with Cleo Laine singing '*Oh Lady Be Good*'. I took another sip as my foot started tapping the bar stool again. Hattie was right. I should eat something. I should break out the moroccan primero hashish raisin cookies when I stop by the apartment. ("The secret is using an excessive amount of the richest immunoglobulin 'A' butter", Dr. Johnson said looking at his fractured reflection in the mirror. Boswell interrupted saying that he wanted, "...some Sus domesticus pachamanca". Dr. Johnson chimed in requesting, "...a tostada of refried beans, with toluca green chorizo smothered in fresh veggies, and a bowl of pork cubes smothered in green chile sauce rich in garlic cloves and jalapenos". I started to excogitate about a plate of brown rice, black beans and ahuacamolli.)

I then noticed that Cleo had stopped singing. I looked over at the bar's clock. I had just enough time to run by the apartment, smoke a couple bowls of Primero, retrieve the thumb drive, a couple of cookies, and then get to the studio.

I drank up, and up, and up, and immediately felt the warm glow radiating from my digestive system.

I took the last couple sips, droplets really, and then took three deep breathes (Nam-myoho-renge-kyo), and then got up to leave. In appreciation of '*Oh Lady Be Good*' I paid the bill and put thirty seven dollars on the bar as a tip.

I started to smile as I remembered tumblers filled to the brim; so I threw down a few more dollars in appreciation on the bar, making the tip forty one appreciative dollars.

As I left the bar I started to wonder if the picture the Arawas always talked about, that was the cover photo of the Hotel AllBustedNow pool, was being exhibited this week, or next, at La Cour Visconti. On the progressive gallery wall's bottom left Götterdämmerung quadrant one would expect.

As soon as I got outside and took three steps on the sidewalk I stopped, and then looked up at the dark sky.

I don't know why but it made me remember what the Twelvers had tagged on the cliffs of Naqsh-e Rustam last Sunday, just about three miles south of Starkville, down the Honkawa river.

It was the typical gang green orange spray painted tag. A proclamation to the multiverses for a fellow gang member and last year's Starville Exodus-Sinai Blues Music Marathon Festival runner-up King Darius: '*The spliff of a persian man has gone forth far. A persian man has delivered his best blues eight bar battle far from persia to the stoner neighborhood plataeans at Club Militades.*'

328

The wind was gently swirling from an undetermined direction throughout the dark streets.

No doubt nature wanted to remind me of the atmospheric forces phenomenon, or perhaps it was just the dissipating breezes of the natural union of a team of winged horses and their charioteer Phaedrus, or just as probable, nature merely wanted to mess up my hair and make my pants flutter.

I started to walk the streets back to the neighborhood thinking of Rasool Rev. Davis sermon last Sunday that, '… the wind don't have no mercy, wind won't stay away from nobody in this neighborhood, it won't stay long, you look in the aquarium and find some fish gone, wind don't have no mercy in this neighborhood'.

Chapter 31   Urban Planning rev. II

Blue sky with high cirrus was a memory. It was dark. I kept looking up at the sky which now was partially covered with outlines of moving clouds having varying grayscale, say in sixteen bits per sample from black to black. Blue was immediately regulated to the hypothalamus, although that might have been due in part to single malt scotch.

I started singing one hundred thirty six E flat notes from an old german tune.

Suddenly I felt like I had been playing a vintage 1975 off broadway character actor playing the role of Masayuki Moni in some unauthorized biographical play filmed by Andy at the Factory in black and white.

I was merging two famous celluloid roles of Hakuchi and Ukigumo and the play actually now had a running time of over ten hours and twenty three minutes in my spacetimepoints.

My sidewalk assumption of the role quickly became weary due to directions the Executive Producer Leni Riefenstahl; sent by the middle eastern investors to watch costs or possibly just to scout for clitorisless preteen actresses).

Leni was angrily berating the director David Lloyd George in front of everyone on the lot for spending way over budget. Leni always insisted that the studio was not a welfare state, and that 10:22 was too long for smaller markets like Svindax.

Suddenly I felt very tired, spiritually exhausted, Andy Déjà SleepVu cinema reducere. I just wanted to get to the studio. Like Ludwig van said, "Music is the marijuana which inspires me to regenerate, I am a grower who harvest buds for mankind and makes them spiritually multiversal".

Boswell and Dr. Johnson began arguing about the believability of the composite character. This was interesting for about a half a block of walking.

Then I remembered Kurosawa's advice of 'cutting it lengthwise'. I slowed my gait, and when Boswell was making what I am sure was a salient point about Kinji Kameda's too late realization of the fleeting nature of love, I quickly crossed the street leaving them to their differing concepts for Kinji's checkered silk coat in the final scene's set design for next week's opening night's stage production at Starkville's old and small hiphopdance theatre on the third floor of 646 N. Franklin Street.

The bicycle path over the Aioi River to the shima byouin hospital was directly adjacent 646 N. Franklin. A jazz bar had recently relocated from the west coast to a space in the lobby of the building between a Chinese restaurant and Izanagi and Izanami Limited. Izanagi and Izanami's capitalistic enterprise occupies part of the first, and the entire second floor at 646 N. Franklin Street. Izanagi and Izanami have been internationally famous jewelry designers since Toyko Post Style Editor Gil Sullivan gave the paper's Mikado Prize to the firm in 1885.

The last two generations of the firm's founders have since updated their business model based on Milton Friedman's, '*Belaying the IRS on the Mount*' Chapter's 5 – 7, in response to the pagan cults of MarxLeninMaoStalin, GobineauHitler, and Hassan al-Banna Khomeini (LandoftheverysmallpenisAryans).

This month's lead sale display is an exceptional jewel edged black hand mirror. It is inlaid with hand cut mother of pearl depicting an early morning mist on Mount Fuji, with a red sun rising over the mountain. The display's sales theory is part of Mr. Friedman's theocratic directive to build rugged individualism into the value of the Izanagi and Izanami brand.

I appreciated that the mirror was placed on a red silk slip North Song Dynasty Pillow with an incised decoration in pearl.

The pillow was place in front of the triptych print '*yokohama tetsudō jōki shussha no zu*'. A single ceiling spotlight lit the display.

(Dr. Johnson shouted across the street to me that, if I '...would play the Kinji character then he would design a neck muff of colobus vellerosus fur perfect for every scene'. Boswell and Dr. Johnson had a good laugh at colobus vellerosus's non-endangered-species-listing expense.)

I looked back and over across the street at Dr. Johnson and Boswell, but at that exact spacetimepoint moment, some highly ionizing particles arrived at my hypothalamus, so I could not tell their stage design lists apart: wwd *vs.* wwf or fww *vs.* dww.

My thoughts felt light as helium, well minus a neutron or two. I ignored them again. I started walking back to get the thumb drive of the saxophone and cello tracks of S.E.U., which I had recorded in G major allegretto grazioso at the studio last night. Damn fine work, airy but dark burned out undertones.

My thoughts were floating through my central nervous system as if notes from Etude Op. 10, No. 4. I wanted a cigarette. When I took a cigarette out of the pack, my thumb drive and a large joint fell into my hand. I stopped walking.

How the thumb drive got in my cigarette pack was not in my memory banks. I stood there for thirteen seconds with all systems idling except memory.

No use – no zeros and ones, or Four Corner Method, painting a spacetimepoint. I put the cigarette back in the pack with the thumb drive, and put the pack back in my pocket in front of some hashish. I took three deep breathes.

As I exhaled the last breathe I looked up and down the street - dark glass buildings reflecting dark glass buildings.

There were a few groups of citizens walking to the theatre, a late diner, or to some bar with live music.

333

I lit the joint and began the last leg of my present journey to the studio to finish mixing the music. My most important contribution to society: the perfect mix of 16 bars for 499 seconds, instruments and vocal tracks fused.

(Or as Boswell brags, '...dirty lyrics to a fat beat'.)

The joint sharpened my consciousness, and my rational faculties, with each inhalation.

I wondered what Lynda Marie Child was doing at the moment. No doubt the absence of her children was some punishment the gods were visiting upon her for their sick pleasures.

The frenchkisser was just one in a long line of usurpers of reality imposing sick fucking degradations upon us mere mortals who just want to go to work and do something worthwhile with our hands, and then, after eight hours go home to a family and a joint, and the internet.

This was my prescription: Northern Lights out the internal rage caused at the mere thought of the acid throwing jihadiiiiiiiicriminals.

('Liberum Arbitrium?' Boswell said to remind Dr. Johnson and myself.)

It was the minimal of a number of tracking and mixing suggestions made to me at brunch last Sunday by HipHop-o-krates, while we were eating baby back pork ribs, and drinking tsikoudia at Kos's Bar-B-Q over on Rigas Velestinlis Boulevard.

(Dr. Johnson spoke up opining that, "JD, you would be a perfect choice as colonel of the Starkville atheist militia due to your education, suppressed rage, and dehumanization of one billion homo sapiens sapiens deeply held beliefs.". Boswell, always the brit, seconded according to Robert's Rules.)

The motion having been recorded, I accepted.

As colonel, I decided to take Khamenei up on his televised proposal of spreading division among Islamic nations.

I realized Khamenei's proposal was merely a clever diversion to distract everyone from islam's main enemy, in each and every one of the JCvisioninstitutedkeplerhubblespacetelescopemultiverses , women educated in science.

(Dr. Johnson corrected me, saying, *"'Khamenei said the main enemy was Starkville and Israel'*, totally missing the point, as academics always do in debating mythical foreign policy internet beliefs, and especially in fighting hand to hand combat under the bed sheets in the culture wars".)

I was just about to cross Agha M. Khān Qājār Avenue, heading the last couple of blocks out of Phil's part of town onword toward the neighborhood and the studio, when I decided to just sit down for a moment at a bus stop bench to relax and savor smoking the joint. ()

I started humming one hundred thirty six E flat notes from an old german tune.

I noticed a softly lit display window in the street level store of a dark glass box building directly across the street from my publicly financed transportation feeder apparatus seat.

("Mitotic"? inquired Boswell in a gaige kaifang strategy session revelation.)

I took another hit off the joint as I tried to focus on the display.

I could make out three paintings in the display. They appeared as they were painted in the Kulturkampf style popular in 1912 and 1913, or possibly completed no later than 1923, or 1925.

I recognized one as the Karls-Church in Vienna, another was the mother mary with her child jesus christ, and the last was a mountain scene with a wayside cross as subject.

(Boswell became agitated. I think from the lack of any sign of human compassion in the brush technique used by the artist of the paintings. Boswell snarled, "The militia should start with the Taliban art historian Wakil Ahmed Muttawakil, and then his students - those unwashed very small penises that have anal sex with each other, and then abuse girls who read *'Zur Quantentheorie der Strahlung'*.)

I appreciated the enthusiasm of the troops, but a disciplined strategy of double envelopment would be required for this campaign.

The militia would deploy Moses Nichols to insure all Islamic countries couldn't hit some kill switch, or activate a firewall to filter the internet. Sam Herrick would insure that all muslim cellular, radio, and television devices would receive streaming NPR broadcasts into all Islamic countries without jamming.

(Dr. Johnson and Boswell stated their belief, that only the popular midnight web casts show that is dual broadcast on the internet and satellite radio should be spared.)

David Hobart would be charged with getting books and print media into all islamic countries, of course scientific texts and periodicals had priority, but due to the ignorance of the populations copies of those texts might be delayed as they were to be transcribed into the '*comic book format*', so even the moslim men could understand the concepts.

Thomas Stickney was to be charged with the smuggling into all islamic countries all the instruments necessary to have a world class philharmonic orchestra; priority to every population center of over five thousand people, (including the sheet music of all the western classic symphonies).

Art classes in painting the human form would be a secondary front established D plus 13.

(Boswell was not satisfied, he wanted, "...O.S.S. and S.I.S. Direct Action with immediate concurrent military strikes and high body counts". He reasoned aloud that you had no choice but, "To kill all the true believers in jihad. If you kill enough of them, they'll stop fighting", he stated dryly, quoting the brilliant Four Star General Curtis Lemay. Dr. Johnson agreed, and then added while he was still reviewing Lemay's DD Form 2807-1, "A star for all four steel testicles.")

We will use Khalid ibn al-Walid's strategy at the Battle of Walaja against them, a military strategy of double envelopment; and the destruction of jihadists and acid throwers plan would work I assured them both.

336

The kkkoran contains the lynchpin of Victory for Clitoris day, verse 36:59, *'And all you Mujrimun single malt scotch drinkers who are disbelievers in islamic clitorisless monotheism, you 8 and 16 bar Shayatin begena players whose faith in the wicked evil scientific method, get you apart this Day'*.

The military strategy is quite simple; separate the prokaryotic jihadist clitoris haters from homo sapiens sapiens.

Space debris worshippers would be drawn out by merely posting cartoons of mohammad raping his child bride in the public squares of the population centers for the practitioners of the religion of peace to admire.

As the fanatics rioted in celebration of the cloak less orphan's humanity and scientific understanding, six waves of MQ-9 Reapers would send them to their mythical virgins.

Knowing what cowards the imammies and leaders of the typical frenchkissing groups like harakat al-muqaqamat al-ilslamiyyah, fatah, tailban, and the society of moslim brothers are, sixty one minutes after the Reapers strike - we do an air drop of thousands of kkkorans into the public square.

Then thirteen minutes later an airdrop of barbecued haitian creole pig ribs and entrails on top of the kkkorans.

That should bring out the jihadimmammies and their brave burkqa wearing warriors who send preteen girls strapped with explosives to blow up buses and schools out for their last cleansing ritual with native georgia clay pigeons, (Columbidae GBU-43/B phylum), released during the last of the haloed MQ-9 Reaper's *'wudhu-ghusl-tayammum'* Médecins Avec La Moral Frontières sponsored flight amongst the virgin cirrostratus cirrus.

No doubt justice and retribution paid for from the all taxes on sanitary pads sold in the Pakistani stores in the neighborhood.

("Besides", An Khe village corpsman Dr. Johnson stated enthusiastically, "if that fails we can just take the GTO over and finish it ourselves.")

I finished the joint and threw the last of it into the street gutter for some spiders to find and enjoy. It is curious that ever so often, I revert back to the giving street offerings to nature.

My burnt green budda offerings are more likely given when singing the chorus to Phil Collins's *In The Air Tonight* with Boswell, Dr. Johnson, followed by Genesis 22.2, from the original sheet music.

(Dr. Johnson stated that, "1st, I was going to be late getting to the studio; and 2nd, the plan need to be written down so logistics could be planned as Rommel had said, '*The battle, is fought and decided by the quartermasters before the shooting beings*'."

Boswell took offense at the mention of the Field Marshall; "Kraut had to shoot himself due to his belief in super race politics. Gentlemen we are being killed in hotels, in bars, in buses, in office buildings, on our streets. Let us leave our Shambhala neighborhood and go to Tehran, Media, Mecca, Karachi, Kuala Lumpur, Jakarta, Mir Ali, Kunduz, and all of North Waziristan to die fighting. I'll follow Patton or Cota in a large scale high intensity fight. I'd never follow an IRGC officer of an army of frenchkissing holocausting tree and rock inspectors.")

I got up and stretched. I look up at the stars, no moon yet. It did look like some rain clouds were moving over the city.

I turned and started toward the studio.

Maybe seventeen minutes or so later, when I crossed over and started walking up Khnum Avenue, and I was just getting up to the Latino part of the neighborhood, a light rain from the east began.

It was gently soaking the streets.

The studio was in an old four story red brick public school built in 1905, close to a corner of an intersection of three streets; Anthony, Cross, and Orange.

The intersection of Khitan Court and Sultan Lane was a block to the east.

The building was abandoned during the 1975 recession, and then renovated into the Werner-Heisenberg Studio in the mid 1990's.

This part of the neighborhood was the poorest. By that I mean the least in economic income – not in human spirit or human compassion. Latinos are born catholic. Latinos die catholic.

("Well, it is mostly due to the strong character of the Latinas", Dr. Johnson postulated.

After a couple seconds Boswell stated, "Except for the Latinos who are soul less heroin or meth dealers. Those Latinos are probably the most violent sociopaths here in Starkville. Regardless that is a concern for catholic educators. To implement the double envelopment plan we will have to travel to the Middle East, Europe, or Asia, to go after the jihadist cowards lurking around waiting for the imaginary well dwelling boy".

Dr. Johnson then wondered out loud, "What is it with the islamonazijihadists and catholic parish priests and the kissing young boys thing? Islamonazijihadists and catholic parish priests must loath reading Titus Flavius Clemens famous editorial in the Mecca Chapter of NAMBLA's Annual Charshanbeh Suri issue from 2001".)

I did the only thing I knew I could to change the subject. I started singing Mississippi John Hurt's '*Spike Driver Blues*'.

I sang as I walked. After Mississippi John, I continued my imitation of the strolling troubadour Eusebius, by giving witness as I sang the words from the great philosopher-king Mathis James Reed's singspiel, '*I'm Leavin*'.

Chapter 32   Anthropomorphic Hypothesis

The light rain was forming small puddles here and there in the dark streets. The light katabatic wind felt good blowing against my face and tussling at my hair.

I was slowly walking up the sidewalk humming along with Dr. Johnson and Boswell to the Reverend Gary Davis's prophecy, '*Death Don't Have No Mercy*', while carefully avoiding the broken glass, syringes, used condoms, and a lot of garbage cans overflowing on to the sidewalk with used baby diapers, and yesterdays copies of Achoo Baytiiiii Version News Agency Journal.

Damn it felt great finally getting to the studio, Gene Kelly singing in the rain great. I did not need Dr. Johnson to diagnosis this strange fleeting feeling from some previous multiverse, spacetimepoint contentment.

An obese orange green tom cat was sitting on some garbage cans pushed against the side of a corner building at the next intersection. As I approach the tom cat from about almost a half a block away, the tom cat started hissing at me. I ignored the cat.

Khnum Avenue intersected with Orange Street, with Almack's Dance Hall on the northern corner, adjacent was the Juba Saloon, next was the studio, so I was getting excited, and I felt the best I had in over a week.

Halfway down the next block is my opportunity to make something, do something useful, mix music tracks. I couldn't wait to make some strong dark coffee and then get behind the huge Everett-Bohm mixing board.

I am not delusional, thinking that I could share a mixing board with either Monk or Coltrane; although I'm pretty sure Ric Rubin wouldn't mind sharing the board with me.

Most of my work gets played in the three local junior college bars, and in the neighborhood's juke joints. Quite a few of my hip hop mixes get played in rotation at the Starkville Gentlemen's Club.

The Mexicans had moved into this part of the neighborhood in the mid 1990's. Doc Baumann still calls this part of the neighborhood 'Dammeśeq'. All I hear spoken from the Khnum Avenue storefront weavers of sackcloth for export is spainish, arabic, armenian, aramaic, and caircassian.

Now these streets were almost exclusively the domain of the illegal's and the gangs. As I walked through the last couple of streets I had noticed there were Norte's on every corner.

Some of Madness's crew were way down the street standing outside a franchise taco restaurant. I think I recognized Antonio, Carlos, Cesar, Rafael, and possibly Jesus-Ernesto.

Some of the buildings on the block had their windows open. Strains of different noreno bands playing filled the air. Corridos echoing throughout the rain soaked street. Muted and slightly damp corridos were blending and reverberating throughout the side alleys.

Unlike Erwin Schrodinger, my neighbor who resides in the penthouse of 14 North Moore Street, I've never been much of a cat person.

The stray tom sitting on top of his throne of garbage reminded me of what the great Sir Winston said, "*I like pigs. Dogs look up to us. Cats look down on us. Pigs treat us as equals.*"

While the cat was still hissing at me, I decided to avoid it by walking away from it.

So I step into the street and walked a couple steps, until I was amost in the intersection of the streets when I remembered that Sir Winston had also said, "*Fear is a reaction - Courage is a decision*".

"Hey sahābiyy JD", a couple familiar voices laughingly yelled at me from a dark storefront doorway directly across the street I had just walked by. I thought I heard one shout something – '*Cattle*' or maybe '*Kaffar*'.

I definitely heard through the laughter, '*Oy gevalt Al Khadir*', and thought it damn weird of them shouting to me like that.

I wondered what the fuck, is it like Dr. Ken Bainbridge said, "*Now we are all sons of bitches*"?

The studio was so close that I really did not want to stop. I told myself it would only be a momentary delay. I turned around to step back up on the rain soaked sidewalk right by the damn hissing orange green tom cat

i can barely open my eyes. The back of my head hurt. i could smell wet baraka hashish. Rain drops were splashing in small oily street pavement puddles. In the puddle next to my face, the rain drops caused tsunamis of small blue gold concentric circles. Three red micro streams were crashing and overlapping the puddle. i felt something burning. i shut my eyes and started to dream at *3.14159265 THC encrusted protons per cubic meter of consciousness...*

i got a nicodemus's hyssop troche out of my cargo pants left pocket and threw in my mouth as i was walking down to the Ōta river on my way over to Sin's side bar at 646 N Franklin Street.

my mind's cobwebs cleared as soon as i got inside the bar. i walked right through multitudes and corps d'elite at the bar, and went and sat down next to Anasah, Zaman, and Louis de Broglie out on the terrace.

After i ordered sake, Louis to my everlastingly momentary appreciation, offered me a dark Vuelta Abajo Parejo. It was cut, lit, with the first three draws savored, before the hot sake was brought out. i sat back in my chair and started listening to the Jay Mcshann Orchestra play *'Relaxin' at Camarillo'*.

After Stockholm, **Sin's Room** had become the Restaurant at the End of Christianity. Sin bought the place from the Italian, (after the old Italian had developed a debilitating stockholm revolving door syndrome psychosis), and it was moved to the windy western cliff of Ras Muhammad.

The warm gulf waters lapped at cliffs below the Restaurant's outside terrace where we were sitting. You could see both the Suez and Aqaba Gulfs from our table.

Shen Kuo, Nasir al-Din al-Tusi, Johannes Kepler, and Isaac Newton were sitting a couple of tables away drinking a 1963 Graham's Vintage Porto and a Isole e Olena Chianti while eating ham and cheese on dark rye bread sandwiches. Kuo and Kepler were doing some reverse polish notation calculations on a HP-35.

Louis was updating ' *De Rerum Natura* '. i think he was a secret 'auch Dreieinigkeitsfest' because he had a glass of rich red tuscan, a premier grands bordeaux, and a Airen based brandy.

Anasah and Zaman were drinking some Euphrates water out of Mycenaean terracotta goblets, while i continually sipped hot tamon-in sake from a bottomless eleven inch Meiji Era Jade Sake bottle.

Louis, Anasah, and Zaman took a couple bar napkins and began diagraming some calculations showing that there **was empty space in which pair production occured**. i took interest when i heard pair production, thinking through the sake that they were talking about women, they weren't.

i got bored in a nanosecond and quit listening as i was pretty sure it was just some trinitatis trigonometry hypothesis about a photon in haploid state asexually masterbating a pair of particles.

In my present state of mind they were snoooooooooooooooooooooozzzzze particles – boring. i was having a chemical reaction to the Parejo: its neuropeptide *NP Cuban* was (master) sating different parts of my cortex, disrupting my memory neurons and entroping all curiosities.

Naguib and Shrin were sitting at a table adjacent to Louis, somewhat listening to the pair production discussion. i could tell both were being distracted by the sunlight reflecting off the shimmering blue waters in the gulf.

Martín Pinzón and his brother Vicente Pinzón were standing a few feet away from Naguib. They were looking at a 13th century sailing ship entering the gulf off to the left. Vicente thought it was the '*La Gallega*' for a second, but Martin pointed out it was just a caravel of Moulay Ismaïl Ibn Sharif's Black Guard from the Kasbah of the Udayas.

Naguib knew that Orhan, Garmeen, and Yunus had been at a book signing at the Mirrabooka International Hotel and Shopping Complex. The unusually credible phone texted word from the arab street soccer hooligans was, "...that Orhan, Garmeen, and Yunus were running late at the Ras el-Amoud checkpoint", Shrin told Naguib and then added, "It would be nice after supper to take the train to Guizhou, Gansu, and then to the Haibao Pagoda in Ningxia". Naguib thought, "It might be nicer, if the weather did not change, to accompany Mr. Stevenson on his walking travels with his donkey in the Cevennes."

"Boring!", i commented to both tables, " ...as i prefer walking travels in the Land of Nod ".

Boswell and Dr. Johnson smiled in agreement. We toasted one another with, ' *to haqq with the time-space continuum* ', and then laughed heartily as we downed another five rounds.

Unexpectedly, at least to me, was that Hissa and Shohreh had come out onto the terrace. They were walking by my table going over to the edge of the patio to look at the gulf.

i was a huge fan of both of them for their outstanding professional work. i could not take my eyes off either of them.

Dr. Johnson and Boswell then started doing some inappropriate pantomime *staccato is legato* violation of the 10th commandment of moses, (who i thought was jewish not islamic).

Then, going completely over the top, Dr. Johnson and Boswell beganing singing "*Pur ti riveggo, mia dolce Aida*", as only Egyptians and Ethiopians can.

Colorado State College of Education graduate Hajji Sayyid Qutb, Yale Worthy Samuel F. B. Morse, Chief Justice Roger Taney, and Editor Henry A. Reeves were sitting at a table about thirteen feet away from us with their table umbrella spread open to block the sunshine.

Sayyid was accompanied by a persian prostitute. Dr. Johnson was sure she was a mullah owned penny-a-marriage girl, to which Boswell nodded his head in agreement.

The Yale worthy was on a blind date with Ms. Louisa Piquet, whose attention was split between looking at the shimmering waters of the gulf, and reading a worn copy of Ben's *'A Conversation between an Englishman, a Scotchman, and an American, on the Subject of Slavery'*.

It was apparent that the date was not going well as the Yalie was visibly intimidated by Ms. Piquet's logic and her personal narrative.

Morse laughed at something Sayyid had said, and then high five'd Sayyid. Morse then spoke up, intentionally so to be overheard saying, "Right, the way I stated it as commencement speaker in my June 3, 1963 address to the graduating class of Hillhouse Hill School, I think the crux of the speech was, '....slavery or the servile relation is proved to be one of the indipensable regulators of the social system, divinely ordained for the discipline of the human race in this world, ...the great declared object of the Savior's mission to earth'."

Hearing the yale educated nativist idiot, i knew it was yet again empirical proof of Hayek's chapter on ' *why the worst get on top* ' in his tome – 'road to islamonaziserfdom'.

Then i said so to Boswell and Dr. Johnson loud enough for the Yale Worthy to hear. Dr. Johnson agreed and then offered, '...every imammie as further proof'.

Boswell looked over at me then, and he balefully smiled as he stated, "El último suspiro del moro, Uma", as a toast.

Then Boswell finished off his goblet of a youthful Tennessee whiskey; (it had only been aging in a reddish white, with some faded blue swirls, oak cask since April 1st, 1979).

Dr. Johnson spoke up then to remind me that, "After supper you're supposed to meet Sergeants Sedwick and Hurcomb of the London Regiment at the Mort Homme Gentlemen's Club on N.W. Verdun Street for billiards and scotch".

Boswell leaned over and asked me to get up and go over to Jay Mcshann and, "...ask him to play Leroy Carr's '*In the Evening (When the Sun Goes Down)*', or if Eva Cassidy is off her break, I'm sure everyone here would really appreciate '*Danny Boy*'."

i was really missing Rosa. i had enough Sake in my circulatory system so that my lymphatic vessels had all sank, enabling me to stand up then and there while blurting out, "Why the Haqq do Homo sapiens sapiens who are raised as muslims suck so much at science?"

346

Boswell grabbed my forearm and pulled me back down into my deck chair while angrily saying i "...*was beyond the wire*". Dr. Johnson looked down at his 'R. Buck Rogers and Trigger' wrist watch compass as he grabbed on to my other forearm. Dr. Johnson leaned over and nodded his head toward the water saying, "Thermopylae is miles away in that direction".

Then both Dr. Johnson and Boswell quietly threatened to cut off my bar privileges if i started a conversation regarding wild creole pigs, california ursidae mohammads, 0 – 400 gold scale iblis qibla compasses, the tetragrammaton, or '*especially the empty space in which pair production occures*', before supper was served.

Sitting on the table adjacent to me were Muon, Tau, Krypton, Xenon, Oney, Austin, Hercules, Giles, Aris, Sheels and Moll; who all were nodding their heads in unison while they continued eating the appetizer of toasted leptocephali.

i looked at everyone for a yoctosecond. i wanted to ask them, 'Since the begena player was but a rasool, and there have been several rasools before him, have you turned your backs on mississippi delta and chicago blues since his death?'

i didn't ask them, nor i did i see a maid and group of bystanders to ask, or even an irish bartender. i knew what they were thinking just from the not almost surprised look on their faces - that muslims are a stiff-necked people practicing another sicko religion of beheading science and philosophical thought, you dumb wild ass attorney.

Parvenez, being an infidelas, i wanted to tell them all inshallah, but thought it could wait until after la cena pasada del conquistador, mucho mas tarde.

347